THE POWER OF LOVE

Lina Langley and Sydney Blackburn

Dedicated to

James. For everything. – Lina

Our wonderful editor Stacy Jo,

who cared for our manuscript like it was her own. – Sydney

Chapter One

VINCENT SILVA BREATHED a sigh of relief when he saw his grade posted on the bulletin board. He'd already passed the entrance exams to be at Camp Hologram, but the on-site test was vital.

He didn't recognize the names of the three other guys in Cabin One, but he never expected he would. Kids with power-gifted parents were raised to protect their identities, for everyone's safety. He didn't want anyone to know who his father and stepmother were. *Especially* his stepmother, though he hated to use that word. It went the other way as well—he used his mother's maiden name on his application so his father and alleged stepmother wouldn't know he was at the camp.

A sharp lack of noise brought his attention to a classroom that reminded him too much of high school—being lectured by Mister Mister, who used to *be* somebody. His power was mimicry—for a few hours he could have the power of any gifted person he touched. Five years ago, he'd run afoul of the villain Chameleon. Vince wasn't sure exactly what had happened—the media reported only that somehow his stepmother had managed to defeat Mister Mister, after which he'd retired from active duty.

The resemblance to high school ended with Mister Mister, who didn't look anything like a teacher. For a start, his gray hair, still thick and wavy, was shoulder length, and he wore an olive drab T-shirt the same color as his canvas pants. He had tattoos down his arms and over the backs of his hands. He was also more physically fit than any of Vince's high school teachers had ever been.

"Welcome to Camp Hologram, gentlemen. You wouldn't be here if you hadn't mastered a general control over your powers, so the focus of your training will be learning independence and teamwork. How to maximize your strengths, minimize your weaknesses. How to survive without any powers at all.

"It takes strength of will, and discipline...."

Vince tuned out the boring "why you're all here" speech. He knew why he was there. He was born with powers and a determination to never be the kind of person his father was. Being the son of a villain didn't mean that was his only choice.

"Weekend leave is in the city of Guilford, but don't get too excited. There's a volunteer element to your grades. I believe most of you have ignored the pamphlet of rules you received before arriving so let me reiterate: booze, drugs, and gambling are not permitted here at Camp Hologram. Lights out is at 10:00 p.m. Reveille is at 5:00 a.m. sharp. You are expected to make up your bunks and keep your gear in your lockers. This afternoon you're to stow your gear and get to know your cabin mates. When you hear the klaxon, get to the mess hall or go hungry. Now grab your packs and go to your assigned cabin."

Finally! Vince leaned down to grab his duffle, a heavy canvas bag almost as long as he was tall and stuffed with everything he owned. Whatever he did at Camp Hologram, fail or graduate qualified to be an official hero, he wasn't going back home. Guilt made him flinch as he thought of his mother. She deserved a chance to make a life without his father screwing it up, and that meant a place with immaculate security. The kind only money could buy. Money popular heroes earned through sponsorships and licensing fees.

The first step was to ace his training.

He listened to the other guys grumble as they shuffled out, most of them with much less luggage.

"This is so lame," someone said.

"Piece of cake," someone else said.

Vince didn't say anything. He followed the others out of the administration building. It was a large complex, holding the showers, the shitters, the kitchen, and the dining hall, along with the lecture room and who knew what else. Stuff the trainees didn't need to know. Might be in the paperwork Mister Mister rightly guessed he hadn't read.

VINCE WALKED INTO the small building marked "One" and had to stop himself from sighing. It didn't look big from the outside, but he didn't expect it to be this small. There were two metal-framed bunk beds on each side of the wooden room and, as far as he could see, nothing else.

He wasn't sure where he was supposed to put his stuff. He had barely registered that there were already people inside when someone bumped into him.

"Sorry."

He didn't sound sorry at all to Vince, but it was enough to get Vince to move out of the way and turn to his right. There on the wall beside the door were four full size lockers in a tidy line, which he'd missed coming in.

"I call top!" he heard someone say from behind him.

"Too much information," said the guy who'd bumped into him.

"Pervert," someone else replied.

Vince glanced around the small room with a smile and tried to stuff his bag into the one empty locker while the others chose bunks. As long as he got one, he didn't care which. His powers had nothing to do with strength, and while he worked out, it wasn't easy for him to carry most of his belongings around with him.

His bag was far too big to fit. He'd need to unpack some of it, put some things on the upper shelf. Still, that wasn't going to stop him from trying.

"I hope your powers have nothing to do with your spatial abilities," someone said.

He turned around, ready to snap back with a snarky remark. The guy who had spoken was sitting cross-legged on the top bunk, a bright smile on his face.

"They don't," Vince replied, smiling back at him. The cabin was dim compared to outside so all he could see was a kind smile and symmetrical features.

"Oh, leave him alone," someone else said. Vince's gaze shot down to where the voice was coming from. This was the other guy who had gotten a bottom bunk. He was leaning on it and looking at his nails, his face covered by artfully uncombed blond hair. "Some boys need to take their toys everywhere. And by toys, I mean—"

"Oh my god," the third guy said. He wasn't on his bunk, he was sitting down on the floor and sorting through the stuff in his bag. "What are you, a walking cliché?"

The blond guy laughed, shrugging. "Is your name really Bartholomew Jameson Cockburn?"

"It's *Co-burn*," the guy replied. "You don't pronounce the 'ck'. It's silent. Also, you can just call me BJ."

"You want us to call you BJ Cockburn?" the blond said, biting his lower lip. Vince had to put his hand in front of his mouth to stop himself from laughing, too.

"Co-burn," he reiterated. "And yes, please."

"Oh I heard you. I'm just really immature," the blond guy said.

"That's becoming clear," BJ said, looking up at him. "And you're supposed to be putting your stuff away."

The blond snickered. "Is that in the rulebook?"

"We were just told," BJ said. "Weren't you listening? You were supposed to put your stuff away as soon as you got in the cabin. Like, um, he's doing." He pointed at Vince.

"Well, *he* doesn't have a choice. Look at that ridiculous fucking bag," the blond replied. "And he has a name. Which I'm sure he'll tell us any minute now."

"Vince Silva," Vince said. He hefted the bottom end of the bag onto the floor and pushed the top in under the shelf. "And yeah, I know the bag is ridiculous. Who are you?"

"Cass Talbot," he said. "So that means the guy who's bullying you must be Car —"

"Locke," the guy on the bunk interjected. "Everyone calls me Locke. And I wasn't bullying him. I was making conversation. Isn't this training camp supposed to be about teamwork or something like that? That's what I'm doing, dude. Teamwork."

"See?" Cass said, turning to BJ. "They get it. This is our last real day of freedom, so we should be spending our time bonding."

Locke pushed off his bunk, landing in a graceful crouch. He stood in front of Cass and right across from Vince. In the light coming in the cabin's window, Vince could see the guy—Locke—was gorgeous. Blond curls that fell to his shoulders, big light eyes; maybe green. Vince couldn't tell from where he was standing, and it was important that he find out.

He shoved the bag one final time and slammed the locker door, only to have it bounce off the bag. He could fix it later.

Cass pulled out a bottle of rum. "I guess if this is against the rules, we should bond over getting rid of it," he suggested.

"Jesus, Cass. Didn't you just hear Mister Mister say no booze?"

Vince was glad BJ said it before he did, because both Locke and Cass were glaring at BJ.

"Right," Cass said. He draped an arm over BJ's shoulders. "No booze. We're getting rid of it. And bonding. Like he said. If you help us, it'll be gone faster."

BJ's mouth tightened, and it looked like he might shrug off Cass's arm, but instead he said, in a grudging tone, "I guess."

Which helped Vince relax. If someone as serious as BJ was willing to go along, then it couldn't be bad enough to get them all kicked out. He slid a look toward Locke, but his gorgeousness was rooting in the locker farthest from the door.

"I got this," Locke turned around with a tacky necklace that had a plastic shot glass on it.

"Classy," Vince said.

"Bottle's good enough for me," Cass declared. The cap made a cracking sound as he twisted it off and took a swig. He swallowed and coughed a little.

Vince stifled a laugh.

"I'm not drinking from the bottle. Who knows what you guys have," BJ said, crossing his arms over his chest.

"Fine," Locke said, giving BJ the plastic necklace. "You use the cup. Gimme that," he said to Cass.

Locke tipped the bottle with caution, made a face, and handed it off to Vince.

Vince knew how to shoot rum, not that he made a habit of it. It never paid to be less than one hundred percent around his father, or worse than that, his father and his father's girlfriend. But he gulped down a shot and passed the bottle to BJ, who poured his shot with exaggerated dignity.

After wiping his mouth with the back of his hand, and giving Locke a sidelong look, Vince said, "So apart from being willing to bend the rules to swill cheap rum, what else do we have in common?"

"You mean, in addition to having super powers?" Locke asked, a smile in his voice.

Vince gave him a long look, and smiled. "Yeah. That, too."

Within minutes, the four of them were sitting on the floor, offering tidbits of information, like age and hometowns. The rum bottle went round and round, and Vince felt himself getting a nice warm glow. The rum, not anything to do with how Locke's hand kept falling on his knee.

"My power is metal manipulation. It's sort of magnetic, but more than that," Cass told them with a lazy smile. "Maybe I'll demonstrate it for you later. What about you guys?"

Vince looked around. He'd had it drilled into him to never talk about his family or his powers, so it was hard to say, "Mine is sound."

"Mine is so lame," Locke said. "Light." He nudged BJ with his foot. "What's yours?"

"I'm a healer."

"Sweet!" Cass exclaimed. "Can you cure hangovers?"

"No." BJ scowled as he drained the bottle into his little cup.

The conversation was starting to drop off, and Locke's hand was resting on Vince's knee for longer and longer moments when a loud ringing scared the shit of them.

"Meal time," BJ finally said. "We're supposed to go to the hall."

"Fuck. Smell my breath," Locke leaned in towards Vince.

"Dude. Yeah, I get it. We reek."

Locke backed off and Vince supposed he ought not to be thinking that, boozy breath and all, he could have wished Locke to move closer. He shook his head.

"Fuck!" BJ pushed to his feet. "I knew this was a bad idea."

"Chill," Vince said, standing up as well. "I got mints. We're good, I just gotta...." He walked to the locker in a relatively straight line and tugged the upper end of his bag until it flopped on the floor with a thud. He half expected to see cartoon dust puff up.

The noise sounded again, and everyone was on their feet. "Hurry up, Vince," Cass said, his tone not carrying a whole lot of urgency.

Vince tugged on the zipper, trying to remember where he'd put his mints. His powers were tied to his voice, so he had a variety of mints, lozenges, and sugar-free candies to soothe his throat and keep his mouth from getting too dry. He pulled out a hoodie and a couple pairs of underwear fell out.

"Sexy drawers, Vince," Cass drawled.

Locke chuckled in agreement and Vince felt a flush burn his face.

"Yeah, whatever." He tried to focus on his bag and thrust his hand inside, looking for the ziplock bag with his stash. He yanked it out and waved it like a victory flag.

"Gimme that," BJ said, snatching it from Vince.

"Easy, dude, I need those. Not exactly any vending machines here, y'know."

BJ found the mints and to Vince's surprise, he handed them out before tossing the lot on Vince's bunk. "Come on, we'll be late."

Locke met Vince's eyes and smiled.

Chapter Two

LOCKE LOOKED DOWN at his tray for a second, wondering what his food *was* and marveled at how steady the tray was in his hands. He was used to mixing his rum with sodas, not swigging straight from the bottle.

He had not paced himself well, and he didn't want to get in trouble. He needed to find somewhere to sit, because he was pretty sure he was going to start bumping into walls or people at any second.

Luckily, his best friend wasn't hard to spot. He had mermaid hair—that was what it was called, so he had been informed every time he said it wrong—and he had recolored it right before camp.

Locke walked over to Ariel, who had seen him and was waving. He sat down next to him, bumping his knee on the table.

Ariel looked at him and frowned. "Hey, you okay?"

"Yeah," Locke said, looking down at his food. "I'm good. What even is this?"

"Oh my god, you're drunk," Ariel said, sounding far too loud.

"Dude!"

"Sorry," Ariel said, laughing quietly. "Okay, your cabin seems so fun. What's everyone like?"

"I don't know. Normal. What's yours like?"

"Fine." Ariel shrugged, taking a bite off his fork. "I guess. So far the best part about being here is Mister Mister. It's so awesome he's our trainer! Do y'think we'll get to see him demonstrate his power?"

Locke had to laugh. He and Ariel had grown up together, collecting and swapping "Heroes and Villains" cards. He could always come out the better if he had anything Mister Mister to trade.

"Maybe. But apart from him, any interesting guys or cool powers?"

Ariel rolled his eyes. "I asked you first."

"They're all hot, I guess, but this one guy," Locke replied. "He seems almost shy, and—"

"Aww," Ariel said. "You're so cute when you crush on a guy."

"Dude, shut up," Locke replied. "I shouldn't have told you. I don't know why I ever tell you things at all."

"Because you love me?"

"Ugh," Locke said. "I don't want to talk about it anymore. Who's in your cabin?"

Ariel sat up a little straighter, looking around the room. "See that guy, with the tats? He's in my cabin. Says his name is Brayden, but he brays assholery. That could be his power. And the cute one with the glasses, he's there too. He's got like, electronics power or something. He didn't go into how it works."

"That's it?"

"No, but I can't see the other one anywhere," Ariel said. "He has dreadlocks, so he's kind of hard to miss." He practically inhaled a few forkfuls of the stuff on his plate and added with a whine, "I can't believe they didn't put us in the same cabin, though. That's so unfair."

"I don't think it was on purpose," Locke replied, trying to eat some of his own food. He was feeling queasy and the lumpy brown mush on his plate wasn't helping. It tasted kind of salty and greasy. He pushed the tray away from him and resisted the temptation to put his head on Ariel's shoulder. Maybe he could nap after dinner. His gaze fell on Vince, directly across from him but one table over.

"It's good to know that you miss me too," Ariel said.

"C'mon, I didn't mean it like that," Locke replied. "Of course I miss you. I'm just looking forward to getting to know everyone."

Ariel raised his eyebrows. "Everyone?"

"Yes, everyone," Locke said.

"That's why you're looking right at that guy, huh?"

Locke's face warmed as he realized he was staring. Vince was between Cass and someone whom Locke didn't recognize. He was pushing his food around with his fork, apparently finding it as unappetizing as Locke did.

"I wasn't," Locke protested. "He's in front of me."

"Whatever," Ariel said. "I give it a week, maybe two because of being at camp, until you get him out of your system. You want me to number them in the order you'll go through 'em? See how well I know you, right? Not easy, though, so many hot choices around here."

"You know, Ariel, when you say stuff like that," he started to protest, but then what Ariel had said hit him. "Wait, you think I'm going to get him out of my system? Do you think we're going to hookup?"

Ariel sighed, shaking his head. "Both your talents *and* your looks are wasted on you."

"What do you mean?" Locke said, looking right at Vince. This time, he wasn't trying to hide it.

"You know, you could probably sleep with anyone here, even if they think they're straight," Ariel said. "But that guy will be easy—he already wants you."

"How do you know?"

"Because he keeps sneaking glances this way whenever he thinks you're not looking," Ariel said. "And he seemed a little, I don't know, confused, when you decided to sit with me and not with him."

Locke laughed, throwing his head back. "But we're just friends."

"Yeah, I know that," Ariel said. "And you know that. But Hottie over there, he doesn't know it. You're going to have to tell him."

"Tell him what?"

"How do you even survive without me?" Ariel said, turning to him. "That's not a joke, it's a serious question. How do you do it?"

Locke rolled his eyes, but he smiled at Ariel. This was his version of being protective, which Locke always appreciated, even when it wasn't particularly useful. "It's always hard when you're not around and I have to lift furniture." Ariel's power was strength, which seemed bizarre in such a small, slender package.

Ariel rolled his eyes right back at him. "Whatever," Ariel said. "Mark my words. You're hitting that, like, within the week."

"What? No, I'm not," Locke said. "Vince is out of my league."

"He's so in your league. Cute, big brown eyes, great jaw. He's just your type," Ariel countered with confidence.

Locke shook his head. "I don't have a type. And I'm not here to rack up any numbers, jeez."

"Oh my God," Ariel said, putting his hand over his chest. "That's so cute. Anyway, you'll hit it and forget it. You'll move on to someone else. That guy."

He pointed his fork at a random guy on the left side of the room.

"Why that guy?"

"Because he's hot as fuck," Ariel replied. "And you're a commitmentphobe."

"I'm not a commitmentphobe, I've never found somebody I like enough, though," Locke replied, his voice a whisper. "You know, yet."

"And you think Vince is it? Are you going to eat that?" He was pointing at Locke's abandoned plate.

"No," Locke said, shaking his head. "I didn't say that. And no, here, have it. It's so gross. Even if Vince goes for guys with my dashing blond looks, it's not like I'm the only blond here. I'm not even the only one in our cabin. That gorgeous blond he's sitting next to? Cass. In our cabin. I'm not into blonds and I think he's hot."

"If you say so," Ariel replied, swapping his tray with Locke's. "You wanna put your money where your mouth is?"

Locke considered it for a second and shook his head. He wanted Ariel to be right. That, and he hadn't brought that much money with him to camp. He couldn't waste it on wagers he was hoping to lose.

Chapter Three

VINCE WAS BURNING with jealous curiosity over the twink with the brightly colored hair who practically hung all over Locke. None of his business, of course, but it seemed kind of unfair. He forgot about that, though when he and the rest of his cabinmates saw their door hanging open.

"Shit," Locke muttered.

"What the hell?" Cass shot nervous looks at each of them, as if they knew something.

BJ rolled his eyes and pushed inside, Locke right on his heels. Vince followed as Cass came up behind, dragging his feet.

Inside, they formed a ragged line in front of the waiting Mister Mister. He was just standing in the middle of the small room, holding the empty rum bottle by the neck, tapping the base into the palm of his other hand. "I thought I said no booze. And what the hell is this mess on the floor?"

"Sorry, sir," Vince said, "my bag spilled as the dinner bell rang."

"And this?" He held up the bottle.

BJ cleared his throat, but Cass stepped forward. "That's mine, sir. I brought it to camp before I knew the rules against alcohol." He glanced back at the other guys. "As soon as we had our gear stowed, I pulled this out to get rid of it. But then Locke reminded us all that we were to be getting to know each other, so I thought, you know—two birds, one stone."

"I see." Mister Mister glared at them. "And you all just happened to go along with this?" His gaze settled on BJ.

Vince stole a glance sideways. BJ was looking at the ground, clearly not pretending to hold any high ground. Vince liked that. He liked that Cass took responsibility. Maybe these guys would be better bunkmates than he'd anticipated.

Mister Mister was staring hard at Cass, his expression difficult to read under the light, salt and pepper beard. "It's not the worst story I've ever heard."

"Thank you, sir!" Cass replied cheerfully.

"It wasn't a compliment, Talbot."

"Call me Cass, sir, we're going to be spending lots of time together."

"Flirting with me won't help you, Talbot." He pointed the empty bottle at each of them in turn and shook it at Cass. "You won't be bringing any more booze to camp, right?"

"No, sir! I promise I will not bring any more booze to camp. You have my word." Cass was giving their trainer the most angelic look Vince had ever seen. He was sure, pretty as Cass was, he was no angel.

"Good. Clean this mess up. I see your cabin like this again, I don't care whose shit it is, you're all pulling extra toilet cleaning shifts. Understood?"

"Understood, sir!" they repeated in a chorus.

He pushed past them like a man on a mission and Vince wondered if they weren't the only cabin to fail inspection. He sighed and started sorting out his stuff. To his surprise, Locke got awkwardly to his knees and started helping. "Hey, you spilled it in the spirit of saving our butts. Least I can do."

"Thanks."

"I'd help, but there doesn't seem to be much room for a third," Cass said, still cheerful. "Maybe we can work on that."

"Don't be a dick." BJ spoke just loud enough for Vince to hear.

"This is gonna be interesting."

"Yeah, I think it is," Locke agreed, giving him a quick smile.

They managed to fit everything in the locker, leaving the big canvas bag mostly packed, so that the door closed tight.

"If you two are through being domestic," Cass said.

Vince turned. Cass was holding another bottle of booze. "Is that tequila?"

Cass grinned as BJ raised his voice to demand, "What the fucking hell?"

"It's the last bottle, I swear! I promised I wouldn't bring more, and I didn't. This was already here," Cass protested, pulling his innocent look on BJ. "So we gotta get rid of it, right?"

Locke started to laugh. "Damn, Cass. Lights out is at ten."

"We better drink fast then."

VINCE AND LOCKE were side by side on the floor, leaning against the back wall. Cass was on Vince's other side, more toward the middle of the room, while BJ was near Cass's bunk. As the tequila went down fast, conversation had turned into giggles and flirtatious looks, or at least Vince thought Locke was giving him flirtatious looks and maybe Cass, too.

He thought he should be surprised when Cass slid across the floor until their legs were touching. "You guys are so cute. How well do we want to get to know each other?"

BJ wavered to his feet, or so it appeared to Vince. "C'mon guys, you can't."

Vince didn't know what they couldn't.

"I think he means I shouldn't kiss you," Locke said with a smile.

"I don't mind." Vince hadn't been kissed in a while. His last boyfriend had cheated on him, and the girlfriend he'd had before that hadn't lasted more than a month before she dumped him for someone better. He wasn't bitter—he thought his father likely helped them decide how to act—but he hadn't tried to date in over a year. This was something he'd never had a chance to experience—drinking, casual sex. Not that he was going to have sex on the floor, he thought foggily.

"I kind of want to kiss you too," Cass said, or maybe he meant "you two."

"Okay," Vince said, dizzy and elated and a little nervous in spite of all the alcohol he'd consumed. Locke kissed him, a warm, wet kiss that was nice all the same.

"My turn," Cass murmured against his neck, and Vince turned his head for another kiss.

It was strange and odd, being between two blonds and he giggled. "I think I need kissing practice."

"I think you're doing fine." Cass smiled encouragingly at him.

"You're cute," Vince said. He turned to look at Locke on his other side. "I think you might be cuter, though."

"My poor ego," Cass said.

Concerned he'd hurt Cass's feelings, he turned his head once more, with some difficulty. Cass was grinning.

"S'okay, dude. I'd be happy in the middle, too, but you two have a thing. Jus' seems a shame to waste all these happy feelings."

He heard Locke's voice in his ear. "Vince?"

"Yeah?"

"Do you want to stop?"

He thought about it for a second and shook his head. "No, I just—I've never done anything like this before."

"Oh, a virgin!" Cass said, clapping his hands together.

Vince laughed. He wondered if he was blushing. "No, that's not what I meant."

"We'll be nice to you," Cass said. "I promise. Right?"

"Yeah," Locke said. "Really nice."

"Oh my god. Seriously?" Vince heard BJ say.

"What? We're getting to know each other," Cass said, his voice low and smooth.

"Ugh, no way."

There was a sound, of BJ getting up, Vince assumed, though Locke was kissing him again and whatever BJ was or wasn't doing didn't seem all that important.

"Count me out." The door opened and a brief gust of cool night air ruffled Vince's hair before the door closed again.

"Damn," Cass murmured. Vince had stopped caring about Cass at that point, focusing instead on the way Locke was kissing him, hungrily, as though he couldn't get enough of him. Vince kissed him back, his heartbeat quickening along with his breath. He was barely aware of Cass next to him until he felt hands that weren't Locke's pulling at his shirt.

Locke moved away from him, catching his breath and biting his lower lip. "Oh man. I don't know if I've had enough to drink for this. Or maybe too much."

Vince nodded. He wanted to say something, but he wasn't sure he'd be able to form a coherent sentence if he tried. He helped Cass along as he took off his shirt, while Locke kissed him on the mouth again. Then he could feel Cass's lips on the nape of his neck, his fingernails tracing Vince's shoulder blades and down his back. His body wasn't used to this many sensations at one time, and he thought maybe Locke was right about too much or not enough.

Locke moved away from his mouth and kissed down his chest while Vince moaned.

"God, so delicious, such madness," Locke said, sprinkling Vince's stomach with kisses while Cass continued licking and nibbling his neck.

Vince groaned. He was trying to say he couldn't move, but no words would come out of his mouth. Locke's mouth left wet trails on his skin, down to his navel and back up until Cass and Locke kissed each other over his shoulder.

Cass broke the kiss and chuckled in Vince's ear. "This is so hot, but you guys are way too drunk for me to keep going with this." He kissed Vince's shoulder and added, "I hope we try this another time. But I gotta clear my head, dudes."

The night breeze wafted over them again as Cass stumbled from the cabin.

Locke pulled Vince across his lap and kissed him again, a slow kiss, of gentle tongues, accompanied by trailing fingers across his skin. "He's pro'ly right, y'know. We have diminished capacity. You're gorgeous an' I don't want you to wake up tomorrow regretting anything."

"Yeah," Vince said, his voice thick. He wasn't sure he agreed, but the idea that Locke didn't want him to have regrets kept him from arguing. He didn't want Locke to have regrets either. "Okay." But he didn't move either, just rested his head on Locke's shoulder.

LOCKE WAS ON the verge of passing out. Vince was so sweet in his arms, but the floor beneath his ass and the wall at his back were both hard. He had to move. God, Ariel would find this hilarious.

Vince stirred in his arms, raising his head from Locke's shoulder to give him a sexy, confused look. Locke smiled at him. Yeah, this was something to be continued. Sober. On a bed.

"We should—"

The cabin door slammed open on his words.

His eyes widened as he realized it wasn't Cass or BJ, but Mister Mister glaring at the two of them. "What the hell is going on in this cabin? Locke, I thought between you and Cockburn, this would be one of the better-disciplined cabins! And now look at this!" Mister Mister threw out his hand to indicate something. Locke wasn't quite sure what it was. Vince was blushing hard enough it was obvious in the dim light of the cabin as he scrabbled for his tee.

"S-sorry," Locke mumbled, trying to get to his feet.

"I was just in here a few hours ago reprimanding you about booze! Where did this come from?" Mister Mister was waving about the empty tequila bottle.

"Um."

Vince was sitting up, his hair tousled, his eyes clear of confusion. At Mister Mister's question, though, Vince looked at Locke.

Locke didn't need to be a telepath to understand the question in his eyes—*Do we rat out Cass?*

"Sir." Locke cleared his throat and began again, "After you reiterated the no booze rule to us, we realized we had to get rid of the stuff we'd brought before we were aware of the rule."

"Since when does 'get rid of' mean consume irresponsibly?"

"If we were responsible about it," Vince offered in a quiet voice, "there'd still be some left."

"Very funny, Silva. I'm sure your sense of humor will go a long way to helping you on kitchen patrol. Which is now Cabin One's job for the next two weeks." Mister Mister narrowed his eyes. "Is any *more* of this pre-existing liquor gonna show up?"

"Um, no, sir," Locke said, hoping he was right.

"I'll give you till reveille to make certain of that. If I find anything—anything!—out of order on the morning inspection, you'll be in for more than KP duty. Do I make myself clear? I mean abso-fucking-lutely crystal?"

"Yes, sir," Vince muttered at the same time Locke did.

"Good. Now air the stench out of this cabin."

Chapter Four

REVEILLE WOKE LOCKE with the brutality of a super villain with invisible punching powers. His head thumped so hard he thought his brains might spill out his ears. He sat up and rolled out of bed before he remembered he was in a bunk, and the top bunk at that.

"Fuck," he groaned, clutching his head as he rolled on the floor. *Now my knees hurt, too, damn it.*

"Shu'up," Cass moaned from his bunk.

"Ughnnnn," mumbled Vince.

Vince. Locke squinted at Vince as he used the rails at the head of the bunk to haul his sorry ass upright. Vince looked as rough as he felt, hair messed, eyes screwed up in a squint, and traces of drool on his cheek. Yet somehow still hot. "Fuck," he muttered again.

"Up and at 'em," BJ said, his tone irritable. "We have to get to the kitchen."

"'N whose fault is'at," Cass said.

"C'mon," Locke told Vince, shaking his shoulder. Not that he needed to, but he was right there.

"Ye-nnn. Stop yelling." Vince rolled over, his sheet falling away from his chest.

Locke averted his eyes. "Get up. God knows what Mister'll have us doing if we screw this up." He put on a pair of sweatpants and pulled the sheets and blankets on his bunk into some semblance of made. He'd do better after his head stopped pounding.

"If you guys hadn't turned the drinking into an *orgy*," BJ muttered.

Cass rolled out of bed, literally, and dragged himself to his feet. "Is'at what you think happened?"

BJ sniffed. "Doesn't matter now, does it."

"Gawwwwd," Vince drawled. "Can't we just do this quietly? Puh-leeeze."

"Does anyone even know how to cook?" Locke asked. "C'mon, guys. We gotta get over there. BJ can make coffee."

"Why do you think I know how to make coffee?"

"Because you're so fucking smart," Cass growled.

Locke waited for everyone to get moving—that was teamwork, right? It had nothing to do with wanting to watch Vince get out of bed and stumble around in his underwear. "Ugh," he mumbled aloud. They were going to be cooking without time to brush last night's liquor out of their mouths.

His gaze fell on Vince's mouth. His memory was quite vivid on that.

BJ was once more first through the door. Did he think he was leadership material? Ha! Locke fell in last, so he could watch Vince with no one watching him. Last night had been weird. It wasn't his first time in a ménage, though it wasn't his preference. Technically it hadn't been a ménage, as they'd realized they were too drunk, but he thought he might not have regretted going further with Vince. He grimaced. In any other circumstances.

The kitchen was big, all chrome, with a very prominent note from Mister Mister on the prep table. BJ was opening bins, and Vince had found the big coffee urn. He looked like he wanted to hug it. BJ said, "I got it, dude. I know how these work. Find me the coffee."

Locke read the note out loud, *"There are recipes in the binder in the pantry. Coffee is in there, too. You'll no doubt need it. Start simple, and remember to have food on by six. The entire camp is depending on you.* Great," he added. "No pressure."

"Ugh," Cass said. Locke looked at him, expecting him to agree, but instead, Cass was holding a hair net. "We have to *wear* these?"

"Yes," BJ replied. He was making coffee, with more noise than necessary. Vince was standing next to him and switching between glaring at BJ and rubbing the bridge of his nose. "Unless you want hair in everyone's food, and I'm sure *that* wouldn't get us in any more trouble. I told you guys this would happen."

Locke sighed, fumbling when Cass tried to toss him the hair net. It wasn't a very good toss, and Cass was too far away, so the hair net fell on the floor and Locke had to walk over to where he was to get it.

"When did he even come back?" Cass said, more to himself than to anyone else in the room.

"I dunno," Vince replied. "You were gone and BJ was gone and Locke and I were, um—"

Cass chuckled. "I bet."

"No, we were just—" Vince was blushing and looking at the ground. He was smiling, too. "Kissing. That's all we were doing."

"I didn't think Mister Mister would check on us again," Locke said, walking over to the pantry and getting the binder out. He brought it over to where all the other guys were, mostly because he didn't want to make the decision of what to cook by himself. Something to do with teamwork. There was also the fact he couldn't cook, at all, but he wasn't going to admit he wasn't good at something in front of Vince. "After he left. You know, the first time."

"I'm so glad I wasn't there," Cass replied. "I mean, for the getting caught part."

In other circumstances, Locke would have laughed, but his head still hurt. BJ was concentrating on something and Vince was struggling to put his hair net on.

"Where'd you go?" Locke said, not because he wanted to know. He just didn't want to pick what they were going to cook and none of the other guys seemed eager to choose, either.

"By the lake," Cass said. "It's pretty around here. I'm pretty sure weed falls under the no drugs rule, so if I'd gotten caught...." He shrugged without finishing the sentence. "No more getting-to-know-you sessions," he said with a wink.

"Here," BJ said, ignoring Cass. He was standing next to Locke, looking at the binder. "Give me that."

Locke handed it to him, glad it wasn't his problem anymore. "So, where were you?"

"I went for a walk," BJ replied, annoyed. "Because I don't get off on group sex."

Cass snickered. "I don't know whether to be offended or sad."

"Wait," Vince said. "So if you were out smoking near the lake, and you went for a walk, how did Mister know to go back into the cabin?"

"He could probably hear you," BJ said, flipping through the binder. "Moaning and groaning. What about scrambled eggs? We could make scrambled eggs."

"Sure, BJ. You make scrambled eggs," Cass said, rolling his eyes. "We'll do whatever you want. Since you seem to think you're so much fucking better at anything than the rest of us."

"I didn't say that," BJ insisted in a low voice. "I'm *trying*. Unlike all of you."

"You told," Cass said. "Didn't you?"

"Don't be ridiculous!" BJ said, shaking his head. "I just didn't want to be part of that."

Locke sighed, getting between them. He didn't want to be breaking up fights first thing in the morning, so it would be better if he could talk them out of it before anyone started throwing punches. "Look, guys, why don't we relax here? Whatever happened, it—"

For the first time since they had started talking, Locke noticed Vince was humming a tune softly, almost to himself. He'd said his powers were sound, hadn't he? Or was he just cheerfully hungover?

"BJ," Vince said in a soft, compelling voice. "You want to tell us what happened, don't you?"

"Not really," BJ said.

Vince started humming again for a few seconds. "C'mon, just tell us."

BJ sighed as he directed his gaze to the smooth tiled floor. "It was an accident. I was just walking by the obstacle course when Mister Mister saw me. He asked why I was out late and I—I panicked. I didn't mean to say anything, but you guys did kind of drive me out of the cabin by having an orgy." His eyes widened. "Oh my god, what the hell?"

"You were *invited* to participate, and it *wasn't* an orgy," Cass said indignantly to a confused looking BJ, as if that changed anything. "You know I could have gotten kicked out, right?"

BJ exhaled through his nose, sneering. "That's your fault," he replied. "What idiot brings pot to camp? You don't even have to read the rulebook, that's common sense."

"You're such a dick," Cass muttered.

"Yeah, that's not cool," Vince added, crossing his arms over his chest. "If you didn't want to get in trouble, maybe you shouldn't have told?"

BJ looked at Locke. Locke wasn't sure if he wanted an ally or if he was being defiant, but it didn't seem to matter. They were there, and they had been caught. Locke shrugged. "Yeah, dude," he said. "Next time you don't want to get in trouble, you should keep your thoughts to yourself."

BJ looked confused. "I, uh. Yeah."

Vincent walked to the large fridge doors and pulled one open. "Whoa. This is huge."

Cass snickered. "That's what Locke said."

Locke rolled his eyes.

"Hey Cockburn," Vince called, pronouncing it wrong, "how many eggs does that book say we need?"

"Three dozen. And five pounds of bacon and five pounds of sausage. And it's Co-burn."

"Whatever. Somebody grab these, please?" Vince held out three cartons of eggs.

Locke took them and put them on the table. "Cass, you wanna find a bowl big enough to scramble these?"

"And a big frying pan…?" Cass asked, looking through the items stashed under a griddle.

"I think we use that thing you're resting your hand on," Locke observed. He at least knew a griddle when he saw one, even if he'd usually been looking from the other side of a breakfast counter.

"I meant to wallop the snitch," Cass said.

Somehow, they managed to fill the trays in the buffet table. Locke could've used his powers to make it look better, but that wouldn't make it taste any better. The bacon was good, but short of burning it, he didn't know how anyone could screw up bacon. The waffles were from a mix, but somehow they'd managed to only cook a few all the way through—whilst burning the edges.

They had a brief discussion about who was going to refill the trays—no one wanted to risk being on the same side of the counter as the guys forced to eat their cooking—until Locke said, "I'll do it."

He was a little surprised no one threw any food at him, but that didn't stop a big muscular guy with some nice bright ink on his right arm, from remarking very loudly, "Can't tell who's gettin' punished—Cabin One, or us!"

Locke rolled his eyes, preparing to make his escape back into the not-as-unfriendly kitchen. At least Vince was there. Before he could turn around, he saw Ariel approaching.

"Hey," he said, smiling. At least Ariel was always nice to him. Mostly. "Back for seconds?"

"God, no. That was awful. I never knew scrambled eggs could be that rubbery," Ariel said with a vigorous shake of his head.

Locke sighed. Ariel had an amazing appetite. It had to be bad if even he didn't want seconds. "We tried."

"Yeah, okay," Ariel said, rolling his eyes. "Whatever. I just wanted to ask you if what I heard was true."

Locke swallowed, looking away from him. He didn't mind talking about his lov— sex life—with Ariel, he just wished he didn't have to do it in front of a dozen people hating on him, for good reason. He also knew Ariel wouldn't let it go, even if Locke told him they would talk about it later.

"What did you hear?" Locke said.

"I heard they caught you, you know, balls deep in someone in your cabin," Ariel said.

Locke laughed, though he glanced into the kitchen behind him to see if his cabinmates were listening. "Is that what people are saying?"

Ariel shrugged, looking around and dropping his voice to a whisper. "Well, no. I heard people say it was two guys."

"Yeah," Locke replied, leaning in so he could whisper. "Well, I mean, no. There was threesome kissing, then twosome kissing, but we were all too drunk—why am I telling you this? Honestly, it was the tequila that got us in trouble."

"Tequila, threesomes, and not one measly text," Ariel said, shaking his head. "Sometimes, I feel like our friendship is one-sided."

Locke laughed. "Yeah," he said. "Same here."

"So, who were they? Was I right?"

"About—"

"Did you get to bang the cute brown-haired guy who was making eyes at you yesterday?"

Locke shook his head, trying not to smile. "No banging happened. We just made out a little." Just thinking about how sweet Vince was the night before made him forget about how much the punishment sucked.

"Nice!" Ariel said. "Who else?"

"The blond," Locke replied. "Cass."

"Dude, good job," Ariel said, back in full voice and holding his fist up. Locke was about to roll his eyes and tell him to put it down when he saw the guy with the tats staring at them, and he knew he couldn't leave Ariel hanging. He gave him a weak fist bump and tried to think of a way to excuse himself without making Ariel feel like he didn't want to talk to him. "So who's next? Two down, one to go, right? If you wanted to do it in cabin order."

Locke shot another glance into the kitchen, and saw Vince approaching the counter with a fresh hot tray. He smiled, shaking his head. "No, it's not—"

"Yo." The muscular guy with the ink spoke again, this time over everyone there, which, as far as Locke could tell, took some effort. "You, the one in the hair net."

Locke pointed at himself, and the guy nodded, standing up and walking closer to him.

"Y'know," he said, shoving Ariel out of the way with his shoulder. Ariel glared at him. "There's something I wanna know."

Locke swallowed, looking between Ariel and the guy with the tattoos. "What?"

"This dweeb," he said, setting his gaze on Ariel. "Does he have to suck you off so you'll pretend to be his friend?"

"What? No, he's—"

"A loser," the guy with the tats said. "So tell me, does he?"

Locke shook his head. He didn't want to get involved with this, but if Ariel decided to defend himself, things could turn out much worse. "Yeah, dude. He's sucking me off right now. Is this the asshole who you said was in your cabin yesterday?"

Ariel nodded. "Yeah," he replied. "This is Bray."

"Brayden," the guy with the tattoos said.

"Look, Bray, if you know what's good for you, you should back off," Locke said, rubbing the bridge of his nose. "Seriously."

"That's so cute, you don't want me picking on your boyfriend," Bray replied. "What are you going to do?"

"Me, nothing, but if you keep pissing *my boyfriend* off, you're going to have to deal with him," Locke replied. "And I don't think you want to do that."

"I'd like to see him try," Bray said. Locke wasn't paying attention to him anymore, he was looking at Ariel, who was still glaring at Bray, his hands in fists at his side.

"Walk away, Ariel," Locke said, ignoring Bray. "He's not worth it."

Ariel shook his head, his nostrils flaring. "But I could—"

"But you won't," Locke replied. "Walk away. Seriously."

Ariel looked at Locke, exhaled and nodded. He turned around and walked back toward his table. Locke stifled a sigh of relief. Ariel could have broken the muscle boy in half without chipping his manicure.

"Good job," Bray said, winking at Locke. "You just saved him from a world of pain."

Locke rolled his eyes. "Sure," he replied. "I saved somebody and I'm already regretting it."

VINCE HAD A fresh tray of scrambled eggs they'd managed to not turn into yellowish brown chunks of rubber and was about to pass it across to Locke when he heard the cute little guy from the day before congratulating Locke on "two down." What was that supposed to mean? Was Locke bragging about sex they hadn't had?

He lifted the tray to slam it down on the scratched, stainless steel counter and froze when a burly guy strutted up to talk smack. He'd been pretty sure, last night, that the cute twink with rainbow hair wasn't Locke's boyfriend after all, but now he wasn't so certain. Open relationships were a thing, right? For some people?

Instead, he shut his mouth as Locke de-escalated the scene then he announced with fake cheerfulness in a loud voice, "Fresh eggs! No rubber!"

Which changed some of the grumbling into laughter and shouts of "That's what *she* said!"

"That joke is so old." Locke rolled his eyes as he took the tray.

Vince wouldn't meet his eye, he just mumbled, "How are we for bacon?"

Locke brought him the tray of rubbery scrambled eggs to dump and said, "Yeah, could use more bacon. He's not, you know. My boyfriend. And I'm not, um. You know."

"Yeah, cool, whatever," Vince said, his voice also low. He didn't know, though. He studied Locke through the veil of his eyelashes. Locke had killer good looks and a kind of confidence Vince envied.

He'd been foolish to think Locke had meant anything more than exactly what he'd said about having no regrets. *You just met the guy. What's the big deal?*

True. He wasn't at Camp Hologram to find a boyfriend.

You keep tellin' yourself that.

SOMEHOW, THEY MADE it through breakfast without the other trainees doing more than bitching. Justified bitching, but still. They'd used more of everything than they were supposed to, with enough food waste to make Vince feel guilty.

"This sucks, man," BJ said, staring at the garbage. "There were times my family would have killed for crappy food like this."

Vince and his mother had had some tough times after the divorce, too. A huge house meant nothing when their cupboards were often empty. Still, that didn't mean he was going to forget it was BJ who landed them in this situation to begin with.

"We should make a list of what we got left and figure out how to supplement it. Like maybe fruit cocktail or more hash browns or something," Locke said.

"This is fucking wonderful," Cass said, slumping forward on the table. "We gotta do that, clean up the shit those fuckers threw on the floor. Then, we have to clean our cabin. We'll be lucky there's any hot water left by the time we hit the showers." His own words seem to perk him up. "Showers. Maybe we'll get to find out if BJ's cock really does burn."

"Shut up, you ass," BJ said. "I wouldn't fuck you if you were the last person on earth."

Cass smirked. "A bottom, huh?"

"Knock it off, you two," Locke said as he rolled his eyes. "We have work to do."

"I'll do the floors and tables," Vince volunteered. No one else would want to do it, and he could get a grip on his feelings.

By the time he had the floor clean, the tables wiped down with Clorox, and the buffet table put away, the other guys had the dishes done—not hard with the dishwasher—and the pantry surprisingly organized for the week. Every meal and ingredient was laid out and labelled, quantity of food required notated against quantity of food on hand. Now if only their cooking could be so impressive.

Vince had also managed to convince himself nothing happened last night, nothing of any significance at least. Just a lark between guys with too much liquor under their belts. No big deal. He kept repeating it to himself as they tidied up the cabin and collected their clean clothes and toiletries for the showers.

He kept his head down in the locker room as they all stripped and tossed their clothes into overflowing hampers. Laundry duty was probably a worse punishment than kitchen, he thought absently. Then he caught sight of Locke and Cass heading into the shower area. Fuck, but they were both gorgeous. Right, both of them.

Vince forced himself to look away and found BJ walking awkwardly with a washcloth in front of him. He snickered. *Someone* must have gotten BJ's attention, though he'd need some damn good luck to compensate for the stunt he'd pulled.

Vince took a deep breath of his own and walked nonchalantly into a room already filling with clouds of steam.

There were six showerheads, two on each of the walls surrounding the doorway. Each of the three walls had one guy already there, with BJ nearest the door on Vince's left, Cass in the corner on the far wall, and Locke, he was pleased to note, in the corner opposite Cass, back to him. Which meant Vince would be on the same wall as someone.

Cass threw a glance over his shoulder and winked. "Got an opening for you here, hot stuff."

"Oh god, shut up," BJ said.

This wasn't going to turn into a reprise of last night, was it? Because he wasn't drunk enough for that. Staying by the door seemed the safest bet, which would put him beside Locke. At least Locke could put sentences together that weren't either complaints or innuendo.

Vince turned to his right and put his soap and shampoo in the metal rack, resolutely ignoring Locke. He turned the water on, adding to the general noise in the room, and almost missed Locke saying, "Ariel's been my friend since forever. He's like a brother to me. That's, uh, why I was warning that blowhard off."

"Oh. Not your boyfriend?"

"Ugh, no. Too high maintenance." Locke grinned at him, the water pulling his hair down over his ears in a dark-blond cap. "He's pretty high maintenance as a friend. He's got no filters."

"So what did he mean when he said you had two down?" Vince asked casually, sticking his head under the spray so he had a reason to close his eyes.

"Oh god, he made me sound like such a slut," Locke replied with a laugh. "I'm really not. And, um...."

Vince grabbed his shampoo and cracked one eye open to look over at Locke. It was so strange how he could go from Mr. Confident to hesitant. What did he have to hesitate over?

"When we get our leave on the weekend, I was wondering if you wanted to, um, maybe go to dinner or something?" He laughed again, but it didn't sound as easy as his first one.

"Ooo," Cass called over the noise of the spray. "Can I come, too? We can finish what we started."

Vince lathered his hair as he thought about it. It was just a date, there was no way his dad or Rebecca would ever know about it. After all, Locke wasn't asking him to get married. He replied in a voice he hoped only Locke would hear, "Yeah, that'd be... It'd be nice."

"Jesus, Cass, does everything you say have to sound like sex?" BJ complained.

"Want me to whisper in your ear so you can find out?"

Vince turned his back to the wall to rinse his hair, forgetting that would give everyone else in the room, except Locke, a full frontal.

Cass turned off his water and said, "You are so fucking hot, Vince. I could eat. You. Up." He punctuated his words by poking Vince's chest and stomach.

Vince jumped back and reached out a hand to steady himself, grabbing Locke's arm in the process.

"And as for you," Cass said, his voice heavy with innuendo as he pressed into BJ's back, "We'll—"

Cass bent double as BJ shoved his elbow back into his gut. Cass used all the profanity Vince had ever heard in creative strings as he staggered into the locker room.

Vince turned away to hide his smirk and met Locke's matching expression. "Want some help?" Locke offered, gaze travelling down Vince's torso.

Vince's cock responded, and he felt the sudden heat in his cheeks as Locke's tongue darted across his lower lip. "Um."

"We should conserve water," Locke suggested, as BJ turned off the water to his shower head.

"Um," Vince repeated, wondering where the hell his power of speech had gone. "N-no." Not like this, not with an audience.

"No?" Locke jerked his head to look into Vince's eyes, surprise evident.

"Not into putting on a show," Vince mumbled, turning away.

"No problem," Locke said, shutting off the water and moving to stand nose to nose with Vince. Something shimmered, or maybe he was seeing things. Locke said in his ear, "No one can see us now."

Vince opened his mouth to stammer a protest—BJ and Cass were just in the next room and there was no door—when he got it. This was Locke's power, bending light.

Locke covered Vince's open mouth with his own, kissing him softly. "Of course," he added in a whisper, pressing his body to Vince's, "You still have to be quiet."

Maybe he should have protested, but he couldn't. Locke pushed him back against the wall, out of the direct shower spray and Vince gasped—the tiles were *cold*.

Locke, however, was warm and wet and Vince wrapped one hand around his waist, the other around his neck, returning the kiss with hunger.

"Wh-which one of us is turning around," Vince managed to say, failing to make it a proper question.

He could see Locke's Adam's apple move as Locke swallowed. "Not today. Not like this."

Chapter Five

LOCKE HAD A nagging sensation that Vince was going to turn into an addiction. He'd have to ask Ariel if that was possible. Ariel was promiscuous, but he still had more dating experience. Very dramatic dating experiences, Locke recalled with a wry grin.

He hadn't meant to sit beside Vince, but there he was anyway. He smiled again, for no reason he could think of.

Vince glanced over and smiled at him. Locke's smile grew and he winked before turning his attention to the front of the room.

Mister Mister was a retired hero, with a lot of rumours about the incident that led to his retirement. He was the same age or younger than most of their parents who were still actively working, or at least Locke's were.

When Locke and Ariel were younger, Mister Mister was Ariel's favorite; he'd had collector cards, the Mister Mister backpack, hoodies with Mister Mister's characteristic pose on them, among a variety of other things.

Locke's father had disapproved of Mister Mister, though he'd never say why. Only that "that man's merchandise is never ending up in this house." Locke's father, known to the public as Sting, had very particular ideas on right and wrong, the duties of a power-gifted person, and what powers were appropriate for "dignity." Locke hadn't known what that meant until his own powers kicked in, along with a voice change and pubic hair. His powers of light manipulation were lacking in dignity.

Duke Fusion was a more appropriate object of hero worship for a youth, in Locke's father's opinion. That had only made Locke more curious about Mister Mister. He doubted he'd learn much about the man during camp, except what a hard-ass he could be for training.

As if invoked by Locke's thoughts, books hit the desk on his other side and Ariel sat down. "Didn't you see me? I saved you a desk."

"Sorry, I was trying to be—"

Mister Mister cleared his throat and asked in a very pointed voice, "If we are ready?"

Locke ruffled Ariel's hair, knowing it would get him a scowl. He mouthed the word "later."

"First, I want to clear a few things up, like why Cabin One is being punished."

"We're all being punished," Bray yelled.

"I'm sure your first time in the kitchen will be stellar, then," Mister Mister said calmly. "Clearly some of you have read the rule list mailed to you before your arrival—sex is officially frowned upon. But let's get real here—you're young, you're fit, and I'd be surprised as hell if any one of you is straight. We all know that for some reason powers tend to be associated with non-hetero orientations. Sex is going to happen. It's not going to be punished unless or until it affects you negatively in training. If you fail to save someone's ass because yours is sore from the night before, you'll be cleaning toilets for a month and sleeping with a goddamn chastity belt."

Mister Mister didn't so much as crack a smile as he waited for the whoops and cheers to die away. "Drugs and alcohol are a different matter. This is your last warning. Going forward there is zero tolerance, and the next bottle of booze I find will see someone on permanent leave. Anything that can impair your ability to make a good decision—besides your own stupidity—will from this day forward have your asses sent back home until you're responsible enough to be here. This isn't a kiddie day camp. Any questions before we proceed?"

"Yeah. Where are the girls?" Bray asked.

Mister Mister frowned. "The *women* are in Camp Synergy. They're being trained by Scarlet Jade. If you'd read the history of the training camps, you'd know that officially the reason for the segregation is some sexist bullshit about the women being more vulnerable. As we'll be sharing some training exercises with them in the new year, I want you to get any such notions out of your head. Scarlet's young women will be trained as hard as you."

"So what's the real reason?" asked the guy with dreads.

"That's Ace, he's in my cabin," Ariel whispered, though he was listening as attentively as the rest to what Mister was saying.

Mister Mister's frown deepened. "An outdated notion that the offspring of two power-gifted people will have twice as much power. So. It's important to know who you're working with, their abilities and their weakness. To start, we're going to head outside for some demonstrations, and our first exercise. You will not," he added sternly, "be able to pick your teams, so don't ask."

Nothing happened for a moment as all the guys seemed to look at each other.

Mister Mister waved his hands in a shooing motion. "Outside. Move your asses."

THE TRAINING GROUNDS at Camp Hologram were extensive. Locke knew *that* from the map, but this was the first chance he'd had to really look. There was an obstacle course, the large open area they were gathered in, and a sandy beach leading to a sizeable lake. If they hadn't had KP this morning, he and his hungover cabinmates probably would have seen it at 5:00 a.m. It was nice enough, being August, but would they have morning calisthenics outside in the winter?

Mister Mister walked into the center of the group and cleared his throat. "You probably talked a little about your powers in your cabins last night," he said, disregarding the chatter among them. "It's important you see them in use. This is your chance to show everyone here what you can do, so show off. You'll need to use what you learn today in every exercise."

The noise died down as they looked at each other. No one seemed to want to go first, until a good-looking guy with his long brown hair secured in a top knot stepped forward. "Hi," he said brightly. "I'm Mickey Basil in Cabin Three. My power is telekinesis, which I inherited from my father, Duke Fusion," he announced, as if just telling people who your parents were wasn't something they'd been brought up to never do.

Locke exchanged a look with Ariel and sought out Vince's gaze. Vince looked as aghast as Locke felt.

Mickey took a step forward, the rest of them making space for him. Mickey might be a bit clueless, but Locke still thought telekinesis was a pretty cool power. Mickey turned until he was standing right in front of the guy with the glasses, whose name Locke couldn't remember.

Mickey stared at him, clenching his fists and furrowing his brow. For a second, Locke thought he was going to make him levitate. Then the guy's glasses slid down his nose in slow motion and fell on the ground unceremoniously.

Locke heard Cass choke on a laugh. He turned to look at him, but so did Mister Mister, so Cass put his hand over his mouth to stifle the sound.

Mickey, glaring, was two steps toward Cass when the guy with the dreadlocks spoke. "I'm Ace Green, Cabin Two, and I'll show you what I can do," he said. Then he was gone in a blur. He was back in a split second, holding the welcome mat from the administration building in his hands.

"Nice," someone said. Several people high-fived him, but no one seemed eager to try to follow that up. Locke was about to say he would go next when the guy who Ariel had pointed at as being "next" at supper the day before came forward.

He stepped a little away from the group and pointed to the fire pit, heaped with dead branches. With a dramatic gesture, a whoosh of flame engulfed the wood. He bowed. "Better bonfires by Royce Bailey, Cabin Three."

"Wouldn't want to piss him off," someone muttered.

Vince jumped forward with a stuttering cry, almost like a war whoop, which seemed to shake the air and extinguish the fire, leaving only smoke to tendril upward in the late morning air. "Vince Silva," he said. "I can also influence people by singing to them."

Locke was impressed. So that's how he'd gotten BJ to confess.

Ariel demonstrated his power by lifting Locke over his head, something he was more used to than he liked to admit, and Locke, still aloft, made it appear as though Ariel was wearing a beautiful sparkly red gown. Ariel twirled, thrilled, and Locke tried not to feel dizzy. Finally, Ariel curtsied in response to enthusiastic shouts and wolf whistles, putting Locke back on solid ground.

Cass strutted forward with a cocky grin and said, "Cass Talbot, Cabin One. Watch this and be jealous." Everyone with metal buttons on their pants at once found themselves unbuttoned, including Mister Mister. He offered Cass a raised eyebrow that seemed unimpressed and refastened his pants.

Bray created a cloud over them and some fog around them, which elicited a few snickers and a couple of calls for strobe lights.

"BJ, Cabin One," BJ said. He took a few steps forward until he was standing in front of Cass. Locke could barely hear him when he spoke. "Can you lift up your shirt, please?"

"Here?" Cass said, grinning. "Anything for you, darling."

That got a few cheers from the crowd, which were intensified when Cass decided to pull his shirt over his head instead of lifting it up.

BJ looked at Mister Mister. "I'm sorry. I swear this is about my power."

Mister Mister gave BJ a nod so slight Locke almost missed it.

"This would have turned blue in a few hours if I let it stay like that, just so you know," BJ said, putting his hands on the mark his elbow had left on Cass's stomach. He must have hit him harder than Locke realized when they were in the showers.

Cass smirked, exhaling through his mouth the moment BJ touched him.

"Does it hurt now?"

"No," Cass replied, winking at him. "Feels kind of good. Tingly."

BJ rolled his eyes, moving away from him. "I won't heal you next time, Cass. I'm serious."

"So you're telling me there'll be a next time," Cass replied, his voice loud.

Once all the whooping had died down, Mister Mister turned to speak to him, looking bored. "Put your shirt on, Talbot. Not everyone wants to see that."

Cass looked like he was about to say something back to him, but Mister Mister wasn't paying attention to him anymore, so Cass pouted while he did as instructed.

A guy with porcelain skin and thick brown hair stepped forward. "I'm Jamie Kane, a telepath. My power is kind of, well, invasive. I don't think anyone would appreci—oh, okay." He turned to look at Mister Mister. "But I don't wanna tell something you don't want—" Jamie fell silent, staring at Mister Mister, standing there alert but relaxed, just looking at him. "You-your lover was a villain?" Jamie said after a few seconds, shock in his voice.

"Good work," Mister Mister said, unperturbed.

Was that why Mister Mister retired? Surely he wouldn't be training them if he'd crossed the line. He looked to Vince who was staring, slack-jawed.

Locke was too far away to ask, and besides the guy whose glasses Mickey had so *spectacularly* removed was walking to the middle of the group. As he passed Bray, Bray said, "Rudy, Super Dork."

Rudy, right, that was his name. He could be a model, he was so clean cut in his khaki cargo shorts and white tee. He gave Bray a grave look and said, "May I see your phone?"

Bray sent a look of appeal to Mister Mister, who merely nodded. Reluctantly he pulled the device from his pocket and offered it to Rudy.

"That's okay, I don't need to touch it." He studied it for a few seconds. A smirk crossed his face and he looked Bray in the eyes. "I'm surprised you don't write 'dear diary,' but I'm sure you're not alone in your appreciation of cat gifs. Oh, and delete that photo of me you dorkified." He raised his voice and addressed the group. "I'm Rudy Jensen and I have an affinity for electronics."

A red-faced Bray was staring down at his phone.

"Does anyone else have their phones?" Mister Mister asked.

Locke and just about everyone else nodded.

"Give them to me, and tomorrow leave them in your cabins. They'll get broken if you try to carry them around on exercises." He held up a basket as if he knew exactly how this was going to carry through.

As the guys dropped their phones in, Mister Mister said, "On the other side of the lake, there's an old tower where they used to watch for forest fires. I'll be putting you into two teams, and whoever reaches the tower—and I mean inside to raise a flag I can see from here—wins. If any member of your team is caught by the other team, they're out and are to come back here immediately. Cheating gets people injured or killed in the real world, so don't do it here.

"Cockburn, you're the leader of Red team with Locke, Medeiros, Jensen, Kane, and Bailey. Green, you're leading Blue team."

Locke was a little disappointed he wasn't on the same team as Vince, and he didn't understand Mister Mister choices for leadership. Ace Green, the super speedy dreadlocked guy, said, "Red team has six members, Mister Mister. That's not fair."

"If you expect life to be fair, Green, consider this your first lesson. Sometimes you will be outnumbered. I'm not here to teach you how to get along in a fair world, but how to do your jobs in the real world."

Green didn't seem to have anything to say to that. As far as Locke could tell, Ace Green's team was the one with the advantage, considering their leader had super speed. He could get there long before anyone else could. It wasn't like he could protest now, though.

"You have ten minutes to talk to your team before the exercise starts," Mister Mister said.

"Sir?" The guy with the fire powers said. Locke thought his name was Royce Bailey. He should probably keep that in mind, since he was going to be on the same team as him. "I have a question."

"What is it, Bailey?"

"How—um, intense—"

"Don't kill anyone," Mister Mister said. "And remember, I am watching you."

Locke couldn't read his expression behind the beard, but he thought Mister Mister might have been smiling.

Chapter Six

AS THE TEAMS separated to strategize, Locke trailed after BJ, aware of Ariel chattering beside him. Would the losing team get a failing grade? He didn't think his father, a well-respected superhero, would be impressed if he failed his first exercise. Locke needed to prove he could be a superhero too, despite his comparatively undignified powers.

He looked at BJ, expecting him to say something. A leader shouldn't stand silent while his team bickered about what to do.

"We're already two minutes into prep time," Locke said after glancing at his watch.

"I know," BJ said. "I'm just thinking."

"Can you think faster, please?" Rudy Jensen said. "Having a plan would be better than having no plan at this point. Even if our plan is garbage."

"Hey, Locke, do you think I could get away with some sort of electric blue? I'm not loving this nail polish," Ariel said, holding his hand out and completely ignoring anyone else. "It's a bit grim."

Locke looked at Ariel's hand, wondering why he could still find Ariel's inability to focus irritating after all these years. He concentrated on creating the illusion of electric blue nail polish. "Like that?"

"A little lighter," Ariel said. "I don't know, I feel like this might clash with the color of my eyes."

"Jesus. Nobody cares about that shit, Medeiros. The other team seems to have a plan," Rudy said, glancing over his shoulder at the other team. "Maybe Jamie can tell us what it is."

"I can try, but it's kind of hard for me to—"

"Screw them," Ariel said, still looking at his nails. "Who cares about what they're doing? You guys are overthinking this. It's find a tower and put a flag on top. It's not like it's rocket science."

BJ rubbed his temple, looking straight at Ariel. "Right, and how do you propose we do that? One of them has super speed. Most of our powers are useless in this exercise."

"Great," Rudy said, crossing his arms over his chest. "Just what we need. A defeatist as our team leader."

Locke took a step forward. He didn't think he was team leader material himself, but anything would be better than BJ at this point. "Guys, listen," he said, a little more quietly than he intended. He cleared his throat, then continued. "Mister Mister said we're supposed to work together, so I'd guess he meant learn to figure out how to best use the skills and powers of the people we're teamed with."

"And what are you going to do, exactly?" Royce Bailey said, sticking his hands in his pockets. "Are you going to give us sparkly uniforms, so everyone on the Red team can at least look cute when we lose?"

Ariel grinned, looking at Locke. "Ohh, can you?"

"For fuck's sake—"

"At least he's trying, Royce," Ariel replied, glaring at him. "Which I don't see you fucking doing at all."

Royce rolled his eyes.

"We need to figure out where we're going to start," BJ said, raising his voice to drown the others out. "He said it was across the lake, right? So all we have to do is cross the lake first. Once we're there, we're going to need Locke's power to at least slow Ace Green down since he's our main concern."

"What do you mean?"

"We might need you to create a replica of the tower," Rudy said. "I think that's what he means. You'll have to tell us what you're planning to do with it and no one in the other team will know what it looks like, so it can confuse them."

"Yup," Locke said. "No problem."

"The lock on the boathouse is an electronic padlock," BJ said. "I noticed it when I was walking last night. Rudy, you can open that, right?"

"Yeah, but—"

BJ held up his hand. "Hear me out. I think Locke is right. So maybe it's not necessarily about who wins, but about how well we utilize our team. Obviously, Ace has an advantage, but being fast doesn't mean he can *find* the tower." He paused, thinking, and turned to Ariel. "This strength of yours, think it means you can paddle a canoe faster than anyone? Canoe speed is based on the strength of the paddle stroke, I think."

"Then sure. I've never done it before, but how hard can it be?" Ariel asked. Locke didn't think he expected an answer.

BJ gave Locke a triumphant look. "That'll cancel out Ace's speed, right? Like, how fast can he run through trees, anyway?"

Locke nodded, but he still had his doubts.

"What do I do?" Royce asked.

"Well," BJ said slowly, "how good is your control? If we get to the tower first, can you make a fire around the base to prevent the others from coming through? Without, you know, starting a forest fire?"

"Of course," Royce said, offense in his voice. "Child's play."

Jamie, who looked a little green, said, "I should be able to give warning when the other team is close or planning to use their powers. The thoughts people have at the top of their heads are the easiest to pick up," he added with a sidelong glance at Rudy.

"I need to be on higher ground to create an illusion tower," Locke said. "I need line of sight, and those trees are in the way." He shrugged, feeling inadequate.

"Makes sense." BJ frowned, staring across the lake at the dense thicket of trees, then upward.

"What about up there?" Ariel said, pointing to the tire wall on the obstacle course.

"Nah, the other team could see him a mile away," Royce said.

"The roof of the admin building," BJ suggested.

"And how do I get up there?"

"There's stuff on the roof that needs maintenance, shouldn't be too hard to figure out. If you go up there while we're crossing the lake, Jamie can tell us when you've got a tower up and what it looks like, so we'll know the real tower when we see it." BJ looked at Jamie. "You can do that, right?"

Jamie nodded. "Yeah, it's easier when someone's like, thinking right at me."

"So we have a plan?"

Locke had to admit, it didn't sound half bad. They might actually win this challenge. But he'd hoped to have a chance to talk to Ariel and that didn't seem likely, not during this exercise.

MAYBE IT WAS the lingering remains of his hangover, but Vince was tired and overwhelmed. It seemed like half his life had happened in the past—shit, it hadn't even been twenty-four hours. Mickey had teased Ace for being a pussy about bitching about unfair numbers, which Vince agreed with—Ace could run like the wind, they were a shoe-in to win this.

Until Ace schooled them all on the realities of his abilities and limitations. "I try to go fast through those trees, I'm gonna be a red smear on a tree trunk. Mister Mister probably picked this type of thing just to neutralize my abilities, so we need to be smart about this. We need to figure out what the other team is likely to do and counteract that and steal what ideas of theirs we can."

"As long as we can catch one of them," Vince offered, "I can get them to tell us their plans."

"That should be our first goal, then."

"Locke already knows what catching feels like when it comes to you," Cass replied, grinning. "Or was it the other way around?"

Vince avoided looking at him. He could feel himself blushing. "No, we haven't—"

Cass raised his eyebrows. "Awww, you were waiting until we could do a threesome?"

"As much as I'm sure we all love hearing about the sex you guys are having with each other," Ace said, crossing his arms over his chest. "I'm only here because my city won't let me work for them without whatever stupid piece of paper I'll get here. So I need us to win. If you could help, that would be pretty great."

"So what do we do?" Bray replied.

"We watch them," Ace said. "And we grab one of them. Shouldn't be too difficult."

"Unless Ariel tries to fight us off," Vince replied. He didn't mind being a big part of the plan, but he hadn't taken Ariel into consideration. "If Ariel is with the telepath, we're screwed."

Ace nodded. "If anyone's with the telepath, we're screwed. If we can get around Jamie's power, Ariel's super strength shouldn't be an issue."

"But what if they don't split up?" Cass said.

"They have to," Vince said. "Because some are going to try to find the tower and others are going to try to stop us. That makes sense, right?"

Mickey shrugged. "I don't know why you guys are worrying so much about this," he said.

Everyone ignored him. "This sounds like not much of a plan," Bray said, sounding dubious.

"Yeah, okay, fair enough," Ace said. "I'll keep that in mind when you're team leader. Now let's head over behind the boathouse so they'll think we're going around the lake from the south side. Once we see which way they split up, we'll know who to grab."

Vince didn't have any better ideas, so he kept his mouth shut. It seemed like an awful lot was depending on them being able to take out a member of the other team almost immediately, without Red team knowing. "Shouldn't we have some of our team going around the lake?"

"You guys assumed this would be a piece of cake because of my speed, right?"

Vince and the others nodded.

"So they probably will, too. They'll be looking for a fast way to the other side of the lake. We'll just steal their fast way." Ace grinned. "Looks like they're still figuring out their plan, so let's get going, make them nervous."

Ace led them at a brisk walk down to the south side of the boat house. He had them press against the wall while sending Mickey to kneel by the piling at the lakeside. "They're heading this way," he said in a frantic whisper. "All of them!"

"Shit! That doesn't make sense," Ace said with a scowl.

"Can we lose by overestimating them?" Vince wondered aloud.

"Shhh!" Mickey hissed.

"Okay, Rudy, do your thing," they heard BJ say, and then there were footsteps inside the boathouse.

Vince froze, his back against the thin wooden wall, the vibrations of the footsteps passing through the wood to him.

"How do we—?"

"Oh, please," came Ariel's voice, full of scorn.

The footsteps receded, and Vince heard a splash.

"We're not all going to fit in here," someone said.

BJ's voice announced, "Rudy, you stay here. Out of sight. If you see or hear the other team, you, um, think it at Jamie, okay?"

"Why me?"

"You did your part—how many electronics you think we're going to find in the woods?"

"Okay, fine. Off you go, shoo-shoo."

Ace looked at Vince and nodded.

Ace slid down the wooden wall to a crouch and asked Mickey in a voice so low, Vince almost couldn't make out the words. "Where's Rudy?"

"Weeds. Dock."

"Vince, you start down there, quiet as you can. Don't be seen. Once the others are far enough in the water, I'll do my speed thing and get him. Have a song on your lips, baby, we won't have much time." Ace delivered all that in a low urgent voice, without so much as a smile or wink on the last sentence.

Vince didn't bother with an acknowledgement. This might be a game, an exercise, but he found it so easy to take it as serious as if the other team really were—his thoughts stumbled on the word *villains*.

Is this how Dad and his girlfriend do it? Anyone opposing their objective is the true villain?

That was an uncomfortable thought. There was no moral or just-cause in this exercise, just a goal. He stumbled over a hummock of grass and froze, but there was no movement from where Mickey had reported Rudy to be. *Focus.*

Every step he took seemed to rustle grass, but the other team seemed to be having difficulty with their canoe and their increasingly angry shouts covered a lot of the noise of his progress. He was closer than he realized—Rudy's brown hair blended into the reeds and cattails, but he turned his head and his pale skin stood out like a beacon. Vince sat down and groaned softly when he realized the ground beneath his ass was damp.

Eventually the sounds on the water started to fade—Red team's fast way across the lake seemed pretty damn slow—and a blur suddenly ruffled the grasses in front of Vince. He got to his feet and ran to where Ace was holding Rudy, his hand clamped over the pale guy's mouth, his glasses askew.

"Sing!" Ace hissed.

Vince opened his mouth and drew a blank. "H-happy birthday to you," he sang in desperation, ignoring Ace's smirk. "You won't tell the telepath anything, right?"

Rudy and Ace both nodded. Shit, his song affected both of them. They hadn't thought of that. Vince focused on Rudy. "Rudy. You won't yell out when Ace lets go of your mouth, right?"

Rudy nodded again.

Vince sang a few more lines of the birthday song to reinforce his power and said, "Rudy, tell me what Red team's plan is."

Rudy very calmly, but with panic in his eyes, told Ace and Vince the whole of Red Team's plan. "That's pretty fucking clever," Ace said. "What's the fake tower look like?"

Rudy's mouth tightened in defiance, and Vince hummed the first two bars of the song again before saying, "Answer Ace's questions, Rudy."

"I don't know. Locke's going to make it and he'll think the description at Jamie, I'm just stuck here."

"You can unlock the shed for us, right?"

"Yes," Rudy said with a scowl. "Come on."

The three of them walked out of the weeds, and Ace beckoned to the rest of Blue team. Rudy did his thing with the lock and Ace swept the boathouse with his gaze.

"There are the canoes," Bray said.

"Oh, but this is what we need," Cass called from outside. "Check it out. A motorboat. Those pansies will never beat us in that."

Rudy, who had followed them outside again, said sullenly, "I can't make it go."

Cass beamed. "But I can."

"Really?" Mickey asked in high sarcasm. "Your power is good for more than undoing buttons?"

Cass gave him a ha-ha, very funny look and jumped into the boat.

Vince hummed a bit more and said, "Rudy, you'll go turn yourself into Mister Mister." That was the rule and Rudy looked the type to follow the rules, but it didn't hurt to make sure.

Rudy walked off as the motor roared to life.

"Come on, this is going to be fun," Cass said.

"We'll pass those losers like they're standing still," Bray added, hopping into the boat.

"Um, guys? That's the camp's emergency boat." Mickey pointed to the lettering on the side.

Ace grinned. "Well, we're saving the world, aren't we? That's an emergency."

They passed Red team just a few feet from shore, waving and cheering.

Vince liked the motorboat, but of course Mickey was right—it wasn't for the trainees to use normally and there was a remote possibility Mister Mister would dock them for points or something. He had no idea how exercises were scored. He should pay better attention.

They tied the boat to a sturdy looking bush and climbed out. Vince had grown up in a gated enclave, with huge manicured lawns and Olympic-sized swimming pools. Trees grew in the middle of flower beds tended by a specially vetted lawn service. This uncivilized nature of tall weeds and whip thin branches on scrubby bushes was, in a word, awful. He'd never heard of super heroes having to do this kind of shit, but he was at camp because they'd all trained at camp, so they must've done it once. In training.

"Any idea where the tower, the real one, is?" he asked

"Red team's on the ground. Watch out for Ariel."

Vince grinned. In spite of Ariel's demonstration of his power, he found it hard to think of the pretty, slender cutie as probably being strong enough to juggle the entire Blue team.

Bray said, "Fire watch tower, it's likely uphill somewhere."

They pushed into a clearing, staying close to the tree trunks. Red team no doubt knew what their fake tower looked like, so they would probably split up right away, half heading for the fake tower to fool Blue team into thinking it was real, and half looking for the real tower.

Ace said out loud what he'd been thinking, keeping his voice low and warning them once again to watch out for Red team. At this point, their powers were pretty useless, they were going to have to win with old-fashioned intelligence. Vince gave Mickey a sidelong look. *Heaven help us.*

They headed uphill, darting from tree to tree to use the rough trunks as cover. "I see it!" Mickey yelled and darted forward before anyone could say anything.

"Fuck," someone cursed from amidst the trees. "Didn't realize they were so close."

"I got him," said another voice. Royce, the pyromancer, appeared briefly in the trees as Mickey tumbled forward, arms outspread to catch his fall.

"Bray," Ace hissed, "You hear me?"

"Yeah," came the soft reply from Vince's left.

"Give us some fog cover. We can't lose another team member."

"No loss," someone muttered, so low Vince couldn't tell if it was Bray or Cass.

Vince eased forward a few trees. "Um, Ace?" He kept his voice low and moved a few more trees ahead. "I see two tower bases." He wasn't sure what he expected, maybe that Locke's illusion tower would be somehow glittery—which made no sense—but instead all he saw was on his right a criss-cross of wooden beams supporting the base of one tower and on his left, what looked like a tree with a ladder on it.

Bray's fog crept up their legs in horror-movie style, filling the forest around them with damp gray swirls.

Ace made it to Vince's side as the fog fully enveloped them. "Shit," he muttered.

Bray and Cass stumbled through the fog to join them.

"Nice work, dude," Cass mumbled. "I can't see a damn—um, wait. Is that the tower?"

All four of them were staring at the cross-braced tower, which seemed to shimmer in and out of the fog.

"That's the fake!" Vince clapped his hand over his mouth, but it was too late to lower his voice.

"Let's move," Ace ordered in a low voice, signalling them to the left. As they moved swiftly through the trees, the fog, not slowing them down as much as the prior necessity of advancing one tree at a time, slowly dissipated. When they reached the small clearing at the base of the real tower, the cover was all but gone.

"Sorry guys," Bray said, "I need to draw moisture from the lake to make clouds and..." he shrugged.

"Hide!" Vincent yelled the word in as loud of whisper as he could when he saw Red team break out of the woods.

"Fuck hiding," Ace muttered. "We're this close."

Royce flung out his arms and fire leapt between the tower and Blue team, racing in a curve to circle the tower.

"We got this," Ace said with a grin, flashing them a thumbs-up before he was gone in a blur.

The fire completed its circle and Royce turned toward them. "Ha!"

Maybe he'd forgotten how Vince had put out his fire before. He opened his mouth and Cass grabbed his arm. "Wait. Let 'em think they've got us. Right now their fire is covering Ace climbing up that rickety ladder."

Red team went into a huddle and Vince stifled a chuckle. He checked to make sure the ground was dry, and sat down, as if he didn't have a care in the world. The day was hot, too hot for a fire, but the high flames weren't throwing nearly the heat he'd expected.

Cass, grinning so broadly his face might split, joined him, flinging his arm across his shoulders. "We might have time for a make-out session."

Vince couldn't help but grin back as he shook Cass's arm off.

Before the members of Red team began advancing on them, no doubt to get them "out" so Royce could put out the fire and climb the tower, an alarm rent the air, and Mister Mister's voice echoed through the forest, "Blue wins! Return to the yard!"

Ace and BJ shook hands, briefly, grudgingly, after Royce put out his fire and Ace got back to the ground. All of them were tired and covered in scratches, Vince noted, and nobody was saying much. They stomped through the underbrush to the boats and Ariel's disappointed expression lifted. "A speed boat!" He turned big, sad puppy eyes on Ace and said, "Can I ride?"

Bray snickered.

Ariel shot Bray a look and winked, "Wait your turn, big boy."

"In your dreams."

Vince chuckled, which got him a smile from Ariel.

"We might as well all go back in the motorboat," Ace said. "Mickey, you tie a rope to the canoe and we'll tow it back."

"Why me?"

Everyone ignored him, which seemed to be the thing to do, and a grumbling Mickey did as he was told.

Vince helped tie off the motorboat as Ariel practically skipped up the beach with the canoe over his head. Blue team hadn't bothered to close the boathouse door, so Ariel waltzed in and presumably put it back. "We done in here?"

Vince looked up. Ariel was holding the lock on the closed door.

"Yes," BJ and Ace said at the same time, before exchanging wry looks.

Locke and Rudy were already with Mister Mister in the yard where they'd started from.

"Well, if it isn't Loser Locke," Bray said, as if he'd been holding his inner asshole back for the duration of the exercise.

Ariel turned to gape at him, disbelief writ large on his innocent looking face. "Seriously?"

"What are you gonna do about it?" Bray asked, jutting out his chin

Vince could only stare. Had Bray gone insane? He looked to Locke, whose mouth had fallen open *in a totally kissable way—shut up!*

"What's your problem?" Locke asked, taking a step forward.

A yelp of pain swivelled his head back to Bray.

Ariel had Bray's right arm twisted behind his back, holding it with one hand. Bray's face was scrunched in pain and he was on his knees. "You know what I like to do with big, muscular men like you?" Ariel purred. "I like to hold them down and fuck them till they beg for mercy. That'll never happen for you if you keep being mean."

Vince was not the only one staring in astonishment. Mister Mister even looked taken aback. Only Locke seemed to find this declaration normal.

Bray grunted something incoherent and hissed as Ariel released him.

"What? You all think because I'm the prettiest and most fabulous gay here I'm automatically a bottom?" He turned, sticking his ass out and slapping both hands on it. "It takes someone special to get this ass." He straightened and jumped around to glare at everyone. "And so far none of you are even close."

"All right," Mister Mister said. "Everyone calm down. Save it for your exercise tomorrow." He grinned, and Vince thought it might be an evil grin. "I want you to write out an analysis report of today's exercise. Begin with your team's plan and what you think worked, what didn't, and why. Extrapolate the other team's plan and point out what you think they did right and wrong, too. Everyone with the exception of Cabin One, who has to get their sorry asses to the kitchen, so off you go. Now for the rest of you...."

Vince groaned, and Locke, who was the only one of Cabin One who didn't have scratches and bruises from the woods, still looked exhausted. Holding an illusion that far away for that long must have worn him out. Lights out couldn't come soon enough.

Chapter Seven

WEEKEND LEAVE WAS granted in the thriving city of Guilford, which was also a haven for the rich and very carefully not-famous. As soon as the helicopter landed on the helipad of the Roehampton Hotel and Vince managed to exit, he wanted to kiss the ground. Instead, he stood with his hands on his knees as he tried to catch his breath while the helicopter powered down. Like everyone else at camp, he had anxiously been waiting for his first weekend off. There was the extra bonus that he would get to spend some of the day with Locke, away from all the craziness at Camp Hologram. Maybe they would get to finish what they had started in the showers a few days ago.

Just the thought was enough to make his head spin.

He hadn't minded the helicopter taking him into the camp, because he was too busy thinking about how his life was about to change. On the way to the city, though, he remembered how much he hated flying. He had never been good with heights and the flight was worse than he had expected. Luckily it wasn't far, because at one point, he had been sure he was going to hurl on Locke's lap.

Locke had noticed how pale he was getting and put his hand over Vince's. They held hands all the way to the city, and as the nausea started to subside, Vince was starting to see how romantic it had been. He straightened up and tried to find Locke, vaguely aware that someone was shoving him aside with their shoulder.

"Silva," Bray said. "Would have never taken you for such a pussy."

Vince grimaced. "You, on the other hand—"

"Didn't you learn your lesson already?" Locke said. As if by magic, Locke's hand was in the middle of his back and he was looking at Bray with scorn. "Go away."

Bray looked at Locke for a second, his eyes narrowing. Locke glanced at Ariel. Bray's gaze followed Locke's. Bray bit his lips, scoffed, and turned on his heel and walked away.

"Must be handy having a best friend with super strength," Vince said.

Locke laughed. "Trust me, I work hard for it. Are you feeling better? You looked white as a sheet up there."

"Yeah," Vince replied. They were watching the rest of the guys go downstairs, one after the other, until they were the only ones left up on the roof. Except for Ariel, who was standing there with his arms crossed over his chest.

"Hey, go ahead without me," Locke said, waving at him. "I'll catch up with you later."

Ariel's eyes narrowed. "You sure?"

"Yep, positive," Locke replied.

Ariel shook his head, turning on his heels and storming away from them.

"He seems mad," Vince said, more to himself than to Locke.

Locke chuckled quietly. "He'll get over it."

"Ugh, I didn't mean to slow us down."

"I'm in no rush," Locke said, smiling at him. His green eyes shone in the sunlight and Vince had to stop himself from kissing him right then and there. "I wanted to make sure you were feeling better before we did anything."

"We—we're doing things?" Vince said, realizing how stupid it sounded the moment he heard the words. Of course they were *doing* things. He cleared his throat and tried to recover. "I mean, are we still on for tonight?"

Locke looked away from him, his smile turning into a wide grin. "Yes," Locke said. "In fact, there's something I've been meaning to ask you."

Vince tried to swallow down the knot in his throat. Going out for dinner with Locke was what had kept him sane all this time. At least, it had felt that way. He'd thought about what Locke had said in the showers almost every night as he was falling asleep, his voice crystal clear in Vince's head.

Not today. Not like this.

They hadn't been alone since then, no opportunity had presented itself to see things through. Going back to the cabin after a long day of training meant going straight to their bunks and passing out almost the moment they had climbed into bed. Even if they hadn't been so exhausted, the cabin wasn't the right place to do anything. Cass was always watching, always ready with a sexual remark, and always asking why they didn't give each other good night kisses. BJ was angry with Cass just as often, and things didn't seem to be getting better.

He thought that, as they adjusted, things would settle down. Vince knew it was a little early to expect everyone to be used to the way things were now—he wasn't used to it himself—but he hadn't expected it to be that difficult. The fact that Locke was sleeping on the bunk right above his didn't make things any easier.

If Locke was about to cancel on him, things were going to get a whole lot more complicated than that.

"What are you doing today? I mean, I know some of the guys have to run errands and stuff, so it's cool if you have to, too," Locke said. All his confidence seemed to have left him and he was staring at the ground. "I'm not going to be offended if you can't, just so you know, but I thought I would ask anyway."

"I don't know what you're talking about, Locke," Vince replied, a little more sharply than he intended to. He hoped Locke couldn't hear the panic under the irritation in his voice, the last thing he wanted was to appear desperate. "What do you mean?"

Locke took a deep breath. "I'm just saying that if you don't already have plans, we could, I don't know, maybe spend the day together? But I totally won't be offended if you say no, like, if you already have plans. I mean, we're still on for dinner, right?"

"Wait, you want to spend the whole day with me?" Vince replied, without thinking, relief washing over him.

"Yeah," Locke said. He wasn't staring at the ground anymore, though he was looking away from Vince. Still, from his profile, Vince could see how red Locke's cheeks were. It was a little weird, seeing Locke go from his normally confident personality to insecure and mumbling when all he was doing was asking Vince out. It made Vince smile.

He wanted a continuation of their encounter in the cabin, too. At the very least.

Locke exhaled through his nose. "So what do you say?"

"Yeah," Vince replied. "I'd love to spend the day with you."

"So THAT'S A firm no on the Ferris wheel?" Locke said to Vince.

Vince rolled his eyes, but he laughed.

They were at the amusement park on the riverfront, surrounded by games and couples with and without children. The smell of deep-fried food filled the air. They'd spent much of the day playing every game available with not a single badly made stuffed toy to show for their efforts, but it had been a lot of fun. The kind of fun Vince couldn't remember having before.

Dinner had been crazy romantic on board an old sternwheeler riverboat all decked out with trim that reminded him of cake decorations. After dinner had brought them back to the park, on the riverfront promenade, and a bench to sit and watch the sunset.

Vince had been a little shy at first—his experience with relationships was spotty to say the least—but Locke didn't seem to care. He carried the conversation until Vince felt comfortable, asking his opinions of almost everyone at camp, and the conversation had moved from there to their childhoods and their expectations for camp.

Vince had never expected camp to be easy, of course, but Locke struck him as better prepared for it. Maybe it was just Locke's confident approach.

"It looks nicer from up there," Locke said.

"You can make me a sunset," Vince replied, smiling at him. "Right?"

"That's true," Locke said. "I can. But there's a perfectly good one happening right now, so I don't know why you would need me to."

"You're right," Vince replied. "I'm just enjoying sitting on this bench. Uh, you know, being with you."

He looked up at Locke, who was smiling. He put his hand over Vince's. Vince grabbed him, trying to ignore how fast his heart was going. Locke looked stunning in this light, and Vince had held off for long enough. He leaned up to kiss Locke, aware and nervous because, in spite of what had already passed between them, this felt like a first kiss.

Locke looked like he was ready, more than ready, to kiss him back. But before their lips could meet, Vince was distracted by a buzzing noise, which he soon realized was Locke's phone ringing in his pocket.

"Shit," he said, shaking his head. "I'm so sorry. This has gotta be my dad on the phone. I told him I was going to call him as soon as we had our first day off and I totally forgot. I have to get this, I'm sorry."

"It's okay," Vince replied, trying for a smile. "Trust me. I get it."

"I'll just be a minute," Locke said, winking at him. "Then we can keep doing what we were doing."

He watched Locke swipe his fingers over the screen of his phone and bring it to his face. "Hey, Dad," Locke said. "Yeah, I know; I'm sorry, I—"

He moved the phone away from his face as he listened, rolling his eyes at Vince and mouthing the word "parents," then moving it close to his face again.

"I know," Locke said. "No, it's been fine. Yeah, I know. Yup, uh huh. Hey, listen, can I call you tomorrow? I'm kind of in the middle of something right now. No, I will. I promise I will. Okay. Love you, too. Bye, Dad."

He hung up the phone and stuck it back in his pocket, smiling apologetically at Vince. "Yikes, sorry about that. I normally wouldn't have answered, and if it was anyone else, I wouldn't have. You don't know my dad, though, he's, like...."

"Strict?"

"Yeah," Locke replied, nodding vigorously. "Controlling. Don't get me wrong; he means well, but things can get pretty tricky with him. It's like he doesn't know I'm an adult now, and still wants to control every aspect of my life. He can be exhausting."

"I know what that's like," Vince replied. He got exhausting and controlling, though he doubted his own father could be called strict in the sense Locke meant it. He was pretty doubtful on the "he means well" part, too.

"Yeah?" Locke gave him a sympathetic grimace. "Yours, too?"

Vince tried to swallow down the knot in his throat. "Yeah," he said, trying to keep his voice as steady as possible. He *really* didn't want to talk about his dad with anyone at camp, especially not with Locke. He would have to if Locke wanted to do this again later, but right then, it was just a date. They were just having fun, he reminded himself. It didn't have to mean anything else. "He's a handful."

Locke chuckled. "I'm telling you, man. Parents," he said.

Vince leaned back on the bench, closing his eyes. His father. What the hell would he say if he found out about this, whatever this was, between him and Locke? Despite his long-running relationship with a woman who was as bad as him, his father still treated Vince and his mother like they were his possessions. He was like a child, a dangerous child, who didn't like other people playing with his toys, even if he didn't want them anymore. At least there was no way he could know what was going on at camp. He took a few cleansing breaths. Vince hadn't ever been very good at hiding his feelings, but he hoped Locke didn't notice how unsettled he was.

"Hey, are you okay? You're not mad at me or anything, right? I didn't want to pick—"

"No," Vince said, opening his eyes and smiling at him. "I'm not mad at you. I'm feeling a bit... I don't know. It's been a hell of a week, hasn't it? I think it's starting to sink in now."

Locke nodded, sighing and leaning back so he was right next to Vince. "It really has been."

Locke grabbed Vince's hand again and put his head on his shoulder. "Nice weekend, though."

"Yeah," Vince replied, smiling and squeezing Locke's hand. "Great weekend so far."

ALL THE GUYS were at the Roehampton Hotel for weekend leave; the camp had two standing suites split between them. When Locke had suggested they get their own room, Vince's mouth had gone dry and he could only nod in agreement.

But the Roehampton wasn't any hotel. And now they were standing at the check-in desk in sticker-shock at the price being asked for the smallest available room. "Give us a second," Locke said with an easy smile, drawing Vince out of earshot. "I'm not changing my mind or anything, but that's, ugh. My Dad is against a lot of sponsorships and stuff, we're just, we're not rich. Um—"

"It's cool," Vince said, putting a finger to Locke's lips. "I'm not rich, either." Not since his father left him and his mother struggling to make the payments on that fancy house in the gated enclave.

Locke pursed his lips against Vince's finger. He reached up and took Vince's hand, squeezing it.

Vince caught his breath. He really, really wanted this. "What if I just, you know, convinced her to comp us?"

Locke's beautiful green eyes widened. "I think it might be okay. Just once."

It was exactly the kind of thing they *weren't* supposed to do, Vince knew. And Locke's expression said he knew it, too. He sucked his lower lip in and bit at it. "Just once, right?"

"Yeah." Locke's eyes took on a sparkle. "Let's do it."

They returned to the counter, Vince humming softly as Locke began to confidently insist they should get a free room, for... reasons.

Vince could have—he should have—told him they didn't need *reasons,* that telling the receptionist she wanted to comp them the room was enough, but watching Locke's confidence fade into fumbling and his face get redder and redder as he tried to come up with plausible excuses was too adorable.

Once Locke was done talking, the receptionist handed them two key cards and told them to enjoy their stay.

Locke caught Vince's gaze and smiled. Neither one of them wanted to get in any more trouble. A room with Locke, though, a room with *just* Locke, that was too good to pass up.

Vince grabbed Locke's hand and dragged him toward the elevator.

LOCKE TRIED NOT to laugh as he stumbled after Vincent. Delighted wasn't a word that crossed his mind very often. It was more for ice cream in waffle cones with sprinkles or something innocent like that. Except he was pretty sure he was delighted with Vince's enthusiasm.

They held hands while Vince's foot tapped impatiently at the elevator bank. When the first set of dull chrome doors slid open, spilling out people, three others brushed by them to board. Locke took a step and spun about a little as Vince didn't move.

"We'll take the next one," Vince said.

"I thought you were in a hurry," Locked asked with a smile.

A second elevator chimed before Vince could answer, and there was no one else waiting to go up as it emptied. Vince all but dragged him in, jabbing the close door button.

"What's this—"

Vince stopped his words with a finger to his lips, repeating his action from the lobby. "This might sound weird, but I've been wanting to do this all day."

His hand moved to cup Locke's head and Locke stilled, his breath catching.

Vince's kiss was sweet and fresh, like a first date kiss should be, Locke thought, and he found the sweetness of it was a turn on. He let Vince take the lead for a few moments, until the kiss grew urgent. Locke kissed back with the same urgency, grabbing Vince by the hips and pulling his body tight against him.

Who knew what would have happened, if the damn alert hadn't sounded. Who the hell took the elevator from the third floor up? They barely had time to get their breathing under control, and Locke imagined he was as flushed as Vince as a family of three boarded the elevator, towels on their shoulders. Of course—the pool was on the roof.

Locke stifled a sigh, and clutched Vince's hand. He liked holding Vince's hand. More could wait until they collected just enough stuff for the night. They should be able to sneak that out without anyone realizing.

The elevator chimed for their floor and the kid beamed up at them as they exited. Locke couldn't help smiling back before the elevator door slid closed again.

The suite was full. It seemed like everyone was there getting ready to go out and check out the bars, if they were old enough to drink, or movies if they weren't. Locke didn't care what their plans were. He went to the cramped room where he and Royce were supposed to be sleeping and dug out a small plastic bag. He carried several, one for dirty clothes, and one to keep a wet toothbrush from getting everything else wet. He stuffed in a change of underwear, socks, and a clean T-shirt. He added a comb, his toothbrush, and the lube and condoms Ariel had insisted he bring to camp "just in case."

Ariel, oh god, he hadn't even texted him. He picked up the bag and it looked perfectly casual, not like "I'm sneaking off to fuck my potential new boyfriend."

He didn't have to worry about finding Ariel, though, because the brightly colored hair was the first thing he saw when he opened the door. Ariel turned, pushed Locke back in the room and closed the door, lowering the din to a dull roar. "Where the hell have you been all afternoon?"

"Ariel, I'm sorry. I was with Vince. I like him. I didn't mean to blow you off, but—"

"We're not even in the same cabin, Locke! I never see you! I was hoping we could do stuff." Ariel was pouting, his voice an unattractive whine. "You're with Vince all the time."

"It's not the same and you know it." Locke took a breath. "Look, I know I owe you some quality friendship time—I have a lot to talk to you about, too. And I miss you, too! But I was so worried Vince would think I was a flake, and like I said, I really like him."

He grasped Ariel by the shoulders, staring into his eyes to show how sincere he was. The bag he was still holding bumped against Ariel's arm.

Ariel glanced down sidelong at his arm, then up at Locke with a sudden, sunny grin. "You swapped room assignments?"

"Are you kidding? Listen to how noisy those bastards are out there. You think anything that happens in one of these rooms is going to be private?"

Ariel's grin faded a bit. "I wanted to go shopping with you on the promenade. And talk to you, about, you know. The talent."

Locked chuckled at that. "I want to do that, too. And ask your opinion about Vince, but you're gonna have to spend some time with him that's not on exercise to be able to tell me what you think. What say we have brunch, the three of us, and then we'll see? I'd kind of like to bring Vince along with us, you and me, but I don't want either of you feeling like a third wheel. Oh god, I'm getting ahead of myself, aren't I?"

"Kind of," Ariel said with a smirk. "That's why you need me."

Locke grinned. "Yeah, I guess it is. I knew it had to be something."

Chapter Eight

VINCE KEPT LOOKING at Locke as they rode a disappointingly full elevator down to their own private room. Locke kept looking back, with a wink or a seductive lick of his lips.

The room door had barely closed behind them when Vince felt Locke's lips on his. Locke kissed him eagerly, hungrily. Vince kissed him back, his breath quickening. Locke's hands were all over his chest, then down at his waist, undoing his belt. He wanted to get Locke's clothes off, too, but he was already hard and his jeans weren't exactly comfortable.

Locke pushed him up against the wall and continued kissing him, his body pressing into Vince's. Vince fumbled with the buttons on Locke's shirt until he could run his hands over Locke's bare chest. They stumbled, Vince forward, Locke backward, until they both fell on the bed. Vince turned his face away from Locke's for a second, trying to catch his breath.

Locke looked at him, furrowing his brow. "You okay?"

"Yeah, just—just give me a second," Vince replied. He was trying to take it all in, the fact that he would finally be with Locke, *properly*. Not on the uncomfortable floor of a wooden cabin, or while he was trying to be quiet because someone else might be able to hear them. "Gotta take these jeans off."

"Let me help you with that," Locke said. He went to the edge of the bed gracefully, his skin glistening under the dim incandescent light and making every line on his body more visible than usual. Vince only had a second to think about how gorgeous Locke was before his jeans were being pulled down and off his legs. He could feel Locke's breathing on the inside of his legs. Locke kissed his skin, soft and sweet kisses punctuated by playful nibbling.

Every time Locke touched him, every time Locke's lips came in contact with Vince's skin, Vince could hear himself moaning, as if the sound wasn't coming from his own mouth. He was hardly aware of anything but Locke and the way he was touching him. Locke grabbed his boxers and slowly moved them down, his breathing quickened. He looked down at Locke, who was kneeling down in front of him, his mouth open and his eyes glimmering. Their gazes locked for a second. Then Locke swallowed and wrapped his lips around Vince's incredibly hard cock.

Vince dug his fingers into the quilt as Locke's hot mouth slowly, too slowly, took his full length before he eased back. His tongue undulated every so often to send a shiver up Vince's spine and through to the rest of his body. He threw his head back and moaned, Locke playing with his already tight balls.

Locke started to speed up his deep-throating, and Vince could feel himself edging closer and closer to orgasm. If Locke kept doing this for too long, there would be no way Vince would be able to stop himself.

"Wait," Vince managed to say between breaths. "Wait, Locke."

Locke eased away, looking up into Vince's face. "Don't you like this?"

"No, I—I really like it," Vince replied, still trying to catch his breath. "You just said—I wanted to finish what we started in the showers."

Locke swallowed, his Adam's apple moving as he did so. Vince loved to watch Locke's throat work, he loved to watch any part of Locke work, move, do *anything*.

"You're right," Locke replied, getting to his feet. He leaned over and kissed Vince deeply, his lips lingering on Vince's before he spoke again. "You're right, I'm sorry. You're so gorgeous I get carried away."

Vince nodded. He tried to smile, but he wasn't sure whether the muscles in his face were responding. He wasn't sure of anything except the fact that he needed Locke. "I know, I just—I, um, can't hold off for much longer and I n-need—"

"Okay," Locke replied, kissing him on the lips again, this time softly, tenderly. He grabbed the bottom of Vince's shirt and took it off him, his fingertips digging into Vince's sides as he did so. "Okay. Lie down."

Vince did what Locke told him, lying down on the bed and waiting. He watched Locke quickly undo his buttons and take off his pants. The outline of Locke's erection was visible under the fabric of his gray boxers, and Vince thought he may have gotten harder at the sight of him, though he didn't think that was possible.

"There's lube in my bag," Locke said, smiling at him and then slinking away to grab the bag he'd thrown off his shoulder and on the floor the moment they walked through the door.

Vince groaned. "Hurry up."

Locke laughed, walking quickly toward the bed. When he was at the foot of it, he looked up and down Vince's body and visibly swallowed. He knelt down on the bed, while Vince watched him cover his fingers in lube. Locke teased him by slowly running his fingers between his cheeks, making the anticipation almost too much to bear.

"Please," Vince groaned.

Locke smiled, exhaling sharply. He pushed his fingers inside Vince, one at a time. Vince moaned, his hips moving up and down on Locke's hand, every thrust and stroke pushing him closer and closer to the edge.

Locke spoke between sharp breaths. "You ready?"

"Yes," Vince replied. "Yes."

Vince's eyes shot open. He looked down at Locke, who had removed his hand and was now opening a condom wrapper with his teeth. He closed his eyes again, trying to catch his breath. He could hardly begin to process the fact that this was happening at all when Locke kneeled between his legs. He could faintly hear the bottle of lube being squeezed, the way the bed squeaked under their combined weight, the way Locke was breathing; sharp and fast. Everything but his own quickened heartbeat sounded far away. He felt the movement of Locke inching closer, felt Locke's hands gently raise his knees over Locke's shoulders.

Then Locke was inside of him, *Locke* was inside of him, thrusting slowly at first, his hands still on the back of Vince's legs, which were now bent and up in the air. Vince opened his eyes to look at him, to look at his face, at his half-closed eyes and parted lips. Locke wrapped his hand around Vince's cock, stroking him with every thrust, every hip movement. It was much too much. He heard Locke say something, though he couldn't understand what it was, as every muscle in his body contracted, and he was coming, crying out, vaguely aware he was covering both of their stomachs in spunk. Then he heard Locke scream, too, his body jerking against Vince's.

Locke pulled out and collapsed next to Vince, his arm falling across Vince's body. "You're so fucking amazing," Locke whispered into Vince's ear. "I would have waited months for that."

"You're the one who's amazing," Vince replied, swallowing, still trying to catch his breath. "I'm glad you didn't have to wait."

"Yeah," Locke said, nuzzling into Vince's neck. "Me too."

IT WAS A few minutes after midnight when the desire struck for something to drink besides water, along with the midnight munchies. Vince hadn't wanted to leave their room, but both he and Locke were pretty sure the drinks in the minifridge weren't part of their complimentary stay at the hotel, and they didn't want to push their luck. Vince was tired, spent, and thirsty. He also needed some time to process what had just happened.

The vending machine was in the lobby, and he couldn't even contemplate the stairs. His knees were still weak, and his ass was tender. Pleasantly, but he'd feel it tomorrow. It was enough he made it to the elevators. He pushed the down button, going through everything that had happened with Locke in his head. It was hard to believe he had only met him about a week ago, when it seemed like Locke had already become such an important part of his life.

But he couldn't get carried away. Locke was obviously more experienced, and he had been prepared. He had condoms, lube—he was probably always prepared.

Locke almost always seemed so at ease. He had even seemed relaxed when they were on the verge of negotiating a threesome, as though he was used to doing that kind of stuff. Vince wasn't sure how he felt about that, though in his mind the threesome was off the table.

He couldn't exactly ask what they were. They had just met a week ago. And though what had just happened was a big deal for Vince, it probably wasn't for Locke.

HE'D *TRIED* TO have casual sex, but it seemed like a lot more work than the reward was worth. It was a shame, because having a relationship was almost impossible when his dad felt he had a right to meddle. Vince still didn't know, would probably never know, if his ex-boyfriend had wanted to cheat on him or if his dad had made him do it.

Plus, if they got into a relationship, Vince would have to tell Locke about everything. He would have to tell him about his father and about his father's girlfriend, and Vince didn't think Locke would be okay with it. He didn't think anyone would be okay with it.

So maybe it was a good thing Locke wasn't into relationships.

The elevator doors opened. Vince looked up to see Ariel walking in, nodding at him and then pressing the close doors button.

"Needed a break?" Ariel said, smiling.

Vince smiled back at him. "Getting a drink. You?"

"There're too many people in that room, and Cass and BJ won't stop throwing shit at each other. I could have broken it up, but I might have chipped my new polish." Ariel made a show of studying his nails, painted blue with purple stripes. Or maybe purple with blue stripes. He glanced at Vince from under his lashes. "Anyway, I needed some fresh air."

"Yeah," Vince replied, nodding. "I don't blame you."

Ariel looked him up and down, his expression sobering. "You know I could kill you with a flick of my fingers, right?"

Vince's eyes widened. Alarmed was not a strong enough word for how he was feeling, but there was a chance Ariel was just joking. He was Locke's friend, and apart from defending Locke—and Bray had deserved it—Ariel had never struck Vince as a violent person. He cleared his throat, trying to make himself sound more confident than he felt. "Y-yeah?"

Ariel stared at him, his eyes big and intense. "If you hurt him; I will hurt *you*," Ariel said. "I don't mean that figuratively. I don't mean I will drag you on Snapchat or whatever. I mean, I will genuinely, physically hurt you."

Vince swallowed. He had no doubt Ariel meant it. Ariel had proven he was fiercely protective of Locke. "I don't think I could hurt him," Vince replied.

Ariel turned around to look at the elevator doors and shrugged. "Okay," he said. "I'm just telling you."

The elevator pinged as it got to the lobby, and Ariel got off first, holding his hand on the door so it wouldn't close. He turned to look at Vince for a second and grinned at him. "By the way, this whole just-got-out-of-bed look you have going on is super cute," he said. "You look adorable like this. Okay, bye!"

Vince watched him walk away before he remembered he was supposed to be getting off the elevator, too.

VINCE'S HANDS WERE full when he got back to the room. Dinner had been on Locke, and while he couldn't exactly protest when they were on a date, Vince didn't want to make Locke feel like he was the only one spending money. Ariel's threat may have played a part in how much he had decided to spend. Not that it was a lot—it wasn't close to what Locke had spent through the day—but at least now they had drinks and a lot of candy.

He fumbled to get his key card out of his pocket when Locke opened the door for him, wearing nothing but a towel around his waist. Vince thought he looked gorgeous like that, his hair dark from the shower, beads of water still on his skin.

Locke looked at him and smiled, cocking his head. "Do you need me to help you with that?"

"Yeah," Vince replied, shoving some of the things he had bought into Locke's hands. "Thank you. I know I went a little crazy, I didn't know what you like and I wanted to—"

Locke was trying not to laugh.

Vince sighed, embarrassed. "It's too much, isn't it?"

"Right, how dare you bring me too much candy," Locke said, chuckling. Vince closed the door behind him and followed Locke to the bed. Locke dropped the handful of candy on the unmade bed and turned to look at Vince.

"Here," Vince said, handing him a can of Coke. "That's pretty universal, right? I should have asked you what you wanted."

"Yeah, this is totally fine," Locke replied. He opened the can and sat down on the bed, still wearing nothing but a towel. Vince sat next to him, close enough so their shoulders touched. Vince opened his own can and took a sip, trying to decide if he should tell Locke about his encounter with Ariel. Before he could do that, though, Locke reached out and grabbed his hand.

They had already held hands all day, but the feeling of Locke's skin on his, cool fingers around Vince's own, made it real. It made *them* real, and he could forget about everything—Ariel, even his father. He put his drink down on the bedside table and turned to Locke, staring into his eyes. "I love your mouth," he said, surprising himself.

Locke smiled, and Vince leaned closer, licking that smile, before pressing their lips together. Locke tasted of fizzy Coke with just a little hint of Vince.

Locke's mouth was enough to arouse Vince all over again, though they were soft, sweet, prolonged kisses that could have lasted forever and led to nothing else and Vince would have been happy.

He pulled away from Locke, exhaling sharply from his nose. "So are you going to take that towel off or—"

"Actually," Locke replied, smiling at him. "I was kind of hoping we could talk. Before you ambushed me with kisses."

"Talk?" Vince swallowed nervously. Was this going to be a blow-off already?

Locke smiled at him. "Relax," he said, turning slightly so he could face Vince. "It's nothing bad. At least, I don't think so."

"Okay," Vince said. He tried to focus on Locke's hand, which was now resting on his leg, instead of the fact that Locke was completely naked under his towel. "I'm not—okay, you remember what Ariel said to me on the first day of KP?"

Vince nodded. He remembered perfectly. The words were seared into his brain, because they had hurt. It made no sense, though. Vince barely knew Locke back then. He barely knew Locke now. "Kind of. Something about two down—"

"Right, yeah," Locke replied. "I wanted to explain that. I'm just going to put everything on the table here, because I want to give you a chance to walk away now, if you want to. Like, I would be upset, but we would still be friends."

Vince closed his eyes. He felt a little dizzy. "You-you want me to walk away?"

"No," Locke replied, shaking his head. "I really don't. Wait, I'm saying this wrong. I like you, okay? I like you a lot, and it's not—it's something I wasn't prepared for, to be honest. I've just, nothing like that has ever happened to me. I swear, I'm not a slut, I had just never met anyone like you before."

Vince looked into Locke's glimmering green eyes. He wasn't sure if he had heard him right. "You like me?"

"Yeah," Locke replied. "I really like you. I want—I want you. I want this. I want you to learn which candy I like so you don't have to bring a handful upstairs, you know? Like, I don't just want the sex, though the sex is incredible. I mean, like, I don't want to freak you out or anything. I want us to go on more dates and stuff, though, and—"

Vince grinned. "You're so adorable when you don't know what to say."

"So does that mean you're—"

Vince closed his eyes and grimaced. Everything Locke had said was exactly what Vince wanted. He couldn't do that without telling him the truth; if he didn't tell Locke about his family now he might as well be a villain.

Locke must have noticed the expression on Vince's face, because he stopped talking.

Vince swallowed. He put his hands behind him and leaned back to look up at the ceiling. His mouth had gone dry.

"Vince, are you okay? You, um, you—?"

"There's something I need to tell you," he said.

"Okay," Locke said. Vince could tell he was being careful to keep his tone even. He should have been grateful for it, but all it did was make him more scared.

"I'm interested, okay? I'd love it. But there's something you need to know before we even start," Vince said. "My father—"

"This conversation took a weird turn," Locke said, chuckling.

Vince sighed.

"Sorry," Locke said. "I didn't mean to interrupt you. I'm a little nervous."

"I'm nervous too," Vince replied, still staring at the unmoving fan on the ceiling of their hotel room. He couldn't bear to look at Locke, couldn't bear to see his reaction when he finally told him about his father. "Just, let me get through this, okay? Once I'm done, you can say whatever you want."

Locke didn't say anything, which Vince took as his cue. He took a deep breath and tried to keep his voice steady as he spoke. "My father is a villain. He's not just any run of the mill villain either, Locke. He's Pied Piper."

He couldn't be sure, but he thought he heard Locke gasp.

He sighed, shifting his weight forward into a dejected slump. "Yeah, so you know who he is."

"Everyone knows who he is," Locke replied. Vince couldn't read the tone of his voice and he still didn't dare look at him.

"Right," Vince said, his voice barely above a whisper. He was trying hard to speak clearly, keep his tone steady, but talking about this with anyone was hard. Talking about this with Locke was almost impossible. "As if that wasn't enough, his partner is Chameleon."

"Like his business partner?"

Vince shrugged. "Like he wants me to call her mom."

"That is so many levels of disgusting," Locke replied.

"I know," Vince said, digging his fingers into the sheets under him. "Anyway, you need to know. I-I'm not sure, but he may have actively sabotaged my other relationships and they were with nongifted people. So having a relationship with me could be downright dangerous for you. I will totally understand if you just decide to walk away now. We can still be friends, or we totally don't have to be, but I would appreciate it if you didn't tell the rest of the guys."

Locke sighed. They sat there in silence for what seemed like forever as Vince tried to ignore the growing knot in his throat. He felt Locke's hand over his own. "Don't worry," he said. "I'm not going to tell anyone."

Vince expelled a sigh of relief before he registered that Locke had still said nothing to his admission. He had only said he wasn't going to out him as the son of a notorious villain. Vince's stomach knotted, and the room started to close in on him. "I'm gonna go," he said. "You can keep the room."

He shifted his weight to stand up, but Locke pulled him back onto the bed. "Where are you going?"

"To the suite," Vince said.

"Why don't you stay instead?"

Vince looked at him this time before he spoke. Locke didn't look upset or scared and that confused him. "You want me to stay?"

"Yes," Locke replied. "I want you to stay. So what if your dad's Pied Piper? You're not your dad. I'm going out with you, not with your father."

"He's dangerous," Vince thinly replied. "Are you sure about this?"

Locke nodded, smiling. "Honestly, I thought you were going to say something much worse than that."

Vince stared at him. "What could be worse than that?"

"Well," Locke said, looking away from his face. "Considering we just started dating, I don't wanna kinkshame you but—"

"Shut up," Vince replied, trying to stop himself from laughing. "Wait, we're dating?"

"Yes," Locke said. "If you want us to be."

"I really do," Vince replied, his cheeks reddening as he bit down on his lower lip.

"Good," Locke said. "So do I."

"C'MON," LOCKE SAID, after a shower that had left Vince somewhat jelly-kneed. It had been more intense than the fooling around they'd done at the camp, but seeing Locke naked in the camp showers from now on would be hard. He groaned at his own unintentional pun.

"Coming," he called back and groaned again. They had packed up their shit, such as it was, and he just needed to comb his hair before it dried into a natural mess. They left the key cards in the room for housekeeping and Vince limped down the hall after Locke.

Locke turned around with a smug grin nearly making Vince groan out loud again. Locke might have a right to it, but that didn't mean everyone needed to know. "Don't look so smug," Vince said. "Next time it'll be you limping through the morning after."

If anything, Locke's grin grew wider. "Promise?" he asked in a lecherous tone as Vince joined him at the elevator bank.

Vince gave him his best seductive smile in return. "Promise." He was doing his best not to think about the fact that it was Sunday, that they were going back to camp in time to peel more fucking potatoes. But thinking about that was more pleasant than remembering Ariel was having brunch with them in the hotel dining room.

The elevator arrived with a chime he was already thinking of as familiar. Locke took his hand as naturally as breathing, causing Vince to sigh softly in contentment. "I like this." He squeezed Locke's hand briefly.

"Me, too." Locke leaned in and stole a kiss. His smile returned.

Vince couldn't help but return it. Maybe this would be a chance for Ariel to see Vince wasn't just screwing around. He nodded absently, determined to see this as an opportunity.

Ariel was already in the dining room when they walked in, his bright rainbow hair unmistakable in the warm sunlight flooding the room. Pristine tablecloths and gold candlesticks caught the sun and gave the room an elegance that made Vince feel under-dressed. Another glance though assured him no one in the room was wearing anything fancier than jeans and button-down shirts. A buffet was set along one wall, bigger and better looking than the one used at camp.

Ariel bounced in his chair, waving and grinning. Vince reminded himself that as cute as Ariel was, he could easily carry out his threat. He eased into a chair, not thinking, and winced. He smiled, because it was a most pleasant kind of soreness.

"Locke! Hi, Vince! Did you guys have fun without me yesterday?"

"Don't be like that, Ariel. I never take you on my dates," Locke said, ruffling Ariel's hair.

He seemed oblivious to Ariel's scowl and Vince guessed this was part of their relationship. He hid a smirk behind his hand.

Ariel seemed to let it go, grabbing his plate and jumping to his feet. "Did you see the buffet table? It's amazing!"

Vince's stomach rumbled, drawing laughs from both Locke and Ariel.

Ariel smiled. "Okay, let's eat!"

Vince got gingerly to his feet and noticed Ariel staring at him with wide eyes. "What?"

Ariel grinned and tapped Locke on the shoulder. "Way to ride 'em, cowboy."

Locke winced and rubbed his shoulder. "Classy, Ariel. Always classy."

Vince was blushing, but he kept his head high. He had loved every minute of having Locke inside him; he wasn't going to apologize for it, not to anyone.

The food put their poor offerings at camp to shame. The scrambled eggs were soft and fluffy, and there were other kinds available, too, which was quite the trick on a buffet. Biscuits, gravy, Canadian bacon, baked beans, even a weird rice porridge, as well as a huge selection of fresh fruit, all sliced and ready.

Vince's stomach growled again, and he heaped his plate with a little bit of everything. Back at the table, he noticed Locke had done much the same. Ariel had settled for a pile of fruit and a pair of poached eggs on an English muffin, smothered in a rich yellow sauce.

Ariel stuck his fingers in the sauce and licked them clean. "How come you guys won't make eggs benny?"

"Oh, god," Vince said. "We're just figuring out how to not overcook scrambled eggs."

"What's hollandaise sauce even made of," Locke pondered before sticking a finger in the pool on Ariel's plate.

"Eggs," Ariel said. "I think."

Vince watched Locke lick his finger clean. Locke saw him looking and winked. "You wanna try some?"

He dipped his finger again and held it out to Vince.

Ariel rolled his eyes, but Vince licked the rich sauce off anyway, cheeks burning. "It's good," he said, his voice a croak.

"I'll get cavities at his rate," Ariel remarked.

They were too hungry to talk much, and while Vince had grabbed more than enough food to fill him up, Ariel went back for seconds. "Where does he put it all?"

Locke laughed. "He's got a wicked metabolism. Most buffet places in Tupewa have banned him."

Ariel sat down with a plate full of bacon and sausage, and said, "So you two wanna talk hot guys at Camp Hologram?"

Vince wasn't going to touch that one. Ariel might be trying to trick him into saying something that could be construed as a desire to throw Locke over for someone else.

Locke clearly didn't have that problem. "Cass is pretty hot, in more ways than one. I don't think he knows the word no."

"Mmm." Ariel swallowed and replied, "He is gorgeous, and it would be fun to see someone as arrogant as him on his knees for me."

"Royce is pretty cute, too."

Ariel hit Locke in the shoulder, hard enough for Locke to wince. "Since when do I do cute?"

"You are cuteness personified," Locke responded with a smile, winking at Vince.

Ariel rolled his eyes. "What do *you* think, Vince?" He filled his mouth with bacon and stared at Vince.

Vince cleared his throat. "Well, you and Bray had a kind of weird thing there."

Ariel's eyes lit up. "We did, didn't we?"

Locke laughed. "I dunno if Bray would go for that. He reads straight, to me."

Ariel pouted.

"Or there's Rudy. He's, like, almost as hot as Locke."

"Really?" Locke laughed again. "Rudy?"

"Come on," Vince said, defending his taste. "That deathly pale skin is kind of hot. And those glasses, you gotta admit—hot."

"He's so right about the glasses," Ariel said. "But really? Me and Rudy? Ha!"

"Who do you like?" Locke asked, stealing a piece of crisp bacon from Ariel's plate.

"Hmm. Oh! You can help yourself to some bacon, too, Vince. Just no sticking your fingers in my sauce," Ariel said with a wink.

"I can live with that rule," Vince replied, laughing.

Ariel didn't answer right away, and finally Locke said, "I'll flirt outrageously with Vince, if you're not gonna talk." He pushed out of his seat far enough to kiss Vince on the nose, making him blush.

"All right, all right," Ariel said, "No need to threaten me with indigestion. I kind of like BJ, you know, from a purely physical point of view. He's got dreamy shoulders. But he's so hung up on Cass. I mean, oh my god, they were yelling and throwing things around last night—they should just fuck and get it over with. Maybe then I'd have a chance with one of them. Or both," he added with a twinkle in his eye, "since I hear Cass likes that. Oh—Ace. My god that hair, yum-yum. But I'm pretty sure I'm not his type, and he can outrun me," Ariel finished with a bright laugh.

"Is there anyone you'd bottom for?" Locke asked, seemingly genuinely curious.

Ariel shrugged. "I doubt it. A boy's gotta have standards!"

Their table was in a sunny alcove, and while they'd been eating and talking, other guys from the camp, along with other hotel guests, had come, and mostly gone.

"So," Ariel said. "I want to do some shopping before we go. I wasn't going to invite *you*," he said to Vince, wrinkling his nose, "but you clearly need wardrobe help, so you better come along."

Locke's laugh was infectious, and Vince joined in. He didn't like shopping much and he kind of wished for more time alone with Locke, but he suspected this would actually be kind of fun.

Chapter Nine

EVERYONE WAITED FOR the helicopter to arrive on the roof, though Ariel, Vince, and Locke knew they cut it close when they went upstairs to find everyone else already sitting there. Ariel hadn't been joking about shopping, and Vince was already wondering where he would put all the clothes Ariel had talked him into getting. He normally wouldn't have spent that much money, but Ariel had been right. He was a grown-up now, living away from home. He just needed a wardrobe that wasn't made up of just jeans and gray hoodies. He wouldn't do it again, anyway, and it seemed to impress Ariel, which put Vince at ease.

There was also the fact that Ariel was more than willing to carry most of their shopping bags, which was unnecessary but a nice bonus. Having a friend with super strength had some perks. He smiled to think Ariel might be someone he would consider a friend, but Locke was holding Vince's hand and dragging him toward the half wall where everyone else was sitting.

Vince paled at the thought. He was about to protest when BJ walked up to them. "Hey, before I forget, your dad called the suite."

"My dad?" Locke said, furrowing his brow. "But why—"

"No," Vince replied. He didn't need to go close to the edge of the roof, he was already feeling so dizzy. "He means my dad. When?"

"Like, this morning? I don't know. The phone call woke me up, though, so thanks a lot for that."

"Yeah," Vince said. He was glad he was holding on to Locke. "What did you tell him?"

"He told him you were out fucking your boyfriend," Cass said before BJ could answer.

"Jesus," Vince said, trying to swallow down the knot in his throat. His dad wasn't supposed to know he had a boyfriend. He wasn't supposed to know where Vince was in the first place. His father knew, which meant Chameleon knew. He was still there, though. Either they had something they hoped to lead Vince into doing with his power, or he just wanted Vince to know there was nowhere he could go and not be found. He hoped it was the latter.

"Take it easy, Vince." BJ glared at Cass. "Cass is a dick. I told him I didn't know where you were, and I'd tell you about it as soon as I saw you. This is the first time I've seen you all day, so there you go. Message delivered."

"Yeah," Vince replied. "Thanks."

"No problem," BJ said and turned around to walk away.

Vince rubbed the bridge of his nose, trying to take deep breaths in a way that wasn't too obvious.

"Vince," Locke said, his voice quiet. "You're digging your nails into my hand."

"Oh, shit," Vince replied, instantly letting him go. "Sorry. I'm just—I need to call him back."

Ariel gave him a curious look. "Your dad doesn't have your cell phone number?"

Vince hoped his shudder wasn't visible. If his dad had his cell number, he'd probably be tracking Vince's every movement via GPS, reading all his texts, and recording all his phone calls. Then calling all his contacts and telling them to lose Vince's number. Or worse. "He doesn't," he said, aiming for a casual shrug. He couldn't explain any of that. Plus, he reminded himself, he'd done a full disclosure for Locke. "He's a handful."

Ariel scoffed, shaking his head.

Vince sighed, carefully editing his story. "My parents' divorce wasn't exactly amicable and—"

He was saved from having to explain any more, in what felt like earshot of everyone else, as the sound of the helicopter arriving grew louder, drowning out his voice.

LOCKE BOOSTED ARIEL into the chopper, since Ariel refused to let go of his bags. He and Vince had managed to stuff their purchases in the small olive canvas travel bags that were all they were supposed to carry on the helicopter. Ariel's travel bag was not only stuffed, he had a shopping bag overflowing with clothes. "It's my carry-on," he proclaimed and while everyone had rolled their eyes—Locke had never seen synchronized eye rolling before—no one objected.

He climbed into the helicopter and turned to help Vince, taking his bag and giving his boyfriend—wow, did that sound weird but also good— a hand up. Locke sat next to Ariel, and pulled Vince to sit beside him, kicking their bags under the seat.

"Is he okay?" Ariel asked in a loud whisper.

"He gets a little airsick," Locke replied, taking a firm hold of Vince's hand and resting both on his thigh.

"Glad you're between us!"

Locke glanced at Vince on his right as the engine whined into high gear. He didn't think Vince would enjoy the ride just because Locke was sitting next to him, but he hadn't expected Vince to look this bad. He suspected it wasn't just from the helicopter. It was a little hard to wrap his head around the idea someone like Pied Piper could even have a kid, let alone what he must be like as a father.

Locke thought his own father was difficult enough. They could go weeks without speaking after a fight. Locke's father often thought Locke wasn't trying hard enough, no matter how much Locke tried to explain he would have much rather have his father's electromagnetic powers instead of his own bullshit, undignified light related ones.

Locke glanced at Vince. His head was back, his eyes closed. A faint sheen of sweat had formed on his forehead, though it wasn't that hot. His skin seemed unnaturally pale and he was holding Locke's hand in a white-knuckled death grip. It hurt, but he was friends with Ariel—he'd taken worse. If it made Vince feel the slightest bit better, it was worth it.

He was mulling over how to suggest he'd be a good listener if Vince wanted to talk when Vince looked at him. He seemed on the verge of tears but also looked surprised.

"Sick," he mouthed, and before Locke could react or ask Ariel for a bag, Vince threw his upper body forward over his legs and emptied the contents of his stomach on his shoes.

Several of the guys made disgusted faces, but the windows were open to keep them from getting too hot, so the acidic stench of bile dissipated quickly.

Vince lay there for a minute. He sat up slowly, wiping his mouth with the hem of his shirt. Locke rubbed his back, wishing he could say it was okay, wishing Vince would hear him.

Vince gave him an embarrassed, shaky grin, which vanished into misery. He turned to BJ on his other side, as if to apologize to him—both his and Locke's shoes had not escaped the vile barrage—and BJ looked horrified as if to say, point that mouth somewhere else.

Vince was waving his hands in the air, as if to indicate he was okay. Then Vince doubled over, and it started happening again, except this time, it was happening straight onto BJ's lap.

Locke put his hand in the middle of Vince's back, lightly stroking him with the palm of his hand. BJ had a hand over his nose, and a scowl on his face. He put a hand on Vince's head as if to push him away.

Locke glared at him, and BJ's scowl deepened, but he slowly withdrew his hand with a shake of his head.

Once Vince was done, and he was well enough to sit back up, Locke looked around the helicopter. He expected to see the rest of the guys laughing, grinning, or doing something. They weren't, though. Everyone was staring at Vince, some with their mouths open, and some looking concerned. It was a good thing Vince had buried his head in his hands, because Locke didn't want him to see that. He put his hand over Vince's shoulder and squeezed it, hoping it would provide Vince some sort of comfort, however small.

VINCE DIDN'T PAY much attention as the helicopter set down in the small clearing near the camp. He was embarrassed, and he knew he owed BJ and Locke and everyone an apology, but right now he just wasn't feeling it.

BJ stomped off to the showers, and the rest of Cabin One went to the kitchen after stowing their gear and changing their socks and shoes.

"You should see a medic," Locke said, for the umpteenth time.

"I can't believe BJ—isn't he supposed to be a healer?" Cass's voice was slightly muffled as he pulled a utilitarian apron over his clothes.

"I don't—" Vince began, but then he nodded. "Yeah, maybe I should stop by the infirmary for motion sickness meds." He didn't feel nauseous anymore, but he didn't want to say he was going to call his father, either. Locke would probably figure it out himself and no one else needed to know. "I'll be right back, okay guys?"

"Sure," Locke said, a look of relief on his face.

Cass grinned and gave him a thumbs-up. "You're not back in like twenty minutes max, though, you can peel the fucking potatoes for pan fries the rest of the week."

Vince managed a scowl that wasn't entirely forced. "Ugh. No worries."

He made his way down the hall to the office with Mister Mister's name on it and raised his hand to knock at the door. He didn't want to make this call, but who knew what might happen if he didn't? Vince took a deep breath and knocked.

"It's open."

He pushed the door open and stared for a few minutes at the man behind the desk. Mister Mister didn't look like a man who did paperwork. His steel colored hair was too long, and although his beard was neatly trimmed, the T-shirt he wore showed off colourful tattoos. On the exercise yard, he looked right at home, yelling out orders and making snarky, dismissive remarks whenever someone face-planted in the mud of the obstacle course.

Mister Mister put down his stylus and tablet, looking surprised. "Silva. Shouldn't you be chopping onions?"

"Um, yeah. I—" Vince pushed a hand through his hair and took a deep breath. "My father called the hotel while I was out with, um, Ariel and Locke. I... was wondering if I could call him from the camp phone?" He inwardly cringed, waiting for Mister Mister to ask why he couldn't use his cell.

Instead, the older man raised a dark eyebrow and got to his feet. "That didn't take him long."

"Sorry?"

"Pied Piper. I thought it might take him a little longer to find you. You can call him; it's safe enough. It automatically scrambles so the line can't be traced."

He said it so matter-of-factly it took Vince a long minute to understand. "Y-you know who my father is?"

Mister Mister nodded, one short, concise motion of his head. "Not his real name. Identity protection laws and shit. Your mother had to disclose for your application."

"And they let me come anyway?" Vince was incredulous.

"Sure. We altered the camp's security, but we were pretty much Pied Piper proof already. The abilities of all villains are accounted for, in order to ensure the safety of our trainees." He pointed to the phone. "We'll assume he just wants to talk to you as a parent. You've got ten minutes; then I'm coming back."

Vince met the older man's eyes, looking for fear or reassurance. If Mister Mister seemed unconcerned, maybe it would be okay. "Thank you."

Once the door closed behind him, Vince took another deep breath and picked up the handset, pressing the buttons he'd memorized.

He closed his eyes. With every ring, the chance his father wouldn't answer the call increased. If he was sent to voicemail, he could just leave a message. If he could do that, he wouldn't have to deal with whatever it was his dad wanted, and his dad couldn't even get mad at him.

"Hello?"

Of course he wouldn't be that lucky.

"Hi, Dad," Vince replied in a small voice. He resisted the urge to ask him what he needed. He cleared his throat to continue talking. "What's up?"

"Nothing is *up*," his dad replied, emphasizing the last word. "Does something need to happen for me to want to speak with my favorite son?"

Vince didn't say anything. That had been cute, once, when he was seven years old. Since then, it had acquired a far more menacing meaning. He didn't feel like playing his father's games, but as usual, when it came to him, Vince had very little choice. "No, of course not. How's, um, Rebecca?"

"Your stepmother is fine," he replied. "You know how much it would mean to her if you called her Mom."

Vince swallowed, looking around and trying to find something to lean on. That was never going to happen. He shut his mouth and waited for his dad to keep talking.

"Listen," he finally said, breaking the uncomfortable silence. "Are you over in Guilford every weekend?"

Vince shut his eyes tightly. He didn't want either one of them to know where he was going to be hanging around every weekend. His father could always tell when Vince was lying, though, and Vince couldn't exactly take that risk. "I don't know, really," he replied, trying to sound as noncommittal as possible. "I guess."

"Great," his father said. "I'm going to be there next weekend. Business."

"Oh, okay." Vince didn't like where this conversation was going. "Will, uh—"

"It's only going to be me."

Vince almost said good aloud, but he chose to say nothing instead. He had sat through enough dinners with his father and Rebecca—Chameleon—and they ranged from awkward to terrifying.

His father took a deep breath before he spoke. "Listen, Vincent, I know I've not always been the world's most devoted father," he said. "But you're an adult now and I would really like to get to know you. Why don't we have dinner together on Saturday? I can go to the hotel and meet you there at about half past seven. How does that sound?"

Vince thought it sounded terrible, but it wasn't as though he could say no. If he tried, his father would use his power and force Vince to meet up with him. When his father wanted something, he got it. Even if that something was getting to know Vince. Vince hugged himself as a shiver ran down his spine.

"Okay," Vince finally replied. "I'll see you then."

The line went dead.

Vince wasn't sure how long he sat there, stunned, after hanging up. A sharp knock on the door and Mister Mister's entrance startled him out of his daze.

Mister Mister stared at him long enough to make Vince look away, and he realized he was still in the trainer's chair. He jumped to his feet as Mister Mister said, "You got anything you need to talk about, Silva?"

Vince came around the desk, and said, "No, everything's fine," and then froze by the door. Slowly he turned around, biting his bottom lip. "Dad will be at the Roehampton next weekend. I—" Vince felt his eyes widen as he realized his father never asked him where he would be. "He said he just wants dinner with me. He knows we stay there. Is the Roe as safe as camp?"

Mister Mister said calmly, "The suites are. I'll make sure the local law enforcement is on alert."

Vince breathed out a relieved sigh. "Thank you. I better get back to the kitchen. Thanks again." Mister's calm confidence went a long way to easing his anxiety.

ALTHOUGH LOCKE AND Vince had only Ariel's account of the fight between Cass and BJ that had taken place Saturday night, they were treated to a daily recap in the kitchen. Not that Locke didn't have his own issue with BJ—he could have tried to help Vince in the helicopter instead of freaking out and trying to push him away.

Locke could see something was troubling Vince and guessed it had to do with his father. "You know you can tell me anything?" They were taking a walk down by the lake. They were both exhausted from a tough day on the obstacle course and a grueling dinner service. They would be lucky if they stayed awake until lights out, no matter if Cass and BJ tore the cabin apart around them.

"Yeah," Vince said, leaning into him.

The lake had a kind of peacefulness in the setting sun, as opposed to the daytime when it seemed almost malevolent, depending on what Mister Mister wanted them to do.

"My father wants to have dinner with me next Saturday, when we're in Guilford."

That didn't seem particularly villainous to Locke. "So what's the problem? Is he abusive?"

Vince's short, sharp laugh had Locke giving him a reassuring squeeze.

"Not physically, if that's what you mean. But he's never been affectionate, either. He's just very manipulative."

Locke frowned. "You think he wants more than dinner? Are you, you know, susceptible to his power?"

"Not as much as he thinks. Don't worry, he can't turn me into a spy or anything. His influence, like mine, wears off after a few hours. The biggest difference is, if he really wants, he can make you think his suggestions are your own idea. So even after it wears off, you find yourself wondering why you did something so stupid or terrible or whatever. With me, someone knows. Like when I got BJ to confess—you could see he didn't want to say what he did."

"Oh." Locke wasn't sure if that was reassuring or not. "You want me to come with you? Like for support?"

"No! God, no." Vince's vehemence took him by surprise. It almost hurt a bit, like Locke would be of no help. Or worse...

He gave Vince a smile. "I guess it's too soon for me to meet him, huh?"

Vince laughed, but it was a harsh, unamused sound. "God, it's not that. Locke, if he finds out we're dating, you could be in serious danger."

Locke turned to give him a full body hug. It seemed so surreal that Vince's father was Pied Piper. Vince might be right, but maybe a power-gifted boyfriend was just what Vince needed.

Vince squeezed him tight. "I wish...."

"Yeah, me, too," Locke said softly.

Vince cracked a yawn. "God, I'm sorry."

Locked laughed a little and drew back. "It's okay. At least we're getting to know each other."

Vince gave him a crooked smile. "M&Ms."

"Reese's Pieces," Locke said with a grin. "Come on, let's hit the bunks before we fall asleep standing up."

The rest of the week was more of the same, and Locke was so looking forward to Friday. Their last day of KP, thank fuck. Cass and BJ were starting to drive *him* nuts. The worst part was, on the training course, they were calm, cool, professional. But the minute the aprons and hairnets went on, they turned into sworn enemies, and Locke and Vince were caught in the middle as often as not. This time, BJ had asked Cass to hand him a knife, which was enough to get them started.

"I can give you a lot more than that," Cass said to BJ.

"Oh, please. You couldn't handle me if you fucking tried. you're such a loser," BJ snapped back.

"Really? Because that kind of sounds like you want me to show you what I can do."

Locke glanced over at Vince. "TGIF, dude."

Vince's laugh was rueful, but it was a laugh.

Cass walked into BJ's personal space, bumping chests, and put his face nose to nose with BJ. "You just don't have the guts to let me fuck you. You're such a prude."

"Fuck. You," BJ said pushing back against Cass.

"I'm right here, baby. Do your best."

BJ growled, sounding like a dangerous animal, as he grabbed Cass at the waist and kissed him.

Locke's jaw fell open, but before he could figure out anything to say or do, Cass was kissing BJ right back, and it wasn't any kind of gentle kissing.

"That look consensual to you?" he murmured to Vince.

"Uh huh," Vince said, staring.

BJ tore off Cass's apron and the sound of fabric ripping filled the room.

"Ariel said this would happen."

"Maybe we should go tell him he was right," Vince suggested, continuing to stare as he started backing toward the door.

Locke was backing up with him, clutching his arm. "I think he and the others are in the showers."

And then, and only then, Vince looked away from the spectacle unfolding before them to stare at the floor with a blush.

Locke laughed. "My boyfriend is blushing at the thought of seeing my best friend naked?"

"Your boyfriend is blushing at the thought of your best friend seeing what happens to me when you're naked in the showers," Vince said, turning redder. "Let's just get out of here."

Chapter Ten

THERE WERE WARY looks when Vince clambered aboard the helicopter Saturday morning. "It's all right, guys. I took something for motion sickness from the infirmary. I won't be puking on—" he stopped abruptly and stared at Cass. "Nice shiner."

"Whatever," Cass said with a sniff.

Everyone seemed more preoccupied with Cass's black eye than the risk of being puked on, but he was still given an outside seat. Since Locke had no problem sitting next to him, it was okay.

The flight still made him a little queasy, motion sickness pills notwithstanding, but he focused on Locke, and chatted with Ariel about the amusement park. "I could win you a prize," Ariel said loftily.

"No winning prizes to give my boyfriend," Locke said laughing. "Get your own date."

Ariel pouted at Locke and then turned to Cass on his other side. "What about you, cutie? Do you like amusement parks?"

"Maybe next time, darling. I want to find Camp Synergy's floor and check out what we're missing." Cass winked. "I hear BJ's got a sister at Synergy."

"That's just—! Jesus, Cass, you—!"

Cass cautiously tapped BJ on the knee. "Relax, Beej. I'm kidding."

Vince raised an eyebrow at Locke, who gave a little shrug in return.

The landing was uneventful, and it only took maybe twenty minutes for Vince to feel normal again. He accompanied Locke and Ariel for some light shopping—Ariel insisted he needed some lube and a box of condoms for the night—and Vince picked up some motion sickness meds for the flight back.

Vince tried not to think about the dinner with his father, which was putting something of a damper on an otherwise amazing Saturday. He had spent most of the day with Locke, walking up and down the riverfront, feeding the birds they weren't supposed to feed. It would have been incredibly romantic—it *was* incredibly romantic—except he couldn't get the fact that the clock was ticking down and his father would be waiting for him when they got back to the hotel.

They were leaning against the railings, watching the boats, when Vince checked the time on his phone for what felt like the hundredth time that day.

"Hey," Locke said, draping his arm around Vince and holding him close. "Are you doing okay?"

"Yes," Vince replied, shrugging. "I don't know. I'm just not looking forward to dinner with my dad. I'll feel a lot better once it's over with."

"Vince," Locke said after a little while. "I still think you should let me come with you."

Vince looked him up and down. Locke was his boyfriend. While normally that involved a meeting-the-parents scenario, Vince was sure it was okay to skip that when the parent in question was a super villain. He licked his lips before he answered. "No. I'm not going to put you in danger."

Locke shrugged, a hurt expression rapidly crossing his face before disappearing. "I'm not helpless, you know. Besides, you don't have to introduce me as your boyfriend. I can be a friend."

Vince took him firmly by the shoulders and looked into Locke's beautiful green eyes. "Locke. I love that you want to do this for me. Just trust me that my father is every bit as bad as his reputation and being my friend, boyfriend, whatever, is dangerous."

ARIEL LOOKED UP at Locke and slightly shook his head. Locke rolled his eyes and grabbed the next shirt Ariel had laid out for him. "I thought you told me Vince turned down your offer to accompany him?"

Locke nodded. "Is this weird? Stalkerish? I just think if I accidentally show up, or something, I can help."

"Yeah, it's kind of stalkerish. But also sweet." Ariel picked over the clothes spread out on the bed. "Why dress up, though? I mean, how do you explain that?"

"I have to look good enough. If Vince asks, I'll say you and I had plans." He pulled on the steel gray shirt with the black pin stripe and looked at Ariel, who smiled brightly.

"You look fabulous in that one." Ariel's smile faded. "But. I know you don't have a lot of experience in the relationship department, but don't you think lying is kind of the wrong direction to take?"

Locke buttoned the shirt and met Ariel's gaze. "You're right. If he asks, I'll confess." He frowned and studied his appearance in the mirror. "What if he doesn't like me? P-parents," he stumbled as he almost blurted out Vince's secret.

Ariel laughed. "Whose parents don't like you? You look like a model out of a GAP catalogue and you have the best manners of anyone I've ever met."

"I don't know," Locke replied, doing the last of his buttons. "Vince makes him sound pretty scary, Ariel. The scariest person in the world." But it would be two against one, if Locke was there, if something should go as wrong as Vince feared.

Ariel pouted. "But that's the way you talk about your dad," he said. "If you want to seem more respectable, maybe wear your hair back. Do you have a headband?"

"No, it's like, my dad is a little on the crazy side, but his is, um, I don't even know where to start," Locke said. "And no, I don't have a headband."

Ariel rolled his eyes and rummaged in his bag. "Here," he said, handing Locke an electric-mint colored headband. "Wear this. It'll add a bit of color to the whole funeral vibe you have going on and it matches your eyes."

Locke laughed and took it off him. "Why do you even carry this around?"

"Because, unlike you, I like to be prepared for everything," Ariel replied. "You know, he's probably overreacting. You're always very dramatic when it comes to your dad."

"That's cute, coming from you," Locke replied. "How do I look?"

"Great," Ariel said, looking him up and down. "I think you're ready."

Locke went to the door, and Ariel said, "I'll swap the sleeping assignments for you, because I'm that kind of friend."

"Yeah," Locke said with a smirk, "No hidden agenda on your part."

Ariel gave him a wide-eyed innocent look. "Go. Impress people."

Locke went down to the lobby, picking a chair where he could watch the elevators for Vince. His heart skipped a beat when Vince walked through a pair of steel chrome doors. He was gorgeous, in soft cotton black pants with a white button shirt and dark gray vest. Tiny gold rings graced his ears and suddenly Locke felt plain and under dressed. Too late now.

In spite of how immaculately dressed he was, Vince's face wore a cloud of worry. Locke abandoned any idea of trying to accidentally-on-purpose run into Vince with his father. He crossed the lobby floor and smiled broadly at Vince. "Hey."

"Oh my god, Locke. What the fuck are you doing here? My father will be here any minute—"

Locke ignored Vince's distress and caught up his hand, twining their fingers together. "I know, I know. But we're two, and he's one. Strength in numbers, right?"

Vince didn't look in the slightest reassured. He looked furious. "Don't make me use my powers on you."

Shocked, Locke said, "You wouldn't!"

Vince grabbed his shoulder and squeezed. "I would do anything to keep you safe."

"Well, what have we here?"

Vince groaned at the deep, smooth voice, and let go of his shoulder and hand as if Locke had turned into molten metal. "Hey, Dad."

Locke turned around, remembered he was meeting Pied Piper in his secret identity. For the first time, he felt a sense of danger. He hadn't been prepared, and now he knew Pied Piper's identity. He didn't want to think about the implications of that.

There stood an older man, beginning to silver at his temples. His hair was the same rich brown as Vince's but there was no other resemblance. Pied—no, Mr. Silva—had a neat mustache and wore what looked like an expensive business suit with a white shirt and colourful tie. He looked successful and, well, *ordinary*. He was giving Locke a mildly curious look. He would never have guessed in a million years that was Pied Piper. "Aren't you going to introduce me to your," he paused to give Locke a measuring look and finished his sentence with a smile at Vince, "friend?"

Vince paled. "He was just leaving."

"That's a shame," Mr. Silva said, turning to look at Vince, a smile still on his face. "How would you feel about joining us for dinner?"

"I told you, he was just—"

"I don't want to impose," Locke said. Vince's expression was somewhere between panic and fury, and Locke wasn't sure what he was supposed to do. This had seemed like a good idea until two minutes ago.

"I insist!" Mr. Silva replied. "You're probably both sick of the food at camp. I'm sure a meal from a nice restaurant would be a welcome change."

Locke looked at Vince, but Vince was looking away, avoiding him. Vince was already angry with him, and he couldn't exactly get away anymore without coming across as rude. Plus, Vince's dad was right. He was sick of the food at camp.

"If you don't mind," Locke said, trying for a smile. Vince glared at him.

"Of course not," Mr. Silva said. "C'mon then, boys. I'm starving."

They walked into the dining room. Designed to catch the morning light, it looked different now. Curtains were drawn across the windows to keep diners from feeling like goldfish, and the overhead chandeliers cast a warm glow over the room. Candles were in the gold candlesticks and lit on tables with diners.

"I have a reservation," Mr. Silva told the hostess, "Castle."

"This way."

Vince's hands were in fists and he wouldn't look at Locke. Maybe he should have listened to Vince, but it was too late now.

After the hostess seated them and left them menus, Mr. Silva smiled pleasantly at Locke—who took the seat beside Vince—before turning to Vince to politely say, "Aren't you going to introduce me to your friend?"

For a second Locke thought Vince actually wouldn't. "This is Locke," he finally said. "He's in Cabin One with me."

Locke smiled. "Hi, Mr. Silva."

The pleasant expression vanished into a scowl that deepened the lines on his forehead and returned almost immediately. "Castle, dear boy, as in king of the. Silva is Vincent's mother's name."

There was an edge to his voice that Locke had no idea how to interpret. "Sorry, Mr. Castle."

"It's so nice that Vincent has a confidant at Camp Hologram. I'm sure he's told you we haven't had the best relationship?"

"Um," Locke said, licking his lips.

"It's quite all right. Entirely my fault, of course. Never home enough; you know what it's like. I never really got to know my darling boy, and now he's all grown up." He beamed at Vince, who seemed oblivious to this show of paternal affection.

Locke still didn't know what to say, so he smiled and nodded.

"So how *is* camp?"

Vince shrugged and gave a half smile. "It's all right. Tough. You know. Normal."

"And how well are you doing?"

"Okay." Vince reached for his water glass, as if in need of a distraction.

"And you, Locke. What's your family?"

Locke swallowed. Could Pied Piper find out who Locke's family was? "It's probably weird, but my father is strict about not talking about it. I'm sure you understand," he offered with an apologetic smile.

"Hmm, hmm," Mr. Castle said.

Vince glared at his father. "Hmm, hmm yourself, Dad."

He smiled at Vince, but somehow it didn't look like a nice smile in this light. To Locke, he said, "It's so nice to meet a young man who *respects* his father."

The rest of the meal passed somewhat normally, with Mr. Castle carrying most of the conversation. He talked about his business trips to cities around the world, without ever mentioning his business, and Locke began to relax.

Apart from the hair, Locke didn't see much of Mr. Castle in Vince. Then again, he wasn't seeing much of Vince in Vince tonight. Vince seemed guarded and content to let his father carry the conversation. Still the man seemed pleasant enough, if a bit full of himself, but his own father could do that, too, sometimes. And it wasn't like either he or Vince were contributing to the conversation, so he was kind of left to carry it himself.

When the plates had been cleared away, Mr. Castle said, "Well. This has been *most* enlightening."

The waiter brought the check in a leather-bound folder and Mr. Castle hummed a bit before saying in a deeper, lilting tone, "It's on the house, young man. And a bottle of wine for my son and his... friend. Do hurry."

The waiter nodded without hesitation and Locke was feeling uneasy again. That bit of humming wasn't Pied Piper's trademark song, so it took Locke a second to understand what had just happened. That wasn't right. "Never use your powers for personal gain. Even sponsorships are better, if you really need the money," his father had always said. But it seemed pretty low-grade villainy. He and Vince had made an exception last weekend, hadn't they? *Not the same*, a small voice in his head insisted.

"SO YOU'RE STAYING in a group suite?" Vince's father asked, raising his eyebrows. Dinner was over, thankfully. They had walked out of the restaurant, into the lobby, and he was about to leave the hotel. Vince wouldn't have to deal with him again for a while. He wasn't looking forward to the conversation he needed to have with Locke, but at least his father would be gone. He popped in and out of his life every few months, and Vince was looking forward to the relief he always felt whenever he could stop interacting with him.

"Yeah." His father wasn't fond of one syllable replies, but he didn't want to give any more details.

His father's gaze darted between Vince and Locke for a second. "And you're okay with this?"

Vince shrugged. "It's part of camp, Dad."

"Nonsense," his father replied, waving his hand in the air. The movement looked practiced, everything his father did looked calculated. "I'm going to help you out."

He winked at Vince. Vince avoided looking at Locke, who had just reached for his hand. Vince wondered if he should try to talk his dad out of it, but it wouldn't work. It never worked. He would only be doing it for Locke's benefit, because he wanted to show Locke how dangerous his father could be, but that would just extend how long his father would be around.

He looked around the lobby, trying to find any excuse to redirect his dad's attention. A few of the guys were there, talking to each other. He thought about introducing them for a second before he shook his head. Introducing anyone else at Camp Hologram to his father wasn't a good idea, even if they might distract him from Locke.

Locke leaned in to whisper in his ear. "Are you okay?"

Vince glared at him and walked closer to the counter, Locke trailing behind him. He shut his eyes tightly when he heard the rhythmic tapping of his dad's fingers on the wooden counter, accompanied by a hypnotic tune he heard his father hum countless times over the years.

The receptionist smiled at him. "How can I help you, sir?"

"You want to comp these nice young men the honeymoon suite for the night, don't you? They make a very cute couple," Vince's dad said, narrowing his eyes.

Vince swallowed. So his father knew they were a couple. Shit.

The honeymoon suite cost upwards of a thousand dollars a night. He opened his mouth to say something to his father when his dad waved his hand in front of his face, stopping Vince from talking.

"Of course, you will personally take care of any room service they may request," he continued, looking straight at the receptionist. "As well as anything the hotel may normally bill as a surcharge."

"Of course, sir," the receptionist replied, still with a smile on her face. "I do need a credit card—"

His dad's humming got a little louder for a second. Then he cleared his throat. "You don't need one, though."

She nodded, her smile turning into a grin, her movements mechanical. "You're right," she said, setting two key cards down on the counter in front of her.

His father turned around and flashed them a triumphant smile. "Enjoy."

He walked closer to them and extended his hand to shake Locke's. Locke hesitated for a second, his gaze falling on Vince, and Vince nodded. If his father knew that Locke knew who he was, things could turn out much worse for both of them.

"Such a pleasant experience to meet an interesting young man like yourself," his father said.

"Thank you, Mr. Castle," Locke replied in a quiet voice.

Vince caught the wide-eyed look on Locke's face and it wasn't wonder or awe. He cleared his throat, hoping to keep his father's attention on himself. "Do you want me to walk you to your car or—"

"I'm not senile, Vincent, I know where my own car is," he replied. He gave Vince a one-arm side hug that lasted just long enough to make Vince feel uncomfortable. "I will see you both very soon."

He watched him walk away, wondering if that was meant as a threat, until Locke squeezed his hand. "Oh my god, he just—!"

Vince shrugged him off, scowling at him.

"We're not going to take it," Vince said. "It's bad enough we did it last week, but hotel management is gonna notice something like this. That woman, she could lose her job."

"Vince—"

"I think I would prefer to spend the night alone anyway," Vince said.

"I'm sorry," Locke said, quietly. "Your father, he's—"

"I told you what he is," Vince turned and set the key cards back on the desk.

"Can I help you?" she gave him a puzzled look.

Vince started singing softly. "Put the keys away," he suggested, his voice gentle.

"Y-yeah, I should do that," she agreed, staring at the plastic cards in her hand.

He sang a little more, some silly song all about the bass. "Can you believe that guy? Trying to scam a free room?" Vince said louder.

"Yeah," the woman agreed, sounding more confident and a little upset. "The nerve of that guy." She composed her face into her hospitality smile. "Sorry about that. Was there something I could help you with?"

"No, we were just passing by," Vince said, returning her smile. "Have a good night."

"Look, can we talk?" Locke said. "I know that I—"

"I don't want to talk." Vince didn't elaborate. He was pretty sure he was going to start shouting at Locke right then and there if Locke kept pushing it.

He turned around to walk away, only to practically run into BJ.

"Excuse us," Locke said with a disdainful sniff.

Vince walked quickly toward the elevator, not looking back once. He didn't want Locke to think he was waiting for him. He maintained his composure until the elevator doors were about to close behind him. He sagged against the back wall with a whooshed exhale.

He barely noticed the pale hand that stopped the doors from closing.

Locke was standing in front of him, looking flustered. "Vince."

Vince closed his eyes. "Go away."

"I'm sorry, okay?" Locke said, walking toward him and stopping in his tracks when Vince shot him a look. "I didn't mean to—I thought it would be nice for you to have support. You seemed so scared of him and I didn't want you to have to face him by yourself."

Vince rubbed the bridge of his nose, shaking his head. "You said that. When I specifically told you I didn't want to put you in danger and wanted to do this myself, remember?"

"It wasn't that bad," Locke replied, looking down at his feet.

Vince's eyes widened as his heart started beating faster. The evening had just started to sink in. He'd been trying to protect Locke before but now they were alone, all he felt was fury. "That's not the point!" Vince exclaimed. "It could have been terrible. I kept waiting for him to convince you to tell him who your family was or, y'know, that you didn't like me that much. Or who you were. You're so out of your league here and you're so fucking arrogant you can't even see it."

"That's not fair," Locke said. "I was just trying to help."

"Well, next time, you can help by listening to me," Vince spat. "How does that sound? Considering I'm the one who knows how to deal with him, I would appreciate the vote of confidence."

Locke took a deep breath and looked down at the floor. "I'm sorry," Locke said. "I swear I wanted to help. I hated seeing you so scared. I just—"

"How do you think I felt when you were right in front of him? When he was talking to you?" Vince replied, his voice louder than he had expected it to be. "He could have—he could've hurt you."

"He didn't," Locke replied, taking a tentative step toward him.

"He could have, though," Vince said, tears welling up in his eyes. "Or he could have made you stop liking me, or you know, cheat on me, or whatever."

That seemed to startle Locke. "I would never do anything like that."

"You don't get it! You saw him make a woman do something she didn't want to. It doesn't matter what you want or don't want to do," Vince replied, hot tears trickling down his cheeks. He didn't want to cry in front of Locke, but this was all too much. He didn't want to *think* about what his father could do beyond sabotaging their relationship. "You can't do this. If I tell you I have to handle something by myself, you have to let me."

"I know," Locke said. "I'm sorry I was such a dick. I did want to help."

Vince didn't say anything.

"You have every right to be mad at me, just—let me make it up to you, please?" Locke said in a quiet voice. "I didn't think it through."

"You could have listened," Vince said, wiping his face with the back of his hand.

"Yeah, that too," Locke said.

Vince didn't say anything. He pressed the floor button to the camp suite and kept ignoring Locke.

"I don't think you should be alone right now," Locke said.

Vince cocked his head, trying to stop himself from smiling. He was still angry, but he did appreciate that Locke had wanted to protect him. It had been as sweet as it had been foolish. "Are you hitting on me?"

"Well, I do still like you," Locke said, grabbing his hand. "A lot."

Vince gave Locke a shaky smile and rolled his eyes. He pressed the one marked pool. He wasn't ready to face anyone else just yet.

"The pool?" Locke asked with a sly smile.

Vince didn't answer him.

"Hey," Locke said, wrapping his arms around his waist and pulling him close. His face was only a few inches away from Vince when he spoke again. "I *am* sorry. I promise I'll listen to you. I got carried away and did something stupid."

Vince looked into Locke's amazing green eyes. He looked so gorgeous like this, with his hair pushed back, with the ridiculous headband that matched the colour of his eyes. "Okay," he finally replied. "Good. I'm sorry you had to go through that."

"Don't worry," Locke said, kissing him softly, then moving back and smiling. "I did kind of deserve it."

"You did a bit," Vince replied. He kissed Locke again, this time a little more insistently. Their tongues met when Locke opened his mouth and Vince pushed his back to the wall, pressing his body into Locke's. He took a second to take a breath, as the effect of Locke's intoxicating kisses started to take hold over his body. When he went to kiss Locke again, his knee bumped against the paper bag in which the waiter had stuck the wine bottle his father had gifted them.

Vince looked down at the bag and swallowed. "Shit," Vince said, moving away from Locke. "I—I could have tried to talk him out of it, but it wouldn't have worked. It never works."

"Yeah, I gathered that," Locke said. "He's really powerful."

"Yes," Vince said. "My powers are diluted. Not as good."

Locke shook his head. "My dad says that about my powers, too. But your father is wrong. You're amazing and your powers are incredible. You shouldn't listen to him."

"Trust me; I try very hard not to," Vince replied, a little more sharply than he intended.

"Hey, I'm right here," Locke said, bringing Vince's hand to his lips and kissing it softly. "If you ever want to talk about it, I'm here. If you don't want to talk about it, I'm here for that, too."

Vince smiled as he felt his cheeks redden. "And are you here to listen to me when I tell you to stay away?"

"Yes," Locke said, nodding his head. "I swear."

"Okay," Vince replied, kissing Locke on the cheek. "Thank you for offering to come with me, though. I mean, that was incredibly dumb, but it was sweet."

"I feel like you just described me perfectly," Locke replied, laughing. The elevator doors pinged, and they stepped out together, walking toward the pool hand in hand. "Did you bring a bathing suit?"

Vince raised his eyebrows, smiling at him. "Do I need a bathing suit?"

Locke smiled back. "Look," he said, glancing down at the bag he was holding in his hand. "We already have this bottle of wine, right? We aren't exactly going to pour it out. Unless you want to."

"No," Vince said. "I just feel shitty about how we got it."

"Yeah, me too. But it's not like we can return it. So what do you say we crack this open when we get to the pool?"

"Yeah, well" Vince replied, smiling despite himself. Maybe something good would come of dinner after all. "Unless you have a corkscrew in your pocket?"

Locke blinked before tugging the neck of the bottle free of the bag. "Not a screwtop, damn." He let the bottle go and smiled sheepishly at Vince. "We don't need wine to have a good time in a pool. Alone. Without bathing suits."

"And then?"

"And then we can go back to the suite and use the wine as bribe for privacy," Locke said, winking. "You have a promise to keep, don't you?"

Vince grinned.

Chapter Eleven

FAR TOO EARLY Sunday morning, the trainees assembled in the common room of the suite for their volunteer assignments. Locke's head was pounding, probably from the half bottle of wine he drank on returning to the suite and the fact that he hadn't had enough sleep the night before. Not that it hadn't been an unforgettable night. He had spent most of the night in the pool with Vince, their encounter invisible to everyone until Locke was on the verge of orgasm. It wasn't as though he could help it—his powers required a certain amount of concentration and he couldn't concentrate on anything except Vince being inside him, something he had looked forward to all week.

Locke had apologized, once he could think straight again. Vince seemed to think it was funny. They slept together in a bed far too small for both of them, ignoring the whooping and teasing from the other guys in the suite. Not that they weren't occupied themselves — Locke hadn't seen BJ or Cass, and Ariel had probably gotten lucky. He was sure he was going to hear about it after they were done volunteering, but the schedule left on the coffee table in the living room placed Ariel and him together at the soup kitchen from nine o'clock in the morning to noon. There was an address next to the words 'Prosperity Square', what Locke assumed to be the name of the plaza where they were supposed to go. There were bus passes in a blue folder, along with a strongly worded warning in Mister Mister's handwriting telling them they were only supposed to use them to get to and back from their volunteering assignment. *If you're late or absent, there will be consequences,* Mister Mister's note read.

"Why do we even have to do this?" Locke heard Mickey grumble.

He heard a couple of people start to answer as he went to get himself some breakfast. He was going to miss Vince, but he liked the idea of having a few hours of hanging out with just Ariel. Meeting Vince's dad had been a disaster.

BY THE TIME the helicopter landed back at Camp Hologram on Sunday night, Vince was thinking dizziness meds were wonder drugs. He almost felt normal getting out of the damned thing. He was so happy to have some free time before dinner. Maybe he and Locke could check out the lake for a private beach or something. His face flushed with the memory of what they'd done in the hotel pool. Somewhere in Guilford, a security guard was probably regaling his buddies over beer about what he'd seen on the hotel cameras, but fuck it. It had been so worth it, he'd happily do it again next weekend.

Mister Mister clapped his hands and said, "Right. Everyone's present and accounted for, so stow your gear in your cabins. Cabin One, you're on KP this week."

"What?" Vince couldn't stop his protest. He'd been so grateful to think his apron had been turned in for at least a month.

"You got a problem with that, Silva—talk to your cabin mates."

Cass and BJ were very pointedly looking at the ground, both of them with tight, stubborn mouths.

"Great," Locke muttered. "Fucking peachy."

The four of them marched to the cabin with their travel bags surrounded by a thick, resentful silence. Inside, that silence was broken only by the hard slamming of locker doors, all four of them.

Locke seemed equally fed up with Cass and BJ's antics.

The thick cloud followed them back to the kitchen.

Locke finally spoke, his voice controlled, but Vince could hear an edge to it he'd never heard before. "You two mind telling me why I am putting this fucking apron on for the third week in a row?"

"You tell 'em," BJ mumbled, turning away to pull his apron over his head.

Cass sighed heavily. "I knew you guys would be mad, that's why we agreed not to tell you."

"You two *agreed* on something?" Vince was amazed.

"Tell us now, or you'll both have black eyes."

BJ snorted but didn't say anything.

"After service on Friday," Cass began, "Beej there got a little frisky."

"Oh, god," BJ groaned.

"Yeah, we caught the opening act," Locke said impatiently.

BJ snorted again, his jaw tense.

"Well, Mister Mister caught the finale," Cass said, looking somewhat repentant.

"And stuck us with kitchen duty for another week," BJ said in a sullen voice, picking up the potato peeler with defiance.

"Which was when BJ caressed my eye with excessive force," Cass added, smirking.

Vince was torn between annoyance and amusement. He would have loved to have been a fly on the wall when Mister Mister walked in on—well, that part he didn't need to imagine. His amusement quickly faded as the reality of yet another week on KP set in.

The only good thing, if it could be called that, was they had it all down to a science—their waste was minimal, and their inventory was perfect. Nobody booed their food or threw it back at them. The camp recipes weren't exactly Roehampton Hotel quality, but it was more or less nutritious.

As Cass and BJ began their familiar sniping, Locke rolled his eyes at Vince and said loudly, "I thought you two fucked out your aggression? Are you gonna become, like, a couple? Ariel will be so disappointed."

That cut dead the impending argument as both Cass and BJ turned to stare in Locke's direction.

"Which of us does he want?" Cass asked. "Well, me, obviously."

Blessed silence reigned in the kitchen, and Vince smiled gratefully at Locke, who winked.

"Pretty little Ariel," Cass mused aloud.

"All yours," BJ said. "You heard what he told Bray during our first exercise?"

"Aww, you afraid to bottom for a cute widdle twink?" Cass mocked.

Vince drew in a deep breath and sighed loudly. "Would you two, I don't know. Shut the fuck up. For one service."

"What business is it of yours," BJ demanded. "Maybe Cass and I like pissing each other off."

"Argh," Locke exclaimed, "too much information!"

They got the food into the hot table, just as the others began filing in, chatting in happy tones about their day. Bray hooted, "Cabin One should be renamed Cabin Fuckup, as I see you guys are cooking yet again."

Vince rolled his eyes and wiped the sweat out of his eyes as he flipped more burgers. "What kind of volunteer work did you get?" he asked Locke.

"Soup kitchen. Ariel was with me, and oh my god, you won't believe the stuff he was telling me. You?"

"I was at a senior's center right downtown."

"With me," BJ added.

"Which would have been an awesome time to maybe tell me I was stuck in this damn kitchen for another week," Vince snapped back. To Locke, he said, "We didn't have to change diapers or anything, just read to them, played chess, that kind of thing. Talked to them."

"I was at the library to do much the same, only for toddlers," Cass said.

"Someone trusted you with kids?" BJ said in exaggerated disbelief.

"Fuck you."

"Been there, done that." BJ shook out a basket of fries to drain and turned to Vince. "Hey, was that your father I saw you guys with in the hotel lobby?"

Vince put the last of the burgers in the final hot tray and wiped his hands on his now filthy apron. "Yeah," he said cautiously, wondering why BJ was only now asking, if he was so curious. "Why?"

"I know it's not cool to talk about our families, I mean, don't get me wrong...."

Vince rolled his eyes and carried the tray of burgers to the counter.

BJ followed with the fries.

A glance at the table showed they needed more buns, too, so Vince knelt down to grab a bag. When he stood up, BJ was standing way too close. "Dude, in spite of that first night, I'm kind of monogamous."

BJ's brow furrowed, but he didn't outright scowl, and he only backed up a little. "Don't get the wrong idea, Vince. I just—" He lowered his voice and finally said, "He *is* Pied Piper, isn't he? Your dad? I mean, I recognized that song he hummed at the receptionist in the hotel lobby."

Vince froze, staring in horrified shock at BJ. "What?"

A clatter of a tray hitting the floor startled them both. Vince whipped his head around to see Mickey staring at him, eyes wide, jaw slack. "Holy fuck!" Mickey exclaimed in a loud voice. "Is it true?"

"Mickey, shut the fuck up," Vince said, his eyes widening. He wasn't sure what to say. He should lie, but Mickey had caught him off guard, and he was sure his deer-in-headlights look was giving him away.

"Shit," BJ whispered to Vince. "Sorry."

"Holy shit, so it *is* true," Mickey exclaimed. "Vince's father *is* Pied Piper!"

"For fuck's sake, Mickey," BJ said as the rest of the room went dead silent. Heads turned to stare into the kitchen as if operated by a single control. Vince felt like a spotlight was picking him out, highlighting him, the focus of a dozen stares.

He spun on his heel and thank god, there was Locke. Why did Locke look as pale and shocked as everyone else? He took a step toward him and lost whatever grounding he had when Locke took a matching step backward. Locke wasn't going to stand with him. For a seemingly endless moment, he couldn't move at all. Then his paralysis broke and he ran from the kitchen, ran from the building. He just ran.

Chapter Twelve

LOCKE HADN'T EXPECTED the horrified expressions on everyone's faces. What horrified him more was his own reaction. Vince had turned to him and he'd acted like he hadn't known. On the other hand, Pied Piper wasn't exactly a run-of-the-mill villain.

He wanted to run after Vince—to explain, to apologize, but that would mean abandoning BJ and Cass to finish up KP.

"Should one of us go after him?" Cass asked as the room erupted in chatter.

"Nah." Locke looked at BJ, who had a guilty expression on his face.

"I didn't mean to out him to everyone," he said, his face reddening. "I didn't see Mickey there. I just—" His hands clenched. "I thought it was kind of cool, okay?"

But Locke could hear the other guys, snippets of conversation he'd come to ignore as usual horseplay, sexual innuendo, and general complaints about the training, the weather, someone's snoring—typical and boring. Now they were saying things like maybe Vince was a spy, sent by his father to infiltrate the camp. Others were scoffing that no one would let the son of Pied Piper into camp, and it must be one of the realistic training scenarios Mister Mister said would happen without warning.

They were saying different things, but all about Vince and his father.

Locke wanted to interrogate BJ, but he didn't want to add more fuel to the gossip. As soon as everyone cleared out to hit the showers, he backed BJ into a corner.

"Oh, this looks interesting," Cass said, pulling off his hairnet and apron.

"Go clean the tables and floors," Locke replied, voice hard, not looking away from BJ. "Cock-burn and I have to talk."

From the corner of his eye, he could see Cass's exaggerated pout, but once he was on the other side of the counter, Locke demanded, "How the hell do you know who Vince's father is?"

After all, like all heroes and villains, Pied Piper had an identity disguising costume. Otherwise, he'd already be found and imprisoned, or whatever they actually did to villains.

"Th-the song. He's got a signature song."

"He didn't sing anything," Locke said, scowling.

"No, but he hummed it. At the check-in desk. I wasn't spying or anything; I was walking by and heard it. I couldn't believe it. Ever since, I didn't know whether to say anything or not."

"Not would have been the right choice," Locke growled.

"I couldn't help it, I just had to know. I didn't mean for everyone to know."

Locke spat in disgust. He had to find Vince and do something. He wasn't sure what, exactly. Talk to him, obviously. Fuck. Pied Piper.

He threw a rag at BJ. "You can finish up. I need to go sort out your mess."

Locke wasn't sure where Vince would have gone, but he knew their cabin was empty so that was where he started. If Vince wanted to be alone that was as good a place as any, until the kitchen was clean.

It felt weird, but he knocked on the door anyway before opening it. "Vince?"

There was only one small window in the cabin and the evening sun filtering through the trees failed to light it up, yet the light in the cabin wasn't on.

A snuffling sound drew his attention to Vince's bunk and a lump he might not have noticed moved. "Are you leading the movement to run me out of town?"

"No," Locke said, crossing the floor to sit beside Vince, not touching him.

Vince rubbed his arms restlessly but didn't speak.

"I'm sorry for backing away from you in the kitchen. I'm—it was cowardly. It's hard to grasp sometimes that you're related to a guy who robs banks and isn't all that concerned if people get hurt. And everyone's reaction."

"I'm not like him; you know that, right?"

"I know," Locke agreed automatically.

"Maybe I am, though," Vince said bitterly. "I comped us a room, didn't I?"

"It's not the same." That was what he'd told himself at the restaurant, wasn't it? "I think, uh, it's hard to explain. Okay, you should know my dad has always said villainy runs in the blood. I mean, I don't believe it." He hadn't, but this was the first time he'd had to put his beliefs to the test.

Vince sat up, looking at Locke. "So, um, now what? Does this affect us? You said it didn't matter."

"It doesn't," Locke said, but even he could hear the doubt in his voice.

"Yeah. I guess you need to think about it, huh." Vince was out of the cabin before Locke could clarify that a little social stigma and some lingering doubts weren't enough to drive him away.

Should he follow, or did Vince really need time alone? He leaned forward, resting his elbows on his knees and burying his face in his hands. "Fuck," he muttered aloud.

Chapter Thirteen

VINCE WASN'T SURE where he was going. All he was sure of was he needed to go somewhere. Anywhere. Far away from everyone else at camp.

He finally slowed down when he was near the lake. He walked into the woods behind the boathouse, hoping to avoid everyone. He really needed to be alone, and he didn't want to hear anyone's opinion about his father right now.

He swallowed as he considered the possible implications of BJ's revelation. Mister Mister knew, so that alone wouldn't get him kicked out, but he might be forced to leave the camp anyway, if the other trainees or their superhero parents insisted he was a danger to the camp. He couldn't see many alternate career options that could provide the resources he needed to escape his father's influence permanently and allow him to see his mother and let her live her life. Except villainy. He cringed. He never wanted to be his father's son, and villainy would lose him Locke forever.

He swallowed, trying not to think about it. He was walking quickly in the dark, the tears in his eyes blurring what little he could see. That was why he didn't notice the tree branch in front of him, which tripped him up, practically sending him flying. The landing was painful, he barely managed to steady himself with the palms of his hands, which were now burning. His jeans sounded like they had ripped at the knees, too, and he would have been concerned with that, except for the fact that he had heard everything in his pocket flying out of it. He was too busy falling to hear anything land. His phone had been in his pocket. He'd grabbed it when he got on his bunk, pocketing it mostly because it was in his way, wondering if he should try to call his mom. He tried not to tell her too much about his dad, because it worried her, but she still needed to be kept aware of things. Mostly so she could be prepared, especially if Vince accidentally pissed him off, which had happened more times than he liked to admit.

Not that it mattered now anyway, he thought as he sat up. His phone wasn't in his pocket anymore and it was likely it had shattered the moment it hit the ground. His eyes were getting a little more used to the dark, but he still couldn't see very well. If only Locke was around…

No, he had to stop thinking about Locke. He got to his knees and started feeling around for his phone, his hands hurting every time he touched the ground. He was filthy, tired, and he couldn't see a fucking thing. All he wanted to do was go back to his cabin and hug his boyfriend.

If he still had a boyfriend.

"Fuck," he said softly, sitting down on the wet ground and hugging his knees close to his chest. He took a deep breath as he felt warm tears streaming down his cheek.

There was some rustling nearby, but he didn't pay attention to it until someone cleared his throat. He looked up to see Ariel standing there, only recognizable in the twilight because of his brightly colored hair and his slight frame.

"Are you here to kick my ass?" Vince tried to make it sound like a joke. He was pretty sure it didn't.

Ariel walked up to him. Vince looked up, still hugging his knees. He wondered if he should run, but it was probably too late. Even if Vince managed to outrun him, he knew he would tire long before Ariel.

"I was going to," Ariel finally said. "But I don't know; I kind of feel like it wouldn't be exactly fair to kick you when you're down."

Vince sighed. "Thanks, Ariel."

Vince watched as Ariel sat down next to him, careful to brush away the leaves away from his spot before he did so. Vince hadn't expected him to do that—Ariel was always immaculate, and Vince didn't think he'd get dirty for no reason—but there he was, sitting next to him, as though it was a bench outside the hotel or something.

"I told you not to hurt him," Ariel finally said, breaking the silence.

Startled, Vince replied, "Did I? I wasn't trying to, but it's not like I can help who my father is."

"You should have told him before you started seeing each other, though," Ariel said.

Vince swallowed. He didn't want to keep crying in front of Ariel, but if they kept talking about this, he wasn't sure he would be able to stop himself. "I did."

Ariel sighed. "I don't mean in a my-father's-a-prick way, you should have said straight out he's a villain. He's fucking Pied Piper."

"I did," Vince repeated with more emphasis. "Jesus, what kind of person do you think I am that I wouldn't have told him?"

"Bullshit," Ariel scoffed. "Why wouldn't Locke have told *me*, if that were true?"

Vince stared at him, a shadowy figure in the gloom. "Because the more people who know, the worse it is? Because my father is fucking Pied Piper? Because he *cares* about you?"

Ariel stared back. "If you weren't a selfish prick who didn't tell him, why did you think I was here to kick your ass?"

Vince swiped his cheeks, his tears dried up. "Aren't you and the others forming some kind of plan to run me out of camp? Like father, like son, and all that crap?"

"No. It was shocking and they're all talking shit like how you could be a spy or something, but I'm pretty sure they're not going to hurt you. And they say *I'm* melodramatic!" Leaves rustled as he shifted position. "Did you ever consider that maybe, even if you did tell him, dating him might not be a good idea?"

"Yeah," Vince said in a small voice. "But I really like him. And I thought if I gave him the choice, maybe... I don't know. Like, I have all these feelings for him and—"

"Wait," Ariel said, looking straight at him. "Wait, you have feelings for him? What kind of feelings?"

Vince swallowed. He hadn't meant to say anything, especially not to Ariel. Not before he talked to Locke about it, anyway. "He's my boyfriend, Ariel. What kind of feelings do you think?"

"Okay, but like, how intense are these feelings?" Ariel said. "Like, on a scale of one to —"

Vince laughed, despite himself. "I don't know. It's hard to quantify. It feels really intense and big and important, but I wouldn't want to freak him out, right? And this is already weird enough, so, ugh."

"And you don't think this is something he should know?"

He shrugged. "I think now is not the right time. It's too soon, and he's already having doubts."

Ariel looked him up and down. Then he slightly shook his head. "You're wrong," he said. "And if you don't tell him, I will. As much as I hate to admit it, you guys are pretty adorable together."

"No, Ariel, don't—"

Vince watched as Ariel got quickly to his feet. He had already started to walk away from Vince before he could process what was happening. Vince swore softly under his breath as he rose, too, running to catch up to Ariel. He was already singing a nursery rhyme as fast as he could when he did. "You won't tell him anything that I told you," Vince said to Ariel, trying to catch his breath. "Right? Not before I do."

Ariel looked at him, a mix of confusion and anger on his face. "I won't tell him anything."

"Not even that you found me tonight," Vince said.

"Not even that I found you," Ariel repeated.

Vince nodded and sighed. "I'm sorry about this," he said. "I just—I have to tell him. Not you."

"Wow, did you really use your powers on me?" Ariel replied, taking a step toward him. Vince swallowed. The thought of using his power to convince Ariel not to hurt him crossed his mind, but he quickly dismissed it. That was the kind of thing his father did, Vince was sure of it.

"I know. Sorry," Vince said, closing his eyes as he tried to get ready for a punch. Nothing happened, though. When he opened his eyes, one after the other, Ariel was still standing in front of him, his head cocked and his hands by his sides.

"Look," Ariel said when Vince finally looked at him. "As much of a dick move as that was, I think I get it. I'm not going to hurt you right now, partly because I think Locke wouldn't be cool with that, but also because I think you *might* be right. If you're not, though...."

He trailed off. He didn't have to say anything else, Vince understood what the meaning of his silence perfectly.

"Got it," Vince said. "I will tell him. I promise. You just gotta give me some time."

VINCE WASN'T SURE how long he spent wandering the grounds. Part of him was hoping that, by the time he went back to the cabin, Locke would have fallen asleep and he wouldn't have to talk to him. All he could think about, whenever he closed his eyes, was the way Locke was looking at him, his green eyes wide, his arms crossed over his chest.

He was terrified what the doubt in Locke's voice meant.

Lights were still on in the cabin when he returned, but it was late. He wasn't sure exactly how late, because he still hadn't been able to find his phone and there was no clock he could glance at inside the cabin. It wasn't as though he could ask anyone there, either. Keeping his gaze away from everyone in the room was a difficult task, but one Vince was more than willing to tackle. He walked to the locker and grabbed his toothbrush and toothpaste off the shelf. At least the bathrooms would be empty now.

A shower would make him feel better, he thought as he entered the empty room and turned on the lights. He brushed his teeth, and he almost jumped when he turned away from the sink, his shampoo, conditioner and towel in his hands, to see Locke right behind him.

Vince looked at him for a second, wondering if he should say anything, but Locke spoke before he had made up his mind.

"We need to talk," Locke said. "I mean, I need to. Do you want to—I mean, can I? Now?"

"Yeah," Vince replied, nodding. "Look, I know—"

'No," Locke said. "Let me go first. I know I didn't sound very sure that this is what I want, and I am."

Vince felt some of the darkness that had fallen over him recede. "Y-you are?"

"Yeah," Locke said with a shadow of a smile. "Just—I got issues with my own father to get over, so I might be a little weird sometimes, but I'm in this, okay?"

"Okay. Good. I'm glad." He thought about what he promised Ariel but decided it was still way too soon to have that conversation.

"So. I didn't bring any dry clothes, so I'll have to watch you jerk off for me, right?" Locke's smile was now full watt.

Vince returned it. "I guess you will."

Chapter Fourteen

MONDAY MORNING PASSED in a weird kind of silence. Nobody said much as they all threw on clothes and trudged to the kitchen. The trend continued as they prepped breakfast. BJ muttered a few "I'm sorrys" at Vince until Vince glared at him. Locke didn't grab his hand, which was disappointing. Maybe they should have talked more about what he meant by being a little weird.

When the other guys came into the hall, Mister Mister was right behind them.

This is it, Vince thought, every muscle in his body tensing up.

Mister Mister was wearing the olive T-shirt and khaki cargo pants he seemed to wear every day. His arms were crossed over his chest, making his biceps look huge and emphasizing the tattoos decorating them.

Everyone lined up at the hot table in a weirdly silent, orderly fashion. Eyes darted from Mister Mister to Vince and back and Mister Mister just waited. The tension in the whole room mounted, or maybe it was just Vince's own anxiety.

"I don't know when you brats started thinking this was a holiday camp for heroes' kids, and I'd've thought you'd gotten over it by now. Could be I'm not working you hard enough."

Groans were quickly stifled.

"But Camp Hologram is for any power-gifted person who wants to use their powers as a hero. I shouldn't have to tell you again that powers don't always come from power-gifted people and powers on their own have no intrinsic morality. Nobody is 'born good' or 'born evil,' power-gifted or not. Vincent Silva is hardly the only one of you here with villainous relatives. We don't get to pick our relatives."

"But we can pick our noses!" someone called. Maybe Bray? Vince didn't dare look at anyone but Mister Mister. He couldn't believe Mister Mister was standing up for him.

"I don't care what you do in your personal time," Mister Mister responded in a bland tone. "But I don't want my camp disrupted because a bunch of you think you're somehow special. Am I clear?"

They'd spent enough time training with Mister Mister that no one hesitated to return a sharp, "Yes, sir!"

"Now eat up, we've got a busy day ahead of us."

Mister Mister spun on his heel and left the hall.

For the first time, Vince wondered where Mister Mister ate and who cooked for him.

In spite of having that worry removed, and contrary to what they'd told Mister Mister, the other guys continued to treat Vince differently. Avoided him when they could, acted nervous around him when they couldn't.

Locke still smiled at him, but his smiles were cautious.

Still, not everyone treated him like a pariah. Royce, the firestarter, took him aside as they waited their turn to do the obstacle course, and said quietly, "My uncle is Spark. You know, of the villain team Flint and Spark? He tried like hell to talk my dads out of letting me come here. Not like they could stop me really, but you know."

Spark was known by Sparky in a mocking way even by other villains, but Vince appreciated the solidarity. "Thanks, man."

Royce smiled and nodded encouragingly, and they'd continued their exercise.

When Vince found himself climbing the tire wall with Rudy, he was surprised when Rudy said, "Anything I can do to make this easier?"

"Um," Vince replied. "I lost my phone in the woods. I guess you don't do that kind of thing." He felt like a moron for asking, and his face turned red from more than the exertion of the climb. "Never mind," he mumbled.

By supper, Vince was almost wishing he *had* been kicked out. Everyone, even Locke, was acting weird.

SOMEHOW THE POSSIBILITY Vince might get sent away from camp had never occurred to Locke, and he felt guilty as he realized it had weighed on Vince. He'd forgotten that maybe the repercussions for Vince might be more than just losing his boyfriend. Temporarily, Locke hastily added, because the idea of not being with Vince seemed flat out wrong. It was just a matter of wrapping his head around a few things.

In spite of what Mister Mister had said about no one being born good or evil, Locke's father had always insisted villainy was in the blood. Locke had always imagined he was too much of his own person to not make up his own mind on the matter, but now his father's ideas kept nagging at him, even if he knew, intellectually, Mister Mister was right. Theoretically.

How many heroes had come from villain stock? He'd never bothered to research it before, because he'd told himself it didn't matter.

He kept glancing over his shoulder, but Vince hadn't come to the showers with them, and Locke was glad. And guilty that he was glad. Not because he didn't want to see Vince, exactly, but—Locke squeezed his eyes shut and shook his head. He had to sort out his feelings soon.

Vince still wasn't around when he left the showers. Locke dressed quickly and went back to the cabin. He could dick around on the internet with his phone for the first time that day, and that would give him something to do when Vince showed up.

Surprisingly, Cass didn't have much to say about Vince's father, and BJ looked worried. BJ had even tried to apologize to him, saying he hadn't meant to cause trouble.

"It's okay," Locke said, not meaning it. "At least you don't think he's a spy, or under his father's control."

"Well d'uh," BJ said. "Pied Piper's powers don't work that way. That's why he hasn't won. His powers have like a two or three hour limit. Of course, most people don't even know he whammied them in the first place, because he's that good, but seriously, there's no way Vince could be a Pied Piper minion."

"How do you know so much about him?" Cass asked, as if he'd finally given up resisting the urge to talk about Vince's father.

BJ turned red. "I just, you know. Pay attention."

Locke had never thought their entire relationship might be some gambit by Pied Piper, but it was reassuring to know it wasn't possible.

Vince returned to the cabin, hair damp and curly from his shower and Locke pretended he wasn't eye-fucking him from the top bunk. His phone rang, distracting him, and he glanced down. His father. He frowned.

Jumping down to the floor, he said, "Gotta take this outside, guys," by way of explanation, and hit answer as he walked out the door.

"Hello," he said, as if he didn't know who it was. It gave him a chance to walk far enough away from the cabins that he wouldn't be overheard.

"Hello," his father replied, his tone even.

Locke swallowed. He knew what this phone call meant, and he wasn't looking forward to it. "How are you doing, Dad?"

His father tutted. "Not great. I've heard a very disturbing rumour."

Shit, how could he have found out so fast? Locke considered lying for a second, but he knew his father would find out the truth sooner or later. He tried to keep his voice even as he answered. "What's that, Dad?"

"That you've been dating Pied Piper's son." The censure in his voice was heavy and Locke flinched.

"Yeah, um." Locke took a deep breath and said firmly, "Yes, I am."

There was a long, long silence, almost long enough for Locke to ask him if he was still there.

"I don't even know where to start," his father said.

"Vince is not like him, Dad," Locke said. He sounded like he was pleading and he hated it. "He's nice, he's smart, he's funny, he's kind. You would love him."

"He's Pied Piper's son," his father replied tersely.

Locke groaned. "I know. He told me," he said. "Relax, it's not like I'm going out with Pied Piper."

His father sounded as surprised as he did angry. "He told you?"

"Yeah, because I—"

"And you're still going out with him?"

"I'm an *adult*," Locke replied, rolling his eyes. "I can make my own decisions."

His father scoffed and Locke's heart dropped to his stomach. "Yeah, I think we can both see how well that worked out."

Locke closed his eyes, trying to keep his breathing steady. He didn't want to get into a shouting match with his father, not right in front of the cabin. "That's not fair."

"Are you going to keep seeing him?" his father asked, completely ignoring him.

Locke took a deep breath, his hand fisted by his side. "That's my decision," he replied. "And none of your goddamn business."

"Watch your language," his father said and sighed deeply. It was the kind of sigh Locke hadn't heard for a long time, not since finding out about how undignified his powers were compared to his dad's. "I'll see you on Saturday at the Roe. Six o'clock. Don't be late."

Locke was about to protest but his father hung up the phone before he could. He looked at the phone in his hand, the line now dead, until the screen dimmed. Only then did he walk back into the cabin, hoping Vince had already fallen asleep.

LOCKE HADN'T EXACTLY gone out of his way to avoid Ariel, but he didn't want to talk to him either. He rarely kept secrets from him—in fact, he couldn't remember the last time he had done it—but this hadn't been just about Vince, it had been about Ariel, too. He couldn't exactly tell him anything, he was supposed to be protecting both of them.

He didn't think Ariel saw it that way. That became obvious as he walked up to his cabin, behind everyone else, and Ariel grabbed him by the shoulder.

"Are you giving me the silent treatment?"

Locke made reluctant eye contact and shook his head slightly. He was very tired and hardly felt like he could deal with his best friend. It was already hard having to deal with everyone else at camp, especially because he wasn't sure what to do about the sideways looks the other guys were already giving him when he held Vince's hand or smiled at him. He'd started to avoid Vince, which made him feel like shit, especially when he remembered telling Vince he would be there for him no matter what.

"We need to talk."

Locke closed his eyes. "Ariel, I—"

"Unless those words are followed by 'am a huge dick', I'm not interested," Ariel spat out. "What the hell, Locke? I've always had your back. Ever since we were little kids, I've been there for you."

Locke sighed, trying to ignore the lump in his throat. His best friend was right, he had always been there for him. They'd had plenty of disagreements through the years, but Locke didn't think he had ever seen Ariel this angry at him before. He wanted to talk to him about Vince, about what his dad had said, about the rest of the guys at camp, but Ariel didn't seem to be in a chatty mood.

"Ariel," he said again. "I wasn't trying to hurt you. I just wanted to protect you."

Ariel's eyes narrowed, and he crossed his arms over his chest. "Because I can't take care of myself?"

"No," Locke replied. "That's not what I said."

Ariel scoffed, a scowl on his face when he spoke again. "Do you remember what happened last time you thought I couldn't take care of myself?"

"Yes," Locke said, nodding and looking away from him. "You nearly broke Alex Hodges' femur, which was so unnecessary."

"I meant to scare him," Ariel said. "And it worked, didn't it? He left us alone. Plus, I was learning to use my powers. If it had been more recent, I would have just given him a couple of bruises."

"If it had been more recent, no one would have believed him when he said we were a couple," Locke said quietly, setting his gaze on him again.

"Or no one would have cared," Ariel replied, shrugging his shoulders. "You're too good-looking for anyone to bully you now."

Locke rolled his eyes. "This isn't about some middle school bullshit, Ariel," he said impatiently. "This is a real-life supervillain. Someone who doesn't care if people get hurt. You can't just knock his teeth out and expect everything's going to be all right."

Ariel took a step toward him. "You think that's what I would do?"

"I just—I don't know what you would do."

"Right, and you never thought to ask."

"Because I wanted to protect you," Locke said. "Vince also didn't want me to tell anyone, and I really like him, and I—"

"I'm your friend," Ariel whined. "I wasn't going to beat anyone up. All I wanted was to be there for you. Now I find out you're keeping shit from me and—"

"Just one thing," Locke mumbled.

"Oh, yeah, just one thing," Ariel said. "Sure. Don't act like this is some sort of nice thing you did for me. This is something you did because you weren't sure you could deal with the consequences, right? Vince is fine as hell, you say he's a good fuck, and he's interested in you. Why wouldn't you keep it to yourself? You probably wouldn't want your dad to know about it."

"I was going to tell him eventually," Locke said. "I was going to tell you, too. Just—when it was safe to do so."

"Wait, so now you tell me stuff when you tell your Dad stuff? Wow," Ariel said, his jaw dropping open.

"Ariel, can you please not be mad at me right now?" Locke said. "I'm already dealing with so much shit and I—"

"I don't know, Locke," Ariel said. He didn't sound angry anymore, he sounded really sad. "I guess I just thought we were closer than that."

Locke opened his mouth to say he'd done it because he didn't want him to get hurt, but before he could say anything, Ariel was walking away. When Locke opened his mouth to speak, no sound came out.

LOCKE LOOKED AROUND the lobby, relieved when he didn't see any trace of any of the other guys, including Vince or Ariel. He had told Vince he had to do this alone even though Vince had offered to go with him and Vince seemed to have understood. Ariel was still acting like he was a little mad at him, which might have been a good thing. He didn't want Ariel with him for this confrontation if there was a chance he'd back his father. He took his phone out of his pocket to text his dad and ask where he was, but before he could, he felt a hand on his shoulder. He could already smell the familiar scent of the Yves Saint Laurent cologne, one of the few luxuries his father allowed himself.

Locke turned around and tried to smile. "Hi, Dad," he said.

"Hello," his father replied, raising his eyebrows. "Are you hungry?"

Locke shook his head. He didn't feel like eating at all. He'd been dreading this dinner ever since his father had announced it was happening.

"Relax," his dad said, squeezing his shoulder. "I just want to talk."

Locke took a deep, trembling breath. "Okay."

"Not here, though," he replied, looking at the restaurant in the hotel. "That place is a rip off. How do you feel about pub food?"

"I'm not hungry," Locke said quietly.

"More for me," his dad replied, smiling at him.

Locke followed him out of the hotel and across the street to a place called Brickhouse. It was only after they'd ordered and his father was sipping on a pint of Sam Adams while Locke worked on his diet Coke that they started to talk about anything other than the traffic in the city and how overpriced the Roehampton was.

"How's Mom?"

"She's fine," his dad said. "She's busy."

Locke nodded. Having a conversation like this was always easier when his mom was around because she often acted like a mediator between them. Locke didn't think she particularly liked it, but someone had to do it. Maybe she was on his dad's side this time and she couldn't deal with being there. The very thought made him feel guilty.

His dad pinched the bridge of his nose and took a deep breath. "You know why I'm here."

"Yeah," Locke said, biting down on his straw.

"You're still seeing him?"

Locke looked down at his drink and nodded, ever-so-slightly. Lying wasn't a consideration, his father could always tell when he wasn't telling him the truth if they were face-to-face. It was easier on the phone.

"Before we start talking about this, I want you to know I trust you," his father said, his tone measured. "Concerned does not begin to cover how I feel about this."

Locke shook his head. "You don't understand, Dad. Vince is really nice," he said. "You should meet him. He's a—"

His father held his hand up to stop him from talking. "I don't care if he's the nicest guy in the world," he said. "He's still Pied Piper's son."

Locke's eyes widened. "Yeah, but I'm your son," he said. "That doesn't guarantee I'm going to be a superhero or anything of the sort. I mean, Ava and Frey—"

He saw a flash of anger on his face, just for a second. "Your siblings would never do anything like this," he spat out. "You were the only one of our children lucky enough to have powers and you go and do this."

"Do what, Dad? Date someone I like?" Locke said. He was starting to feel as angry as his father looked. "I don't think I have to apologize because I'm the only one that can get a—"

"This isn't about that!" his dad replied, slamming his fist on the table and startling Locke. "There are things you don't know, things most people don't know, about Pied Piper. About what he's capable of. Carey, you are in over your head."

Locke almost flinched at the sound of his first name. He'd been going by his surname for years, but of course his parents wouldn't call him that.

Locke shook his head. "I really like him," he said. "Maybe if you met him—"

"You want me to meet him? You want me to meet Pied Piper's son?" His dad answered, his jaw dropping open. "I suppose you also want him to meet your mother? Not to mention your siblings. Who cannot defend themselves against the power-gifted, in case you've already forgotten."

Locke stared at him. He'd never seen him like this. His dad's fury was evident on his face, but there was something else and Locke couldn't quite put his finger on it.

"This isn't fair," Locke said. "He's the first person I've ever...."

Locke wasn't sure how to finish that sentence, but it seemed to calm his dad down a bit.

"I know it isn't fair," he said. "And I'm sorry about that. But this is the life of a hero. This is what you're here for. You have to make sacrifices to keep your family safe. You think I don't do that all the time?"

Locke sighed. "I know you do."

"It will hurt less if you stop seeing him now," his dad said. "It's your responsibility to keep us safe now, too. To keep yourself safe. I don't even want to think about what would happen to your mother if you were hurt—"

"You said that was an occupational hazard," Locke replied automatically, recalling his send off to Camp Hologram, which included a lengthy and awkward talk that covered everything from superheroing to STDs.

"It is," his dad said. "You're supposed to minimize the risk by not being foolish. That's part of your job. From the moment you go to camp until the day you die; you're supposed to protect yourself and your loved ones."

Locke finished his drink and kept sucking on his straw, though there was nothing left in his cup but ice.

"Like I said when we started this conversation," his dad said evenly. "I trust you. I know you'll do the right thing."

Locke didn't nod, he didn't say anything. He turned around to look as the waiter arrived with their food. "Service is quick here," he said quietly.

His dad nodded. "I thought you weren't hungry."

"I was wrong," Locke replied with no conviction. He was glad his dad had ordered him a burger, after all, eating was better than talking about this. Then again, anything was.

Chapter Fifteen

VINCE WASN'T SURE how much time he was supposed to give Locke after seeing his father. He had expected maybe a few hours. Or overnight. Locke's father couldn't possibly be as bad as Vince's. But Locke left the hotel early Sunday morning, presumably with Ariel.

Vince was picking through the complimentary continental breakfast included with the suite when Ariel joined him, hair damp from the shower. He looked like he'd slept poorly, too. "Where's Locke?" Vince blurted out.

Ariel spared him a glance. "How the fuck should I know?"

"He had dinner with his father last night, said he needed to do it alone. Since I gave him hell for showing up after I asked for pretty much the same thing. Anyway, I haven't seen him since."

"Are there any chocolate muffins left?"

Vince bit the corner of his lip. "Did something happen between you two?"

"I'm just mad at him for not telling me who your father was." Ariel's voice was slightly muffled behind the cover of the muffin box. "Ah ha!" He held aloft a chocolate muffin.

"Why, though? I mean, I asked him to keep it a secret. It wasn't his secret to tell."

"Maybe," Ariel said around a mouthful of muffin. "It's nice of you to care. I wouldn't worry too much about what his father might have said. Now that Locke knows how strong your feelings are, he'll...." Ariel must have seen the flash of guilt in Vince's eyes. "God, you're so stupid."

Vince didn't know what to say to that.

Ariel finished off his muffin and poured himself a coffee into a Styrofoam cup. "I better go find him."

Vince didn't see either of them again until they were on the helicopter back to camp. He climbed in last and found the only available seat beside Bray, who flinched away from him. Whether it was because Bray thought he might get airsick again, or because he believed villainy was contagious, Vince didn't know. It wasn't until Monday night after supper that he'd been able to catch Locke alone outside the cabin. "What the fuck is going on?" He winced at his own words. "I'm sorry, I mean—you're going out of your way to avoid me and I-I don't even know why."

"You know why," Locke said, his voice wooden.

Vince felt his eyes well up and he blinked furiously. "You said you were okay with that. You said you'd stand by me." He spun away. "For fuck's sake, Locke, if you were breaking up with me, you could have at least had the guts to tell me."

"I just think it's better we stop seeing each other for a while."

"Yeah," Vince said bitterly. "Better."

After a few minutes, he heard the cabin door close and he turned around and rested his head on the outside cabin wall. He ignored the strong urge to bang his head against it.

"Yo," Cass said, putting his hand on Vince's shoulder. The sudden touch startled him.

"Hey, Cass," Vince said, smiling thinly at him.

"Just so you know," he said, so quietly Vince could hardly hear him. "We're cool. At least as far as I'm concerned."

Vince raised his eyebrows. "We are?"

"Yeah," Cass said. He looked Vince up and down and winked. "And I'm totally willing to hang out with you. Amongst other things. You know, if—"

"I don't know if you've noticed this, Cass, but I'm in a relationship," Vince replied automatically. Hearing the words coming out of his mouth made him feel dizzy, though. "Okay, I guess maybe I'm not."

"Yeah," Cass said, glancing over at the door. He'd probably seen the whole thing. Maybe even heard it.

Vince tried to swallow down the knot in his throat. "Yeah."

"Anyway," Cass continued. "I thought you should know. I'm pretty new to this whole thing, I think, at least compared to everyone else here. That whole secrecy, villain or super-hero bloodline thing? It's like, so weird and archaic. I'm still trying to wrap my head around it. So I'm on your side."

"You're new to this? You mean you're the first person in your family to be power-gifted?" Vince replied, his eyes widening in surprise. "But you always seem so, well, you know."

"Confident? It helps that I'm cute," Cass said, laughing and winking at him. "And I want to make the world a better place or whatever. But I'm pretty sure it's mostly the cute thing."

Powers generally manifested with the onset of puberty, which was a thing the power-gifted learned when it happened to them. Vince wasn't entirely sure how it worked with people like Cass, but in his case, the International Alliance of Enhanced Abilities came in and arranged some intensive work to test the limits of his abilities and ensure he knew how to use them. Vince's powers weren't the kind he could use accidently, since he had to hum or sing in a very particular pitch, but other kinds were different.

Camp Hologram was where people trained once they decided they wanted to use their powers to benefit society. People with powers like BJ's healing weren't necessarily suited to the law enforcement kind of superheroing and often went into medicine. Depending on the country, a doctor with super healing powers could make a fortune, if that's what mattered.

Vince's father had always thought that was what mattered. Withdrawing financial support after he left, leaving Vince and his mother to struggle with the bills on a four thousand square foot house in a gated enclave was his way of teaching them the importance of money, or so he'd claimed.

That wasn't the lesson Vince had learned, but he doubted his father would understand.

By Wednesday, nothing had changed. Mister Mister set everyone up on a "buddy" exercise, with Ariel and Bray getting Mickey, while everyone else was in pairs. Locke and Vince were teamed together.

Locke didn't protest, which Vince considered progress. "You two are rescuing a kidnapped child," Mister Mister said, handing them a crudely drawn map with a directional indicator and little more than an x marking the location of the imaginary child and a "you are here" dot. "The longer it takes you to find her, the more likely she is to die." Great, they'd be marked on how quickly they did it, too. With nothing more to go on, they set off.

After a while Vince said, "Do you suppose this happens often, you know, in the real world?"

"Kids get kidnapped all the time."

"Yeah, but hauled out to the woods?"

Locke shrugged. "I guess we're just to show how good we are at reading shitty maps?"

He still wasn't the friendly, enthusiastic Locke he could be with other people. Vince wondered if Locke had added "for a while" merely to soften the blow. Maybe he could ask how long "for a while" might be.

So they went through the woods in silence. Vince had become accustomed to the unkemptness of raw nature. The woods were lumpy, hills and hollows all trying to trip one up. When he saw a narrow trunk stretching across a particularly low point, he walked across it. It wasn't the smooth iron rails he'd played on as a boy, but it was close enough.

"How'd you learn to do that," Locke asked, wiping his brow when dragged himself out of the hollow.

"Other kids were riding their skateboards over the metal rails of the library steps, I was walking on 'em."

"Seriously?" Locke sounded impressed.

"Yeah. Before my powers kicked in, I was into parkour and stuff. I guess I figured I'd be in the circus, but you know." He chanced a grin at Locke. "Nobody wants to watch a tightrope walker who can't go higher than three feet off the ground. Not that I ever learned to walk on anything as small as a rope."

Locke grinned back. His grin immediately faded. "We should get going, kid's not gonna save itself."

"Right." Vince stifled a sigh.

Their path had been generally rising since they'd set out, but now it grew steep enough that sometimes they had to pull themselves up by grabbing on to branches. Without warning there was nothing ahead of them but a rope bridge across the river, which to Vince looked very far away.

"Looks like your circus skills will come in handy," Locke said.

"I can't. I can't cross that." Just looking over the edge had his stomach churning and his head spinning. He hadn't realized he'd been backing away until he hit a tree trunk. The sharp end of a broken branch scraping across his skin was nothing compared to the maw before them, waiting to swallow him up.

Sympathy warred with impatience on Locke's face. "Can't you just, I don't know. Sing to yourself that you're not afraid?"

"It doesn't work like that. I can't use my powers on myself and even if my—I could be forced to cross, but it wouldn't make me any less dizzy or terrified."

Locke scowled at the close reminder of Vince's father and turned to look at the spider web of a bridge.

"You finish the exercise. Mister Mister can dock me points for not—"

"Pretty sure that's not how it will work."

"There's a time limit, Locke. If the imaginary kid dies, we'll both get fail marks."

"That's a pretty shitty phobia for a superhero to have."

"It's not like my powers are flying." Vince was far enough from the edge that he was starting to feel sort of normal-ish, but remembering the chasm sent a shiver through him. Even if he could force himself onto that tiny bit of rope, could he control the dizziness and nausea that would have him trying to puke over the side and very likely fall to his death? "Just go already."

"Close your eyes."

"What?"

"No time to argue, Vince, just do it."

Confused, he closed his eyes.

"Okay, now look. No ravine. You can do this."

Vince opened his eyes and stared ahead in confusion. The gaping chasm was now filled with grass and trees.

Locke waved him impatiently over to the posts marking the rope bridge. It crossed a meadow no more than a foot below it. "Piece of cake, right? Come on."

"Um…" He gingerly took hold of the rope and stared at the grass carpet ahead of him. Swallowing, Vince hurried across the bridge, one foot in front of the other, grasping the sides tightly and feeling silly as his eyes told him there was nothing to fear. He was still breathing hard when he got to the other side, but Locke slapped him on the back and said, "Come on, we're almost there."

"Thank you."

"Whatever. That's part of what we're learning right? To utilize each other's talents?"

Vince stifled a sigh. Of course it was foolish to think it had been anything but training. This side of the river was a lot rockier, less underbrush, but more dangerous underfoot. "Listen," Locke said.

The faint sound of a child crying and calling for help came to them. They shared a glance. The scenario was creepily real, but it had to be a recording. They stumbled around following after the sound and finally realized it was coming from a crevice in the rocks. Locke sank down to a sitting position and said, "Fucking Mister Mister."

"What?" Vince gave him a wary look and then started down the crevice. It was steep, and if anyone did bring a child there, they wouldn't be able to do it alone. He looked up to see Locke still staring at the hole he was already half inside.

"How does he know our weaknesses?"

"After I threw up on everyone in the helicopter, I think mine was kind of a no-brainer. Are you afraid of like, caves, or small spaces?"

"Not really. I mean if that was a cave we could walk into, it would make me nervous, but not sitting here." Locke's voice was strained and he couldn't seem to tear his eyes away from the hole. "It's underground. I-I have nightmares about being buried alive. How can he *know* that?"

"Look I got this one, okay? Can you maybe throw me a ball of light to use once I'm down?"

Locke looked relieved. "Yeah. That would still be using my power to help, right? It won't last long once it's out of my line of sight, but yeah, I can do that."

Vince resumed climbing down. The solid ground in front of him, the awareness of it behind him kept his own phobia from triggering. "Maybe it's in your IAEA file," he called up as his feet touched the bottom. The edge was maybe his height and half again above his head, no big deal.

"Maybe." Locke had edged closer to the hole, but he was lying on his stomach looking in, as if to prevent himself from falling.

"The crying seems to be coming from back there." Vince gestured into the dark. He looked up. "Light?"

"Here. Catch."

Vince didn't know how to hold light, but he managed to catch the ball of it anyway. He gave Locke a thumbs-up and followed the sound.

It wasn't very far away, behind a rock, a lumpy looking thing, but before Vince could figure out how to turn off the crying or otherwise activate the signal that they'd found their victim, Locke's light sputtered and faded. "Shit," he muttered.

He inched forward, using his hands to guide him around the rock and fumbled with what felt like a fifty-pound bag of rice. Did that mean he had to actually carry the "child" out? In the dark?

Vince ran his hands over the bag, unable to find any playback or signaling device. So if they were going to succeed at this, he had to at least get the bag into the light.

"Vince?"

"Yeah?"

"Everything okay?"

"I guess. I don't know. It's dark." He pulled at the bag. The floor of the cavern was too rough to drag it.

"This help?" A light flared, back at the base of the hole, shedding just enough light that Vince might actually be able to keep from killing the "child."

"Yeah, thanks."

"I can maintain this one. I-I should have thought of it before. Why is our victim still crying?"

"I guess because she's not rescued yet," Vince said, more irritably than he meant. He managed to get back to Locke's light with only a few scrapes on his shoulder, from using the wall of the cavern as a guide.

He plopped down the wailing rice bag.

"We found it, why is it still crying?" Locke asked again.

"I guess technically it's not rescued until we get it out of this hole." Vince hefted the rice bag over his head. "Can you reach it?"

Vince thought his arms would break, it took so long for Locke to say, "No."

"You're gonna have to come part way down."

"I—no. You and the ravine? That's me and that hole."

The rice bag continued wailing and Vince was aware the clock was ticking. There was nothing he could find to make it stop. It was probably triggered by surroundings.

"Use your power on me. Make me come down."

"What? Are you fucking nuts?"

"Look, Vince. You and the ravine, yeah, there was a chance you could have fallen and died, right? Perfectly rational fear. But I know there's not the slightest chance I'm going to be buried alive in that hole. Totally irrational. But we have to get the bag out of that hole." Locke's voice was strained, but matter-of-fact.

Vince scowled. He might have tried to talk Locke through it, because he only had to come half way down, and he could brace his back against the opening and grab the bag. But how long would that take?

"I don't want to do this."

"It's okay, Vince. It has to be done. We're on the clock. I officially give you permission to use your powers on me." Locke smiled a little. "Hurry up."

Vince started humming and blushed a little when he realized it was some pop love song he'd heard a million times on the radio. "Come down the hole, Locke, just halfway. I'll be right here," he added before he could think Locke might not find that reassuring.

He only had a brief glimpse of the paleness of Locke's face before he got up and did as Vince suggested. When he was in position, without looking down, Locke said thinly, "Hurry before I puke on your head."

Vince grunted and heaved the bag of rice up into Locke's grasp. But Locke seemed frozen in place.

Vince climbed up the rough opening, all hands and feet, careful not to bump Locke. He took the rice bag and tossed it on the ground, where it abruptly stopped crying. He grabbed Locke's hands and pulled him out.

Locke was trembling. Vince pulled him into a reassuring hug. "It's okay. We did it," he said softly.

Locke shoved him away, almost falling to the ground. He smiled apologetically and said, "Yeah."

Vince opened his mouth to say something, but he wasn't sure what he could say. It didn't matter, anyway, because Locke had already turned away from him after grabbing the rice bag.

It would have been pointless to talk to him then.

Chapter Sixteen

IT WAS LATE and Locke was dirty, tired, and his head hurt. KP had never been fun, but it was particularly bad that dinner service. Things were different, though, and Locke knew it was in no small part due to what had happened during the exercise. Vince had almost been defiant about being in Locke's face, the sad puppy dog look had been wiped clean from his expression and he had stopped addressing him—unless he absolutely had to.

Lights out would be soon and they were all busy getting ready for bed. Locke didn't like being there, in that tight space, trying to avoid Vince's gaze every time he looked at him. He had texted Ariel, who had gotten back to him and told him he would meet him outside his cabin. Ariel's text read *OMG, we have so much to talk about.*

Whatever that meant. Locke didn't want to be in the cabin, and Ariel had news of his own. He could have happily spent all night outside talking to Ariel if it meant he didn't have to be around Vince.

He climbed down the ladder, careful not to touch Vince's bunk as he did so, and walked outside, saying nothing to anyone.

Ariel was standing right outside the door, a huge smile on his face. "Hey! Walk and talk?"

Locke glanced at the cabin and nodded. He didn't want anyone inside to hear them. "I don't think we have much time before lights out."

"We don't," Ariel said. "So, tell me, how did it go? Did he tell you?"

"Huh?"

"Was it, like, *so* romantic? Oh, was it during the exercise? That would have made sense," Ariel continued, ignoring the question. "You have to tell me everything, okay? Start at the beginning."

Locke cocked his head. "Ariel, what are you talking about? Did who tell me what?"

"Vince. Wait, he didn't tell you?" Ariel said. "He said he was going to tell you."

"Ariel, I still don't know what you're talking about," Locke said. "Nothing happened. He was nice and sweet, and I pushed him away."

Ariel's eyes widened. "Why?"

"I can't, Ariel," Locke replied. "Being with Vince means I'm not a good superhero because I'm putting my family at risk, because I'm putting you at risk, and I can't do that. I've wanted this all my life. I don't think I'd be good at anything else."

Ariel sighed deeply. "You shouldn't have to make that choice."

"My dad said it's what I signed up for," Locke murmured.

They stopped walking when they reached the open area near the lake, the first part of camp Locke had seen after his first KP. The morning after he had been with Vince for the very first time. Vince's presence was in every part of camp, everywhere Locke looked. He had tried to ignore it, but it hadn't worked.

"I just thought things had changed," Ariel said.

"I don't know why you thought that," Locke replied.

His father's words played like a song on repeat in his head. His resolve had been tested when Vince had hugged him after retrieving the crying bag of rice, but he couldn't let his father down.

It was hard, but Locke was doing the right thing. He was. This was what doing the right thing was. Or so he'd been trying to tell himself ever since he'd spoken to his father.

"Because he was *supposed* to tell you," Ariel whined. "And I can't, and ugh! This is the worst. How much longer do I have to put up with the two of you fighting? This is the first guy you've ever gone out with that I actually like."

"Okay, well, thanks. Your approval means a lot," Locke said, chuckling quietly. "But why can't you tell me? You tell me everything."

"Yeah," Ariel said, sarcasm dripping from his voice. "Like you tell me everything. I just can't, okay? I can't even tell you how I found out."

"Why?"

"Because." Ariel shrugged. "I'm going to shut up now. I shouldn't have assumed he told you anything."

Locke's eyes widened as he realized what Ariel was telling him. "Did he use his powers on you?"

Ariel's gaze darted away from Locke's. "Well, he—"

"You're telling me he used his powers on you, he didn't tell me about it, and he's the only guy I've ever dated that you actually like? I don't know that much about villains, Ariel, but it kind of sounds like something Pied Piper would do. Doesn't it sound like that to you?"

"Honestly, I don't think he's the one who's acting like his father in this situation," Ariel said so quietly Locke almost couldn't hear him.

"Maybe that's not such a bad thing," Locke said, his voice trembling.

"Stop being gross," Ariel said. "Anyway, I'm sorry I said anything. We better head back."

"Yeah," Locke replied, biting his lips. "Let's go."

BY FRIDAY MORNING, Vince's anxiety had reached a boiling point. Locke kept avoiding him, but it wasn't just that. He wasn't just treating him coolly anymore. Ever since Wednesday, Locke had seemed angry at him. It surprised Vince, but it didn't matter, because now he was angry too. How long was he supposed to wait for Locke to make up his damn mind? They needed to have a conversation.

On the way to KP, still half asleep, Vince had already made up his mind. He was going to talk to Locke. If nothing else, he needed clarification on what "for a while" meant. If it was a euphemism and they were never getting back together, he needed to know, even if hurt like hell.

Locke was walking ahead of everyone. Vince trailed behind BJ and Cass, who were already bickering over something, though the sun had barely come out.

He quickened his pace to get past them and grabbed Locke by the wrist. He hadn't intended for the gesture to seem aggressive, but it came across as territorial. Locke looked at him, his green eyes widening, but he didn't shake him off.

"Can we talk?" Vince said, though it barely sounded like a question. "It's been days."

"I don't know," Locke replied. BJ and Cass glanced at them and stopped talking for a few seconds. They left, not saying anything. They would have to start KP by themselves, which was kind of a shitty thing to do to them, but Vince needed to talk to Locke.

Vince sighed, talking only when the two guys were out of sight. "Look," he said. "I don't know what changed, but I need to know if we are ever going to be...to move forward. If not, maybe you could, you know, have the courtesy to say it straight out and tell me why Pied Piper being my father wasn't a deal breaker and then suddenly it is."

"It's not," Locke said. "I told you I needed some time, okay? There's no need for you to keep pushing. Not after what you did."

"What *I* did?"

"You used your powers on Ariel," Locke replied, his voice an angry hiss. "Did you think I wasn't going to find out? He's my best friend."

Vince's heart dropped to his stomach. "He told you that, but not why?"

"Does why matter?"

Vince's fear of losing Locke was turning into anger. "No, of course why doesn't matter. I'm the son of a villain, so I must be a villain. Using my powers for any reason not Locke-approved is evil. You know, I really cared about you, I thought we had—but I guess it was all just me being stupid. God, and I thought my father would have to use his powers on you to turn you against me. It didn't even take that." His eyes were burning again.

"Your father didn't have to turn me away," Locke replied, looking away from him. "Your actions were enough to show me the kind of person you are."

"My actions were enough? Do you even hear yourself?" Vince replied. He didn't care he had raised his voice, and that the other guys could probably hear them in their cabins. "Once again, you have no fucking idea what you're talking about."

"This is why I wanted you to give me space," Locke said, holding his hand in front of his face. "I was thinking maybe things would be okay, maybe I'd get over how everyone is acting at camp because maybe you aren't like your dad after all. That's what I wanted to believe, anyway. Then I find out about the Ariel thing, and fuck, like, what do I even know about you?"

"I told you everything!" Vince snapped back. "You think I'm like my dad?"

"Actions speak louder than words," Locke replied. "I was trying to find a way around this, but I just—I don't know if I can."

Vince swallowed. "So what am I supposed to do? Keep waiting until you find the balls to end it permanently? This isn't fair," he said. His voice was steady, though he felt like he was about to implode. "I'm not like him. If anyone's being a dick here, it's you."

"Oh, I'm being a dick," Locke replied. "Yeah, I'm totally being a dick, using my powers on your friends. I'm sorry I'm being such a dick."

Vince closed his eyes and took a steadying breath. "Fuck you, Locke."

He waited for Locke to say something, to apologize, but nothing happened. He could hear the rest of the guys talking, starting to make their way to the showers.

Vince swallowed, his heart beating hard in his chest. "Look," he said, his voice breaking as he spoke. "If you really think I'm like him, then maybe we should call it quits."

Locke sighed deeply, but his arms were still crossed over his chest and his face was now turned away from Vince. "If that's what you want."

Vince laughed, no humor in his voice. He was already choking back tears. "What does it matter what I want? If you've made up your mind, I've no choice."

For a second, Locke looked like he was going to say something, like he was going to apologize or try to argue with him. Instead, he turned around and quietly spoke. "C'mon," he said. "We need to get to the kitchen."

VINCE DIDN'T THINK anyone would notice he wasn't getting into the helicopter Saturday morning. When everyone left Cabin One that morning, Vince went last, without his travel bag, and went inside the admin building. It wasn't uncommon for someone to do that, take a leak before the flight or whatever. He stood inside the reinforced glass doors and watched everyone board.

It wasn't, as far as he knew, mandatory to go have fun in the city. Still, he came outside as the helicopter rose into the air, lifting a hand to shield his eyes from the wind of the rotor.

He could see Locke—hard to miss that golden blond hair—by the window, hands gesturing, probably talking to Ariel. He didn't expect Locke to turn and look out. Their eyes met and held. Locke seemed... what? Surprised? He shouldn't be surprised Vince would prefer to be alone among the crowd.

The moment passed, and Vince slumped. Staying at camp probably made him more suspicious in Locke's mind. Well, to hell with him.

"There's no other way to Guilford," came a voice behind him.

Vince turned and mustered a wan smile for Mister Mister. "Nothing for me in Guilford that I can't find here. Except for the dining room."

Mister Mister shrugged. "Kitchen's yours for the weekend. Just keep it clean and inventory what you use for Cabin Three next week. It might be a long weekend, but everyone's coming back tomorrow night, same as usual."

Vince nodded. "Are we training on Monday, then?"

"Haven't decided. Everyone probably expects that, so maybe not." Mister Mister smiled. "Can't be too predictable." He half turned away, as if to disappear to wherever he was quartered, when he stopped and looked over his shoulder at Vince. "You wanna talk about your father, or anything else, knock at the office door. If I don't answer, text the admin line."

Vince nodded, dropping his gaze to his feet. He'd forgotten about replacing his phone. It wasn't like he used it much since coming to camp anyway. He could reach his mom by the camp phone—and he should, so she didn't panic if she tried his cell and couldn't reach him. Otherwise he was in no hurry. He set off for the obstacle course at a jog.

He had some thirty hours to figure out how to move on with Locke sleeping right over his head. He couldn't keep waiting to use the showers when everyone else was done. If Locke would at least treat him like he treated Cass and BJ and the others, but no, he acted like it was hard for him to be barely polite.

He climbed the tire wall. It was surprisingly easy, when he didn't have to do it in thirty seconds with ten other guys fighting for space. He wasn't going to drop out. He wanted to be a hero, at least in the sense of fighting for law and order. It wasn't just because he felt he needed to make up for what his father had done, and was no doubt plotting to do again. His father's choices made him ill, as ill as heights.

Besides, it paid well enough he might be able to get his mother to a place where his father wouldn't be able to ruin her relationships and job prospects. His mother. His heart broke a little more. Maybe when he was asking Mister Mister to use the phone, he could ask for a cabin reassignment.

Chapter Seventeen

VINCE WAS AT the lake Sunday evening when the whup-whup of the helicopter returning beat the air. He didn't bother to move from his spot on the dock. He was in his shabby old jeans that Ariel had been so disdainful of.

He was still in Cabin One—Mister Mister had refused to consider a switch even after Vince humiliated himself by confessing the reason he wanted it. At least his mother knew how to reach him.

He had a pile of pebbles beside him and, every now and then, he threw one in to watch the ripples in the water. He had some vague philosophical thoughts about the ripples being the reaction to actions, and how they spread, but relating it directly to his life seemed almost silly—after all he didn't pick his sperm donor, so was it really an action? Yet it seemed to have some weird ripple effect.

He didn't look up when he felt the dock move as someone walked along it. He hoped it was Locke. If he didn't look, maybe it would be Locke.

"Do I need to break your legs or what?" Ariel asked dropping gracefully to sit beside him.

"Might be a blessing," Vince replied. "I mean, I'm sorry I didn't tell him like I promised you I would, but when I tried to talk to him, he said he couldn't trust me." He gave Ariel a sidelong look. "Thanks for telling him I used my power on you, by the way. That helped."

"I don't get it," Ariel said. "I mean, I thought he really liked you. Strong feelings, you know. Reciprocal."

Vince threw a pebble into the lake.

"Would you fight for him? If you thought you still had a chance, I mean?"

"I guess," Vince said again. "It's not that I don't want to. Only I don't know how. I've never... My last boyfriend cheated on me, and I'm not sure it was all his idea. And he was kind of my second relationship, y'know, ever. My second fucked up relationship. So I'm not exactly sure how this relationship stuff is supposed to work."

"Not his idea?" Ariel sounded confused.

"That's another thing," Vince said. "My father is such a controlling dick, if he decided he didn't like Locke, he could make Locke break up with me anyway. What's even scarier is that he said he *likes* Locke. Maybe it's best we don't, we aren't—" he choked off his words and swallowed hard. "I don't want to hurt him, Ariel. And maybe this is the best way to do that."

"Shouldn't Locke have a say in that?"

Vince snorted. "I think Locke's made it clear what he has to say about it."

"Maybe," Ariel said, rising to his feet with the ease of a dancer.

Vince thought maybe he'd be alone a while longer, after Ariel left, but no, the dock started vibrating under his ass again and the thumps of two sets of feet set the water around the dock rippling outward.

A body dropped on either side of him and Vince did a double take as he realized who they were. Royce, that wasn't such a shock, since his uncle was a villain. He hadn't exactly been chummy the past week, but even he'd been friendlier than Locke. But Ace on his other side surprised him. "Hey."

"So," Ace began. "We noticed you didn't come to town."

"Yeah, dumb move," Vince said, like it was nothing. "I busted my phone. Should've gone to the city to buy a new one." He still had money for that. The IAEA gave each of the trainees a token paycheck for incidentals and Vince had used some of his own savings for his clothing splurges with Ariel and Locke, not that he wanted to think about that.

"Anyway, we noticed you've been getting the cold shoulder from, um, some of the guys and we thought of a way you could maybe get them over it."

"It was mostly Ace's idea," Royce said, "But even though my uncle isn't anywhere in the same league as your dad, and hardly anyone knows about him anyway—"

"Royce keeps to himself," Ace said.

Royce kicked one foot over the side of the dock. "Yeah, well. I might not have a bestie here," he said, his voice holding an edge that suggested he'd had this discussion before, "but no one avoids me. The point is not about me, though, okay? We were thinking if you like did something cool for the camp, you could get more people to see what a great guy you are."

Vince turned to look at him. "Like what?"

"The camp has a budget for like four social events per training year," Ace answered, and Vince whipped his head around to his other side. "So we thought, what if you stood up and organized something? Like a Halloween party."

"Seriously? Isn't that kind of fifth grade?"

"C'mon, it'd be fun. We could have a costume contest. Give the guys a chance to test out some ideas for graduation, y'know?" Royce said. "Like I'd be in for that."

Vince looked him up and down. Royce always seemed to be wearing the same thing, a dark short-sleeved shirt and well-fitting blue jeans. He didn't strike Vince as someone who was particularly fashion conscious or interested in dressing up. If *he* was interested, maybe they were on to something. He didn't think it would help with Locke in particular, but maybe he could get some of the other guys to come around. It wasn't the greatest plan, but it was better than his own.

Waiting it out might have seemed like an okay idea when he didn't have to sleep in a bunk directly under his ex-boyfriend every night, while everyone else seemed to go out of their way to avoid him. He had been having a hard time keeping track of what was happening with everything else around him when Locke had been there. The weekend had provided him with some much-needed time to get away from Locke, but he would see him again soon, and he was sure all the progress he had made—if he had actually made any progress—would go down the toilet.

Vince was ready to put his head down and spend the upcoming semesters with few friends, because that was what he was used to. But maybe what Royce and Ace were telling him was that he didn't have to. If he had friends, he could at least take his mind off Locke.

"If this Halloween party is where everyone is getting ideas to what they're wearing to graduation, graduation's going to be kinky as hell. Not that I'm complaining," Ace said, interrupting his thoughts and flashing a smile at both of them. He fanned himself with his hand. "It's so hot right now. The images in my mind aren't helping."

Royce laughed lightly, shaking his head. "You're all a bunch of pervs," he said. "I was thinking something classy, like movie glam or something. Imagine that, looking all dapper in a tuxedo."

Ace's smile turned into a grin. "I'm imagining it. But I don't know. That seems a bit overdone. Vince, what do you think?"

Vince closed his eyes. "Yeah, okay," he replied.

Ace clapped him on the shoulder. "Nice. Guess you'll have to think of a theme."

"I'll think of something," Vince said, smiling weakly at him. He wasn't looking forward to adding to his workload, but it wasn't as though he had anything else to do. *At this point,* Vince thought, trying hard not to glance back at his cabin, *it's not like I have anything to lose.*

Ace got to his feet, not nearly as gracefully as Ariel, and pulled his T-shirt off. "I'm going for a swim. It'll be nice to cool off before dinner." He hooked his scuffed sneakers off with his toes. "You guys coming?"

Royce looked up, alarm on his face as Ace undid his jeans. "Uh, you're going in naked?" The last word was squeaked out as Ace pulled down both his jeans and his briefs.

Vince tried to not stare, but Ace's crotch was at his fucking eye level. Shit. He glanced away as Ace said, "Christ, you guys see me naked every day in the showers, what's the big deal?" He dove into the water, without so much as a splash.

"Sometimes this place is more like a fucking sex camp," Royce muttered.

Vince chuckled. "He's just swimming."

"Yeah, well, it's a lot of temptation for a sweet little innocent virgin like me," Royce said with a rueful shake of his head.

"You're not really a virgin?"

"You guys should come in," Ace called, shaking water out of his face. "It's fucking great!"

Vince had gone swimming plenty over the weekend, still not liking the way the lake weeds would sometimes brush against his legs, but it was a great way to cool down when he didn't have the luxury of staying in an air-conditioned hotel with the others. There were no weeds in this part of the lake, he knew.

Besides, it wasn't like Ace was inviting them to fuck around in the water. "What the hell," he said, getting stiffly to his own feet. "It's just a swim."

"You guys are too hot," Royce muttered.

"That's why we're getting in the lake," Vince said, pulling off his own clothes and leaving them in a pile beside Ace's.

His dive wasn't as clean, but damn, the cool lake water felt good. And a swim would keep him from having to face Locke just a little longer.

On the dock, Royce got to his feet and waved. "See you guys at supper."

As he walked away, Vince realized Royce had never answered his question. He didn't think it was possible a guy like that could be, but then again, who was he to say? He'd been sixteen before he'd even kissed someone.

Ace grinned at him and hit the surface of the water with the flat of his palm, splashing Vince in the face.

Vince yelled and retaliated.

It had been a long time since he'd *played*.

SEPTEMBER WAS OFF to a lousy start. First, Vince staying at camp alone had made Locke's heart ache a little. He'd looked so small and alone as the helicopter rose. And Locke had been so set on sitting next to anyone but Vince, he hadn't noticed until they took off.

"So-ooo," Ariel had said as they wandered the streets of Guilford, just the two of them. "If you're done with Vince, would you recommend him? I can recommend Ace, though he needs a," Ariel paused and smirked, "firm hand."

"What? No!" The idea of Vince and *Ariel*!

"C'mon, it wouldn't be the first time we swapped fuck buddies."

"Vince isn't a—I mean, he wasn't—Just no." The idea of Vince and *anyone* was bugging him, but he'd given up any claim or right he had to make on who Vince spent time with.

Ariel had chuckled knowingly, but hadn't said anything more all weekend. He dragged Locke to the amusement park and they went on every ride, like little kids, and all Locke could think about was how much more he'd enjoyed it with Vince.

THEY DIDN'T HAVE kitchen duty so Cabin One wasn't forced to spend as much time together, and that was helping, but now Vince was being ostracized a little less by the other guys, and that was making Locke question his decision.

Vince wasn't the same guy he met, all withdrawn and quiet. The day before, they'd been given a free day at the camp, which was kind of weird and left Locke feeling a bit at loose ends, though Vince managed to find things to do away from Locke.

Today training had resumed and it gave Locke a feeling of relief, because training kept them busy. It was mentally and physically exhausting. It didn't leave him much time to miss the easy intimacy he'd shared for such a short time with Vince.

It also didn't stop flares of jealousy when he saw other guys talking with Vince, when he could see from their body language that they were aware of Vince as a hot, fuckable guy. Whom Locke had cut loose.

Vince and Ace had been teamed up for this exercise, while Locke was with Mickey. Everyone knew—everyone but Mickey—he had barely enough of a power-gift to qualify being at camp and being buddied with him was a sure way to do badly on an exercise. Whoever was with Mickey had to basically do it all on their own, unless there was nonpower related things to do. Even then, Mickey had his limitations.

Locke stared at Vince and Ace, thinking about Ariel's recommendation of Ace. Seeing Ace smiling at Vince. Vince smiling back. Vince hadn't smiled since Mickey had blurted out for the whole camp to hear that his father was Pied Piper.

Mickey must have seen the direction of his gaze. "We should at least beat them. They'll probably be too busy fucking each other's brains out to complete their mission properly."

Locke whipped his head around to stare at Mickey. "What?"

"God, you must be the only one in camp who doesn't know they hooked up Sunday night. They went swimming," Mickey added with air quotes. "Then they disappeared for a couple of hours yesterday."

So. Any imagined sadness on Vince's part was just that, Locke's imagination. Why didn't that make him feel better about his decision to break things off with Vince?

"THIS IS RIDICULOUS," Ariel said, poking Locke hard in the arm. "It's been three weeks and you still follow him with your eyes. Why don't you just talk to the guy?"

"Why do you even care?" Locke asked, hating the flush in his cheeks.

"I dunno. You two seemed to have something. You know, more than usual."

"Yeah," Locke said bitterly. "That's why he's off fucking Ace, Royce, who knows who else."

Ariel opened his eyes wide and stared at Locke. "He's *what* now? Who told you this?"

"Everyone knows."

"Dude, are we living in alternate universes? Because in mine, 'everyone knows' Royce don't fuck around. In my universe, Ace is a filthy braggart who can't keep his mouth shut about who he's fucked and been fucked by." Ariel didn't sound like he thought that was a problem.

Locke gave him a curious look.

Ariel's answering grin was smug. "He's talked me up quite nicely. It's been very useful." His grin vanished. "But he hasn't said anything about Vince."

"Maybe because he knows you're my best friend."

"Whatever, dude. River in Egypt."

THE WEEKS OF September passed easier than Vince would have thought. He found it hardest when Mister Mister would team them together, because at those times Locke treated him like a person, even smiled at him once or twice as if he couldn't help it. Following those exercises, Locke became twice as cold and distant, as if he regretted treating Vince like a friend for just a few hours.

Even Cass had stopped teasing them, but Vince had seen Cass and BJ exchange weird looks now and then. He wasn't sure if they were still hooking up, or what. If they were, it wasn't in the cabin.

He spent a lot of his free time with Ace and Jamie, whom Royce had talked into joining the party planning committee. They were letting him have complete control over it, as much as Mister Mister granted, but were happy to let him bounce ideas off them and delegate jobs to them. He knew he'd have to announce a theme soon, so they could start thinking about costumes.

On the last weekend of the month, he replaced his phone and let his mother know his new number. He called her the moment he activated his new phone. "We hardly have time to use them at camp, so I didn't feel compelled to replace it right away." He thought about telling her about Locke and decided there was nothing to tell. "Are you okay?"

"Yes," she replied, but her voice was strained. "Vince, listen. I've found a place. One I think your father won't be able to find. But you know what he's like, so I won't be calling you for a while. I'm safe; I want you to know that."

Vince felt a strange mix of relief and disappointment. "Are you sure it's safe?" He wanted it to be. But at the same time, she'd been his only support. Still, if she was safe, at least as long as it took for him to become an income-earning hero, that was one less worry.

"Yes. I won't say anything more about it. You know your father. And Vince—he knows where you are. Be careful."

"I don't think he knows where I am location-wise."

"It's just a matter of time."

"Ma, there's at least a dozen power-gifted people here. He's one guy."

"And all he has to do is get you all in one room and sing a little song. Remember that."

Vince shivered and it had nothing to do with the cool September evening. Maybe he should talk to Mister Mister again. "Love you, Mom."

"Love you, too, *meu bem*."

Vince walked back into the suite at the hotel, sighing and looking down at the floor. He knew there was very little chance he was going to run into Locke, since he spent most of his time hanging out with Ariel out of the hotel and in the city. Vince couldn't blame him, though it still felt like Locke was trying his best to avoid him. It hurt, but not as much as before. Now that he knew his mom would be safe for a while, he could focus on moving on with his life. It was going to be hard to do, but he had to.

He was glad Royce and Ace had come up to him and asked him to plan the Halloween party. He hadn't thought of a good idea yet, but he was sure he would, and he was glad he could focus on that instead of on his parents. Or Locke.

"Hey," Ace said from behind him, startling him. "You're here. We've been trying to find you."

Vince looked at him, cocking his head. "You've been looking for me? Why?"

"Because the party planning committee is going out," Ace said. "And also, you're our friend. Weirdo. Oh, did you get a new phone? Oh my god, finally. Here, give me your number."

Vince smiled as he took Ace's cell phone and punched his new number in.

Ace cocked his head when he got his phone back. "Yo, Vince, are you okay?"

"Yeah, fine," Vince replied. He wondered if he should tell Ace about his mom and then decided not to. He didn't want to ruin anything by reminding his friends of his parents, and by extension, his father. His friends didn't seem to care, but Locke had said he didn't care, either, and that hadn't been true. "So, what do you guys have in mind?"

"I'm voting for a club, Jamie doesn't care, Royce wants to go to a bar. You're the deciding vote," Ace replied, flashing him a smile. "Wear something nice, anyway. You know, just in case."

Thanks to that shopping trip back in August, Vince had nice clothes, and Guilford was the only place worth wearing them anyway, so most of them were in his travel bag. He smiled a little as he dressed—skinny black jeans and a long-sleeved button-down shirt that was ostensibly black, but printed with bright, confetti-like shapes in a rainbow of colors. When he came out, Ace whistled and said, "Club, huh?"

"Nah, too early for a club. Let's start in the hotel bar and figure it out from there. I'd even go for a promenade pub crawl," Vince said, referring to the street fronting the hotel and running several blocks along the river.

Ace pouted. He was wearing skinny jeans, too, a black vest with silver buttons and a white shirt under it. For the first time since they had met, Vince noticed his lobes were stretched and he was wearing black plugs. It was subtle, and since his hair was long and he tended to wear his dreads down, Vince wasn't surprised he had missed them until now.

"I thought you were eighteen," Vince said as they walked together toward the elevator.

"You're not wrong," Ace replied, typing something on his phone. "Sorry, not trying to be rude, just texting the guys to meet us at Brickhouse. I don't know where they are right now, so. I mean, they could be in the lobby, but who knows?"

"That's my point, aren't you a little young? Like, are they going to let you in?" Vince replied, ignoring the last part of what Ace had said. He wasn't looking forward to spending time in long lines only to be turned away.

Ace rolled his eyes, laughing and sticking his phone in his back pocket. His jeans were so tight Vince marveled that his phone fit into them at all. "It's not like a bouncer can catch me if I try to sneak in."

Vince looked him up and down. It was minimal, but the idea that Ace was using his powers to do something for his own benefit didn't sit right with him.

He was about to say something when Ace started to laugh. "Oh my god, relax," Ace said. "You should have seen your face. I'm fucking with you. I have a fake ID, like any normal teenager. Seriously, I'm not going to get you in trouble."

He wondered if Locke had his own fake ID. Since he was only two years older than Ace, Vince assumed he would need one if he wanted to go out. Ugh, he needed to stop thinking about Locke. He looked up at Ace and flashed him a tenuous smile.

"Are you okay?"

Vince's smile widened as he shook his head. "I wasn't really worried about me, to be honest," he said. "Well, only enough to wonder if I should have brought a jacket. It's getting a little cold now."

Ace rolled his eyes. He was about to say something when his phone pinged in his pocket. "Jamie says Royce is already drunk," he said. "This should be fun."

Vince hadn't been looking forward to going out, but Ace's good mood was contagious.

Vince grinned and patted his pockets again. Shit, he'd forgotten mints. If he was going to be drinking he needed to baby his voice. His other option was to make every second drink a bottle of water, which had the added benefit of keeping him sober. He wasn't sure he wanted to stay sober—getting drunk sounded like a good idea.

"I gotta stop at the hotel gift shop for mints," he said.

"Oh?" Ace gave him an arch look. "Should I buy some, too?" He laughed at Vince's confused look. "So the mints aren't in case kissing happens?"

Heat flooded Vince's face. He hadn't thought of hooking up, it seemed wrong still, but moving on would eventually involve someone else, if only for a good time. "Kissing might happen," he said with a small smile.

Ace whooped and said, "I'll keep my fingers crossed."

Vince blinked, surprised by Ace's enthusiasm, but remembered that flirting among the guys of Camp Hologram was like breathing. "So," he said, clearing his throat and looking away from Ace. "What's the plan?"

"We'll go to the bar here, get a drink, and meet them there in a bit," Ace said. "I think we're too sober to hang out with them right now. We have to fix that. Unless you had any other ideas?"

Vince smiled, digging his wallet out of his jeans. He was pretty sure he still had some change. "No," he replied. "That sounds good."

Chapter Eighteen

VINCE AND ACE sat in the windows of the hotel bar, which had the tongue-in-cheek name The Office. Vince didn't imagine anyone called home to say "I'm at The Office," but he supposed it was cute to people of a certain age. That didn't mean the bar was full of older people, though. It was a decent age mix, as one might expect to find in a hotel like the Roehampton.

Vince's shoes didn't have a heel to hook on the rail of the bar stool, but he rested his feet there anyway as a waitress brought them a pitcher of amber beer and two large glasses. Draft was cheap, and neither of them could afford bar prices for decent booze, or at least Vince couldn't, and Ace seemed content to split a pitcher with him.

"So, can I ask you something personal?" Ace said after taking a sip of his beer.

Vince nodded, though he wondered if this was going to be a question about his dad.

"Do you like Jamie?"

"Um, sure," Vince replied. "He's nice."

"No," Ace said, shaking his head. "I didn't mean it like that. I just thought you had a type, that's why I was asking."

Vince smiled at him. He liked Jamie well enough, but he had never seen him as more than a friend. Vince hadn't been able to stop thinking about Locke, so talking about this felt weird. Talking about anyone *but* Locke felt weird. "My type is cute."

"Oh, good," Ace replied, winking at him. "I thought your type was blond and I wanted to tell you Jamie doesn't fuck around."

"Okay," Vince replied, cocking his head. He wasn't sure why Ace was telling him that, because Vince was sure he had never expressed any romantic interest in Jamie. He hadn't expressed any interest in anyone that wasn't Locke.

"Oh, all right," Ace said, rolling his eyes. "If you want to know the truth, I was worried I didn't have a chance."

Vince could feel himself blushing again. Ace had always been nice to him. He was smart, and good looking with a lean physique. That was Vince's type. He wasn't into huge muscles like Bray or BJ had. Vince wanted to flirt back, but it still felt wrong. Locke had made his decision, though, and he had been clear about what he wanted.

"I—uh, you have a chance," Vince quietly replied, taking a sip of his drink.

"Good," Ace said, grinning. "I have a lot more questions, but I think we're both still too sober for those."

Vince laughed, grabbing the pitcher. "Easy fix."

"Right," Ace said, nodding. "Easy fix."

By the end of the pitcher, Vince was feeling relaxed, and the sore spot on his ego from Locke's rejection was being soothed by Ace's unabashed interest. His heart didn't feel any better, but he didn't want to be a maudlin drunk—not that he was drunk yet, not by a long shot—so he concentrated instead on how good it felt to have Ace's admiring attention. Ace seemed to understand Vince wasn't just going to fall into his arms.

After they were done with their second pitcher, they decided to go meet their friends before they were unable to walk. Mostly before Ace was unable to walk, since he seemed to be putting beers away at a much faster rate than Vince.

Brickhouse was a small pub, but it was pretty, and being on the riverfront, it was more expensive than somewhere Vince would normally go. Luckily, Jamie and Royce were already sitting at a table in the back and had ordered a pitcher themselves. They were happy to share, at least that was what Vince managed to gather between laughter.

"Heyy," Royce said, clapping Vince on the shoulder. "I thought you guys were gonna be here earlier."

"Sorry, got caught up," Ace replied, his eyes glimmering. "Can't blame me."

Jamie laughed. "After we're done here, we should go to karaoke."

"Wait, you can sing?" Vince replied.

Jamie laughed again, throwing his head back this time. "Oh my god, no, absolutely not. But you do. You can. Whatever, you know what I mean."

"What? No," Vince said, casting his gaze toward his feet.

"You do, though," Ace said, taking a sip of his beer. "I've heard your incredible rendition of Happy Birthday."

"Shut up," he replied, smiling despite himself.

"Wait," Royce said, waving his hands in front of his face. "If you sing, will the whole bar fall under your spell?"

"No," Vince said, shaking his head. "It doesn't work like that. I mean, it could, but it has to be a specific pitch and—"

"Okay, I have to see this," Jamie said. "Please. This sounds like so much fun."

"I don't sing in public." Especially under the influence.

Royce smiled. "Oh, bullshit," he said. "It totally works like that. You're like, the most powerful of all of us, and you're so hiding it."

Vince stared at his drink. "Nope," he said. "I'm serious, it doesn't work like that."

"Whatever," Royce said. "I don't believe you."

Jamie rolled his eyes. "He's not doing it; he's shy," he said. "He might do it if you bribe him. Sorry, Vince, I try not to drink too much because it makes me say whatever's on my mind, which is usually whatever's on someone else's mind."

"It's, uh, okay," Vince replied, looking away from him. He wasn't used to everyone in a group paying attention to him, and he didn't know if he liked it. He tried not to sing in public, and he was pretty sure that adding singing to his drinking night was going to hurt his voice, but they were his friends, and he was trying to let loose.

"Oh, c'mon," Royce said.

Vince shook his head. "I don't know," he said. "This doesn't seem like a good idea."

"I'll buy your drinks," Ace said. "Please. I really need to see this."

"Yees," Royce added, grinning. "I'll help. Jamie should too, since it was his idea."

"Fuck that, I'm poor," Jamie said. "I can barely buy my own drinks. I shouldn't be drinking, anyway. Tomorrow is going to be awful. But I can read someone's mind if you want me to?"

"No, that's—that's fine," Vince replied. "I'll do it if you guys start talking about something else. Anything else."

"Fine," Royce said. "So are you going to tell us what happened with Locke or are we going to have to keep guessing?"

Vince felt his cheeks redden. Just when he had almost managed to stop thinking about Locke for the night, someone brought him up. He knew Royce didn't mean anything by it, and he was so drunk he kept almost losing his balance, though he was sitting down.

"Okay, you know what," Vince said, "let's go to karaoke. Let's do it. Right now."

Ace grinned. "You're singing? Right now?"

"Yes," Vince replied. "I'm singing. But you have to promise not to record it. Any of you."

"Cross my heart," Jamie said. "Can't wait to see this."

They found a bar offering karaoke around the corner where Riverfront Drive met Adelaide Street, which lead uphill into Guilford's entertainment district. The four of them mastered their giggles and pretended to be mature and sober, which allowed Ace's fake ID to pass with little scrutiny. They crowded around a single book listing hundreds of songs, and another pitcher of beer landed on the table. The karaoke team must normally deal with better than average clientele, as each song was labelled with the key it was to be sung in.

Most people wouldn't know what that meant, which was part of what made karaoke so awful, sometimes. But Vince found it helpful. He could pick a song he could sing without straining his power-voice.

The 80s section was the biggest—the 80s had given the world a lot of basic but catchy tunes that seemed almost made for karaoke. At least that's what Vince tried to convince himself, instead of admitting even to himself he just plain liked 80s music. His mom had grown up listening to it, and he'd grown up listening to her oldies. He ran his finger down the lists, as the lines of type seemed to waver. Man, he hadn't heard some of these artist names in years.

"Day by Day," he said out loud. That seemed perfect, like a metaphor for his life. He didn't know it, exactly, but he'd heard of the group, Doug and the Slugs. He was pretty sure they'd had one big hit, and "Day by Day" wasn't it. But whatever; if he sucked, the guys wouldn't ask him to sing more, right?

"That's weird shit, Vince," Ace said, but there was no mockery in his tone. "Gimme that thing."

They all picked songs after a little while—Vince insisted. No way he was going to do this alone—and took the book and their picks up to the lady running the gig. She wore a wig with a big puff on the top like from the sixties, or something and wild makeup that made her look ageless. Probably handy, gig like this.

They were on their second pitcher—for this bar, which Vince thought was named TJ's—when Royce's name was called. Good thing, too, as that man was seriously close to being too drunk to stand.

Vince grinned and cheered, though Royce was terrible and missed an entire verse because he was doing some sort of stripper-esque dance. It was hilarious.

Vince wasn't any better, because he'd never heard the song he'd chosen before, but the lyrics, which were about getting on with life, still seemed kind of hopeful to him.

The guys ruffled his hair and thumped him on the shoulders when he sat back down, and he decided to do another song, one he knew. Something sexy maybe, like—he stopped midchuckle as an idea occurred to him. "Wait here, guys, I already know my next song."

He stumbled just a little and leaned close to the karaoke lady to ask if she had the song.

She grinned and nodded, like she was in on the joke. Maybe she was— it couldn't be a secret that Guilford was a haven for the power-gifted.

"What song didja pick?" Ace asked.

Jamie opened his mouth, and Vince stopped him with a finger across his lips. Jamie had nice lips.

Jamie rolled his eyes and sat down. "Idiot."

"You'll see," Vince said, addressing Ace and Royce. Royce was nodding happily. Anything would have made him happy, Vince guessed.

He started sipping his beer, having lost count of how many pitchers they'd gone through, until his name was called. He took the stage and grinned at his table mates, maybe especially Ace.

Then he killed Bonnie Tyler's "Holding Out for a Hero."

"SO GOOD," ACE said, leaning against the mirror. "You're susha good singer."

The elevator was empty except for the four of them and they were all leaning against a wall or each other, whatever kept them propped up. Vince was far more drunk than he had expected to get, but it was easy to get fucked up when people kept buying him drinks and he didn't have to keep checking his bank account.

"Thank you, thank you," Vince replied, waving his hands in front of his face. "Wesha duet next time."

"Oh my god, yes, I'd pay to see that," Jamie said. "And I'm broke."

Royce was leaning on his shoulder, his eyes closed. He mumbled something, but Vince couldn't make out what it was.

Ace shook his head. "I can't sing. I'm—"

"I c'n teach you," Vince said. "See, singing's easy. Your voice 's an ins-insterment, right? So i's hard at first, then's easy. Jus' gotta practice. We can practice and then we can duet. We can do Grease. I can be Sandy. Or Danny...."

"Sandy! Oh, will you dress up in leather?" Ace replied, staring at Vince. "Because I would learn to juggle fire to see that."

"I c'n tea'shoe," Royce replied, his eyes fluttering open. "D'you have sticks at the suite?"

"Sticks? No," Ace said, shaking his head. "They're prolly called torches or something."

Jamie shook his head, too, scoffing. "I'm not letting you guys do this," he said. "This seems like a terrible idea. Right, Vince?"

Vince shrugged.

"I know you'd like to see this, but they might set fire to the hotel," Jamie said, though Vince hadn't said anything. Vince thought he could get used to not having to talk in order to communicate, his mouth was dry and his tongue felt heavy. Plus, he was tired.

"I don't see a problem," Ace said. "Place is full of rich snobs, anyway."

Vince laughed. "We sleep here, too."

"You c'n—I c'n per-protect us," Royce replied. "Okay, maybe we could jus' do it on the balcony."

"Do it on the balcony." Vince snickered. "Nah, gotta side with Jamie on this one," he said. "We should proba'ly not do anything involving fire when we're this drunk."

Ace slid down the wall and fell on his ass, giggling. "What about leather? C'n we do something with leather? I want us to go back to this leather thing."

"Not till you learn Danny's parts," Vince said. "And trus' me, I'm not go'n up there till you learn your parts... es. That song is so-oooo high."

Ace laughed. "I din't realize we'd picked out a song already," he said. "This kind of sounds like a date."

"Oh, I—um, maybe," Vince replied, looking at his feet. What Ace was saying made sense, and Vince had pretty much walked into it. Ace had been flirting with him all night, and Vince had no reason to turn him down. Ace was sweet; he was funny—he wasn't Locke, but Vince couldn't have Locke. And the last thing he should be doing was comparing every guy that hit on him to Locke.

Ace was the perfect way to start getting over Locke. He was the complete opposite from him. Locke was cute, pale, blond, with incredible green eyes. Ace had bronze skin, huge dark eyes that looked almost black, and beautiful high cheekbones. His smile was incredible, too. Vince could do a lot worse.

He shook his head and told himself to stop comparing Ace to his ex-boyfriend. That wasn't fair to Ace, and it certainly wasn't fair to himself. He had tried, but Locke had made it clear his feelings weren't reciprocal. Ace knew his history, he knew about his dad, and he knew he wasn't over Locke.

With all of that, Ace was still flirting with him. Ace was his friend, which complicated things, but even if things didn't work out, he was sure they would end more amicably than they had with Locke, who treated him like a stranger on the best of days.

"He likes you," Jamie said, looking straight at Vince and pointing at Ace. "He thinks you're very cute. Also, he always stares at your butt when you walk away."

"Hey!" Ace said, frowning. "You din't have to tell him that."

"Yeah, I'm sure he hasn't already figured that out," Jamie replied, rolling his eyes and laughing. "Hey, have any of you pressed the button? I feel like we've been in this elevator for ages."

"Oh, shit," Vince said, looking at the buttons and trying to ignore how red his cheeks were. None of the buttons were lit up. The lights on the elevator were on, so someone had to have called it, Vince thought.

He pressed the button with the number eleven on it and leaned against the wall, pressing all the buttons down with his back. The elevator made a noise and all the guys started giggling. "Well, I've pressed the button now."

"We'll make it I swear," Royce sang off-key before dissolving into a sloppy laugh.

"We could sleep here," Vince replied. "This elevator is more comfortable than the bunks back at camp, I bet."

"Okay, well, I don't do group sex," Jamie said. "I think that's a Cabin One exclusive."

Vince laughed, holding his belly as the elevator pinged and the door opened. "That, no. That never happened. You mus' all think I'm such a slut."

Ace pouted, crossing his arms over his chest. "Nah, man. I wish."

Chapter Nineteen

LOCKE WOKE UP to the sound of people coming in. He could usually sleep through anything, but it had been difficult lately. It was normal that the guys would come in later on a Saturday night. Ariel had asked Locke if he wanted to go out, but Locke had shrugged and they'd spent most of the night playing scrabble and bitching about boys. Well, Locke had spent most of the night bitching about boys—especially one—and Ariel had spent most of the night rolling his eyes. He was sure Ariel would have preferred going out, but he was obviously trying to be a good friend, which Locke appreciated. He didn't want to be by himself when he was still feeling this upset about everything that had happened.

The suite was divided into five small bedrooms, one with three beds, and a shared living room, dining room and kitchenette. It was, of course, beautifully decorated, much more spacious than the cabins back at Camp Hologram, but the walls were paper thin, and it felt a lot less private. At least he didn't have to sleep right above his ex-boyfriend every night.

Ariel was snoring next to him. Ariel had swapped his room assignment to be with Locke because he didn't want to leave Locke alone. Locke didn't remind him that whoever shared his room would automatically keep him from being alone. He knew Ariel was doing it because he was acting so pathetic.

Ariel knew him too well, made it so easy to be miserable around him whenever the mood struck, which was far more often than he liked to admit lately. Ariel was a good friend, but Locke could tell his patience was starting to wear thin, so he would have to get a grip soon.

Someone giggled right outside his door. Locke got up, crossed the floor, and cracked the door open. He was about to step outside when he saw Vince with the rest of the guys. Swallowing, he took a step backward. He knew he should close the door, but watching was so tempting.

"So, like," Vince slurred, looking at Ace. He was leaning on Jamie, his head on his shoulder, but Locke noticed Ace's arm was also around his waist. Locke's heart started to beat fast in his chest. Had anything happened? It wasn't like he could go out and ask. He had been the one to break up with Vince. But Vince had seemed so devastated, Locke didn't think he would do anything like this.

He tried to swallow the knot in his throat while he kept watching.

Royce was on the sofa, still wearing his shoes and already fast asleep. "How many tattoos ya got? C'n I see?"

"Jus' the one," Ace replied. "Is on my chest. You wanna see it?"

"Yup," Vince said, nodding. Ace took a step to the side and away from him, which made Vince wobble in place. Ace tried to take off his shirt, but he was struggling.

Jamie had started to laugh. "You see him in the showers," he said.

"Yeah, but like, I don't *stare*. I never looked at his tattoo," Vince replied, his voice a whine. Locke didn't think he had ever seen him this drunk before. He wanted to go out there and—what? Do what exactly? Hold him? Put him to bed? Stop all this? He took a deep breath, trying to stop himself from opening the door, though resisting got harder and harder. It wasn't his place to do any of those things.

He had made that very clear to Vince.

"Let's go to your room; I'll show you," Ace said, smiling. Jamie moved out of his way as Ace wrapped his arm around Vince's waist again and grinned at him. "You good?"

"Ya," Vince said, laughing as he tried to walk toward his bedroom, stumbling on his first step. "I'm good."

"Whoa, there," Ace said. "C'mon, we need to get you to bed."

They walked together, both swaying back and forth, until Vince opened the door to his bedroom with his shoulder. Locke kept watching, wondering if he should go out there. Jamie was taking Royce's shoes off, muttering under his breath. It suddenly occurred to him that he could make himself invisible and step outside, but Jamie might still be able to read his mind. He tried to keep his breathing under control. As soon as he was about to shut his door, Ace stepped out of Vince's bedroom, shirtless and unsteady on his feet.

Jamie walked over to him, grabbing him to hold him up. He was giggling when he spoke. "You doing okay?"

"Ya," Ace said, shaking his head. "He—uh, I got him on the bed, but by the time I took my shirt off, he had passed out. I shouldn't, I din't wanna wake him."

"Okay, but where's your shirt?" Jamie said.

"Floor somewhere," Ace replied, sighing and sitting down on the edge of the sofa, trying his best not to squash Royce. "It's never gonna happen, Jamie. He's—so, uh, so cute, an' he proba'ly thinks I'm just a kid."

"Hey, relax," Jamie said, putting his hand on Ace's shoulder. "I think you may have drank a little too much."

"A bit," Ace said, slumping forward as he put his elbows on his knees.

"Seriously, don't worry too much," Jamie said. "He was thinking about it."

Ace looked up at Jamie, his eyes shining. "Seriously?"

"Yeah," Jamie said, smiling back at him. "But don't tell him I told you. I'm sure you can talk about it on your date, right?"

"Right, good point," Ace replied, putting his head on his lap. "G'night."

"Nope," Jamie said, laughing and shaking his head. "Come on, let's get you to bed."

LOCKE HADN'T SLEPT very well, and the sun wasn't making him feel any better. It was almost October and it was unseasonably warm, which made him feel sleepier. Vince looked terrible. Fuckably hot, but terrible. He wore dark sunglasses and a tight black T-shirt over jeans Ariel had scoffed dismissively about. He had barely spoken to Locke, though he wasn't sure if it was because of how hungover he was or because Locke had given him every reason to think that's what he wanted.

"Rough night?"

Vince grunted, stabbing an empty coffee cup with the garbage stick they'd been supplied with.

"Don't feel like talking, huh."

"The fuck do you want, Locke?"

Ouch. Good question, though. He couldn't say, *I don't want you to date other guys* because he didn't have a right to. "Just making—" He stopped himself. He didn't want to just make conversation, either. "Look, Vince, I—" Jesus, why was this so hard? "So you and Ace, huh? Wasn't just fucking around?"

Vince groaned. "I have no fucking clue what you're talking about. I am so not in the mood to play games, especially with you." He stabbed at more garbage, as if he'd rather be stabbing Locke.

"You and Ace aren't dating?" Locke tried to sound like he didn't care.

"No. At least not yet."

"So it's just sex?"

"Not that it's any of your business, but no, I haven't had sex with Ace, okay? For fuck's sake, pick up some garbage, would you?"

Locke looked away, hiding his relief. "I'm sorry," he blurted before he really knew he was going to say it. He knew, no matter how he decided *he* might feel about it, his father would have a very strong opinion on him dating Vince. Maybe his father was right, but Locke was starting to become more certain he wasn't. Vince wasn't his father, he was a good person, and Locke had hurt him for no reason. He felt like shit about it.

That was if Vince was even interested anymore. And using his powers on Ariel, well, Ariel hadn't seemed bothered by it, though he had never said *why* Vince had used his powers.

"Whatever," Vince said, turning away.

Locke threw down his stabby stick and marched after Vince, grabbing his arm. "I said I was sorry!"

Vince angled his head to stare at Locke's hand, until he let go. "I don't even know what you think you're sorry for. It's been a month, Locke. Over a month since you said we weren't done, you just needed some time, and a month since you told me you couldn't get past my father being a villain," Vince said bitterly. "Like my father is my fault, like I had a choice. Like you didn't have a choice, like you didn't fucking know. So what the fuck is it you're sorry for?"

Locke looked down at his feet. He tried to think of a good answer. At that point, anything that would have made Vince stay and listen to him would have been good enough. The problem was he didn't know if talking to Vince would help matters, and he was less than impressed with his apology. He swallowed before he spoke. "Look, can we just—can we talk, please?"

Vince looked him up and down, his lips a straight line. Locke didn't need to see his eyes to know he was furious. "Fine," he replied after a torturous second. "Talk."

"I don't mean right now. I want us to sit down and have a cup of coffee or something," Locke said in a small voice.

Vince laughed, no humour in his voice. "Yeah, so I'm still trying to figure out what the words 'a while' mean when you say them. I'm not waiting for you anymore, Locke, I'm done. No, if you want to talk, it's happening right now," he said. "And it's only because I'm being nice. I should walk away from you. I have no reason to listen."

Locke sighed, pinching the bridge of his nose. "I know that," he said quietly. "It's just, I don't know, I miss you a lot."

Locke watched as Vince's jaw dropped open, then he scoffed. "Wow," he said, turning away from Locke. "Seriously?"

"No, wait," Locke replied, getting in front of him. "I'm serious. I didn't mean to hurt your feelings, I just...."

"You just what, Locke? You just what?" Vince wasn't quite yelling, but his voice had gotten louder and people were starting to look at them.

Locke opened his mouth to answer, but he couldn't think of anything, so Vince shook his head.

"That's what I thought. You don't miss me. You're annoyed I've finally started to move on. See, it's all great when I'm pining after you or trying to avoid you, isn't it? It's great when everyone else is giving me the cold shoulder and everyone's flocking to you and asking you if you're okay, as if I'm some sort of fucking psychopath. But when I start to have friends, when someone starts to show interest in me, when I'm ready to move on, that's not allowed. That's not okay. I'm only allowed to be with you, but if I'm not with you, I'm not allowed to be happy. Did I get that right? Is that what you're trying to tell me?"

"What? No!" Locke said, trying to ignore the sudden heat in his cheeks. The rate at which Vince was rattling off accusations was making it hard to keep track of them, and he didn't think he would have been very good at defending himself, either. Vince was furious, way angrier than Locke had ever seen him before, and Locke couldn't blame him. He just wanted them to sit down and have a cup of coffee together, but he had forfeited that right when he had made a decision about Vince.

"No," Vince repeated flatly. It wasn't a question, and he seemed to have gone from angry to uninterested in a split second.

"No, that's not it," Locke replied, his voice breaking. "I just miss you, okay? I was wrong."

"You were wrong," Vince said, shaking his head. "Okay, cool. I'm glad you know that now. I'm going to get back to work."

He turned and started to walk away, but Locke got in front of him again. Vince crossed his arms over his chest. Locke watched his throat work as he swallowed. He wanted to grab him, kiss him, show him how sorry he was through the way he touched him.

But he couldn't do that. He didn't have the right to do that anymore.

Locke sighed, pinching the bridge of his nose. "I want things to go back to the way they were," he mumbled.

"The way they were before everyone found out about my father, right? When only you knew, so you could pretend you didn't have to deal with it. The way things were when you thought I was just some other guy at camp. When I was just someone who made *you* feel good."

"That's not fair," Locke said. "That's not what I meant."

"You know what's funny about all this, though? You told me you thought I was like my father and—"

"I didn't mean that," Locke said, raising his voice over Vince's. "I swear. I just, I don't know. I was a bit freaked out because, and you'd used, you know, on Ariel, and I was still trying to wrap my head around the whole thing. If you hadn't done that, I don't think I would've, well, I don't think this would have ever happened."

Vince laughed again, this time shaking his head. "I'm done with this conversation."

"Wait," Locke replied when Vince turned away and started to walk away from him. He grabbed his wrist and Vince turned his head to look at him. "Vince, I'm so sorry I hurt your feelings. I'm—"

"Stop," Vince replied, looking at his wrist. Locke knew he should let him go, but he couldn't. "You're making it worse. You know that what I do wears off after a couple of hours, right? So Ariel could have told you what happened, but he chose not to. Did you ever stop to think about that? No, you didn't. All you thought about was how it affected you, never what it might have been about. You never stopped to listen even though I was trying to tell you."

"Trying to tell me what?"

"It doesn't matter anymore," Vince said, shaking his head. Locke loosened his grip as Vince moved his arm to his side. "I'm leaving. You can finish up here, report me, I don't care. I can't be around you right now."

VINCE STALKED DOWN the promenade, anger and something else keeping his muscles as taut as high-tension wires. He kept going, past the amusement park until he reached the small beach, which was mostly rocks, and a sign warning about the river current. There were people lying out all the same—call it a beach, and a halfway decent day and people would be out working on their tans—but they ignored Vince. He sat on a hillock of grass just off the boardwalk and every muscle began to spasm and tremble.

How dare he? How dare Locke try to—which one of them was more like his father now, huh? How stupid to try such mundane manipulation on the son of Pied Piper. Vince had developed some resistance to his father's manipulations, surely Locke didn't imagine his unpowered attempts would work?

The worst of it, the absolutely worst, was part of Vince wanted to believe. He clenched his fists and beat into the ground until his knuckles bled.

Chapter Twenty

REPORTING VINCE HAD never crossed Locke's mind, not even as Vince was storming away from him. Vince had every right to be angry, but Locke had never seen him like that, and Vince had done his best to ignore him ever since they had gotten back to camp. It was easy now that Vince had other friends, guys who seemed to surround him almost every time Locke walked up to him. Locke wondered how much he had told them. Then he had tried to tell himself he didn't care what they thought about him.

Even if Locke had managed to find a way to talk to Vince, there was nothing he would have been able to say. Vince had made a decision already, and Locke couldn't blame him for wanting to move on.

Thinking about Vince being with someone else hurt. Ever since they had talked, the possibility had seemed more and more likely, and Locke was starting to feel worse.

It was a good thing training seemed to be getting harder, because at least he could concentrate on that instead of on the fact that Vince wouldn't even talk to him.

A few days had passed since they had gotten back from the city. They were all standing outside, near the lake, and Mister Mister was just about done briefing his team.

The instructions were clear. Their mission was to extract a team of hostages from the opposing team. It was from a burning building, but Vince had already shown he could take care of a fire, so the entire thing seemed simple enough. Locke might have time to try to talk to Vince once they were done with the exercise, since they had been placed on the same team, along with BJ, Mickey and Cass.

He wasn't sure what the opposing team was supposed to be doing, but it wasn't any of his business. All he wanted to do was finish as soon as he could.

"Okay," BJ said. "How are we going to do this?"

Vince looked around the group, his gaze darting away as soon as it found Locke. "Okay, well, we're not sure who the hostage is and who is holding the hostages. We also don't know how many people we're supposed to extract, only that they're upstairs."

"Right," Locke said. "The first thing we need is to figure out how many people we need to get out. Mister Mister said we only had to get the people who were on the second floor, right? So I could turn invisible and go in there. Whoever is on the first floor is whoever we're up against, so it would be a matter of a simple headcount. The problem's the fire."

"Sure, but if Jamie is down there, he'll be able to read your mind," Cass said. "So they'll know we're coming for them."

"They already know we're coming for them," Mickey replied, turning to look at Locke. "We shouldn't discuss the rest of our plan yet, at least not with you."

"Guys, I can turn invisible, but I can't walk through fire. That's the problem," Locke replied, rolling his eyes.

"That's okay, I can put out the fire downstairs," Vince said. "Then we can come up with something better. Royce is good, and he has to be the reason behind the fire, so I will only be able to hold him off for a bit. A headcount seems like a good start."

"Okay," Locke replied, his heart beating fast in his chest. "We can—"

"You guys can follow us," Vince said. "Just stay a few feet behind us. We don't know the range of Jamie's power."

"Right, good point," Locke said, his mouth dry.

As they walked up to the building, Locke wondered why he had never seen it before. It wasn't big, but it wasn't small, either, and there was no way he could have missed it in the morning. The camp was well equipped, so the idea that a building would have been built specifically for this exercise wasn't entirely ridiculous. The closer they got, the hotter it got, and there was black smoke coming out of the windows.

The fire was loud, too.

They had all seen Royce's power before, but never to this extent.

Locke stood next to Vince. He dropped his voice to a whisper before he spoke. The last thing he wanted to do was make it seem like he didn't believe in Vince, especially in front of the rest of their team. "You sure you're going to be able to deal with this?"

Vince nodded, his hands clenched at his sides. "Sure," he replied, not looking back at Locke, who thought he didn't seem sure at all.

Mister Mister was standing next to them, his arms crossed over his chest, watching the cabin with narrow eyes. The fire seemed to be getting bigger, and Locke wasn't sure if that was part of the exercise. Mister Mister had said they had to extract hostages from a burning building. There had been nothing in their briefing about having to break through a fire and smoke barrier around the building.

Mickey cleared his throat. "This is getting bigger, we should—"

Before he could finish, he was interrupted by Jamie's clear voice in Locke's head. *There's something wrong, help us! Please!*

Locke looked around, wondering if he was the only one who had heard Jamie's plea, but everyone was staring back at each other with the same panicked look in their eyes.

"Uh, sir," Mickey murmured. He had walked over to Mister Mister and was tugging at his sleeve, like a little kid. "Is this part of the exercise?"

Mister Mister looked at Mickey, opening his mouth but saying nothing. Locke didn't think he had ever seen him like this. He was normally either disinterested or angry, but he seemed scared, which terrified Locke. The interaction couldn't have lasted more than a few seconds when Locke turned to look at Vince, who was muttering a swear word under his breath. If he had known what Vince was going to do, he might have tried to talk him out of it, but there was no time for that. Vince started running toward the fire, and Mister Mister took off after him, running just as fast. Then Vince screamed, so loudly it made all of them cover their ears, but he only managed to put out the fire in front of him. The fire was spreading, and there was no way Vince was going to be able to put all of it out.

Locke's heart was in his throat as he watched Vince walk into the small building, followed by Mister Mister. They were only there for a minute, maybe less, but Locke felt like crying the moment Vince walked in.

He hadn't hesitated, he hadn't even said anything. As soon as he had known something was wrong, he had gone in and put himself at risk, not even questioning that something might happen to him. And something could happen to Vince. Locke wasn't sure what had happened, but he knew if Ace was okay, he should have been able to leave, at the very least. He was fast enough the fire wouldn't touch him.

Vince came out first, his mouth still open. Bray was leaning against him, and hadn't quite passed out, so Vince was going slowly. Mister Mister came up behind him, carrying Ace around his shoulders.

Ariel came up behind them, coughing. He was carrying someone around his shoulders, too, but Locke couldn't see who it was from there.

Ariel doubled over and the guy on his shoulders tumbled onto the ground. Locke started to run toward him, barely noticing that everyone else on his team was running alongside him.

Before he could say anything to stop him, Vince turned around and ran back inside, Mister Mister running a few steps behind him.

Locke kneeled down against Ariel, who was doubled over coughing. "Can you breathe?"

Ariel nodded weakly. His gaze shot back to the building, his eyes watery. "There's more—I couldn't—"

"It's okay," Locke replied, putting his hand on Ariel's shoulder. "Don't worry, they got this."

He was covered in a sheen of sweat and streaks of soot, his clothing singed, and he was still gasping for breath. Locke was both grateful and terrified at once. Ariel was okay, but Vince had just gone back inside. Locke had been able to tell Vince was struggling the moment he had walked out with Bray, who was also on the ground coughing, and gasping for breath.

BJ was going around the guys, kneeling down and murmuring things Locke couldn't hear. He lifted his head and yelled, "I need somebody to get the oxygen tank from the infirmary, now!"

Locke didn't even have a chance to get to his feet before Mickey was off at a run. He watched Mickey for a minute and then glanced at the guys Vince and Mister Mister had brought out. Most of them seemed to have avoided a serious injury, as far as Locke could see.

"Jamie," Ariel gasped. "And Royce. They're both still in there."

Locke looked around for BJ, glad to see he was on his way over. "It'll be okay," he said absently to Ariel, trying to believe his own words.

BJ ignored Locke and took Ariel's hands. "Any burns?"

Ariel shook his head mutely.

"Hurts when you breathe?"

Ariel nodded, his breath coming hard and raspy.

"They're fine, right?" Locke asked, watching the building. Why wasn't Vince out already?

"Yeah, but they need some oxygen. Smoke inhalation is the biggest danger in a fire."

"What happened?" Locke asked.

Ariel shook his head, still gasping for breath. "Don't know."

A yell drew Locke's attention back to the burning structure as Vince stumbled out, almost dropping Royce. Mister Mister, carrying Jamie over his shoulders, bumped into Vince and BJ was on his feet in a flash. "Come help me get them away from the fire, idiot," he said with a glare at Locke.

Locke felt a flash of embarrassment. He was supposed to be a hero-in-training and in his first real emergency, he'd been reacting exactly like a bystander. He ran to help BJ, along with Cass, and the three of them got everyone clear of the fire. BJ took charge of Royce, who was bleeding from a gash in his forehead, but otherwise seemed untouched.

Locke guided a choking Vince to the ground. His clothes were singed, a sure sign his powers had been affected. The smoke—Vince had to breathe to make noise, so the smoke would have played havoc with his voice. He dropped a kiss on Vince's forehead and eased him onto his lap.

"You were amazing," he said softly. "And oh my god, you scared the hell out of me." He wasn't sure Vince could hear him, and it didn't matter. Vince's breathing was labored, wheezing, far worse than Ariel's and it didn't make him feel any better when BJ waved for Mickey to bring the oxygen tank over as he went to check on Jamie and Mister Mister.

Mickey pushed the mask onto Vince's face and Locke watched, worried. "He'll be okay?"

"Like I would know," Mickey replied. He looked almost as worried as Locke felt. "BJ!"

"Mickey, bring that tank over here," BJ said, and then Mickey was off with the tank and BJ was kneeling over Vince. "Fuck."

"What?" Locke asked, resisting the urge to clutch at Vince.

BJ spared him a glance. "Nothing." Still holding one of Vince's hands, he put the other over his chest. After a few seconds, he nodded to himself, his hand moving upward to Vince's neck, where it rested another few seconds. "I'll send the oxygen tank back soon, but he's out of danger."

"Th-thank you."

BJ gave him a strange look but was off before Locke could say anything else.

All the truths he'd been denying for the past six weeks came spilling out of his mouth. "I'm sorry, Vince, I feel like I've wasted so much time. More than wasted time, I've lost the best relationship I ever had. My father is wrong—you're not a villain, and I think I always knew that, but when you grow up hearing it—no excuse, I know." He wasn't sure Vince could hear him, but he couldn't stop himself. "Watching you run in there, into danger, I realized you could die—die, Vince!—and that it doesn't matter if you can't forgive me for being a dick, as long as you live and be happy. My jealousy was selfish, and I want to fight for you, to keep you, but I don't know how and I guess it's too little too late, but live, Vince, I beg you...." his voice trailed off into silence as tears choked him. He managed not to sob aloud, but his tears were tracking in the soot on Vince's face. "Just live, and be happy even if it's not with me."

APART FROM CALISTHENICS for the guys on the team outside—who hadn't breathed in smoke—exercises for the next few days were off. Vince was relieved. His throat was still raw and he had dreams of choking to death on smoke. As his voice had given way to the smoke, the flames had left some slight burns, but thanks to BJ, he and the other guys were healing quite rapidly, some more so than others.

Now that everyone was back on their feet, Mister Mister wanted everyone in the lecture room.

Vince let Locke help him to his feet, annoyed at how electric he still found Locke's touch. He'd heard—or maybe he only wished to have heard—Locke's words after the fire, and in spite of his determination to not let Locke get under his skin, he felt his resolve crumbling with each kindness.

It wasn't as if Locke was pressing him for anything, which made it even harder. If Locke would pressure him, he'd be a hell of a lot easier to ignore, but no. He had returned to being the same kind, smiling, gorgeous Locke he'd been before and nothing more.

I will not let him see me waver.

Locke hovered a little until Vince took a seat. He smiled almost wistfully at Vince and went to sit beside Ariel, who was almost fully recovered. Maybe it was part of his stamina power.

Not paying attention. He took a deep breath and coughed. He looked around the room, and noticed Royce was slumped, with a red mark on his head that had been raw and bleeding. His fire powers must give him some kind of immunity, because Vince had pulled him from the middle of flames that would have killed anyone else. Jamie was looking a little rough, too, but not so bad.

He couldn't even look at Ace right now. Did he still want to go out with Ace? *Why wouldn't I? He's gorgeous, funny, smart. Just like Locke.*

Shut up about Locke already.

He was flattered Ace wanted to go out with him, but he wasn't ready to date again; he'd been thinking, if he remembered clearly, about just hooking up. Now that he was sober—*and Locke had confessed his feelings*—but no, Locke had nothing to do with it. He liked Ace. As a friend. And he wasn't sure he could ever like him more, so wouldn't a date be kind of misleading?

Mister Mister walked into the room and tapped the lectern with a pointer stick. He usually cleared his throat to get their attention, but he'd gone in with Vince, riding in the bubble of safety of Vince's powers, to help the guys and he—Vince tilted his head. Mister Mister had gone upstairs to get Jamie by himself, though, hadn't he? They'd clasped wrists at the base of the stairs and shared a nod and then he put out the fire on the stairs by using his voice.

"Gentlemen, what happened a few days ago was an unfortunate accident. We don't often get trainees with fire powers, so that exercise wasn't standard. I had the staff throw together a quick structure that wasn't meant to do more than be a framework for Royce's fire." Mister Mister paused and took a drink of water, not something he normally did. "Royce, you should know if there is fault to be had, it's mine. I never thought about what might happen with the overhead beams, there should have been a lot more foresight into the construction of that shack, for the safety of you all.

"For the rest of you, a beam broke free in Royce's controlled burn, and knocked him out, leaving the fire to burn on its own. Fortunately, Jamie was able to let us know something was wrong before it was too late. Vince and BJ, I want to commend both of you as well, for your quick thinking and rising to the occasion like true heroes."

There was something a bit strange about Mister Mister's speech and it took Vince a second to pin it down—he was addressing them by their first names. His voice was, if anything, gruffer from the smoke inhalation, but he sounded... sorry?

Mister Mister took another drink of water. Vince knew the feeling—his own throat still ached and he didn't dare test his powers yet.

"This incident demonstrated we cannot do without a full-time doctor on staff, even if they twiddle their thumbs most days. I've put in a request to have that changed.

"As much of a disaster as this could have been, I hope you all learned something—a real life fire emergency is not going to have a controlled burn, with heat shielding and smoke controls. A fire out there is going to be dangerous to any of you, so no rushing in without consulting with local fire fighters on the scene.

"I want you all to write up a thorough review of the exercise, blaming me if you must, but also evaluating the reactions and behaviors of your fellow trainees. I'll be available for one on one counselling, if any of you need to talk through your feelings about this exercise.

"Leave this weekend will see all of you volunteering on Sunday at the Guilford Memorial Children's Hospital, so let's be sure to bring our funniest tricks. Cass," he added sternly, "something child appropriate."

A few laughs went up, followed by coughing.

"The rest of the week will be set aside to allow full recuperation from the fire rescue exercise. Those of you unaffected will be expected to work on your obstacle course skills—as you are aware of, there will be situations where your gifts will not help you. You need to be physically and mentally strong. New KP duties are posted according to ability; check the boards on your way out."

Vince stood up as the guys began to file out. "Um," he said. He cleared his throat and pitched his voice higher—to get attention, not a power sound. When all eyes were on him, questioning eyes of brown, hazel, blue, and green, so green, but he wasn't thinking of that, he said, "The Halloween party theme is masquerade. Costumes are mandatory, so you guys might want to start thinking about that now."

The whole mood of the room lifted a little as the guys filed out. Even Royce looked better. Vince grabbed his shoulder as he walked by. "Hey, man. You okay?"

He gave Vince a wan smile. "I will be. Probably."

"Silva."

Vince turned to find Mister Mister behind him. "We should have a chat in my office."

It wasn't a request, but neither did Mister Mister look angry, so he nodded.

When everyone else had gone, Mister Mister gestured ahead of him. Inside the office, scattered throughout with a surprising amount of paper, Mister Mister said, "We need to talk about your father."

Vince nodded reluctantly. "You don't think my father had anything to do with the fire?"

"No, that is on me. But he's been calling, leaving messages that are supposed to convince me to give up the coordinates of the camp. I'm not suggesting you're complicit in any way, but I need to know what you think his play might be?"

Vince frowned. "You think he confides in me?"

Mister Mister shook his head. "I'm pretty sure he confides in no one. But nobody knows him like you do."

Vince bit his bottom lip, nodding slowly. "It's not to get me out. Too simple. I'll have to think about it, sir. His motivation could be grand or petty. He's like that." It could be as simple as finding out if Vince knew where his mother was, or he might be planning to take the entire camp hostage.

He remembered what his mother said, but his father would have to find them first, and Mister Mister said the security measures couldn't be easily bypassed. "I promise, if I figure it out, I'll let you know right away."

"Thank you." Mister Mister didn't look pleased, but at least he seemed to understand Vince was not his father.

Vince met Mister Mister's eyes, seeing his trainer as a person for maybe the first time. The lines of worry mostly hidden by the usually neatly trimmed beard gave him a hint of vulnerability Vince would have been happy not to see. He wanted to believe someone stronger, more competent, was going to ultimately take care of them all and he recognized how ridiculous and immature that was.

None of them were children anymore. That's part of what Mister Mister was trying to teach them. Vince nodded and broke eye contact.

As he made his way out of the admin building, he wondered why Mister Mister was at Camp Hologram. This was a tough job in more ways than one. Tougher than even being a superhero liaison to law enforcement, he imagined.

Outside, Vince rubbed his arms in the cool air and saw Ace sitting across from the doors, on the edge of the part of the obstacle course not-so-fondly known as the mudpit. He didn't look like he had been hurt by the fire, but he did look more serious than Vince had ever seen him.

"Hi," Ace said, looking up at him and smiling. "Do you have a minute?"

Vince nodded. He had a good idea what the conversation was going to be about and he wasn't looking forward to it at all. He liked Ace. A lot.

As a friend.

He was smart, cute, and funny, but Vince knew he wasn't ready to date. If Ace had been interested in something a little more casual, maybe Vince would have thought about it. But even then, that would complicate their friendship, and the last thing Vince wanted was for things to get even more complicated.

"So I was thinking," Ace said as Vince sat down next to him. "Maybe a Grease duet is a bit much for a first date, but how about we go to the Halloween thing together? We don't have to do matching costumes or anything, but I don't know, it could be fun."

Vince sighed, leaning forward. "Okay, listen," he said. "I know I said I would go out with you, but I've been thinking about it a lot, and I don't know if I can."

Ace turned to look at him, his eyes wide. "Aw," he replied. Vince expected him to ask why, but Ace shrugged instead. "All right. I get it."

"You do?"

"Yeah," Ace replied. "Just tell him I'll kick his ass if he hurts you again."

Vince chuckled, a knot forming in his throat. "We're not back together, Ace," he said quietly. "We're just—I'm not ready to do any of this. All I'd be doing is comparing you to him, and that's not fair. To any of us."

Ace nodded, smiling at him. "I told you; I get it."

"So you're not—you're not angry with me?"

"Because you turned me down?" Ace replied, rolling his eyes. "You must see me as such a dick if you think that."

"No, 'cause I changed my mind," Vince said, looking down at his fidgeting feet.

"Yes, how dare you," Ace said, laughing and shaking his head. "No, I'm a little stung, but I'll get over it. Lucky for me, you're not the only cute guy here I want to take on a date."

Vince scoffed. "Ouch. I'm not even special."

Ace winked at him. "You are," he said, getting to his feet. "I promise. I should go. I gotta start planning for this party. Date or no date, I'm going to be fabulous."

Chapter Twenty-One

LOCKE FOLLOWED ARIEL into the fourth store of the day, sighing. He didn't mind shopping, and he was excited to prepare for the Halloween party, but the more he thought about it, the harder it became to face.

He wouldn't be going as Vince's date. In fact, Vince might have someone else as his date, and Locke would just have to live with that. He was happy Vince had survived and recovered after running into the fire. Locke didn't think he had cried as much since he was a little kid. It hadn't just been when Vince was gasping for breath after walking out of the fire, it had happened a few times since then, when Locke was least expecting it.

The important thing was Vince was going to be okay.

He was going to be okay, even without Locke. Because Locke had screwed everything up.

"Come on," Ariel said. "Cheer up. This would be so much more fun if you didn't have that look on your face all the time."

"Sorry," Locke replied, flashing a weak smile at him. "I'm looking forward to the party. I swear."

"Yeah, I can tell," Ariel replied. "You're going to look *amazing*. I promise."

Locke nodded, looking away from him. He knew it was true, because Ariel was in charge. He wouldn't let either one of them show up to a costume party wearing anything that didn't look absolutely spectacular. His worries had more to do with Vince; what Vince would be wearing, who he'd be arriving—and leaving—with.

"Ugh," Ariel said, turning to walk out of the store. Locke followed him, confused.

"What was that about? I thought you really wanted to go in there," he said.

"I did," Ariel replied. "I do. But you're making costume shopping not fun, and we need to talk. So that's what we're doing, before we continue our shopping trip."

"But Ariel—"

"No," Ariel replied, his voice high. "I'm not letting you ruin this for me."

"Okay, fine," Locke said, sighing and looking at his feet. He didn't want to have this conversation, but it made sense Ariel would know something was wrong. Locke didn't want to burden him with it, especially after the fire. "It's about Vince."

"*Quelle surprise*," Ariel replied, trying to stifle a yawn. "I mean, I'm not trying to be a dick, but things have been this way for weeks. I thought you'd be feeling a little better by now."

"Yeah, I know," Locke said. "I was feeling better, but then I realized how much of an idiot I was being. You know, publicly."

"Right," Ariel said. "So this isn't about Vince. This is about your ego."

"No," Locke replied, shaking his head.

"It kind of sounds like it," Ariel said.

Locke sighed. "You don't understand, though. Everything changed after the fire," he said. "The first thing I thought when we heard Jamie's distress call was oh my god, Ariel's in there. And I wanted to save you—and the others, but you're my best friend and sorry if that's selfish—but I froze. I didn't know what to do. I turned into a *bystander*," he said, like it was a dirty word. In the superhero business, it kind of was. "And Vince just ran in. I couldn't breathe. As soon as I saw you both come out, I was so relieved, and I knew if you could still carry someone, you'd be okay. And Vince, he was coughing, but he was okay. Everyone I loved was okay.

"Then he turned around and ran back inside and—" Locke stopped, because remembering brought back all the trauma of the day itself. "He was inside so long, it seemed, and when he came out, his clothes were smoking and Ariel, I was so scared. I never felt so helpless as I did then, and while I'm not sure he was conscious, I just—I don't know. I told him everything. It spilled out."

"Everything."

"Like how I cared enough that what I really wanted was for him to be alive. And be happy. Even if that meant without me. Ariel, I screwed up, didn't I?"

"What have I been saying?" Ariel said, punching his shoulder.

"Um, why *did* Vince use his powers on you? You never said."

"You never asked. And then it turned out you didn't even give him a chance to talk to you, so I feel like he was right to do so."

"But why?"

Ariel pursed his lips. "You ask Vince. If he still thinks you should know, he'll tell you. It's up to him."

"I know I should. I'm scared, though," Locke replied in a whisper. "Maybe he won't want to talk to me. Or maybe it's too late. Maybe he's already moved on. Ace was flirting with him pretty heavily. What if they're together now?"

Ariel's eyes widened. He smirked and shook his head. "Um, yeah, I don't think so. I was going to ask Cass if he'd go to the party in drag so everyone wouldn't know who I was and he was busy. With, uh, Ace."

Locke glared at him. "When was this?"

"Like two hours ago?"

"And you didn't tell me?"

Ariel shrugged. "Didn't see how it was relevant." His smirk returned. "It's not like I joined them. Cass is such a sweet bottom, though."

"Ugh." Locke clapped his hands over his ears. "TMI, dude!"

"Bullshit. You've been with Cass."

Locke dropped his hands and elbowed Ariel in the ribs. "He's a good kisser, that's all I know."

They shared a chuckle and Locke wondered if this was a good time to ask Ariel about the fire. Ariel, who loved to talk about everything, hadn't said much about it. If it had been terrifying for Locke, on the outside, it must have been worse for Ariel inside.

"Ariel, about the fire. You know if you want to talk about it, right?"

"Soon. Like, I talked to Mister Mister, and okay, part of me was like oh my god, I have an excuse to talk to him personally! He used his power mimicry, you know, to yell out the fire like Vince."

"I've never seen him use someone else's power before," Locke whispered.

"He's so cool," Ariel said, ignoring him. Then he blinked. "But yeah, it was intense. Like, we heard this crack and didn't even have time to think about what it was before the heat swept over us like nothing I've ever felt. And the smoke, my god, it was *everywhere*. I'm so glad Jamie was there because I don't know how long it would have taken you guys out there to figure out we needed help. Like it was so fast, even Ace just didn't have time to react, you know? Royce has amazing power. All I could think of was stomping it out, right? But on the second floor, I could have accidentally stomped the whole floor down on Royce and we knew he was in trouble already. We were all coughing so hard, even though we knew to get down, but the fire was everywhere... I don't know, Locke. Still processing. It'll be a while before I... I mean, it was kind of like... scary but not just because of the fire and smoke?"

"I get it. I mean, not exactly, because I was on the other side." Locke didn't mention that it probably would have taken them too long to realize something was wrong if not for Jamie—no need to freak Ariel out over something that didn't happen.

"Cool, so can we talk about our costumes for the party?" Ariel was already bouncing on his seat, his irrepressible grin spread across his face. "I swear, you'll look so pretty you'll knock Vince's boxers off! You know, if he's wearing any."

"God. There's a thought."

"You're welcome."

Locke shook his head. He did feel better. He got to his feet. "All right, let's go. I'll focus on the important stuff."

VINCE LOOKED AROUND the room. He was nervous even though Mister Mister had given them all afternoon to prepare. He had never hosted a party before and he wanted it to be as close to perfect as possible. It had stopped being about making people like him again—everyone seemed to be over the shock of his father being Pied Piper. The guys had been warming up to him even before the fire, but after the fire, Vince had found himself in a unique position, one he was not prepared for. He was suddenly popular.

He had never *quite* been an outcast growing up, but his father had been very choosy about who was good enough to play with Vince. Once puberty hit and it was clear Vince had powers and was bi, he saw no one that his father didn't see first. Vince couldn't confide in his friends, because his father would find out, so he'd gotten a reputation as stand-offish. Dating was even worse.

Now everyone at camp knew his father was Pied Piper and they didn't seem to care. Half the guys at camp had either asked him out on a date or made a pass at him for a hookup. Word had quickly spread he wasn't interested in going out with anyone.

Then there was Locke. He was finally treating Vince like he did everyone else, friendly, cheerful, casually flirting, but never pushing for more. Vince wondered if Locke knew Vince was turning people down, and if he knew why. Part of him wanted to ask about what had happened after the fire, but he didn't want to find out it was just wishful thinking on his part. The thing was, without Locke being cold, it was hard to stay angry and that meant the physical attraction he'd felt right from day one was back.

"Earth to Vince," Ace said from behind him. "Okay, dude. What do you think?"

Vince turned to look. He, Ace, and Royce—as the planning committee—had decided that instead of bringing dates, they needed to act as hosts, so they'd brought their costumes to the mess hall, now transformed into a Venetian ballroom. Or as close as their miniscule budget could make it. Ace was emerging from behind a dressing screen Mister Mister had loaned them—god knew why a man with tats who never wore anything other than khakis, camo, and T-shirts would have a four panel, silk-painted folding screen, but there it was.

Ace was transformed. His dreads were wrapped in metallic ribbons of pink, green and blue, making them stand away from his head on either side in an upside down fan shape. A white, full-face mask was painted with one dramatically arched eyebrow, lashes and a rouge spot on the left side, left side of the mouth painted in a curving red smile, while the right side was stark with its side of the mouth straight and black.

He was wearing something Henry VIII might have worn—a tight jacket with lots of trim, bubble shorts, and tights, except the left side of the bubble shorts was a ribbon skirt, the same colors as the ribbons in his hair. He looked outlandish, and even a little frightening, yet the clothes showed off an attractive body. "Nice legs," Vince said.

Ace laughed and stuck out one leg, pointing his toes. "Thank you. I think I could still run in this getup. Who's next to change?"

"Royce hasn't brought his costume in yet, so I guess it's me." Vince picked up the large bag that held all the parts of his costume.

"Let me know if you need any help undressing," Ace said.

Vince chuckled. "I'll do that."

"I'm going to see if Royce needs a hand carrying his stuff so feel free to wait naked behind that screen for us."

Vince shook his head. "I feel like Royce isn't on board with this plan."

"Don't worry," Ace replied, his wink barely visible behind his mask. "I'll get him to be," he added confidently as he walked away.

Vince rolled his eyes. He hadn't hung out with Royce for that long, and he didn't know if he was a virgin, like he had said, but he didn't fuck around. He wasn't interested at all, and he seemed to be one of few guys at camp who shut people down when they flirted with him, though he was never a dick about it.

Vince pulled out the pieces of his costume—a fancy rented red jacket with lots of gold embroidery across the collar, down the front opening, and around to the bottom of the tails. He'd been a bit iffy about going as the Phantom of the Opera in his Red Death costume, because of the villainous aspect of the character, but he hoped people would see it as ironic. The rest of the costume was from various thrift stores in Guilford, because the costume shop's costumes were kind of, well, costume-y. He didn't care that the red velvet pants were women's yoga pants or the knee-high boots with their one-inch heels were women's boots—they fit the character, they were his size. It was all good. A sheer red curtain panel worked for the cloak. He'd considered a plastic rapier from the dollar store, but decided it would be in the way if he wanted to dance.

His mask was phantom shaped, but decorated with fine gold braid and decoupaged sheet music, just in case anyone at the party needed help to guess who he was supposed to be. Not that they needed to "be" anyone, but he wanted people to get his costume choice.

NIGHT HAD JUST begun to fall when people started to arrive. Vince's nerves slowly seemed to settle down as people kept filing in, some by themselves and some in groups. Vince was fiddling with Ace's phone and trying to put the music on. Ace had said he would sort out the playlist, and Mickey had lent them some USB speakers that looked expensive.

"Hey," BJ said from behind him. "Good job putting all this together."

Vince turned around to look at him. BJ was wearing a simple costume with black pants, a blue jacket with white trim and a white cotton jabot with lace trim, along with matching white cuffs. His face was half obscured by a blue mask, which matched the color of his jacket. It was a simple disguise, no hat or wig, and Vince would have worked out who he was fairly quickly even if he hadn't recognized BJ's voice.

"Thank you," Vince replied, smiling. "You look good."

"Not as good as you," BJ said. "That costume looks like it took a lot of effort. It's clever, too."

Vince's smile widened. "You think so?"

"Yeah. How do you think I knew it was you?" BJ replied, with a wave to Vince's mask. "Power of the voice and all that. By the way, have you seen Cass?"

"Not yet, not that I know of. He's been very hush-hush about his costume. I can tell him you've been looking for him, if I figure it out?"

"Don't!" BJ exclaimed. "Sorry, uh, don't. Please. Things are kind of weird between us right now and I'm trying to avoid him."

Vince laughed. "As if Cabin One needed to get any more awkward. Do you want to talk about it?"

"Not much to talk about," BJ said, shrugging his shoulders and swallowing. "It's just that I don't do casual sex for a reason. And Cass, well, I think that's the only thing he does."

Vince's mouth dropped open. "You *like* him?"

"Yes," BJ whispered back. "Don't tell anyone, okay? He already knows and it's—yeah, awkward."

"Yikes," Vince replied. "Sorry."

"It's okay," BJ said. "I don't have feelings for him yet or anything, but I could see it happening. Which sucks, because I also happen to think he's a real jerkoff."

Vince laughed. "Yeah," he said. "I know how that is."

BJ laughed along with him. "Fucking superhero camp."

"Tell me about it."

"I'm going to go get myself a drink," BJ said. "Do you want anything?"

"Nah, I'm good," Vince replied. "I'll get something in a bit. I'm still trying to sort out the music."

"Okay," BJ said.

Vince watched him walk away, his gaze shooting to the door of the mess hall as the costumes caught his eyes. Locke was recognizable, because despite his amazing costume, he had opted not to wear a wig. That made his bright blond hair stand out against the rest of his outfit, a Prince Eric costume with tight blue pants, a white jacket with gold buttons and blue sleeves. He was wearing black boots, too, and white gloves. He was also wearing a white mask—or maybe it was gold, Vince couldn't tell from where he was standing— that covered half his face.

Vince would have been happy to keep staring at him all night, but the person who caught his attention was the one Locke was walking arm-in-arm with. Whoever Locke had brought as his date, because that was obviously who this person was, was wearing an intricate black and gold mask that covered his face. The rest of his outfit was instantly recognizable. Vince had seen *The Little Mermaid* dozens of times, at least, and the pink gown with the white skirt was perhaps the most iconic one in the entire film and this person—Locke's date—had gone all out. He was wearing a long red wig that went all the way to his waist. Vince didn't know much about wigs, but he knew that one looked expensive.

"Here," BJ said, standing next to him and putting a glass in his hand.

"I said—"

"Drink. You look like you need it," BJ replied. "I brought one for myself too."

Vince scoffed. "Great. Thanks."

The two of them stared in unison at Locke and his mystery date, until Bray—unmistakably Bray—walked in. He was wearing a mask and body paint to look like a statue, but it failed to fully cover his tattoos. A white loincloth and a pair of sandals completed his costume. He certainly drew the eye. It was amazing, Vince thought, how ridiculous a nearly naked man of Bray's superb physical condition could look, with enough effort.

BJ coughed and turned so he couldn't see Bray. "I'm not laughing," he said. "Straight boy's got no style sense."

"Well," Vince said, squeezing his palm to his face to force his muscles into a serious expression. "It's not Cass." A snicker escaped him.

BJ snorted.

The two of them erupted in childish giggles. They were just winding down when the person trailing after Bray walked in. His identity was obscured by an all-white mask. He wasn't wearing a wig, but his hair was covered by a small white hat with golden trim and a white feather. The sleeveless jacket, which went down all the way to his knees, had buttons on each side, which meant they weren't functional, but they still looked amazing. The jacket was breathtaking in and of itself, with exquisite silver and golden embroidery thread on the flaxen fabric. The outfit was completed by a long turtleneck white shirt with ruffled sleeves.

"Wow," Vince said, trying to focus on the guy in the costume instead of Locke and his date. "Who do you think that is?"

"No clue," BJ replied. "But I'm going to go get another drink. Don't want to be around if it's Cass."

"Wait," Vince said. "I'm going with you."

Vince hadn't planned on getting drunk that night, but he could see Locke was stealing glances at him already. It was already difficult enough to be around Locke, but now he had a date, and Vince wasn't sure how he was supposed to deal with that. He hadn't been ready to move on, but Locke had been the one to break up with him in the first place, and even if Vince had heard Locke right after the fire, it didn't mean anything. *Just live and be happy even if it's not with me.*

It was obvious Locke was trying to do that—or he was already there—but things were harder for Vince. He was annoyed with himself, too. He had been so guarded when it came to Locke he'd allowed him to get in another dig, another extra humiliation.

He normally managed to pace himself well, but there was no reason for him to. They were supposed to have the day off the next day and maybe what Vince really needed was to loosen up enough to find the courage to hookup with one of his prospects.

And stop thinking about Locke.

It was well into the night when Locke managed to catch him alone. Vince tried to stand up and walk toward the bathroom, but he was too drunk and nearly stumbled over. Locke gracefully grabbed him and stopped him from falling, saying nothing.

"Thanks," Vince mumbled. He wasn't sure if he wanted Locke to hear him.

"No problem," Locke replied, in a normal tone of voice. He didn't even seem drunk. "I've been trying to talk to you all night."

Vince shook his head. "I'm right here," he said, sitting back down.

"Yeah, you basically run away every time I come near you," Locke replied.

Vince sighed, his gaze settling on Locke's lips. God, he was so beautiful, even with his face half covered. Vince really wanted to kiss him. "If I talk to you, will you stop following me? I'm trying to have fun tonight." *And forget about you.*

"Yes," Locke replied. "I promise."

Vince waved his hand in front of his face. "But you're—I mean, does your date know you're talking to me? Shouldn't you be trying to chase after him?"

Locke's eyes widened for a few seconds, and he bit his lower lip.

"This isn't funny," Vince snapped.

"My date? Do you mean—"

"Well, yeah," Vince replied. "We all know who you both are supposed to be."

Locke choked back on a laugh. "No, Vince. I didn't come with a date. Ariel is, you know, Ariel."

Vince closed his eyes, feeling his face burn hot with embarrassment. He'd thought Ariel was the one in the blonde wig, full face mask, and some sort of *Gone with the Wind* dress that left his shoulders bare. Whoever that was, he kept throwing himself into people's arms and tossing his head back dramatically.

"Vince, I know maybe I shouldn't say it, but there's been no one for me since you." Locke laughed self-consciously. "Anyway, I don't want to do this here, I mean in the hallway by the toilets," he added, rushing his words. "It should be on a balcony, you know? But no matter how beautiful you made the mess hall inside, it's still... Oh shit, I'm babbling, aren't I?"

Vince realized Locke was nervous, though his drink-fuzzy brain couldn't quite work out why. "Kind of," he said.

"Um, so, would you like to take some night air with me?" he asked, in exaggerated formality, bowing slightly and offering his arm to Vince.

He would probably regret this later, but he took it. A small sigh escaped him before he could stop it. He had fallen far deeper and faster than he'd ever thought possible, getting over it seemed impossible, especially now Locke was being so nice, and Vince was constantly reminded of what he liked about him in the first place.

"You did a wonderful job with this party, by the way. And did you see Zorro? I think that's Mister Mister, but only because of the chest hair. He is, as Ariel has been telling me, dreamy."

Vince chuckled. "Yeah, hotter than any instructor I've ever had before. My father has a particular dislike of Mister Mister." He immediately wished he hadn't brought up his father, but Locke just laughed along with him.

"Yeah, mine, too."

Vince swallowed before saying, "Your dad's not a villain."

"No." Locke glanced at him and pushed his mask to the top of his head, allowing Vince a good look at the green eyes he was so fascinated with. Locke opened the door to the cool night air. "My dad is Sting."

"Oh." Vincent didn't know what else to say, but he now had a much clearer understanding of why Locke felt he needed to stay away from Vince. Sting's infamous lectures on right and wrong and the perils of gray morality were the subject of much mockery from Vince's dad, and he knew many heroes also felt like Sting took his stance a little too far. He'd always kept up on all the gossip, looking for a role model the opposite of his father. Sting had never been it. "Oh."

"Oh, indeed," Locke said with a sigh. "We're grown ass men, about to take on more responsibility than most guys our age, and I let my father's feelings, his *approval*, blind me to my own happiness. I can't tell you how sorry I am." He pulled away from Vince and gave him a big smile. "But maybe I can show you."

He pulled out a small bag and gave it to Vince, "I was going to wrap it, but that seemed—and I didn't want—I mean it's not a bribe or anything. It's just, I was thinking of you when Ariel was dragging me around to all these stores, and I realized I didn't know when your birthday is or was, or whatever, and, um, yeah. No strings."

Vince blinked, wondering how much he'd had to drink. Was he already passed out and dreaming? Everything seemed to be in some kind of weird slow motion as he opened the bag. Inside was an mp3 player, with a coil of earbuds. "I don't know if I can accept this."

"It wasn't that expensive. I mean, who uses them anymore? And you can see it's opened. I just, you know, put some music on there for you. I mean, you know I'm not rich like some of the guys here. Shit even half this costume is DIY." he gestured down his body. "These ridiculously tight pants are from Ariel's everyday wardrobe, and barely fit."

"They look really, really good, though." Vince *was* dreaming, because he wouldn't have said that if he was awake, he was pretty sure.

Locke blushed. "Um, anyway, the reason I wanted to do this outside is over by the obstacle course."

"Oh. You weren't trying to seduce me?"

"Well, I'd love to, but you know I care about more than sex. Will you come see?" He held out his hand.

Vince took it and stumbled after Locke. He cared about more than sex? Maybe there'd been another fire or something. He wanted to believe he was hearing all this, experiencing all this, but could he?

"This isn't to seduce you. It's because I want you to know I think you're special, and I, um, have a lot of feelings for you, and—" He was holding a paper lantern and reached in his fancy jacket for a lighter.

Vince stared, certain now he was dreaming, as Locke lit the candle.

"This is for you. Because you're my hero." He held the lantern aloft and as the candle heated the air inside the paper, it floated up into the night sky.

Vince had no words. He reached for Locke's hand and held it as they both stood watching the lantern fly higher and higher.

Finally, he turned to Locke and, still without speaking, drew him into his arms. It was too dark to see the color of Locke's eyes, but he could see the contour of his face and the way his lower lip trembled. Vince, too overcome to speak, pressed his lips to Locke's.

The kiss started off sweet, but quickly grew intense, hungry, lips opening to tongues as they pressed their bodies close. Vince struggled to remember why he hadn't done this already, after the fire. He wrenched his head back, or so it felt, difficult to stop kissing Locke. "My father is still my father."

"I don't care who your father is. I only care who you are." Locke reached out to push Vince's mask up, off his face. "Do you think you might want to, maybe, go out with me?"

"Yes," Vince finally said, in little more than a whisper. "And sex, too."

Locke squeezed him tight, laughing like he was relieved. "Our cabin's empty now, um, if you're sure. You've been drinking and I don't want you to—"

Vince nuzzled his neck. "I'm sure."

Locke groaned. "Good. Yes. Me too."

They took turns pulling the other to the cabin, and Vince kept thinking, *I hope it's not a dream, I hope it's not a dream.*

Inside Cabin One, Locke pulled him against the cabin door and ran his hands under Vince's plush red jacket. "So many clothes," he muttered against Vince's mouth.

Vince shrugged off the jacket as he kissed away any more words. He helped Locke unfasten the buttons on his waistcoat, until Locke began to whimper.

"I gotta take these pants off, Vince, or my dick's gonna lose circulation."

"Poor baby," Vince mumbled, licking the column of Locke's throat as he helped open the tight pants.

Locke's cock sprang free, unencumbered by underwear. "Commando?"

"Couldn't fit underwear in those pants."

Vince nodded, sinking to his knees. He tugged the pants off Locke's strong legs and said, "Damn boots. Get the rest of your clothes off, while I'm busy down here."

He heard Locke gulp, followed by a gasp as he swirled his tongue over the head of Locke's cock. "Vince! I...."

Vince ignored him. He'd missed this, missed the smell and taste of Locke. He squeezed Locke's gorgeous ass and sucked Locke as deep as he could.

"Vince, I'm gonna—"

Vince pulled off quickly, squeezing the thick base of Locke's cock. He could make a song of that, Locke's cock. "No, you're gonna fuck me, and we don't have time to make it long and loving."

"Oh. Oh."

He looked up at Locke, all shadows and contours in the dim light coming in the window from the compound. "You're gorgeous."

"You are wearing way too many clothes, Vince Silva," Locke said in a husky voice. "And I don't think I can move with those pants around my knees.

Vince began to giggle. He helped Locke to his bunk and pulled off his boots, the pants. He stood up and removed the rest of his clothes. "Condom, lube?"

"My locker, top shelf."

Vince got the supplies, aware of Locke's gaze on him.

"Come here," Locke said, his voice husky.

Vince stood between Locke's knees, holding onto the upper bunk as Locke kissed his stomach, his hips, his thighs, everywhere but his cock. "Please," he begged.

"Yes, my love," Locke whispered back, teasing the head of Vince's cock and licking up the underside. "You taste wonderful."

"Missed you," Vince managed to say before Locke swallowed him down. He clutched at the upper bunk, knees locked to hold himself upright, and gasped when Locke slipped his fingers between his legs, stroking his balls, then behind his balls.

He whimpered a little when Locke's hands disappeared, only to gasp again as Locke changed the speed of his sucking, distracting him. He almost didn't hear the pop of the lube cap, but he felt Locke's slick fingers, prepping him.

"Sorry to rush this."

"No, I want it, Locke. Need you. Just you."

"We gotta switch places. This bed is so narrow."

"You'll be on top of me. It'll work."

"God, you drive me crazy, Vince, in all the best ways." Locke climbed onto the end of the narrow bunk, between Vince's legs, and lay down on top of him, sliding their cocks together as he kissed Vince.

Vince twined his tongue with Locke's, licked his lips and broke the kiss to whisper, "Hurry, before someone comes."

Locke chuckled and slid down Vince's body, dropping kisses all the way. He pushed Vince's legs apart, and Vince drew his knees up. He wanted this so bad. His hips lifted as Locke kissed his cock, then his balls.

He shivered when Locke moved to put the condom on, each sound of preparation playing on his nerves, heightening his anticipation. Then Locke was leaning over him, kissing his stomach, licking his nipples and whispering, "Are you ready?"

"Oh god, yes," he groaned. "Please."

It burned a little, when Locke pressed his cock inside. Locke paused until Vince lifted his hips in silent plea to continue, and then he was in. Locke's breath came hard and fast when Vince cried out in a strangled voice, "Locke, please, move."

"Vince, you're so...."

Locke moved, slowly at first, hooking Vince's legs on his shoulders. Vince closed his eyes, feeling like the world was right for the first time in two months. He was with Locke, Locke was insi— "Oh *Locke*," he yelled as Locke's movement stroked his prostate.

So perfect, such bliss, and as Locke's thrusting grew harder, more out of control, Vince's orgasm broke over him in a wave, his cock jetting cum across both their stomachs.

Locke made a few inarticulate sounds or shouts and came soon after, collapsing with an exhausted whimper on top of Vince. "I, Vince. You."

"*You* Locke. Me Vince," Vince managed with a thready laugh, still trying to catch his breath.

"Uhn." Locke agreed. He eased out of Vince, tied off the condom and tossed it into the middle of the cabin. "Jus' gonna cuddle a bit," he mumbled, lying back into the miniscule space between Vince and the wall.

"'Kay," Vince agreed. "Missed you. That was so right."

"Mmm," Locke agreed. "I'm sorry."

Vince thought about maybe cleaning up, but he was tired and Locke's arms and legs entwined with his was comforting. Comfortable, warm. Perfect.

Chapter Twenty-Two

A HORRENDOUS SCREAMING sound ripped through Locke's skull and he jerked awake. Vince howled and buried his head under the pillow. "Make it stop," he cried out.

Locke was glad he was between Vince and the wall or he'd have fallen out of the narrow bunk. He didn't have time to think about how much any discomfort had been worth sleeping in Vince's arms because the sirens—he recognized them now he was awake—were still shrieking through the camp.

Cass was already on the floor, wearing just his briefs and some wildly spiky hair.

BJ rolled out of bed immediately after and started swearing. He tossed Locke's discarded condom—which he'd had the foresight to tie off—into the trash can with a disgust that the sirens overruled.

Vince seemed to realize this wasn't a unique hangover torture and sat up, allowing Locke to roll out of bed.

"Are we under attack?" Cass yelled.

Somehow he had already managed to pull on sweatpants and a T-shirt, and was now tugging socks over his feet. BJ was reaching for a hoodie, and Vince was sitting up, sheet forgotten. No one seemed to notice the pair of them were stark naked.

Locke scrambled for clothes. He threw some at Vince, who was holding his head and looking both pained and afraid.

Cass and BJ were already out the door by the time they got some clothes on, and Locke said, "Do you think it's your dad?"

Vince shook his head. "Not his style." He sounded doubtful, but maybe it was just his hangover.

They weren't the last ones out, but there was no Mister Mister on the calisthenics field. Instead, armed men, ungifted, were very much in evidence. Locke knew they'd always been there, part of the camp's security, but he'd never actually seen them before. Even the fire incident—the trainees and Mister Mister had it all under control before anyone showed up to extinguish the fire, and by then, Locke was more concerned with Vince. And the other guys, of course, but mainly Vince.

It was weird to see them, all in black, full tactical gear, in contrast to the trainees who were in various states of dress, mostly sweatpants and rumpled tees, with tousled hair and worried faces. To his surprise, it was Mickey who marched up to one of the men and demanded to know what was going on. Mickey's powers were laughable, and there was a quiet rumour he wouldn't even be training at Camp Hologram if not for his father's influence.

Having Mickey on a team was at first considered playing with a handicap, but while he still refused to admit his powers weren't all he claimed, he never hesitated to do what was asked of him in any nongifted capacity. And a lot of their training scenarios required them to work without their gifts.

Locke watched Mickey talk to them, trying his best not to look at Vince, though he was right next to him and didn't seem to want to move. Locke thought about reaching out and grabbing Vince's hand. They were officially dating; he could do that now. But Vince had been drunk the night before and even though everything had seemed perfect, Locke knew they still had things to talk out.

That didn't mean he couldn't enjoy Vince being around him, even in the midst of chaos. He turned to look at him, opening his mouth to say something, but before he could, Mickey had ran back toward them and was now standing in front of the group, his eyes wide and his fists clenched at his sides.

Locke and Vince exchanged a glance.

"Are you going to tell us what the fuck is going on?" Royce asked.

"It's Mister Mister," Mickey replied, his voice shaky. "Nobody can find him."

Bray scoffed and Locke turned to look at him. "What do you mean nobody can find him?"

He hadn't bothered to remove his makeup before he'd gone to bed so his face was still covered in white paint. Now that he was wearing a white T-shirt and sweatpants, Locke could see the appeal of the look.

Mickey shook his head. "What I just said. They don't know where he is. He's missing."

"He's allowed to leave the camp whenever he wants," Rudy said from behind Bray. "Honestly, I don't see what the big deal is. Mister Mister got drunk and must have gone to hookup with someone else."

"We're in the middle of nowhere," BJ replied. He looked at the group of masked men in front of them. "I don't think anyone leaves camp without them knowing."

"That's my point. I spoke with a guy who calls himself Agent Smith, and he said the perimeter was breached somehow and they're staring at the security data, but the only person missing is Mister Mister. Now they know we're okay, he said they're going to resecure the perimeter. Smith said in order to keep the camp safe, there's just him and 'Agent Jones' to help us find him," Mickey said, making air quotes around Agent Jones's name.

Locke swallowed. "Us? Well, yeah, I guess," he said, answering his own question. "That's what we've been training to do, right?"

"He's probably fine," Rudy said, rolling his eyes and crossing his arms over his chest.

Locke glanced at Vince for the first time since Mickey had come running back to them. Vince looked so pale even under the soft light of dawn. The second their eyes met, Vince shook his head, his lips a thin line.

"Yeah, probably," Locke replied, trying to keep his voice as steady as possible. "But we still need to find out what happened to him. Just in case."

Rudy nodded. "I guess I find it hard to believe something could happen to him," he said. "Okay. So who saw him last? I left the party before he did."

"It was me," Mickey said. "I, uh, yeah. I mean, you can't blame me, he's hot."

"Okay, wow," Cass replied, a smile on his face. "I have so many questions."

"Which we have no time for right now," Locke said, though he had to admit he had a lot of questions himself. "When?"

"Last night," Mickey replied. "We left together. I went back to his—well, I talked him into letting me go back to his place with him."

Cass laughed, "Did you stay there?"

"No, I was only a little bit drunk, but he wasn't having it," Mickey said, twisting his lips. "Which was a shame. Anyway, he told me to go back to my cabin. He said I needed to sleep it off. That was a couple of hours ago."

"How was he acting?" Vince asked.

"Normal," Mickey said, shrugging his shoulders. "A little standoffish, but that's pretty standard."

Vince nodded, swallowing. He turned to look at Locke, getting close to him and whispering in his ear. "My dad. He could have made him walk off with him."

Locke shook his head, though he suspected something like that had happened. "No way," Locke replied. He hoped he sounded more convinced than he felt. "You said this wasn't his style."

Vince shrugged. "That was before I knew what was going on."

"So you think Pied Piper might have taken him?" Ariel asked. He wasn't quiet about it so all the guys set their gaze on Vince, who looked at Locke like he was pleading. Locke had never wanted to punch Ariel as much at that moment, but he got his concern. He just wished he had been a little quieter about it.

"No, don't be stupid," Locke said. "He would have had to get in here first. Getting in here is difficult. Getting out of here has to be a thousand times harder."

BJ nodded. "You're thinking he's still at camp."

"Just that, if someone did take him, they wouldn't have gotten very far," Locke replied. He sent a significant look toward the helipad where the helicopter still sat. "They'd be hiking out of here."

"We can help the security guys find him," Vince said, his voice so quiet Locke was sure only he could hear him.

Ariel perked up. "What do you suppose they look like under all that gear?" he said, nodding to the men in the tactical suits.

"You have a gift for the irrelevant," Locke replied, ruffling Ariel's hair before he could duck away. "I know we're all tired and none of us got enough sleep, but it's what we've been training for since we got here. If we don't help and something happens...."

He didn't need to finish the sentence.

"Fuck," Jamie muttered. "Where do we even start?"

"I have an idea," Rudy replied. "We need to retrace his steps before he went missing. So the last thing we have is Mickey's account, and no one saw him after that, right?"

Nobody said anything.

"So we need to go where he was last seen," Rudy continued. "Which is wherever he sleeps. Mickey can take us there. And if he has a laptop or if he left his phone behind, then I can dig up some clues. It would take those guys ages to look through everything."

Ariel grinned. He caught Locke's gaze, expecting a smile back. While the idea of going into Mister Mister's space was enticing, it also felt wrong. "So you're saying we break into his room?"

"It's an apartment," Mickey said. "And I can take you there. There isn't really anything—"

"I'm sure we can judge that for ourselves," Bray interjected. "You must have been too busy to look around for clues, huh?"

"Is that the first time you've been to his apartment?" Ariel asked.

Bray snorted. "Obviously not," he replied. "Did you really think there was any other reason why this loser would still be here?"

"That's not fair," Mickey replied. "It's not what you think, anyway—"

"Look, as much as I want to hear all about your relationship with Mister Mister, the longer we stand here debating what to do, the more likely it is that whoever has him manages to get away from camp," Rudy said. "I have a lot of questions. All of which can wait. C'mon, Mickey, lead the way."

"It's in the admin building," Mickey said.

"It's a big building; show us," Rudy replied, his impatience obvious.

Mickey turned his head to look at Rudy and nodded. Locke could tell he was relieved. They all started walking together, following Mickey. Locke tried to focus on the chatter amongst them instead of how hard his heart was beating. Vince was still next to him, but he hadn't reached out to touch Locke. He was being friendlier than he had been before the Halloween party, but that didn't mean anything, he reminded himself. He wouldn't believe Vince wanted to be with him until he told Locke as much, and it wasn't the right time for that. Not when it was obvious Vince was worried about his dad breaking into the camp and dragging off their instructor.

"Why would he do something like this?" Locke asked Vince in a whisper.

"Your guess is as good as mine," Vince replied. Then he shrugged. "It may not be him. This just feels a little bit like it's about me. My mom is doing okay and that's not, ugh, it's not allowed. This is the kind of stunt he would pull to remind me that I'm never free of him. No matter how much I try."

Locke couldn't hold himself back anymore. He put his hand on Vince's shoulder and squeezed it. Vince's gaze shot up to his face and he smiled thinly.

"Don't worry," Locke said. "We're going to find Mister Mister. He can't have gone far."

Vince sighed. "Yeah, okay."

Locke dropped his hand to his side. He wanted to say something else—anything else—to make Vince feel better, but he couldn't think of anything to say. They were standing in front of the admin building now and Mickey was pointing at a white door Locke had always assumed led to more offices.

"Is it locked?" Jamie whispered. Locke turned to look at him. Everyone had been chatting all this time, but it was the first time he had heard Jamie speak. He looked terrible, too. There were dark bags under his eyes and he kept rubbing his temples.

Mickey shrugged. He turned the handle as the guys waited. The door opened and Mickey took a step forward. Locke hesitated. Even if Mister Mister had been kidnapped, going into his space like this felt wrong. He hadn't ever even gone into his father's study and he knew his father.

"He wouldn't leave his door unlocked, would he?" Cass asked.

Mickey shrugged. "I don't know. I wasn't paying attention to the door when I was with him."

"C'mon," Vince said, taking a step in front of him. Locke swallowed and nodded, stepping into the apartment as Mickey turned on the light. Locke looked around the small apartment, trying to see if there were any signs of struggle. Other than looking very clean and more like a showroom than a place anyone lived in, there was nothing remarkable about Mister Mister's apartment.

The door led them to an open concept area, a small kitchen with an equally small island and a big window open to the back of the compound, a little bit of grass and a lot of trees. There was a small desk in the dining area, instead of a dining table, but it only held a closed laptop and a mouse. Not even a printer. There was a sofa, a chair, a coffee table and a big TV in a wall unit. A colorful rug provide the only hint to a unique personality, and—"Something was here," Locke said, pointing to behind the sofa.

Vince looked as Rudy pushed past all of them to run his hands over Mister Mister's laptop.

"I think that's where he keeps his fancy dressing screen. I think it's still in the mess hall. He loaned it to us."

"Yeah," Mickey confirmed. "He never said where it came from or whatever."

Locke felt a little disappointed. He'd thought he'd found a clue. "Anything else look out of place?"

Mickey shrugged. "Not really, no."

"What about the bedroom?"

Mickey blushed. "We, ah. He never. It wasn't like that."

Cass snickered and pushed the bedroom door open. "Bed made, not military style. Looks homey. No sign of a fight." He closed the door and called, "Rudy, you got anything?"

"Not much. Did you know he can watch all the security cams from here? There's some notes about upcoming exercises, nothing specific. There's another password that links to our scores, and whatever our boy Mickey is up to, it's not getting him high marks."

Mickey once more blushed a bright, beet red. "I wasn't trying for high marks. I just—for fuck's sake, it's none of your business."

Rudy smirked. "I can pull up the security footage of last night, or early this morning, I guess. Like from almost anywhere in the camp. Including all the exits from this building. So maybe we can get a bead on which door he left and with whom. Has anyone seen his phone?"

"It wasn't in the bedroom," Cass said. "Unless he puts it in a drawer."

Locke stared at him.

"All right, I'll check."

A few minutes later, he emerged from the bedroom and closed the door again. "No phone."

"What *did* you find?" Ariel asked, curious.

"That was a bit weird," Cass said, "because where else would a guy keep his lube and condoms? But not in his night table like a normal dude."

Ariel turned to Mickey, who was tight-lipped and still red. Locke clamped his hand over Ariel's mouth. "Don't. Ask."

He let go and said, "When we were growing up, you were a big fan; is there anything you can think of that might seem out of character for Mister Mister?"

"Besides fu—" Locke's hand covered Ariel's mouth again.

"I think we can take that as a no."

Vince spoke up, "Should we watch the security video here? Wouldn't it be better to watch in the office with, um, agents Smith and Jones?"

Jamie said, voice strained, "If we watch it first, then ask them about it, maybe I can get something from them."

Bray nodded. He, Ace, and Royce were in the small kitchen poking around cupboards. "That's a good idea."

"You don't really think they were involved?" BJ asked.

"You know what Mister Mister keeps telling us—question everything," Royce said. "Everything looks normal here. Except he eats way too much yogurt. That's totally not normal."

"Yogurt sounds good to me," BJ said.

Locke met Vince's eye, hoping to see support. "Let's check the video footage. We'll go to the mess hall afterward. Mickey and Jamie," he paused, "and Bray will talk to Smith and Jones. Me and Vince and Ariel will whip up some food for anyone who feels like eating, and then we can figure out the best way to approach this. And if it *is* Smith and/or Jones, we'll look like we're doing something relatively harmless."

Vince nodded, a small smile on his mouth.

"Yeah," Rudy said, "There's no cameras in the mess hall. Some just outside, in the hallway, but not in the actual room. It'll be safe. Someone wanna turn the TV on?"

BJ pushed the button.

"Okay, this is from the emergency exit off the infirmary," Rudy said as the video began to play. He frowned. "Looks like someone tried to turn the cameras off or something."

All they could see were Mister Mister's legs, still clad in the black tuxedo pants he'd worn for his Zorro costume, as he dug his heels into the ground, fighting whoever belonged to the two pairs of denim clad legs on either side of him.

"Just two people," Vince said.

"Two that we can see," Ace pointed out.

"It would be hella hard to move a lot of people across the ground surrounding this camp," Rudy said.

Everyone turned to look at him.

"It's all laid out on the hard drive. If there's more than two, yeah, it's gotta be an inside job. So let's be careful what we tell the men in black, all right?"

Locke nodded. The idea that someone inside camp would be involved in all of this, it was kind of scary to think about. That meant they were all vulnerable. If Mister Mister had been taken, none of them were safe. It didn't matter then. Because they were still beginners, they were barely a blip on anyone's radar. As soon as they graduated, though, they were going to become more than just a little complication. A smart villain would pick them off one by one, eliminating them before they became a real threat. That was why the camp's security was so tight. If someone had managed to breach it, they could have taken any of them out.

They could have taken Vince out, he thought with a twinge of panic as he looked at him. Vince was talking to Ace, quietly, so Locke couldn't hear them. They were both looking around the apartment; maybe trying to find if something was out of place. He felt a twinge of jealousy over the something that had almost happened between them because Locke had been so stupid.

He walked over to Vince, putting his hand on the small of his back, his heart beating hard in his chest. So many ways he could have lost Vince.

Vince turned around to look at him, a smile crossing his face. "Hey," he said. His smile faded when he saw Locke's expression. "Are you okay?"

"Fine," Locke replied, hoping he sounded sincere. "Just a little concerned. If this is an inside job...."

"We were just talking about that," Ace said. "If some villain is going to attack us, it'd make sense for them to take Mister Mister first, right?"

Locke nodded and dropped his voice to a whisper. "I'm sure a lot of the guys are going to come to the same conclusion because it's not a stretch. Could we keep it between us though? Everyone's already a bit frazzled and—"

"My lips are sealed," Ace said with a wink.

"Don't worry," Vince added. "We've got your back."

"For sure," Ace said. "Is there anything else I can do to help?"

Locke smiled at him despite himself. Ace had always struck him as a nice person, if a little arrogant. Part of him wanted not to like Ace, since he had almost swept in and stolen Vince away from him, but it was hard when he was standing there, obviously trying to be as helpful as possible. "No, don't worry about it. Let's go eat. We'll feel better once we have breakfast."

VINCE DIDN'T LOVE that Locke had decided they be the ones to make food. He had spent far too much time in the Camp Hologram kitchen. He knew the logic behind it, though. Locke and Vince had been doing KP for so long they could practically do it in their sleep and while they never managed to provide anything one would call tasty, at least their food was edible. Cabin Three was currently on KP and everyone was pretty unhappy, including its occupants.

He was grateful Locke had told him to stay nearby, too. What had happened the night before had been magical, but even with Locke's apology, Vince knew they needed to sit down and talk things through. With Mister Mister missing, they couldn't, and it made the night seem almost unreal.

He focussed on trying to work out if his father was behind this. Pied Piper was a showman. He liked to be caught on video, singing bystanders into doing his dirty work. That he wasn't on video was reassuring. Still, he hadn't wanted to see Vince out of any paternal affection. He was planning something, but this didn't seem like his father's style.

Putting breakfast together was at least easy. Ariel's incessant chatter seemed to put both Locke and Vince at ease. It was nice to think Ariel was still his friend, even after everything that had happened between him and Locke.

"Okay, Vince. The oatmeal is done, and Locke is sorting out the cutlery and stuff. Is there anything else you need me to do? Do you need a hand with those eggs?"

"No, I'm almost done," Vince replied. "You made coffee, right?"

"Yup," Ariel said. "First thing I did. I have a feeling a lot of us are going to need more than one cup. I'm still recovering a little, you know. That wig was small and I'm sure it's not helping with my hangover."

Vince smiled. Of course this was how much Ariel talked when he was hungover.

"You looked cute, though," Vince replied.

Locke walked back into the kitchen and glared at Ariel, but there was a smile in his voice when he spoke. "I leave you two alone for a minute."

Ariel winked at him. "Hey, I didn't do anything. Not this time."

"I know you better than that," Locke replied, shaking his head and chuckling. "Come on. All the trainees are seated and we need to talk to them."

"What did the men in black say?" Vince asked.

Locke shrugged. "Not sure yet. You're going to burn those."

"Shit," Vince replied, looking down at the scrambled eggs. "No, it's good. We're fine. They'll be a little rubbery, but they can deal."

Locke laughed again, winking at him, and then Vince watched him walk away with Ariel. It seemed like things were back to normal between them, like maybe Vince hadn't imagined it. If his father *did* have anything to do with Mister Mister's disappearance though, he imagined Locke's attitude toward him would quickly change.

He turned off the griddle to finish the eggs, dumped them in a metal container and brought them to the front. Losing Locke's affection would suck, but it wasn't the worst possible outcome of this situation. He needed to concentrate on the bigger picture.

He finished with prep and went to join the rest of the guys, some of whom were already eating. The mess hall was guaranteed to be chaos once they were done, but Vince knew they couldn't stick around to clean it up. Not that Mister Mister was there to punish them when they didn't, he thought with a shudder.

He went to sit down next to Locke, but Bray was already on one side and Ariel on the other, so Vince settled for sitting across from him as he listened to the conversation.

"Nothing, huh?" Locke said, twisting his lips.

"Nothing," Mickey replied. "They said they appreciated our help, but they didn't know how or who had breached the perimeter."

"Yeah," Bray agreed. "They also said we should stay out of their way. Something about how they're pros and we should let them do their job."

Vince shook his head. "I don't understand," he said, ignoring his grumbling stomach. He wanted to go get some food, but this seemed more important. "They asked for our help. Did you get anything, Jamie?"

"Absolutely nothing," Jamie replied. "There must be some sort of blocking device in their helmets. It was like trying to read turnips."

Ariel stifled a snicker.

"I have a bad feeling about this," Bray said.

"Bray, don't be paranoid," Mickey replied, shaking his head. "Jamie isn't the world's first telepath and it's a good thing they are protected. They said it's standard procedure when there's a perimeter breach, you know, just in case."

Bray glared at him. "You asked?"

Mickey shrugged. "I wanted to know."

"The fact that there's an SOP for a perimeter breach is scary in and of itself," Jamie said.

"So you guys got nothing useful," Ariel said.

"Except that we can't trust them," Bray replied. "Which we kind of already knew. Now we know for sure."

Vince rubbed the bridge of his nose. His father had plenty of followers, people he wouldn't need to influence at all, and he had managed to get more than one to turn against their employer before. This wasn't entirely outside his usual methods.

He opened his mouth to say something, but Locke started to speak before he could. "Was Rudy able to get anything from the security equipment that he couldn't from the feeds we found in Mister Mister's quarters?"

Mickey shook his head.

Vince frowned. "If no one was seen getting in—could it have been someone with powers like yours, Locke?"

Locke frowned. "Maybe? Wouldn't security take that into account though? Use infrared or something?"

"So it has to be someone at camp," Vince replied, his heart dropping. "It's definitely an inside job."

Locke sighed, pinching the bridge of his nose and closing his eyes. "This means we have even less time than we thought," he said. "Because if they take him out of camp, well, they know how security works inside and out."

Bray shook his head. "I don't understand. Where would they take him?"

"I don't know, but it's hard to get out of here. If we're lucky, they're hiding him somewhere until they can sneak him out when we're distracted."

"Do you mean like now?" Ariel replied. "Because we're distracted."

"Yes," Locke said. "Like now. We're going to have to split up and hope they haven't managed to get him out of here yet. I'm going to assume the men in black have a better understanding than we do of the terrain, considering we never go out of here without using the helicopter, so we're going to have to work fast."

Ariel looked at him. His skin looked almost chalk white, which made his colorful hair stand out more, and he was biting his lips. For the first time since Vince had known Ariel, he thought he looked scared. Even when the fire had happened, Ariel had seemed more upset that he hadn't been able to help than afraid for his own life. Vince was sure he had come to the same conclusion he had been discussing with Ace earlier, so he jumped in. The last thing they needed was for everyone to panic.

"Okay," he said. "So what do we do?"

"We need to split up," Locke said. "Search the woods or anywhere they might have hidden him."

"Splitting up is how people die in horror movies," Royce said. Vince had barely noticed he was there, standing up behind him, his arms crossed over his chest. There were dark bags under his eyes and his lips were a thin line.

"Those people don't have powers," Locke countered, his voice harsh. "Look, I get it. You guys are afraid; I'm afraid too. We don't know what this means. We need to contain the situation as soon as possible."

He didn't say anything else, but he didn't have to. Mister Mister could be dead, and one by one, they could follow. The guys started chattering among themselves once the weight of what Locke had said began to sink in, but Locke held up his hand and everyone in the room went quiet.

"Mickey, I need you to go back out there and talk to the security team. Ask them how the perimeter was breached. Maybe we're wrong; maybe it's not an inside job. That should also give you some idea of what the rest of the security team is doing. Take your phone and make sure to send me updates."

"Gotcha," Mickey said, nodding. His voice was bright, but his hands were tight fists at his sides.

"Royce should go with you," Locke said. "I have a feeling poking around and asking questions may get dangerous. He can protect you. Right?"

"Yes," Royce replied in a small voice.

"Rudy, I need you to go into the admin building and start looking at their files. Not just Mister Mister's, anyone's. Anything sketchy—"

Jamie cleared his throat. "I'm sure the people who work here go through extensive background checks."

Locke glared at him and Jamie looked away.

"Sorry," he said. "If I have a better idea, I'll be sure to let you know."

"I don't want to know so much about their background," Locke addressed Rudy again. He was sitting next to Vince, his shoulder touching him and his gaze on Locke's eyes. "Just anything weird that may have happened lately, sick leave, I don't know. Anything. As we all know, personal tragedies are a good catalyst for turning to villainy. Start with their names. If anything comes up, let me know. Ace should go with you. You can look inside all the other rooms in the admin building while Rudy finishes up, can't you?"

"Yup," Ace replied. "No problem."

"Maybe there's something in Mister Mister's office we missed at his apartment," Rudy said. "I can start there."

"Great, start with that," Locke said. "Bray, you're good at navigation and you can always cover yourself with fog, so I need you to start looking for Mister Mister in any places where we might have missed him. The woods, anywhere. Mickey will let you know where the security guys are so you can avoid them."

Bray sighed. "Can I take Ariel?"

Locke shook his head. "No, sorry," he said. "I need him for something else. You're with Cass."

"Cass? Oh, great, yeah, give me the urbanite," Bray replied, rolling his eyes. "I have to be sneaky while city boy there wonders why he can't get his phone on the complimentary Wi-Fi."

Cass rolled his eyes. His long lashes were sticking to each other from the mascara he hadn't taken off. "They're wearing steel toed work boots," he said. "And there's gotta be metal in their helmets. You might be better off with me than you are with Ariel."

"Speaking of," Locke said, turning to his best friend. "You're going back to his place. You know him better than all of us do—"

"Except Mickey," Ariel said with a grin.

Locke ignored him. "So I need you to go back there, check his drawers, his medicine cabinet, his books. Anything out of the ordinary, let me know ASAP. Jamie, go with him."

Jamie didn't say anything. Ariel might have been Mister Mister's fan, but Jamie was the only one who could read his mind.

"BJ, Vince and I will check the perimeter, too," he said to Bray. "Vince's power can come in handy if we run into one of the security guys. And BJ, well, he can help."

He didn't have to say anything else.

"Let's go, guys," Locke said, standing up. "Go to your cabins, get some granola bars or whatever, and some jackets. We don't know how long we'll be out there. Make sure you have everyone's number."

Everyone looked at him, saying nothing.

"And remember that defending yourself is not a crime," he finally added. "You're a superhero. That's what your powers are for."

"Should we meet back here in, I don't know. Four hours?" Vince asked.

Locke shook his head. "As long as we're staying in constant communication with our phones, it might not be a good idea to be all together."

"Not that great of an idea to split up, either," Royce mumbled, but he didn't try to stop the group from dispersing.

When it was just the three of them, it was BJ who broke the heavy silence left behind. "Let's go."

IT TOOK THEM longer than Vince expected to even *find* "the perimeter." It was probably not obvious for good reasons. The first being wanting it difficult to find, the second so bad guys would be caught before they realized they'd crossed it. He couldn't think of more, but those two seemed pretty good.

The perimeter was actually a series of cameras, B-movie worthy pit traps and trip wires, and a laser system Vince was sure he saw in an Indiana Jones movie he'd watched with his mother. They'd have walked right into it if Locke hadn't been flashing random bursts of his power ahead of them.

Once they found it, another thing became obvious. After an hour more of thrashing through underbrush and stumbling over tree roots, there was no way in hell the three of them were going to be able to check the entire perimeter in one day.

"Maybe we should split up?" BJ didn't seem to feel confident about the suggestion.

Locke immediately replied, "No. Royce wasn't wrong about splitting up being a bad idea. I mean, we didn't send anyone out alone, and we shouldn't. We won't. So no."

BJ looked relieved.

"So what *do* we do?" Vince asked. "Clearly this part of the perimeter is fine. Does that mean it all is? Do these lasers and cameras work together or independently? I mean if each section is independent, a small area could be, I dunno. Broken. Without the rest being affected?"

Locke sighed, his brow creasing into a frown. A thought must have occurred to him as his frown was replaced with a smile. "We can call Rudy and ask. He looked at all the schematics. God, I love being able to use my phone."

"This isn't a game," BJ said.

But Vince understood Locke's reaction. As Locke pulled out his phone, Vince put hand on BJ's shoulder. "It'll be okay."

BJ shrugged his arm off. "You don't fucking know that."

"No. But if it's an inside job, it's those security dudes and they're not power-gifted."

"That we know of," BJ added, his tone ominous.

Vince stared at him. "You are so depressing, dude."

Locke, who'd wandered off a few feet in order to hear, rejoined them. "Okay, this is odd. Rudy says it's both continuous and relay, whatever that means, but more importantly, he says nothing was down this morning when he was poking around. So either Smith and Jones were lying, or they fixed it, I guess, before sounding the alarm." He frowned again. "But I thought the alarm was *because* the perimeter was breached?"

"We didn't actually ask," Vince realized.

BJ groaned. "So what now, hotshot?" he said to Locke.

Vince joined in the frowning, wondering how his father could be a part of this. In order to get to the guards, it would have to be through the phones. Hadn't Mister Mister said his father had left singing messages for Mister Mister, trying to get him to reveal the camp's whereabouts?

But surely the security systems would have taken that into account. His father was no has-been villain. Pied Piper was still at the top of his game. It would depend on what Rudy found while searching personnel files, but that was a little too subtle for Pied Piper. His ego demanded everyone know when he was responsible for something.

Relief that it was most likely not his father was quickly replaced by guilt—*someone* had taken Mister Mister, and who knew what would be next? Maybe it would be better for it to be Pied Piper. At least Vince could predict his actions to a degree.

But to assume it was Pied Piper meant abandoning other courses of action. He sent a desperate look to Locke, wishing they could have just woken up normally, in each other's arms, and the most uncomfortable thing about it would have been the narrowness of the bed. They could have had a soft, sober conversation and—*stop being so selfish!*

"I'm pretty sure it's not my father. Which, unfortunately, makes this even more complicated."

"Or less," Locke offered with a smile that maybe was supposed to be reassuring.

"Which leads me to ask again," BJ said, "What do we do now?"

Locke seemed to shrink in on himself. "I'm not—I never expected to be some kind of leader. Most heroes work with local law enforcement, right? We're not a bunch of vigilantes making these kinds of decisions on our own. I—"

Vince didn't feel much like a leader either, but he did have an idea. "Mister Mister had us do all kinds of rescues. So we have about what? Fifty places we know of where somebody could be kept. Like the crevasse where we rescued that bag of rice remember, Locke?"

Locke's shoulders straightened and a thoughtful look crossed his face. "Yeah. We should get our bearings. Figure out which spot is closest to where we are now."

"And where *are* we now?" BJ asked.

AFTER A LONG day of looking around half a dozen places they thought Mister Mister could be with nothing to show for it, Locke's confidence had drained away to almost nothing. Taking charge had felt good. He had been sure they were going to find something, but everyone had checked in and no one had found a fucking thing. Even Vince, who had looked so fucking perfect and had been so sweet through the day, seemed to be getting grumpier.

Locke needed a shower. He was exhausted, his head hurt, and he was hungry. The two granola bars, the lone packet of chips, and the bag of gummy bears they'd shared had not been enough. He wanted to keep looking, but he needed to eat. They all needed to eat. BJ's negativity had petered out through the day as the exhaustion seemed to get the better of all of them. Vince hadn't been inclined to talk. There were only so many times a person could say "third time is the charm," with a huge smile on their face, after all.

Locke walked into the dining hall first, rubbing his temple and closing his eyes when he saw everyone else was already there. He wanted to go back to the showers, eat something he didn't have to make himself, and get into bed. Not that he thought he would get much sleep.

"Hey, guys." His voice was quieter than he knew it should have been, but part of him didn't want the guys to hear him. "So did anyone find anything?"

Rudy turned to him. "Nope," he said. "We didn't find anything else. I mean, don't get me wrong, I know people's credit scores and stuff now. So that'd be great to know if I was getting married to them. I'm not sure how it helps us find Mister Mister, though."

Next to him, Ace tied his long dreads up in a ponytail. "Like I told you earlier, there was nothing interesting in the admin building either. No leads. I know how everyone's doing, though, so I'm happy to tutor some of you guys."

"Shut up," Royce said, his brow furrowing. "This isn't a joke. I know you guys seem to think it's fucking hilarious but it's not."

Vince shook his head. "None of us think this is—"

"A joke?" Royce replied, raising his eyebrows, his nostrils flaring. "Yeah, you fucking do. All of you think this is a joke. You're sitting there, making cracks about people's grades and getting married, like this isn't someone's fucking life. I obviously need to remind you guys about this, but if it wasn't for Mister Mister and for Vince, about half of us wouldn't be here. We'd be dead."

They all quieted, everyone's gaze on him. Locke's heart beat in quick tempo. He wanted to say something to stop Royce from freaking out, but he had every right. They hadn't found anything. Everything Royce was saying was true.

Royce took a deep breath before he continued. Locke thought he might never stop. "You guys don't understand, but think about it. I'm just a student. That's it, I'm here with you guys, and I could have fucking killed us all with my power."

Ariel turned to look at him. "But your power is—"

"Not fully realized," Jamie replied, glaring at Ariel. "That means any villain we're after, anyone we're after, they're going to be so much more dangerous than all of us. I mean, for all we know, someone literally plucked Mister Mister from the sky. While we're sitting here making jokes, they could be hurting him or—or worse."

Rudy shook his head. "You don't understand. This place is locked up tighter than a maximum security prison."

"No, you don't understand," Royce snapped back. "If Mister Mister's not here, there's a reason for it, and I'm willing to bet the reason is he's dead."

Locke swallowed. "Come on, Royce," he said. "Let's not get carried away. Yeah, we didn't find him today, but—"

Royce scoffed. "Who made you boss, anyway? You've shown us you're no good in a crisis once already."

Locke's eyes widened. Vince glanced at him for a second, saying nothing, and Locke felt the heat in his cheeks.

"I just thought—"

"Your plans have uncovered so much," Bray said, rolling his eyes. "So far, we know Mickey was sleeping with Mister Mister and Royce probably has PTSD. Which would be totally justified if he wasn't being such a little bitch about it."

"Guys," Vince said, taking a step forward. "I know we're all tired and discouraged, but we can't keep going if we're going to—"

BJ interrupted him. "They're right, though! I mean, they're being real fucking jerkwads, but they're right. Locke may have had the best of intentions but none of his plans have yielded any real results. Of course you're going to defend him, you're so far up his ass you can't see the light."

"That's not fair," Locke protested.

"You know what isn't fair?" Bray said, standing up and walking over to him, his face so close to his own that Locke could see the wrinkles in his furrowed face. "That you seem to have decided everyone needs to listen to you. When that seems to be a huge fucking mistake."

Ariel was next to Locke so quickly Locke felt like he hadn't even blinked.

All of them were talking over each other, voices rising in volume by the second it seemed. Locke looked around, desperately seeking an escape and saw Jamie, eyes squeezed shut, hands over his ears. He looked as sick as Locke felt.

Locke walked over to him. He was about to put his hand over his shoulder when Jamie's eyes shot open. "Will all of you shut up?"

No one seemed to hear him. If anything, they grew louder. Locke was about to say something when Jamie stood up, his chair crashing backwards with a loud clatter as he slammed his fists on the dining table in front of him. "Why don't you all just shut the fuck up!"

Locke looked at him, shocked. Everyone fell silent, staring at Jamie.

Royce spoke first. "Jamie, are you all rig—"

"Shut up," Jamie said, his hands over his ears again, his eyes shut, pain evident on his face. "Shut up, shut up, shut up! You guys are so fucking loud all the time. All you ever do is argue. That's not gotten us any results, has it?"

Bray shook his head, rolling his eyes. "Hey, man. Chill. There's no need to—"

Jamie's eyes shot open. "I'm not freaking out," he said. "You would be able to tell if I was freaking out. If I were freaking out, I'd be telling everyone how insecure you are because you feel like no one at camp likes you because you're straight. You're right, no one does like you, but it's because you're a dick! Ariel feels a bit sorry for you sometimes, but you're such a bully!"

Ariel turned to look at him. "Okay, that's a little harsh—"

Jamie scoffed. "Where do I even get started with you? Royce is right about you, you think this is all a joke. You can never focus on the fact you might, you know, literally die because you decided this is what you wanted to do. You might be super strong, but the moment you see a guy wearing skinny jeans and a shirt that shows off his muscles in front of you, you become useless. Don't think Locke doesn't know you wanted to fuck Vince. By the way, he doesn't think it's fucking cute at all."

Ariel looked at Locke, who looked away from him. Before Ariel could say anything, Jamie continued spewing words.

"What is cute is how none of you are saying a fucking thing now. Because you're scared. Please, it's not like I'm saying things you don't all already know. Like, Mickey, you think you're hot shit but your powers are ridiculous. The only reason the guys here put up with you is because you know how to do shit unrelated to your powers. But no one, literally no one, cares your dad is Duke Fusion. No one can figure out why you're here in the first place!"

"Ouch," Mickey said. "Is that what you guys—"

"Leave Mickey alone, Jamie, he's just a kid," Royce started. "He—"

"Don't lie to him, Royce," Jamie said, his gaze shooting toward him. "Though, I mean, it's par for the course, isn't it?"

"Look," BJ said. "I know you're tired, Jamie, if you have a headache or—"

"Hah! A headache!" Jamie sneered. "You'd fucking love it if you could cure everyone here, wouldn't you? Because you'd be the best of all of us, the only one who takes it seriously, right? The only one who actually deserves to be here!"

When Cass spoke, his voice was quite. "'C'mon, Jamie. He didn't say—"

"He didn't have to," Jamie said. "And stop trying to defend him. He's already upset enough and it's kind of cruel to pretend you like him when you're still trying to get into Royce's pants. Still! Which, by the way, is never going to happen. Royce's partner would not be okay with it and all he does is think about them."

Ace looked at Royce, cocking his head. "I thought you were single. You're not?"

Royce shrugged.

"Oh, please," Jamie said, rolling his eyes. "It can't be that much of a surprise. You think just because you're smart you know everything about everyone here. But you don't. If you don't want to be here, you should fucking walk out. Nothing is stopping you, and I mean, you're an adult, right? At least that's what you tell yourself like, every single day."

Rudy shook his head. "That's enough. We didn't mean to—"

Jamie glared at him. "Ariel should thank his lucky stars he didn't loan you his phone when yours ran out of battery. Your crush is impairing your judgment."

Rudy looked down, his cheeks red. "I wasn't going to do anything."

Locke cleared his throat. "Rudy is right. That's enough."

Jamie's eyes narrowed. "Oh, please," he said. "You're the worst of them all. You and Vince. Hey, guess what, geniuses? The only way to work out relationship problems is to talk to each other. This will-they-won't-they shit is driving me crazy. Either get together for good or split up, but make up your fucking minds! You are obviously in love, so can't you just fucking talk to each other?"

Locke looked at Vince, who was looking away from him, his cheeks as red as Rudy's.

"Maybe," Jamie said. "If you all talked to each other instead of keeping everything to yourselves, we would have already found Mister. Maybe. I know it's a wild fucking hypothesis, but maybe we should fucking test it?"

The silence in the room was deafening, weighted with embarrassment.

Locke wasn't sure if he dare speak, but he didn't feel comfortable thinking anymore, either. It was easy to forget Jamie's powers weren't something he could turn on and off with a switch. Locke cleared his throat and said, "Okay then. What did we see that we *didn't* mention?"

Bray, not looking at anyone, said, "The boathouse is unlocked. But there's no way to leave camp from the lake, so it didn't seem important."

"The lock's electronic," Rudy said. "So it would have had to be opened by a key."

"Unless *you* opened it," Mickey suggested, his tone dark and sullen.

"He didn't," Jamie said in a curt tone. "None of us in this room had anything to do with this, so don't waste time being resentful and petty."

Vince, color still high, offered cautiously, "We checked all the places where our rescue exercises have been conducted, between all of us. Haven't we?"

"What about places we haven't yet had exercises?" Cass asked, looking at Rudy.

Rudy shook his head. "There was nothing on Mister Mister's laptop or the one in his office about future exercises."

"Isn't that kind of odd?" Ace asked.

No one was looking at Jamie. "For fuck's sake," he said, in a normal tone of voice. "It's not like I can read your minds all the time. You're just so loud, you think so damn loud."

"If he's a bomb," Ariel said, "he's already exploded. So, let's move on."

"It's late, we're all tired and hungry," BJ said. "Why don't we eat, shower and regroup at 6:00 a.m.? Locke's the only one any good in the dark and he needs food and rest as much as we do. Otherwise, we could end up \missing something."

"Jamie," Locke said. "I'm sure we'll all talk about our personal problems after we find Mister Mister and, uh, sorry?"

Jamie gave him a glare. "It's just so stupid, all you had to do was talk in the first place and I wouldn't be getting all this angst overload."

"Right, right," Locke said hastily, glancing toward Vince. He loved him? He cut his eyes toward Jamie and blushed. "Sorry."

"Whatever. Who's cooking?"

Chapter Twenty-Three

BREAKFAST DUTY HAD been decided last night, but this time of year 6:00 a.m. was still well before daylight. Mickey went off to find Agents Smith and Jones—*like those are their real names*—while someone, who was thankfully not Vince, overcooked the eggs.

The center table had Vince, Locke, and some of the other guys clustered around. "Okay, so Bray said a boat's missing—"

"I uh, didn't actually check inside. I just—"

With seven pairs of accusing eyes on him, Bray gulped and said, "I'll go do that now. But yeah, um."

Vince almost felt sorry for him. Then he felt guilty for not *actually* feeling sorry for him. He'd known what it was like to not fit in—his controlling father had made him the freak kid long before his powers manifested. If he was being honest.

"Please," Jamie said, startling him.

Was Jamie responding to his thought? Jamie wouldn't want them to all be paranoid around him. *Mister Mister. That's the priority.* "What would the significance of a missing boat be? I mean, Bray wasn't wrong. There's no way to leave camp by water." The lake did drain into a shallow creek that eventually became the Brightsand River, flowing through the city of Guilford toward the sea. Upstream from the lake was a white water nightmare all flowing the wrong way to get out of camp.

"We must be missing something. Some place we haven't checked," Locke insisted.

"Not the fire house," Royce said dryly. "I burnt it to the ground."

"Not your fault," BJ said.

Rudy said, "Mister Mister blames himself. It was in his notes," he added when Vince gave him a questioning look.

Jamie nodded. "He's not wallowing in it, though."

"So," Locke said, frowning. "We checked the ravine, the rice bag baby crevasse, the caves, the old hunting cabin root cellar."

"Come and get it while it's hot!" Ariel called from the kitchen.

Vince noticed the guys were choosing to sit as far from Jamie as possible and he was about to say something to Locke when Cass emerged from the kitchen, still wearing his hairnet and apron and sat down opposite Jamie. He offered a good-natured grin. "No hard feelings, right?"

Relieved—because he still hadn't time to process what Jamie had said, and he was afraid of angsting on Jamie by accident, though he didn't have too much angst left. Except about what might happen to Locke if Vince's father decided to... ugh, he couldn't think about that at all. He'd be able to protect Locke from his father's powers with his own; ever since his powers had emerged his one goal was to learn to block his father's powers. He wasn't sure he'd ever fully achieve that. One of his father's many disappointments was that Vince's power seemed a diluted version of Pied Piper's.

Bray came in the door and announced into the relative quiet, "A canoe is missing. I looked all around the lake perimeter with the binoculars from the boathouse and couldn't see it, so whoever took it hid it. Maybe to throw us off the trail." He said all that as he walked across the floor and helped himself to food.

Locke dropped his fork. "The watchtower."

"We didn't rescue anyone from the tower," Ariel said. "We just lost our flag."

"Yeah, but did anyone check to see if someone was there?"

"Here's the funny thing about a watchtower. You sit at the top, and you can see everyone coming," BJ said, obviously making an effort to contain his sarcasm. "If whoever took him is there, then we can't sneak up on them."

Locke nodded. "Yeah, but they can't get away before we get there."

"*If* they're there. *If* they haven't moved during the night to one of the places we already checked," Ace added, looking as glum as he sounded.

"*If* they don't have a gun to pick us off as we try to climb the tower," Bray added.

Mickey joined them. "All I could get was, the perimeter is secure. Mister Mister and whoever took him are somewhere within the perimeter. There must be some place with shelter where they're waiting for us to assume they're gone, so they can, uh, I don't know. Steal a helicopter?"

Locke shrugged.

Vince wished Jamie could have held off on his revelations. Taking charge wasn't easy and Locke had stepped up when no one else had. Now, he seemed to be hoping someone else would take over.

"At the risk of sounding irrelevant," Ariel said, "someone's been messing with the pantry inventory. Cass and I are not going to take the blame for that."

Vince rolled his eyes.

"I can go up the tower," Locke offered.

"What? No!" Vince exclaimed. "Did you hear Bray? We're not bulletproof!"

"I can bend light around me, become effectively invisible. You know that."

"And what if he's not up there?" Ace asked, though he didn't sound skeptical, just curious.

"I don't know. Maybe we can see more of the terrain from up there."

The others were nodding in thoughtful agreement.

"It might be just as lousy a plan as all my ideas were yesterday," Locke warned.

Everyone crowded around. "Tell us what to do."

Chapter Twenty-Four

DAWN WAS STILL breaking, and the guys were paddling across the lake in the three remaining canoes. They'd left the motorboat as too noisy and started early to avoid being obvious to anyone who might be in the tower. They'd all learned so much since that flag-capture exercise. It was a lot colder now, though, and unlikely to get too much warmer.

Vince was wishing he'd saved some of his clothing budget for a new winter coat. And thermal socks. "I'm not so sure it was a good idea for us all to do this," he whispered.

"Shh."

The canoes drew up to the opposite shore with minimal splashing and thrashing in the underbrush. They pulled them out of the water and tossed forest litter over them—many of the leaves had fallen already, which meant they had a lot of bright colours to hide the shape and colour of the small boats.

It also meant they'd be easier to see from the watch tower.

The plan was to surround it, from the cover of the trees, each ready to unleash their power as the need arose. BJ was to stay close to the ladder in case Mister Mister was there, hurt. Vince didn't want to think about any worst-case scenario.

He kept thinking about what Bray said, about someone up in that tower maybe targeting them with a weapon they'd never learned to counter. Could he vibrate the air fast enough to stop a bullet? Could he even react fast enough to attempt such a thing? Since he could think of no strategic reason not to, he stuck with Locke and BJ.

Locke stopped walking. "Wouldn't Jamie be able to tell if, um, who's up there?"

Without waiting for an answer—and Vince had to admit the question made him feel relieved Locke might not be going up there after all—Locke chased after Jamie, pulling him aside to whisper words Vince couldn't hear.

Locke looked grim when they rejoined Vince and BJ. "Jamie says he can't get a read on anyone up there."

"So there's no one there," Vince said, relieved. Why was Locke still looking so serious?

"Or they're wearing the same helmets as our security team."

"Mister Mister wouldn't be wearing one," BJ suggested, as nervous about this as Vince.

"If they knocked him out, uh, they might have shoved one on his head. It would make sense. If they know enough to pull this off, they have to know we have a telepath."

Vince's heart sank. It did make sense. An awful, eerie sense. "Be careful," he said to Locke.

Locke gave him a crooked smile. "Now you know how I felt, watching you run into a burning building."

Vince yanked Locke into a tight embrace and kissed him hard. "Be careful," he repeated.

"Oh please," BJ said. "This is so not the time."

Vince released Locke as Locke said, "I will."

Locke gathered the rosy glow of dawn around him and was gone.

ONCE HE STARTED to climb the ladder, Locke felt his nerves fall away. This was something that had to be done, and he was the one who could do it. He had no time for nerves to get in the way of his judgement. When he was about halfway there, he looked down for a second. Vince was looking up the tower, shielding his eyes with his hand. He seemed so nervous, it was probably unkind to keep him waiting.

The sooner he got back down there, the sooner he'd be able to talk to him. They needed to talk.

He looked back at the ladder and kept climbing. If Mister Mister was there and he was knocked out, they'd have to take him down. Ariel's super strength would come in handy again, since Locke didn't feel comfortable with throwing a man who was twice his size and seemed to be built entirely of muscle over his shoulder, especially with Vince looking up at him and worrying. If Mister Mister was up there and hurt....

He couldn't think about that. He was almost at the top of the tower, which was a good thing, because his arms and his legs were aching. Coming up was a tough climb. He wondered how the men in black had done it, if they had done it, but the longer he kept climbing, the more it seemed like it was impossible.

He hoisted himself up onto the floor of the tower, trying his best to be quiet as he did so. If someone was there guarding Mister Mister, Locke would not be in any state to fight them. All his muscles ached and he was starting to get a headache. Making himself invisible was mentally taxing and especially difficult when he was doing something physical. There was also the whole not getting shot thing, that seemed pretty important. He wondered if he had enough energy to shine a light into the inside of the tower, because it was still kind of dark up there, but he decided not to risk it. Instead, he took what he hoped was a quiet deep breath and looked around.

There was a thick brown blanket on the floor next to a crumpled sleeping bag. Locke's brain couldn't make sense of what he was seeing at first. A small single burner propane stove was overturned, and a plate of food had been spilled. He released the light around him as it was obvious no one was there, now.

Unlike Mister Mister's apartment, it looked very much like a struggle had happened. Locke wasn't going to trust his own on judgement on that. He sent a text to all the guys he had numbers for and silently asked Jamie to advise the others that shit was definitely wrong.

A wave of dizziness took out his knees and he fell to the floor. "Oh god," he said faintly, staring at a bright red spot on the floor. "That's blood."

AFTER A BRIEF argument and the realization that none of them had a fucking clue what to do next, Vince suggested the only thing he could think of. "We know that even if this started as an exercise, it's more than that now."

BJ had been able to confirm the blood was Mister Mister's, which made his healing powers seem a lot more impressive. Vince didn't think their trainer would go that far for an exercise.

"We don't know who to trust," Bray said, sounding as frightened as any of them.

Vince sighed. "Locke. We should, maybe, call your father?"

"Right," Locke said. He took his phone out of his pocket and stared at it.

"I called mine," Mickey said, looking depressed. "He seemed to think this was part of the exercise. I couldn't convince him. I don't think he takes me very seriously. I guess there's no reason why he should."

Cass slung an arm across Mickey's shoulders. "You totally kick ass on the obstacle course, dude."

Vince ignored them, though if Duke Fusion wasn't going to help that made it all the more important someone else did. "Locke. Mister Mister watches us on our exercises, to make sure we don't get too far into trouble. He'd, um, if this was an exercise, he'd come out now. He might fail us all, but he wouldn't let us panic like this." Vince tried to stay as calm as his voice, but he couldn't help feeling like they were in way over their heads. And it didn't matter that they were adults. Right now, they were half trained, barely grown, and dealing with something beyond their experience, if not their ability.

"Right," Locke repeated, seeming to snap out of his daze. "Right." He swiped and tapped and put his phone on hands-free. "Dad? We're in trouble."

Although he was a disembodied voice in the room—the trainees had returned to the mess hall—the change from concerned parent to superhero on the job was evident as they listened to him ask questions about the security team and the powers the trainees could bring to bear.

"Rudy, is it? I need you to conference this call with your phone and then send me the files on the security personnel."

"I don't think that's—" Rudy began.

"I have an IAEA emergency authorization code, don't worry."

"Okay, sir. On my way."

"Wait a second. Ariel. Christ, your mother would kill me if she heard me now. Go with him. Watch his back."

"Easy," Ariel said, looking chipper again. "He's a got a very nice, uh, I mean yes, right."

Locke looked at Vince with a grin as the two left the room. Their grins vanished as Sting said, "Which one of you is Pied Piper's son?"

"Um." Vince cleared his throat and said, "That's me. Vince."

"Pick up the phone. I'd like to talk with you in private."

Without a word, Locke picked up his phone and showed Vince how to switch it. He mouthed the words "good luck" and kissed Vince's cheek.

In the hallway, Vince said, "Yes, sir?"

"What are the chances your father's responsible for this?"

"I honestly don't know. Mister Mister said the camp was secure against him and—" had he mentioned his father's girlfriend to Mister Mister?

"And?"

"His girlfriend. Chameleon."

"Oh, this just gets better and better. Does my son know about her?" Sting sounded a lot more like a parent right now.

"Yes, I told him everything he needed to know, to decide if he wanted. But she just projects illusions, and we already tested the perimeter for defenses that would detect illusions." Sort of; if Locke throwing light balls to detect lasers counted. "I think."

"You know Chameleon is the one who injured Mister Mister?"

"Um, yeah."

"And you still think there's a chance your father's not involved?"

"I, uh, don't know," Vince said, eyes burning. He didn't want to be scolded by Locke's father, like he was somehow responsible for his father's actions.

"Christ," Sting continued, almost to himself, "after what he did at Kicking Horse, I can't believe they'd let anyone associated with him near the rest of us"

Vince blinked. What was he talking about? "What's, uh," He hesitated, not sure he wanted to know. "What's Kicking Horse?"

There was a long silence on the phone. "If you really don't know, this isn't the time or place to go into it. Give the phone back to my son."

Vince walked back into the mess hall and handed Locke his phone without a word. Locke raised his eyebrows at him, but Vince said nothing. What was Kicking Horse? What was Locke's dad talking about? He probably shouldn't worry about that right then, but as he watched Locke pale while he listened to his father on the line, it was all he could think of.

Locke nodded a few times, eyes squeezed shut. "Yes. Got it. Okay."

He put his phone on hands-free again, the rest of the guys crowding around him.

"Has anyone been in touch with Camp Synergy?"

Vince glanced at BJ, who looked pale. When no one said anything, Locke finally answered. "No."

"Okay," Locke's dad replied. "We'll contact Scarlet Jade and tell her to lock down."

The trainees exchanged concerned looks with each other. BJ was the one who was looking down, his gaze locked on his fidgeting hands.

There was a long pause before Locke's dad spoke again. "Take me off speakerphone."

Locke did as he was told. He listened to his father say something else and smiled without humor. "Thank you."

He ended the call and put his phone back in the pocket of his jeans. He glanced at Vince for a second, his eyes wide, and Vince reached out to grab his hand. Locke flashed him a grateful smile.

"My pa—Sting and Null are on their way," he said, his voice loud and clear. "It'll take them a few hours to get here. We're supposed to wait, gather documentation so—"

"Hours?" Ace said. "What if something happens to Mister Mister in the meantime? Shouldn't we be out looking?"

Locke shook his head. He looked calm, but he was squeezing Vince's hand even tighter than before. "This is out of our league," he said. "Also, superheroes have to do paperwork."

"This is bullshit," Bray shouted. "We're just supposed to sit here and do paperwork?"

"We're supposed to sit here and stay safe," Locke replied. "Only for a few hours."

"Fuck this shit," Bray said, walking toward the door.

"Bray," Royce said in the voice of calm reason. "How are you going to find Mister Mister if you're hurt? Or if you are, y'know, dead?"

Jamie nodded. "He's right," he said. "We can't trust anyone out there. We never could. We have to stick together. That's the only way we are gonna be able to stay safe."

Bray swallowed, walking back to his seat and groaning as he sat down. "I hate feeling so fucking useless," he said. "So powerless."

"You're not," Vince replied, letting go of Locke's hand. "We have a map to work on."

LOCKE DIDN'T MIND calling his parents. In fact, if anything, he was grateful for the idea. It hadn't seemed real, none of it had, until BJ had climbed up and gone to inspect the blanket, even though Locke hadn't asked him to do that. He was just sitting there, doing nothing, being useless.

When he finally pulled himself together enough to climb down the ladder again, he noticed Vince was gearing up to go up to the top of the watch tower, looking like he was going to puke if he even grabbed on to the ladder.

Now that Locke knew his parents were coming, he felt a lot better. At least about Mister Mister. As the clock ticked down, Locke realized this would be the first time his dad had ever met Vince, who was busy with Bray but still looked a little bit scared whenever Locke caught his eyes.

They would not get a chance to talk once his parents arrived. Locke had never seen them at work, but he had heard plenty about it, and to say they took it seriously would almost feel like an understatement. If he wanted to talk to Vince, he would have to do it then.

He walked up to him and brushed his shoulder. "Hey," he said. "Do you have a minute to talk?"

Bray looked up from the map, glaring at him. "Really? This is hardly the time."

Locke smiled at him. "C'mon," he said. "You've been hard at work too. Take a break."

Bray rolled his eyes, but he put the pen down on top of the orientation brochure they had been using to mark the spots they had already checked.

When Locke noticed a few of the guys were scowling at him, he tried to flash them a smile.

"We won't be long," he said, trying his best to sound cheerful despite the looks everyone was giving him.

"Won't even leave the building," Vince added, smiling at him. Locke took a second to look at him. Vince was wearing dark-blue jeans ripped at the knees, a blue shirt and the gray hoodie he always wore. It was the kind of thing he always wore, a kind of normal, down-to-earth outfit Locke had never really taken the time to appreciate. It made his face look even better, with his big brown eyes and beautiful lips, and for a moment, Locke considered talking about what Jamie had said.

"I'll stand guard by the door," Ariel said, winking at Locke. He was pretty sure he just wanted to overhear the conversation between him and Vince, but it didn't matter. He appreciated the gesture all the same.

Vince got to his feet, hooked his arm around Locke's, and they walked to the hallway together.

Ariel walked past them, a smile on his face. "Don't get too dirty," he said. "I can still hear you guys from the outside."

Neither one of them said anything. When Locke was about to push the doors to the mess hall open, Ariel turned back and grinned. "On second thought, please get as dirty as you want."

With that, he turned on his heels and walked out the double-doors.

"He knows how to make an exit," Vince said, smiling. He hugged himself, his expression sobering. "Maybe he doesn't get that we're in danger."

"He knows how serious the situation is," Locke said, trying to swallow down the knot in his throat. "I think he's just trying to be a good friend."

Vince's smile widened. Locke took a deep breath. "I need to tell you something."

"Is everything okay?" Vince asked, cocking his head and frowning.

"Yes," Locke replied, grabbing Vince's hands and stepping closer to him. "This isn't about that, if that's what you're talking about. I just—I made a stupid decision once before because I chose not to talk to you. I'm not doing that again."

Vince watched him, saying nothing.

"You should know this." he said, his gaze darting around as he scanned the hallway for anyone who might have slipped out of the mess hall. He leaned in close to Vince as he whispered, "You know my dad is Sting, but I don't think I've told you my mom is Null. So if they act weird, that's why."

Vince's eyes widened as Locke moved away from him. "Oh," he said. "Okay."

"Also," Locke added, "I'm pretty sure they don't know we're together."

"What?"

"I just—okay, my dad talked to me, and then I freaked out a little bit, okay?" Locke answered without taking a breath. "I didn't know if you were going to take me back and I just haven't had a chance to talk to either one of them about you yet."

Locke couldn't be sure, but he thought Vince looked like he was about to cry all of a sudden. He turned away from Locke and licked his lips, letting go of his hands at the same time. "So do you want to act as if nothing is going on when they are here? I'm still Pied Piper's son and if—"

"What? No!" Locke said, his jaw dropping open. "No. Absolutely not. I'm not ashamed of you, Vince Silva."

Locke grabbed his hands again and brought them up to his mouth, pressing soft kisses on them. Vince smiled at him, his cheeks reddening as his eyes shone.

"I just wanted to you to know because I didn't think it would be fair to spring that on you without warning," he said. "And I, um, fuck. Vince, what Ja—"

"Sorry," Locke's father's said. Locke didn't think he sounded sorry at all. "Are we interrupting?"

Vince instantly let go of Locke's hands as they both turned to look at him. His mother was standing next to him, wearing her costume, saying nothing. The upper part of her face was obscured by a silver mask but Locke could see she was smiling.

Ariel ran in behind them. "Incoming!"

Vince shook his head. Locke's mom started to laugh.

Chapter Twenty-Five

VINCE WASN'T SURE how he was supposed to react to meeting his boyfriend's parents, especially not when they were practicing superheroes, who already seemed to hate him.

At least Locke's dad did.

Then again, this wasn't the right time to be worried about that.

Vince watched as the rest of the trainees gathered around the only adults in superhero costumes. Locke lagged behind, staying with him and flashing him a wan smile that told Vince nothing. He was grateful Locke had taken the time to reassure him despite the tense situation, but he knew talking to him would have to wait.

Vince tried to swallow down the knot in his throat and took a step forward as he listened to what Sting was saying.

"First of all," he said. "Let me start by saying how well you've done. We already have so much intel because of everything you have done so far. I also want to commend you for reaching out for help. One of the most important things you can learn in this job is that you don't have to act alone. There's nothing shameful about asking for help. It was the right thing to do."

The guys looked at each other, some with smiles on their faces. Mister Mister had told them a time or two, but it sounded better from an active superhero. Vince wondered if Sting had practiced this speech on the way there, when he was in the plane. Even then, he had to admit Sting's speech made him feel less helpless.

When Null spoke, her voice was loud and clear. "Did you finish the map?"

"Yes," Bray said. He handed her the orientation brochure he and Vince had been working on and she smiled at Bray. She had a pretty smile. Vince could tell Locke took after his mother, even though half her face was covered.

Null and Sting were quiet for a few seconds as they both looked at the map.

"Have you been to the ruins?" Sting finally asked, breaking the silence. It was the first time all of the trainees had been quiet, at least ever since Jamie had freaked out and blurted out everyone's thoughts.

"What ruins?" Locke said. "There are no ruins around here."

Null and Sting exchanged a brief look. "Has Mister Mister ever taken you into the woods?"

"We've been to the woods lots of times," Locke said. "We've done a bunch of exercises and—"

"But you've never seen the ruins," Null said.

"There are no ruins on the map," Vince replied when it seemed like no one else was going to say anything.

"That's gotta be where he's keeping him," Sting said.

Null nodded. "Okay, everybody. Listen up," she said as she grabbed something out of the canvas bag hanging off her shoulder. "We studied everyone's power on the way here. We're going to split up into two teams. The rescue team is coming with us, the support team will stay here. It's very important you stay here and stay safe if you're part of the support team. Do you understand?"

Vince heard murmurs of assent coming from some of the other guys. The rest just kept watching her. She took out a ziplock bag and threw it on the table in front of her.

"You're going to wear these ear plugs at all times," Sting said. "In case Pied Piper is involved."

He said it very matter-of-factly while he looked at all of them, but Vince was sure Sting's gaze lingered on his face. As each one of the trainees stepped up to take their pair of earplugs, Vince could feel the knot in his throat growing. Sting and Null seemed convinced Pied Piper was the instigator. Vince had been working to counteract the effects of his father's powers since he found out his own power was similar, but he had always gone out of his way to avoid a confrontation with him.

Now he was going to have to save Mister Mister from him.

"Car—Locke, you're part of the rescue team," Sting started. "Brayden Collins, BJ Cockburn, Royce Bailey, you're with us, too."

"Sir," Vince said, clearing his throat and walking closer to where Sting and Null were. "I think I would be of use with the rescue team."

Sting's eyes narrowed. "Vince Silva," he said, his voice hard. "You're the person I spoke to on the phone."

"Yes, sir," Vince replied. He was glad he didn't sound as scared as he felt. "Ever since my power manifested, I've been working on a song that counters my father's voice. I would be an asset when it comes to rescuing Mister Mister, I don't just know how to counteract Pied Piper, I know how he thinks."

"It would be better for you to remain here," Sting said. "The support team needs to be defended, in case anything happens."

Vince nodded, trying not to sigh. He needed to be there. He needed to make sure Locke was safe.

"I understand," he replied. He tried to think of any argument that would make sense, would make it so he was useful as part of the rescue team. He frowned as it finally clicked. "Pied Piper is my father, though. I might not be able to convince him of anything, but I could be the missing puzzle piece that throws him off."

Vince didn't doubt his father would hurt him if he felt it was necessary, but maybe he'd hesitate a little. Long enough. Sting frowned but said nothing.

"Ariel and I can stand guard here," Jamie said. "I can hear people's thoughts if they're coming and Ariel can kick their ass. Plus, we have the earplugs. We're not leaving the mess hall until you come back anyway."

Vince flashed him a grateful smile. Sting and Null exchanged another look for a second. Null inclined her head an imperceptible degree, and Sting rolled his eyes.

"Fine," he said, crossing his arms and setting his gaze straight on Vince. "Silva, you're with us."

"As far as the support team, your job is to keep in touch with us. You're how we contact the outside world if things get crazy. You need to start looking into the records Rudy pulled up and find how this could have happened. I know you may have already done this, to an extent," Null said. "But not every villain tells you how they managed to do something and it's obvious something needs to change at Camp Hologram."

MUCH OF THE woods surrounding the camp and lake were not as densely thicketed as they had initially seemed to a bunch of trainees who at the most might be suburbanites. The direction in which Sting strode with such confidence was different—it was evident no one had come this way in years. Or so it would have seemed. Null knelt in the tangle of thorny underbrush and pulled free a piece of cloth. "Anyone recognize this?"

They all did. It was a ragged scrap of Mister Mister's habitual camouflage pants. He must have been yanked with a great deal of force through the undergrowth for that tough fabric to tear. Or he might have ripped it himself to leave a clue, Vince considered. Too bad none of them had found it. *We had no reason to look here.*

"Mister Mister," Bray said.

Null and Sting exchanged significant looks. "Not a word from here on in," Sting said.

Vince's heartbeat quickened. The group was covered by fog and Vince didn't think they would be easy to spot, but even being as quiet as they were, his father would probably be able to hear their footsteps coming from a mile away.

He wondered what had happened to Mister Mister. If only he'd never met with his dad. Locke squeezed his hand and interrupted his train of thought. They met each other's gaze, and while Locke's smile didn't strike Vince as particularly sincere, he appreciated it all the same.

Sting glanced at them for just a second, and Locke let go of his hand to walk slightly ahead of him. He was still covered by Bray's fog, and since Vince could see him, he felt a slight sense of relief.

Sting raised his hand as the trees thinned out before them. Null turned to Bray and lifted her hand, palm up, to tell him to increase the fog and send it forward.

Vince sidled closer, until he was in a position to push Locke back or down, whatever it might take. He could see through Bray's creeping mist the broken shapes of a brick foundation. Bright colored leaf litter, dulled only a little by the mist, kept it from looking too dreary.

A glance at the trees showed that anyone moving across that expanse had nothing to hide under. Vince knew Locke had noticed that, too. The idiot was going to—

He didn't even complete the thought before Locke bent the light around him and disappeared. "Locke!" he hissed. What did he expect to do once he got there?

Null grabbed him—how did she know where he was?—and Locke let his power go. "I can nullify your power," she said in a voice so low Vince almost missed it.

"Locke, you can cover the three of us," Vince whispered. He, Locke, and Null, they could—

"No," Sting said with a tone of finality, glaring at Vince.

Right. Vince considered himself a hero-in-training. Sting considered him a potential enemy.

A low moaning cut through the tension. Vince would keep them all safe.

He pushed past the older heroes and rolled across the clearing. Yes—there was Mister Mister. He was bound and unconscious, blood crusted across the side of his face Vince could see. He could just put Mister in a fireman's carry and get him back to the safety of the trees. Then Sting and Null could work on finding his father or whoever was behind this.

Vince frowned. Not his father. His father would have just sung Mister Mister into whatever he wanted—an informant, or an accomplice. Pied Piper would not resort to brute force. Would he?

Bray's fog grew thicker and Vince climbed over the remains of the wall. What he hadn't seen, between the fallen leaves and the curling mist, was the bear trap.

There was a loud snap that echoed through the clearing, accompanied by the most intense pain Vince had ever felt. It consumed him from the inside out until nothing was left but blackness.

LOCKE SHARED HIS parents' stunned disbelief when Vince darted forward. It reminded him of the way he'd rushed into the fire. Like then, he was paralyzed and only able to stare as Vince dropped for cover and peered over the crumbling foundation wall.

Ignoring his father's soft curses, Locke's heart lodged in his throat as Vince pushed himself over the wall. The resounding snap and Vince's blood-curdling scream had Locke lunging forward, only to freeze once more as his father grabbed his shoulder.

Vince's scream had brought someone else out. Chameleon's green suit was unmistakeable even through Bray's fog. It was bright and flared from the elbows and knees just enough to be distinctive while allowing her to easily assume someone else's appearance. If she could touch them.

Like his mother, Chameleon's power relied on touching. Chameleon knelt, presumably to check on Vince. She began to talk, which meant Vince must still be alive, thank god. Locke glanced at BJ, whose hands were clenched into fists at his sides, like he, too, wanted to run out there.

"This is what we're going to do," Sting said in a low, urgent voice. "Collins, keep up the fog, it's perfect to muffle our approach. Bailey, I assume you can throw fireballs? Keep an eye on us and don't hesitate to take your shot. Chameleon is worse than you might know, and she'll live. Cockburn—"

"I should go with you," BJ said through clenched teeth.

"No," Null said, her tone gentle.

"You're the healer," Sting explained. "If you get hurt, then what?"

BJ nodded almost instantly, but he didn't look any less concerned.

"Son, I'm sorry I ever thought your power was less than useful," Sting said, and Locke nodded. He pulled the light around them and his mother moved closer.

"I don't want to put you in danger," Locke said.

"Fuck off," Null said. "This is my job."

Sting gave Locke a brief smile. "You get used to that."

Locke returned a smile of equal brevity and expanded the light bending field to include all three of them. This could be reality, if he and Vince were to end up in the same city, working as a team. Always a loved one in danger. He had a whole new respect for his father.

While Chameleon continued to talk and gesture at Vince, or maybe Mister Mister or both, the three of them strode across the open field. Bray's fog muffled the sounds of the crackling leaves underfoot, but it also swirled as they passed through. If he focussed on it, Locke could see Bray was trying to compensate for that.

His father jumped the broken wall, leaving Locke's envelope of bent light.

"Sting!" Chameleon exclaimed. "You weren't—! What are you doing here?" She glared in Locke's general direction. "With your spawn, I guess. Didn't expect the kids to go snivelling to daddy."

Locke could only stare at Vince, whose leg seemed to be mangled up to his hip in sharp, steel teeth. He lay so still. So alarmingly still. Once more he made a move toward him, this time stopped by his mother's grip. She motioned them to go around, behind Chameleon.

"It's a smart, adult thing to know when one is out of one's depth," Sting said. "Where's your boyfriend?"

"Please," Chameleon retorted with scorn. "Do you think Pied Piper's been biding his time as a mild-mannered bank robber since Kicking Horse just to disrupt a kids' camp?"

"You gonna let his kid bleed out?"

Locke's breath was coming in short shallow gasps, trying to get his emotions under control and focus on the problem.

"Be doing him a favor, really. Boy thinks he can be a hero," Chameleon sneered. "You know how futile that is, right Sting? Sins of the fathers? Isn't that your standard lecture? I don't even know why you came. I know you publically condemned Mister Mister for his unwise associations." She prodded Mister Mister with the toe of her heavy green boot. "He is a fool, though."

"He was young and—"

"Where's your idiot son?" Chameleon asked, voice sharp as a knife.

"Why? Light manipulation is his power. It's almost as useless as yours. He can't hurt you."

Did his father really believe that? Locke and Null were behind Chameleon now, as close as Locke dared to go. His mother took two big strides out of his light envelope and said, "I can, though."

Locke's breath caught as his mother and Chameleon struggled, and for a moment there were two Nulls, but he ran to Vince's side and grabbed his hand. He had a pulse. Thank god.

Chameleon's hands were bound behind her with zip ties Locke never wanted to know where his mother hid. BJ and the others joined them. Sting had them organize a tight perimeter and used a small transmitter to signal the helicopter that had delivered him and Null.

Vince helped BJ pry the trap open. Null knelt to help pull him free, but Sting stopped her. "I don't want you to accidentally neutralize his gift."

"You're sleeping on the sofa for a week for that remark," she said, and then Vince was lying next to Mister Mister and BJ was doing his laying on of hands thing.

VINCE WOKE UP in a tiny white hospital room, surrounded by machines and calmer than he'd ever felt, which had to do with the medications he was given, as the doctor told him how lucky he was. Both the tibia and the fibula on his right leg were fractured, but it wasn't too bad, and he wouldn't need surgery.

He would just have to wear a cast for a couple of months and he would need to go to physical therapy. Vince was vaguely aware of the pain he had felt and he was surprised the damage hadn't been more extensive. He was sure BJ had something to do with it. He would have to thank him when he went back to camp.

Mister Mister had come to visit him once, and the next day, they were already leaving. He'd been too doped up the first time to understand what Mister Mister was telling him—except everyone was fine and Chameleon had been captured. Vince was happy that Mister wasn't just alive, he seemed to have made a full recovery.

The next time he saw Mister Mister at the hospital was when he came to pick Vince up. The helicopter ride was silent. Vince couldn't be sure because the camp trainer wasn't the kind of man who opened up about his feelings, but he thought Mister Mister seemed upset. Vince was too preoccupied thinking of Locke to worry about him too much, however.

Vince didn't have his phone—he'd left it in the mess hall before the search party had gone out—and he was concerned Locke didn't know how he was doing. The rest of the camp was waiting for them and cheered when Mister Mister helped him out and handed him his crutches.

"Into the lecture hall with you. We'll have a little chat and the rest of the day is free. Tomorrow we're back to it," Mister Mister ordered, sounding no less gruff than he ever did. He hung back a bit until he saw Locke come over, and then he just nodded.

Locke brandished Vince's phone with a grin. Vince, both hands on his crutches, said, "Thanks."

"I'll put it in your pocket," Locke said, radiating innocence.

Vince caught his breath as Locke put his arms carefully around Vince's waist, sliding the phone into his back pocket. "I don't know whether to be mad at you for being stupid and getting hurt or being impressed at how brave you were," he said before kissing Vince's neck just below the ear.

"Um, I vote for brave?"

"Fucking stupid brave. I thought—you were lying so still, there was so much blood." He squeezed Vince tight and let go when Mister Mister cleared his throat.

Locke waited as Vince didn't quite stumble into the lecture hall, closing the door behind himself when he followed Vince in.

The relief the trainees felt upon finding both Mister Mister and Vince safe was beginning to fade into a mix of anger and fear—for having gone through Mister Mister's private quarters, including his bedroom and all his electronic devices. It was a heady mix of emotions that had Vince checking Jamie out. If he could feel it, it must be awful for their resident telepath. But Jamie was wearing one of the TP blocking helmets, which to be honest, Vince had never imagined could be used to protect a telepath, only protect one *from* a telepath. Jamie looked more relaxed than he had in ages though, so it had to be working.

Mister Mister no doubt knew the full extent of their snooping. He moved to the front of the lecture hall, wearing a sleeveless olive tee and camouflage cargo pants, as usual. Vince wondered if he had taken them to the hospital, since he hadn't stopped at his apartment.

Vince leaned back against the wall of the lecture hall and clasped Locke's hand. Locke was standing next to him and Mister Mister didn't seem to care that neither one of them attempted to sit down.

Ariel was on Locke's other side, the three of them drawing on the bonds of love and friendship for their strength.

Pleased with the idea, Vince wondered if that should be part of his graduation speech. *Yeah, like you're gonna be valedictorian.* The thought was followed by how proud his mother would be that he graduated, and *that* thought had him wondering if she would even be able to attend. Now that his father and his girlfriend knew where he was, his mother showing up at camp could only end the peace Vince hoped she'd found.

Finding Mister Mister safe had made Vince feel better, but that had stopped when he'd found it was Chameleon behind Mister Mister's kidnapping. He couldn't help but wonder what else his father had planned—neither him nor Chameleon ever worked alone. The thought was enough to get his heart pounding again.

They'd gotten lucky this time, but they hadn't been alone. Vince had been so foolish to think his father had done nothing except test the camp's communications security.

"You're so in your head," Locke said in his ear, so close the warmth of his breath tickled. It very effectively brought Vince back to the here and now.

"Yeah, sorry. It all seems kind of surreal."

"Tell me about it," Locke agreed with a shake of his head.

Mister Mister raised his arms for silence, and the guys all quieted, giving him their attention. "I hope this scared you. It should have. It scared all of us," he said. "What you're learning here is going to have real world applications where a happy ending isn't always guaranteed, and a failure is going be a lot more drastic than an abandoned bag of rice. This started out as an exercise, but the camp's security was compromised and we were all in danger. Before we get back to business as usual, I want to say I'm proud of all of you. Realizing the situation was a lot more serious than you thought and calling for help, you probably saved my life. So thank you."

He looked away and cleared his throat before he started speaking again.

"I know some of you are feeling a little nervous for having tossed my place and rifled my computer, but don't." He grinned at them. "The important stuff was on the laptop I had with me. I expected you to look there; I'd be pissed if you didn't."

There was a murmur of relief across the room.

"As with your other exercises, I expect a full analysis from each of you. By Friday."

Another murmur, this one of protest, began to build, but Mister Mister forestalled it with a single raised palm. "If you haven't noticed, those analysis exercises help you strategize. I'm sure everyone here appreciates how important that is. Any questions?"

Ariel raised his hand, and both Vince and Locke turned their heads to stare at him. "Are you going to sign the pantry inventory for the food you took? Because our trainer is a real hard ass when it comes to that inventory."

Locke looked at Vince, rolling his eyes, and the two of them grinned as the other guys chuckled or laughed outright.

Even Mister Mister smiled faintly. "Yes, yes, of course. Good job noticing."

Chapter Twenty-Six

OVER THE NEXT three weeks, Mister Mister introduced the trainees to Camp Hologram's security system. It seemed like they walked every inch of the perimeter, learning exactly what measures were in place. "It's been the habit to leave the security in the background; but I think it's better you all know what's in place and how it's supposed to work." Mister Mister glanced at them. "So it's easier to tell an exercise from a genuine emergency."

"Why so many trip wires and pit traps?" Rudy asked. "They seem, well, primitive."

"Sometimes it's the simplest things that are the most effective. If you think about it, Chameleon's powers don't seem like much, but they were effective enough to get around our high tech." Mister's tone did not invite further inquiry along those lines.

Vince and Locke took some time in the aftermath of the incident to finally talk it all out. Locke acknowledged he'd let his father's belief and expectations dictate his behavior and he'd never believed Vince was a villain. "I really am sorry."

"I know. I understand." Vince did understand, once he'd been able to look at the situation without feeling hurt and rejected. Locke still seemed to feel a little guilty, even though Vince had let his crutches drop to give Locke a tight, forgiving hug.

Neither of them, however, addressed Jamie's words about being in love.

In no time, it seemed, the Thanksgiving holiday loomed. Thanks to BJ, Vince would soon be walking around on his own. He and Locke would sneak out to the lake or obstacle course to be alone, but they still often slept together in the narrow bottom bunk.

For most of the trainees, Thanksgiving would be the first time going home since they'd arrived in August. Sure, many of them had had their family come to Guilford this weekend or that, but none of them had been home.

Locke was excited, and so was Ariel—they had a long history of shared holidays, and both were looking forward to going home.

Vince just smiled and tried to be happy for them. His home was stuffed into his locker in Cabin One. He knew he should talk to Mister Mister about staying at Camp over the long weekend and soon. Before it was too late and he found himself at some no-tell motel in Guilford—all he could afford. He told himself it wouldn't be bad. He'd have the mess hall to himself and could buy one of those chickens-in-a-can with canned gravy and cranberry jelly and canned beans. Instant mashed potatoes. It would be his first independent meal.

Yeah, it sounded pretty good when he thought of it that way.

They were out freezing their asses off on the obstacle course while Vince watched. An early frost had turned the soft, often muddy ground into a sharp obstacle of its own and the guys were wincing as they dug their elbows into it to crawl under the low hanging barbed wire above them.

Vince had come to like the obstacle course, in an abstract way. He almost missed it. He saw it as representing the things they'd likely encounter running down a suspect in an urban environment. Which was good, because so far, all their other training had been in the woods and included things like negotiating that horrible rope bridge, which he hoped never to encounter in an urban setting.

He started as his name was announced over the seldom used loudspeakers— "Silva, come to the office, on the double."

"Oooo, Vince is in trouble," Ace teased.

"Maybe Mister is tired of Mickey and wants fresh meat."

"God, Bray, your sense of humour is the worst. Just shut up, okay?"

Vince ignored the guys, though their comments made him smile. He hobbled toward the administration building. Walking on crutches was still weird, but BJ assured him he'd be done with it by the holiday. "I'll be inside where it's warm," he called over his shoulder.

Inside, he paused for a breath, happy to not see it hanging in the air as he exhaled. What did Mister Mister want with him? "On the double" didn't mean "take your time," so Vince tried to hop to the office as quickly as he could and tapped on the open door.

Mister looked up from his desk. "Your father wants to speak to you." He held out the landline handset. "You want some privacy?"

Vince shook his head. He didn't know what his father wanted, but having some kind of back-up seemed like a good idea. He gestured for Mister to put it on speaker or record it. When Mister Mister nodded, Vince said, "Hey, Dad," in a falsely cheerful tone.

"Vincent," his father returned in the same tone. "I'm sorry to drag you away from your training, but I seem to have lost your cell phone number."

This phone had a security measure added to it that blocked his father's power. A cell phone wouldn't. "That's okay, Dad, because I lost my cell phone." Which was true enough, even though it had been replaced. "What's up? Are you sure you should be calling here?"

"Please, dear boy. You don't think *I* had anything to do with that? Your stepmother acted on her own—you must know I'd never let any harm come to you." Vince looked at Mister Mister, who returned his gaze steadily, without expression.

Before Vince could answer, his father continued on cheerfully, "But that's not why I'm calling. I realized the holiday was coming up and thought how nice it would be if you invited your new boyfriend to come home with you. You could show off where you grew up, fill him in on all the family stories." His father hesitated and then added in a sing-song voice, "I'll make my famous pie. Your mother married me for my pie."

Vince couldn't help but smile. There were two stories that showed his father in a light Vince had never known—courting his mother with pie, instead of using his powers, and using his powers to ease her pain during labour when Vince was born. Vince had spent many hours wishing he'd been able to know that man. "That is pretty tempting, Dad, but we've kind of made other plans." Also true, although not together.

There was an ominous silence at the other end of the line, and Vince crooked his head to reassure himself Mister Mister was still there. His father spoke again, sounding far too casual as he asked, "Are you spending Thanksgiving with your mother? If you tell me where she is, I can send a pie over. It won't be as nice as seeing you and your dear friend, but I understand, after what Rebecca did."

Prickles chased down Vince's spine, and he was glad his mother hadn't told him where she was. Pied Piper might not be able to use his power on this phone line, but he had an uncanny knack for knowing a lie when he heard one. "Mom? No. I don't even know where she is."

"Ah, so she's abandoned us both. I'm so sorry, dear boy." After a pause, he added, "Perhaps in light of that, you'll reconsider? After all, we men must stick together. Since I'll be alone this weekend."

Vince struggled to find something to say that wouldn't antagonize his father into something. "Yeah, I know. But it's only a long weekend, Dad, and Locke is really eager to go home, you know. After what happened. Maybe another time?"

"Given who his father is, I'm rather surprised he invited you to stay the weekend."

Shit. How could he reply without a lie? Of course his dad would have found out who Locke's father was, after meeting him at the Roehampton in Guilford. He sent a silent plea to Mister Mister.

Mister nodded and said with uncharacteristic sharpness, "Wrap it up, Silva. This isn't the country club."

"I gotta go, Dad. I'll call you later." Damn, now he'd have to do that. Didn't say how much later, though. He pressed the button that cut the call and handed the receiver back to Mister Mister. "Thanks, Mister Mister."

"Just get back to it," he said in a gruff voice.

LOCK FINALLY CAUGHT up to Vince at lunch time. "Hey." He glanced around the room and decided it was safe to plant a swift kiss to Vince's cheek. "What was the deal in the principal's office? Everything okay?"

Vince's cheeks were ruddy from the kiss—he was adorable when he blushed. "Yeah, just my dad."

"Oh."

They were shuffling through the line toward the hot table, trays in hand. If Vince wasn't going to volunteer more, Locke had to ask. They'd had enough problems caused by simply not talking. "What did he want?"

Vince sighed. "He *said* he wanted to 'invite' us to spend Thanksgiving with him."

"Us?"

Vince gave him a strange look. "Yeah. You and me. Us."

Locke realized with a guilty start that he'd been so looking forward to going home, he hadn't thought about what Vince was doing for the holidays. He looked down at his tray, thinking hard. It hadn't occurred to him to invite Vince home, not with his father's stance on good and evil being "in the blood" and what he thought of as The Incident.

"What did you tell him?" he finally asked Vince.

"I said no, obviously. I mean, he didn't try to pretend he didn't know what happened. He just said Chameleon acted alone. Don't worry; I'm not going to let him near you."

"I wasn't worried about that," Locke said, defensive even though Vince had sounded merely matter of fact. "Wait, where *are* you going for the weekend, then? Your mom's?"

Vince shook his head. "I don't know where my mother is."

"What?" Locke just about dropped his tray. "Do we need to call someone, send out a search party—?"

"No! Nothing like that. She's found a safe place where my father can't get to her. I can't see her, as long as Dad knows where I am."

"Oh. Okay." Locke couldn't imagine what a guy would want with an ex if he'd already moved on to another relationship. He almost missed Vince's next words; they were spoken so quietly.

"I figured I'd stay here."

Locke started filling his plate with the dubious offerings on the hot table. "I feel like such a dick that it never occurred to me to ask before. But staying here by yourself is not acceptable. I'm going to call my folks and see if you can come home with me." He grinned, as if he wasn't a bundle of nerves inside. He wasn't going to give Vince up just on his father's disapproval. Thanksgiving was the perfect time for his dad to start getting used to the idea.

AFTER EVERYONE HAD gone inside, Locke stood outside Cabin One, hugging himself and seeing his breath in front of him. He was nervous about talking to his father, but he knew it needed to happen as soon as possible. If his father said no, he needed time to convince him. Or maybe he would spend Thanksgiving with Vince at camp.

He pressed his phone to his ear and waited. His father picked up on the second ring. "Is something wrong?"

"Jeez, Dad. Hi to you, too." Locke supposed he couldn't blame his father for being paranoid.

"Sorry, son," he replied. "Glad it's not an emergency. Listen, I'm glad you called, actually. You know we're looking forward to having you home, and your sister wants to make homemade peac—"

"Dad," Locke said. He was starting to lose his nerve. "There's something I need to tell you."

"Is everything okay?"

"Yes, everything's okay. Everything's great," Locke replied. "It's just—"

"Great!" his father replied. "So listen—your mother and I think it would be a good idea if you asked Victor if he'd like to spend the holiday with us."

Locke blinked. "You mean Vince?"

"You know, that's a good idea. Invite him, too."

Locke frowned at his phone. "Him *too*?"

"Too, yes," his father said slowly, as if Locke was being dull-witted. "As in also, additionally."

Locke sighed and pinched the bridge of his nose. "Dad. Please. Is this some kind of code? Because I don't know anyone named Victor."

His father chuckled. "Right. Sorry. Mister Mister."

"You want me to invite Mister Mister to Thanksgiving?" Locke replied, his eyes wide.

"That's what I just said, isn't it?" his dad said. "We have a lot to talk about."

Locke swallowed, wondering how that conversation would go. His father had invited Vince, though, and he should probably get off the phone before he changed his mind. "Okay. See you soon, Dad."

"Bye, son," he replied. "See you soon."

Chapter Twenty-Seven

THE TRIP FROM Camp Hologram to Tupewa, where Ariel and Locke lived involved a helicopter ride to Guilford—which Vince would never be comfortable with, even with Locke's arm around him—a shuttle bus to the airport, and a flight on a plane large enough that Vince didn't feel entirely terrified.

They had three seats together, and Locke insisted on being in the middle, which had Ariel teasingly asking Vince if he wanted the window seat. "Just kidding! Although with Locke between us, all the puke would go on him."

It had been weird having Mister Mister with them at first, but he was sitting across the aisle, his nose buried in a leather-bound book without any words on the cover, and he seemed to be paying little to no attention to them.

At the airport, a man in a chauffeur uniform held up a sign that read Medeiros, and Ariel, pushing the luggage cart as if it were empty, waved.

"His parents always send an armoured limo," Locke explained as he and Vince chased after Ariel and their luggage. "Dad thinks it's silly, but Mom thinks it's safer, and obviously, Ariel loves the celebrity treatment."

In the limo, Locke once again made certain he was between Ariel and Vince and Vince wondered if it was just him finding it a bit odd. Or was it because of what Jamie had said? As if reading his mind, Ariel finally said, "What do you think I'd do, Locke, jump his bones in front of you? Geez, what kind of friend do you think I am?"

Locke blushed and Vince laughed.

"It's not like he could fight you off," Locke muttered.

"Oh so now I'm a rapist?"

"That's not what I meant!"

Vince cleared his throat, aware of Mister Mister smirking across from them, eyebrows raised in curiosity.

Locke blushed, and even Ariel looked embarrassed. "When you, uh, went missing," Locke said, looking at the floor between him and Mister Mister, "Jamie, well he's a telepath—"

"I'm aware," Mister Mister, clearly amused.

"He kind of spilled everyone's secrets," Ariel said. "Even old ones that aren't true anymore. Vince knows what I want to do most to him is save him from his hideous taste in clothes."

"I can hear you," Vince said with a smile.

"Your wardrobe could do with a make-over, too," Ariel told Mister, who had added a white button-down shirt, sleeves rolled up, unbuttoned, over his usual olive tee.

"Why would I wear nice clothes for you clowns?"

"Fair point," Ariel said. "So, can we move on and talk about the important stuff?"

"What would that be," Vince asked.

Locke and Ariel both gave him deadly serious looks and said simultaneously, "Food."

Vince relaxed as Locke and Ariel started describing their favorite holiday dishes and the ride seemed to be over all too soon. They each took charge of their own bags—not much bigger than they'd have taken to Guildford—and walked into a shiny elevator with regular floor buttons and a keypad, Mister Mister bringing up the rear. Locke typed in a series of numbers. "That locks the elevator and takes us straight to the top floor." Locke took Vince's hand and said, "Elevators."

Vince grinned, but he couldn't deny the anxiety beginning to knot in his stomach again. "Locke, are you sure it was your dad who invited me? Because—"

The elevator slowed and the doors slid open. "Oh," Locke said. "You should know—my name."

"Locke's not your name?"

Ariel snickered.

"Yeah, but it's my last name. My family calls me—"

"Car-ey," Ariel sang out.

Vince sputtered. "Carrie? Like the horror movie?"

"No! Carey, like the old Hollywood movie star, Carey Grant. My parents are—"

"Weird," Ariel finished.

"Says the guy named after a spirit in a Shakespeare play," Locke returned before addressing Vince again. "My sister is Ava, and my brother is Humphrey. He goes by Frey—only my mother gets away with calling him Humphrey."

Vince rubbed his mouth, trying not to laugh. "Okay."

Mister Mister felt no such compunction. He chuckled heartily.

Locke looked at Vince's feet and mumbled, "You can call me Carey, if you want."

"I-I'm touched you like me enough to say that, but I think I'll stick with Locke if it's all right with you."

Locke beamed at him. "Yeah. Just not in front of my family, okay? They think it's strange to go by my last name."

"Strange," Vince muttered.

"Well, you guys have fun," Ariel said with irrepressible cheer, bouncing down the hall. "We'll catch up later."

Ariel disappeared into his apartment. Locke grabbed Vince's hands and looked into his eyes. "I was going to warn you my dad can be a bit of a hard-ass, but I think he's—"

"Oh, please," Mister Mister interrupted him, rolling his eyes. "Stanley cries while watching nature documentaries."

They both stared at him. Mister Mister smirked, took a step forward, and knocked on the door.

LOCKE SHOULD HAVE realized when his father referred to Mister Mister as Victor that there was history between them. That didn't explain why his father had forbidden Mister Mister's merchandise in their house when he was young. Still, the stiffness between them—like two cats warily circling—eased quicker than expected, helped a lot by his mom.

Locke concentrated on making sure Vince didn't feel excluded, which wasn't easy to do with his little brother asking him a barge-load of questions. Ava teased him and discovered Vince blushed so easily. It was weird to think Vince and Ava were the same age, and he teased Vince, too, saying, "I hope you don't decide she's the prettier Locke."

"I *am* the prettier Locke," Ava declared.

Vince just laughed and squeezed Locke's hand.

When dinner was over and the dishes done, Ava and Frey left, with Frey exclaiming, "I'm staying with Ava this weekend, so Mister Mister doesn't have to share a room!"

It quickly became apparent this wasn't coincidental when Lettie and Rosa Medeiros, came over. Ariel was as brightly curious as ever, but even he had turkey lethargy.

Once they were all sitting in the living room, Locke's mom offered to pour Vince more wine, which he turned down. She poured it anyway. "In case you need it later," she said, smiling at him.

"I'm afraid we've reached the unpleasant part of the evening," Locke's father started. "You probably all know by now this isn't our standard Thanksgiving dinner."

His gaze fell on Mister Mister, and they stared at each other for a bit until Mister Mister looked away and his father continued speaking. "I think we can all see things are changing again and the magnitude of these changes can't be overstated. We're approaching dangerous times. That much became clear when Chameleon kidnapped Victor and gravely hurt Vince."

He turned to look at Vince. "Speaking of which, I owe you an apology. What happened at camp made me realize you are trying your best, and you would never purposefully hurt my son. You can't choose who your parents are, and unlike some people, you never wanted to get involved with a villain. I can say you're an exception to the rule."

"What rule?" Locke asked.

His father ignored him. "I think I was working under the assumption you knew what your father had done. But you don't, do you?"

"I know he never hesitates to sing a guard into shooting anyone who moves when he pulls off one of his bank heists," Vince said with a wince.

Locke could empathize with that wince. He could imagine how horrible he'd feel to do something so against his nature and trying to reconcile it afterward, even knowing they'd been coerced—there'd been several suicides after a Pied Piper heist, which he thankfully didn't pull too often.

"Mr. Locke," Vince began in a shaky voice after no one replied. He squeezed Locke's hand. "I've never been anything to my father, except something to be moved from his liability column to his asset column, or vice versa. I would do anything to keep him from hurting the people I—" He blinked, about to say he loved Locke. "Anyone I care about."

"That's a nice speech," Locke's dad said, smiling. "Unnecessary, but thank you for it."

"It should be unnecessary," Mister Mister piped up. "Every candidate who goes into Camp Hologram is comprehensively vetted. We know more about them than they would ever want us to know."

"Just like every security agent is comprehensively vetted, huh?"

Mister Mister crossed his arms over his chest, but said nothing.

Locke's mother rolled her eyes at his father. "Let's not point fingers. Even the power-gifted are still only human. Otherwise Chameleon wouldn't have escaped."

"What?" Vince gasped, echoing aloud Locke's own surprise.

"She was about to transferred to a prison transfer truck when some foolish guard got too close to her. My nullification of her power had worn off by then, of course, so she took on his appearance and started yelling about how she tricked him, and could someone get the damn restraints off him." His mom shook her head in disbelief. "It was almost Keystonian. I'm sorry," she added, addressing Vince directly. "She should be punished for what she did to you."

Mister Mister grunted again, as if to remind her he had been bested by Chameleon, too, and Locke's father said to him, "You should have known better."

That didn't make sense—clearly Chameleon had hurt Mister Mister in the watch tower—but his mother rolled her eyes once more as if she found the half-buried enmity between the two men ridiculous.

"Let's stay on topic, please."

"Right," his dad said. "Do you guys know who Flood is?"

Ariel, Vince, and Locke all shook their heads. The adults in the room seemed to pale, glance away from each other or even wince at the mention of the name.

"I guess the International Alliance of Enhanced Abilities does a good job of keeping it under wraps. You need to know this, though. Before Flood, a power-gifted person's marketing team decided whether they would be a hero or a villain," he said with a heavy sigh. "Flood was different, though. We were at Camp Hologram before it was gender segregated with Victor, my wife and a few other people."

"Duke Fusion, Nightingale," his mother said, her tone full of nostalgia. "They weren't called that then, though."

His dad nodded. "We already knew what Flood was doing when we went into training. He was power-gifted and he was killing the power-gifted one by one, for fun, or something. Nobody ever really knew why. To this day, no one knows who Flood was. Who he is. He might still be alive."

He took a deep breath and held Locke's mom's hand.

"Everyone thought he would leave us alone," Locke's mom said when it was clear his dad wasn't going to speak anymore. "We were young, and we were still training, not bothering anyone. Not one of us was active. But Flood got into camp, and—well, we tried to fight him off."

"We were so young. We hadn't spent a month at camp before the attack. We didn't even realize Flood was manipulating the river until he took down Joy, our instructor." Mister Mister said, swallowing. "We were so unprepared for what Flood could do. We tried our best to hold our own, but Flood was a formidable opponent, and he took us all out. One by one, he wounded us, and then—"

"When Joy came back to and tried to fight, Flood killed him," Locke's father said. "Then, for good measure, he killed Julie. She was already out of the fight. He just—he was angry I kept trying to fight him off."

Ariel was the one to break the silence this time. "Who is Julie?"

Mister Mister shook his head. "She never graduated, so she never got a superhero name. She could teleport, though obviously not when she was knocked out, which happened almost instantly."

"We fought him off," Locke's dad said, voice shaking like Locke had seldom heard. He didn't sound proud, if anything, he sounded upset. This wasn't a story Lock had heard before, which he was strange. His father had never been shy about bragging around his family. This didn't seem like the type of thing he wanted to brag about, though.

"That's not entirely true," Mister Mister said, sitting back on the chair and looking at Locke's dad. His expression changed, but Locke found it hard to read. "He took us all down, but Stanley was the last one standing. He fought until he passed out, just long enough for other superheroes, ones with more experience than us, came in to fight Flood."

He turned to address Locke. "Your father saved us all," he said.

"I only did what I had to do," Locke's dad mumbled. No one paid attention to him.

Locked could see by Ariel's gaping mouth and Vince's puzzled frown that they were as surprised and confused as he was. "How does that relate to what's happening now?"

"After camp, a few people, particularly your father and Nightingale," his mother said, "decided to make it their quest to ensure Flood never did anything like that again. But Flood was only the first. Eventually more true villains appeared, most relatively harmless, at least until Pied Piper came along."

Vince cringed, and Locke tightened his hold on Vince's hand.

"Nightingale had singing powers like yours, Vince," Locke's mother said with a kind smile.

"Pied Piper, sad to say, was directly responsible for his death. You boys would have been little more than babies at the time, and after Kicking Horse, no one talked about Pied Piper to keep the secret from the nongifted," Alloy—more familiarly known as Rosa Medieros—said. Both Ariel's moms were also gifted.

Vince looked like he wanted to crawl in a hole and die. Locke began to understand just why his father had such a hard time trusting the son of someone like that.

"What's Kicking Horse?" Ariel asked before Locke could.

His father looked at Mister Mister "Maybe you should tell them."

"Oh for heaven's sake," said Lettie, Ariel's other mom, and Locke's mother grinned at her. "Boys, up until ten years ago, there used to be a month-long summer festival in the mountains at a place called Kicking Horse. It was kind of a neo-hippy thing, all restored Westfalias, impromptu concerts, artists, performers, you name it."

"Clothing optional," his mother added, a smile in her voice as if she'd been there.

"Hush, Emma. I'm telling the story. Ten years ago, a man dressed in motley attire took control of the sound system and sang a little song. A thousand people walked off the cliff at Kicking Horse. The International Alliance of Enhanced Abilities, and our own Department of Special Powers, along with similar agencies around the world, immediately began a cover up."

Locke was stunned, and so, it seemed, was Vince, who was staring slack jawed. "M-my father?"

"I'm afraid so."

Vince let go of Locke's hand and leaned over, grabbing the wine glass in front of him and drank it all at once. Locke didn't think Vince even liked wine that much.

"Vince is not like his father," Locke said quietly. He wanted Vince to hear him, he thought it was obvious no one thought Vince was like Pied Piper, but he had to let Vince know he was on his side.

"We know," Locke's dad said. No one else said anything, not even Ariel.

"Excuse me," Vince broke the silence after putting the wine glass back on the coffee table in front of him.

Locke watched as Vince got up and disappeared into the hallway. Locke went to get up and follow him, but his mom shook her head and he sat back down, his mouth dry. He couldn't imagine how bad Vince felt. He just wanted to hug him.

"Give him a minute," she said. "This is a lot to process."

He nodded, but he didn't take his gaze off the hallway.

VINCE HAD ALREADY been in Locke's bedroom, but only to drop off his luggage. He had paid little attention to the wall-to-wall window overlooking the north side of the city. Tupewa was active even on a holiday, lights blinking on and off in buildings in front of him. Normally, he would have felt sick just being up that high, but he didn't care right then. Already, his heart was pounding and he felt dizzy, plus it was the only place where it didn't feel wrong to stand. He didn't want to get in Locke's bed, he didn't even want to be in Locke's room. He just wanted to disappear. His father—fuck. No wonder Sting didn't trust him.

"They don't open," he heard Locke say from the door.

He turned around to face him, raising his eyebrows but saying nothing.

"The windows," Locke said as he walked into his bedroom. "They don't open. If you're thinking about jumping."

Vince tried for a smile. "Only a little."

Locke sighed. "I didn't think you should be alone," he said, crossing the room to press the button on the white roller shades and brought them down at once.

"I can't face anyone right now."

"Do you want me to leave?"

"This is your room," Vince said in a low voice. "I can hardly kick you out."

"That's not what I asked." Locke put his hand on Vince's shoulder. There was nothing romantic about his touch, not right then, it was just a reassuring hand. Vince was close to tears.

"Do you want to talk about it?"

Vince shook his head. "What is there to talk about? You know, when my father called, I was thinking about his pie. Not about what he had almost done to—not about what he has done to everyone else."

"You didn't know," Locke said in a soft voice. "You couldn't have known."

"I knew enough," Vince replied, hot tears trickling down his face. "My dad makes people do bad things and they kill themselves because of it later. That should have been enough to clue me into the kind of person he was. He is."

Locke watched him, a somber expression on his face. "You were trying to protect your mother," he replied. "You were trying to protect yourself, Vince. You're brave, not stupid."

Vince scoffed. "He didn't just kill a superhero, Locke," he said, his voice a whisper. "He killed thousands of people. Thousands of people. My father is a mass murderer. No wonder your dad hates me."

"He doesn't hate you," Locke said. "He apologized."

"He shouldn't have," Vince said, wiping his tears away with his sleeve. "He was right."

Locke put his arms around Vince and held him close. When he let go, he looked far more serious than Vince had ever seen him.

"Listen to me," he said, his hands still on Vince's arms. "If there's anything I have learned at camp so far, it's that we're not our parents. If I had listened to my dad—if I had kept on listening to my dad, we probably wouldn't have been able to save Mister Mister."

Vince sighed. "But—"

"You kept telling me you weren't your father and I was too stupid to listen," Locke said. "But you didn't have to tell me! You just showed me over and over again. When you went into the fire. When you walked into a fucking bear trap instead of me. When you decided to be upfront about who your father and his girlfriend were."

Vince took a deep breath. "I guess," he said, as if he didn't quite believe it. He had stopped crying, though.

"C'mon," Locke replied, grabbing his hand. He guided him toward the bed and they sat down together, Vince still saying nothing. Locke was his boyfriend. It was his job to make him feel better, but what he was saying did make sense. "If you don't want to talk about it anymore, we can just sit here all night. We don't have to say a word."

"Really?" Vince said.

"Yes, really," Locke replied, smiling at him. "As long as you're here, I'm happy to do whatever you want."

Vince took a deep breath, throwing himself back on the bed. "I guess part of me hoped my dad wasn't as bad as—I guess part of me hoped I could still have a dad, I don't know. It's so stupid."

"It doesn't sound stupid to me," Locke said. "Wanting a dad sounds pretty normal."

Vince nodded, trying to swallow down the knot in his throat. "Thank you for inviting me," Vince said as he sat up. "This has been—well, overall wonderful. Of course my fucking father had to ruin it. Your family is so lovely. Even though I'm—"

"What?"

"You know," Vince said.

Locke put his hand under Vince's chin and tilted his face up so they were looking at each other. "My family is nice because they can tell you're a good person. You're here because they trust you. You're here because you're a superhero."

Vince's chuckle was wry with self-deprecation. "A superhero that's terrified of heights, whose father is a mass murdering maniac."

"Hey, I've heard worse origin stories," Locke said, smiling back at him. "Plus, you're here now. That's what matters. You're not leaving, right?"

Vince couldn't help but soften. Even with the night's revelations, Locke still wanted him around. It was a little weird, and a lot wonderful. "I'm not leaving your side," he replied when he found his voice. "The skyscraper makes me feel a little dizzy, though."

Locke smiled, biting his lower lip. "I'll keep the shades down while we're here. What would be your ideal to place to live?"

"I don't know," Vince said. "Somewhere rural. Near mountains, you know, at the bottom. No ravines. Loads of trees. Maybe a cabin?"

Locke laughed. "Aren't you from Rawdon? If I'm understanding you right, you want to live in a cabin. In the woods."

"As long as it's a ten-minute drive away from the city, for work, food, and internet. I think I'd be okay with that," Vince said. "What do you think?"

Locke turned toward the shades and focused on them. Vince turned to look at what he was doing. When he did, Locke had replaced the dull whiteness with a gorgeous wooded scenery that flooded light into the room. "Something like that?"

Vince grinned. "Yeah," he said. "That's perfect."

LOCKE WAS PLEASED he was able to shake Vince's bad mood. He understood it, but he'd been sincere when he said it wasn't anything Vince could help. Vince could only be responsible for his own choices and Locke hoped he'd helped Vince see that. He stared at the idyllic scene projected on his blinds. Neither of them would be able to afford something like it for a long time.

"Maybe we can be roommates after graduation, until you find your magical cabin in the woods that's only ten minutes from the city." Locke kept his tone light, pretended he wasn't assuming they'd seek work in the same city.

"That sounds good." Vince shrugged and bit his lip like he might say something more, but he didn't.

Locke lay back on his bed and petted his stomach. "So stuffed."

Vince lay beside him. "Yeah. Delicious. Good thing it's a month till Christmas."

"Oh no, Vince, you don't understand. Tomorrow, we get together with Ariel's family and do it all again. Bigger. Louder. Even more food. We will be waddling back to Camp Hologram."

Vince groaned, but Locke could tell he meant it in a good way. Tingles shot through him when Vince took his hand. "Did you tell your dad about the fire—"

"We are not telling him about that. Not that you weren't heroic, but Dad's feelings for Mister Mister aren't entirely friendly." Which, between his father's suggestion to invite him and the story they just heard, there seemed to be a few missing pieces.

"Oh. Right. Because he fell under the influence of a villain?"

"That's what I've always thought, yeah."

He could feel Vince relax beside him. Locke added some fireflies to the scene he'd projected. Fireflies were easy.

"Pretty."

"So," Locke began, tightening his grasp on Vince's hand. "There was one thing we didn't talk about. About, you know. Jamie."

"Aww, you shouldn't be jealous about Jamie, he and Royce are the only two guys who *didn't* hit on me."

"That's... not what I meant."

"I love you," Vince said, his voice low and intense. "It's almost slipped out of my mouth a hundred times already."

Locke whipped his head to the side to look at him. "You do?"

Vince was staring at the scene still projected on the window screens. "Yeah. A lot. Which brings up the other thing we never talked about."

In spite of being stuffed and a little drunk, Locke rolled onto his side and half on top of Vince. He'd been about to say it back, but he stopped and smiled quizzically at Vince. "What? What more could there be?"

"Why I used my power on Ariel. Because he figured it out. He was going to tell you."

Locke was speechless for a long moment before stammering, "Y-you've loved me that long?"

Vince nodded, meeting his eyes, glancing away, meeting them again.

"Wow. I love you too, Vince," he replied, planting a soft kiss on Vince's lips and closing his eyes. "A lot."

When their tender kissing began to grow heated, Locke forced himself to roll away. "Wrong time and place. Do you feel up to joining the others? Mom's making popcorn."

The smell was already invading his room. Vince sat up and gave Locke an incredulous look. "More food?"

"Smells good, though, doesn't it?" Locke got to his feet and held out his hand. "Don't worry, Ariel will eat most of it. He always does." He let his illusions fade.

Vince took his hand, letting Locke help him to his feet. He smiled, lighting up the room better than any fake fireflies.

In the living room, everyone was sitting, open and relaxed, discussing what movie they should watch. Nobody made a fuss as Locke drew Vince into the room. His mom brought in a monster-sized bowl they used for popcorn when Ariel was over and said, "Before we pick a movie, I have a question for you fine young gentlemen. Have you given any thought to the names you'll register as heroes?"

Ariel chirped up, "Oh, Vince, you should be K."

"Like Agent K?" Vince asked.

"No, just K. For karaoke. I heard you can belt it out."

"Oh god."

Locke chuckled. "I was thinking of Lumen."

"Lumen and Special K!" Ariel chortled around a mouthful of popcorn.

"What happened to just K?" Vince asked, but no one was listening.

"I'm going to be Beauty Force!"

"Oh my god," Locke said, as all the mothers laughed.

"That sounds like a sailor scout power," Vince said, snickering.

"I know, right?" Ariel didn't seem deterred at all. "It's awesome."

Vince and Locke began to giggle, then full on laugh, falling against each other as their laughter seem to feed back on itself. It stopped when Vince realized Locke's face was close enough to kiss. So he did.

"A kiss begins with K!" Ariel crowed.

"I hate that name," Vince muttered.

Locke put his arms around Vince's neck. "I think you might be stuck with it. And me."

They just sat there, staring at each other, oblivious until the Disney theme music began.

About Lina Langley

Lina Langley [she/they] is a first-generation immigrant. She currently lives in sunny Florida and spends her time slashing hot strangers while getting coffee.

Her past is haunted by spies, thieves, tyrants, and murderers. A resident of the world, she's lived on three different continents. She first saw a radiator when she was twenty-two years old, and one time she followed a cat instead of going to a house party.

She likes to read, watch TV, and play video games when she's not developing them. The rest of her free time is spent recreating her own characters in The Sims and hoping that people don't look at the back end of her games.

Email: lina@linalangley.com

Facebook: www.facebook.com/lmlangleyauthor

Twitter: @linalangley

Website: www.linalangley.com

Other books by this author

The Whole Trying Thing

"Holy Water" within *Into the Mystic, Volume Two*

About Sydney Blackburn

Sydney Blackburn is a binary star system. She likes candlelit dinners and long walks on the beach… Oh wait, wrong profile. She's a snarky introvert and admits to having a past full of casual sex and dubious hookups, which she uses for her stories.

She likes word play and puns and science-y things. And green curry.

Her dislikes include talking on the phone, people trying to talk to her before she's had coffee, and filling out the "about me" fields in social media.

Besides writing, she also designs book covers for poor people.

Email: blackburnsyd@gmail.com

Facebook: www.facebook.com/SydneyBee

Twitter: @blackburnsyd

Website: www.sbtales.weebly.com

Other books by this author

"After the Dance" within *Beneath the Layers* anthology
The Lure of Port Stephen
Trick or Treat
"Morning Star" within *Once Upon a Rainbow, Volume One*
What it Seems (Coming May 2018)

The #1 rule of superhero training camp is you don't talk about superhero training camp.

Or your parents.

Or their powers, which is the only thing saving Vince's life—he's the son of a notorious supervillain. But the secret could become a deadly deception when he falls into a super-powered entanglement with gorgeously heroic cabinmate Locke.

When their instructor disappears, Vince's father may be to blame. Torn between loyalties, Vince's greatest fear is that his father's taint will corrupt him and poison his heart against Locke.

Vince might be doomed to follow in his father's footsteps, but he hopes love can beat genetics.

A NineStar Press Publication

Published by NineStar Press
P.O. Box 91792,
Albuquerque, New Mexico, 87199 USA.
www.ninestarpress.com

The Power of Love

Printed in the USA
First Edition
March, 2018

Print ISBN: 978-1-948608-32-9

Also available in eBook, ISBN: 978-1-948608-27-5

Also Available from NineStar Press

Connect with NineStar Press

www.ninestarpress.com

www.facebook.com/ninestarpress

www.facebook.com/groups/NineStarNiche

www.twitter.com/ninestarpress

www.tumblr.com/blog/ninestarpress